BONSHEÁ

Making Light of the Dark

D1522889

by Coral Anika Theill
Edited by Judy Bennett

BONSHEÁ
MAKING LIGHT OF THE DARK

iUniverse books may be ordered through booksellers or by contacting:

iUniverse
1663 Liberty Drive
Bloomington, IN 47403
www.iuniverse.com
844-349-9409

Because of the dynamic nature of the Internet, any web addresses or links contained in this book may have changed since publication and may no longer be valid. The views expressed in this work are solely those of the author and do not necessarily reflect the views of the publisher, and the publisher hereby disclaims any responsibility for them.

Any people depicted in stock imagery provided by Thinkstock are models, and such images are being used for illustrative purposes only.
Certain stock imagery © Thinkstock.

Cover photo by Wen McNally Photography

ISBN: 978-1-4759-8181-0 (sc)
ISBN: 978-1-4759-8182-7 (e)

Print information available on the last page.

iUniverse rev. date: 09/24/2021

Contents

In Memory of
Adaline 'Addie' Archer
Aug. 17, 1929 – Dec. 19, 2010
my friend, mentor and adopted mother

Cruel and Unusual Punishment

Two hundred years ago a system of legal slavery allowed for the ownership of human beings as if they were livestock. Children were ripped away from their mothers with as little consideration as separating a calf from a cow. In this country today, extreme forms of paternalistic religion promote an institutional form of slavery where a woman must be totally obedient to a husband who has absolute control of her life. The wife's lot is to obey and bear children. If she rebels and chooses to save herself by escaping from this life, the father – supported by the church community and often by the court system, can forcibly strip a child away from the mother.

For nearly twenty years, I was married to a man who ruled his household with absolute authority. His personal justification for his behavior came from Biblical scripture. During this time, I bore him eight children (and suffered three miscarriages), home schooled, renovated three houses, baked, canned, gardened, etc..... I was treated as a possession (slave). In the course of my marriage, I was drawn (against my will) into several extreme Christian cults that emphasized patriarchal authority and the obedience of women. Physical exhaustion, birth trauma and a home environment that gave no support contributed to my mental and physical collapse in April 1993.

What I experienced during my childhood, in my marriage, in the churches and the court system amounts to nothing less than **hate crimes on a gender basis**. Two years before I finally escaped from my husband, I suffered a breakdown - a partial stroke and severe depression -after the birth of my seventh child. While nearly catatonic, my husband forced me to have sex - his 'right' in the marriage, but **rape** to me - and I became pregnant again. His brutal treatment pushed my health further to the edge. While completely broken down I was ridiculed, exorcised for demons, told I was a 'witch' and cursed by God by my husband, his friends and family, and 'Christian' cult leaders and counselors. After the birth of my eighth child, I recovered physically *and mentally* and divorced my husband.

The treatment I received in Oregon's courts was more abuse and humiliation. Sexual crimes I endured as a child, my breakdown, my fertility and the 'rape' by my husband all became subjects for ridicule in court. Oregon Circuit Court Judge Albin Norblad laughed when he heard I became pregnant when my husband raped me. My husband got custody of all the children, including my nursing infant, and I was ordered to pay child support! When I complained, I received a letter from the Oregon State Bar informing me that I deserved this treatment because I had a breakdown. Removing a mother's children from her, when she has committed no crime, is cruel and unusual punishment.

"A victim's first scream is for help, a victim's second scream is for justice."
- Coral Anika Theill

Photo of half-way house, "Wings of Love" on Killingsworth in Portland, Oregon where I lived in 1994. Note: Barbed wire is pointed inward - to keep prisoners from escaping.

*During this period of time my ex-husband was following the advice of his unlicensed counselor, **Pastor Bill Heard, Roseburg, Oregon and advisors from the Bill Gothard Institute [cult] in Chicago, Illinois. The rat and lice infested half-way house was operated by the pastors of my midwife, Mabel Dzata, in Portland, Oregon.***

During the period of my breakdown/depression in the spring of 1994, my husband and his pastors left me at the *Wing's of Love* half-way house on Killingsworth in Portland, Oregon, to punish and "break me" (their words) to the will of God. The house was a shelter for ex-cons, street people and prostitutes. It was filthy and infested with rats and lice. My husband's debt-free estate, at this time, was over a quarter- of- a million dollars. It was a frightening experience during the period of my illness/breakdown for my abusive husband, his Christian cult leaders and religious supporters to be in charge of my "recovery program." Three months earlier, I had a D & C, due to my 3rd miscarriage, from being raped by my husband. I was helpless and physically and mentally incapacitated during this time due to my breakdown and partial stroke. (Photo Credit: Debbie Dresler)

BONSHEÁ

Making Light of the Dark

is

Dedicated

to
my eight children
Sarah Reneé, Rachel Ellen, Aaron Michael, Theresa Marie,
Joshua Paul, Rebekah Anne, Hannah Rose and Zachary David
and my grandchildren
in hope that someday the truth will help them heal

to my mentor

Barbara A. May, PhD, RN, Professor Emerita of
Nursing, Linfield College, Portland, Oregon
for assisting me in remembering who I truly am apart from my trauma

and to all those who have survived or are suffering personal crisis

BONSHEÁ – Yaqui Indian – *meaning 'out of the darkness into the light'*

"This religion and the Bible require of women everything, and give her nothing. They ask her support and her love, and repay her with contempt and oppression" – *Helen H. Garderner*

Six Decades of Torture and Abuse

BONSHEÁ *Making Light of the Dark* shares my search for freedom and light in a society based on patriarchal religion and laws. It openly speaks about the ideas and beliefs in our society which foster sexism, racism, the denigration of human rights and the intolerance of difference. My documentation exposes the dark side of human nature when all people are not valued. A healthy society must have the courage to address these issues, speak about them, examine them and bring them to light. Indifference encourages, "silent violence"-the type of violence I experienced in my home, in the community, religious circles and judicial system. Nobel laureate, Elie Wiesel states, "*The indifference to suffering makes the human inhumane.*"

After surviving years of childhood and marital abuse and neglect, a woman suffers a physical collapse and severe mental/nervous breakdown. While in a near catatonic state, the woman is physically assaulted and raped. She becomes pregnant.

Toward the final stages of her pregnancy, she fully recovers from her breakdown. She births her baby, and mother and baby enjoy bonding and breastfeeding. The mother cherishes her newborn son. After undergoing several psychiatric tests and evaluations, her physicians state that she is well.

Her abuser, the father of the child, manipulates the judicial system and seeks custody of the baby. With intervention from the religious community and testimony about the mother's prior mental history, the father is awarded custody of the nursing infant. The mother is ordered to pay her rapist/abuser exorbitant child support while suffering from homelessness and disabilities. She is no longer allowed contact with her child. When the baby is abruptly taken away, the mother goes into shock.

*The 'father of the child' has committed crimes against the mother according to Oregon statutes and laws (Chapter 743, Oregon Laws 1971, 163.375), but is embraced and rewarded in our judicial and religious system. **The victim becomes the criminal.***

I am this woman; this baby is my child; and the father of this child is my ex-husband.

The price for my own safety and freedom in 1996 was an imposed, unnatural and unwanted separation from my eight children. The injustice committed against me is not just the physical separation from my children, but the willful desecration of the mother-child relationship and bond, a sacred spiritual and emotional entity.

Forcibly taking a mother's children, and then controlling her emotionally by withholding contact must be publicly recognized as one of the greatest forms of 'mis-use' of the American justice system and one of the greatest hidden vehicles for wide-spread socially approved physical and emotional abuse and control.

A nation is not conquered until the hearts of its women are on the ground. Then it is done, no matter how brave it's warriors, nor how strong their weapons. - *Cheyenne Proverb*

Coral Theill with her eighth child, Zachary David Warner, July 1995, Independence, Oregon.

I have not been allowed to see my son since 1998, nor allowed to write him or send him gifts since 2003.

I have a personal story to tell of childhood sexual abuse, twenty years of marital abuse, mental and physical, condoned within some of the fundamental, evangelical Christian movements (cults) that thrive today. My story is also about injustice, the failings of the Oregon court system, and the stigma associated with mental illness.

A few years ago, I believed by sharing my truth and breaking my silence, my very life would be threatened. Breaking the silence and "telling secrets" takes courage. I have discovered there is more danger in keeping secrets. If violence cannot be talked about, it cannot be stopped. I truly believe more victims would be willing to share their pain, fear and shame if they could expect to be believed, respected and vindicated.

"On March 10, 1996, I was forced, by an Order of the Court, and by my ex-husband, his attorney, his family and religious supporters, to do something that raged against my good conscience, my common sense and against all my motherly instincts. After a temporary custody hearing, a Court Order signed by Judge Norblad forcibly removed my nursing baby and two youngest children from me. I obeyed the Court Order and gave my children over to my ex-husband. I drove to the hospital, rented a breast-pump and later collapsed and went into shock. I could not understand what had happened and why. I have not yet recovered from the shock; perhaps I never will....

In 1999, I legally changed my name and entered a state address confidentiality program for safety from my ex-husband. A federally funded program, to protect my safety, acknowledged I was a victim of extreme abuse, yet the Courts remanded my eight children to a known perpetrator, the children's father.

Mr. Warner and his attorney, Mr. Lawrence, were pleased.... they had taken away my children. They did not know, though, that they would never be able to take away my soul, my dignity, my inner joy or my freedom-those things that are a part of our sacred ground. *No one outside ourselves can rule us inwardly. When we know this, we are truly free.*"

It has long been known by those who seek power over others, Hitler, the Taliban, Genghis Kahn and many others throughout history, that the way to destroy a population is to destroy their connections to their past. The men who would destroy women are not necessarily destroying only the mothers, their intent is to destroy the child. The mother is but a tool in this quest, a tool that serves as proof of the man's past. He must destroy her to break the connection and reeducate the child into a likeness of himself, or destroy the child trying.

Foreword

"Coral, just as important as it is to realize that yearning for chaos is not in your nature, it is equally important to remind oneself that others thrive on chaos. That is their nature. Therefore, any association you have with such a person will necessarily include the chaos they introduce into the equation. I don't think we ever stop exposing ourselves to such people, for it is as much a part of human existence as anything else. What we do learn, however, is how to create healthy boundaries so we do not continue to place ourselves in a situation where we expose ourselves to the greatest degree of injury.

"In a way, it's similar to the lessons we learn about fire. We depend on it, but maintain a safe boundary where we can function without getting burned. That's not to say that there isn't a time when we have to learn the hard way - a time when we touch the flame, and feel the burn. It's just that once we feel the pain, we learn something, and then create a healthier boundary that allows us to coexist. The biggest difference between this "fire" analogy, and experiencing a cruel abusive relationship is that the flame of the fire is easy to see, and lets you know you are being hurt if you get too close. Abusive relationships work in an opposite order." – *District Attorney John Haroldson*, Benton County, Corvallis, Oregon

"Benton County District Attorney John Haroldson introduced me at a speaking engagement in Corvallis, Oregon. He wrote, "Casting religion in a negative light, can often invite a strong reaction mixed with accusations of heresy and un-Godliness. Such reactions can have a chilling effect on those who might wish to express a negative human experience, namely domestic abuse, where religion has been used as a vehicle to enable the abuse. In *BONSHEÁ*, Coral Theill confronts this troublesome dynamic in an anecdotal account, which underscores the degree to which religion, and the legal system, can be used to enable systematic domestic abuse. In doing so, Coral Theill has ventured into relatively uncharted territory in a manner which may well draw detractors, but at the same time offers great validation for those who find themselves entangled in an abusive relationship buttressed with religious justification.

"In addition to broaching this form of religious distortion, *BONSHEÁ* also illustrates the degree to which the legal system can also be used as a vehicle to further perpetuate abuse even after the victim has chosen to take a stand against the abuse. In *BONSHEÁ*, Coral Theill has clearly chosen to take a courageous stand. It is a stand that comes with a cost, but whose dividends are measured in the strength of the soul." – *John Haroldson*, District Attorney, Benton County District Attorney's Office, Corvallis, Oregon, 2003

Fight for Life

by Christine Pahl, MS, *LPC*, Oregon

The beautiful words below could be written for and to any mother who has lost her babies and children through court sanctioned kidnapping. Nothing justifies the minimization or removal of a fit and loving parent from a child's life. NOTHING.

Sadly, Christine Pahl, MS, LPC passed away June 10, 2017 in Mill City, Oregon. Chris was my best friend, adopted sister, and confidant. She was a lifelong activist in service of the voiceless and a post-trauma recovery specialist. Each day she stood up for the helpless, the disenfranchised and the vulnerable. She was one of those few people in life who "gets it."

I am thankful I was able to spend a week with her in September 2016 in Oregon. She made a huge difference in my life and I miss her. She shared with me the week before she passed that she wished to meet and speak with my children and the administration of Corban University in Salem, Oregon. She drove me to Corban University in September 2016 so I could drop off a package with letters and gifts for my children. I left my package with a colleague of my son, Joshua Warner, at Baseball Northwest. He asked me who I was. I replied, "I am Joshua's mother." He said he didn't know Joshua had a mother.

I never received a response from my son, Joshua.

Since we first met, I felt this incredible sense of helplessness in changing the outcome of Coral's tortured life—I say "I" felt a sense of helplessness. Coral, however, has been indomitable. Despite insurmountable odds, lack of a safe place to live and security, lack of any family, legal or emotional support, and a system that exercised traumatic control of her life, she has continued to relentlessly fight back. Her acute intelligence and drive and ability to network are inspirational to all who know her. She thinks deeply and feels intensely. The fervor and passion with which Coral fights back against the injustices that have rained upon her over her lifespan, come from the same deep place from which mothers love and protect their children. Coral Theill is a mother who has modeled for all what love and commitment looks like!

This battle for justice wasn't what was keeping Coral from "healing" or "getting on with her life" as trauma survivors are so often told to do—it was her life, and to give it up would mean giving up life itself.

The need to tell people to "get over it" is born out of our own need to escape the reality of the evil that actually exists in this world. Most trauma writers talk about "blame the victim" mentality and we do that well in this culture.

What people fail to understand is Coral's inability to re frame her experiences in a way that allows her to begin some healing is born out of the incomprehensible nature of what happened to her—and if it could happen to her, it could happen to anyone. People don't like feeling vulnerable or hearing about trauma because they come face to face with man's capacity for evil and the lack of safety in the world.

How do you make sense out of losing eight children? How do you make sense out of a childhood of constant emotional, physical and sexual abuse? Coral never had the chance to have a solid foundation of love, security, trust and safety in her life.

Due to seventeen years of ongoing court trauma and abuse since escaping from her abusive husband, his cult leaders, family and friends, there is no security, comfort, relief, reframing, making meaning—all those things that need to happen to recover from trauma.

I realized, for the first time, that she could not give up her fight and she would not give up as long as there was a breath left in her. The culmination and proof of my understanding of Coral Theill's fight for life was when I saw her pictures with her children and baby. I felt my own twinge of internal pain at the very thought of what she had experienced emotionally losing her children, that the pain of such an experience would be so unbearable one could only fight back to stay alive.

"The ordinary response to atrocities is to banish them from consciousness" writes Judith Herman in the opening statement to her book *Trauma and Recovery*. "To study psychological trauma is to come face to face both with human vulnerability in the natural world and with the capacity for evil in human nature To study psychological trauma means bearing witness to horrible events . . . when the traumatic events are of human design, those who bear witness are caught in the conflict between victim and perpetrator. It is morally impossible to remain neutral in this conflict. The bystander is forced to take sides." (Herman)

Having known Coral for approximately nine years and recently having spent a week with her, she is legitimate!!! I am continually amazed that she functions at all given what she has been through in her lifetime. What I know of Coral is she is a woman with a huge heart, capable of compassion for others, who is thoughtful, resourceful and resilient, but who has endured poverty, homelessness, abandonment and ridicule beyond imagination. Still she keeps on fighting back seeking the validation she has never received from those closest to her!!!

How she has kept functioning all these years in the face of repeated invalidation by people and systems is beyond my comprehension and a testimony to her determination and drive. It is what keeps her alive as so many people would have crumbled long ago and retreated to a world of self-destruction. (We see it every day in mental health systems and homeless shelters.) Luckily, Coral is articulate and extremely intelligent, both assets which I have found present in trauma survivors I've worked with over the years who had survived enormous abuse and still functioned in society.

The question remains whose side are we on—the victim's or the perpetrators? I think in Coral's documentation of what has happened to her, it is quite evident whose side the system and people of power are on. What frightens me is the absolute vulnerability we all have to people in power and the values and beliefs that these individuals hold which could impact every single one of us should we become prey to the system or as Judith Herman wrote "to come face to face with human vulnerability in the natural world and with the capacity for evil in human nature." What happened to Coral is pure evil and a testimony to the vulnerability we all have. Whose side are we on?

Coral, you really are amazing, resilient, determined, inspirational and worthy of enormous recognition for your efforts, and some semblance of justice in the midst of a world of insanity, cruelty and violence and paradoxically a world of love, compassion and understanding. Let's hope that you finally get the love, compassion, understanding and support that is long overdue. Hats off to you, Coral, and know that you are an inspiration to many.

"At times our own light goes out and is rekindled by a spark from another person. Each of us has cause to think with deep gratitude of those who have lighted the flame within us." - *Albert Schweitzer*

Acknowledgments

I want to express my deep gratitude to my editor, Judy Bennett, for her love, compassion and sensitivity while working on this manuscript with me. Judy exhibited patience and listening skills that were beyond expectation. She drew out details needed for story clarity and helped me articulate scenarios of my trauma, when I was at a loss for words.

Judy sat with me in my raw pain without judging, criticizing, condemning or needing to move or change it. While remembering details of my past and reliving them through writing, I had moments of re-experiencing them. Judy's spiritual essence and maturity gave her the ability to understand that these moments of trauma were a justified and normal response to what I had survived. She had a profound gift of gently walking me through some of the more unexplored territory of my life and pulling out unspoken pieces of me from between the lines. She allowed me to see more of myself.

I am especially fortunate that the Universe sent me this gifted woman to be a part of my life. Through her help, I was able to accomplish what I believe was a part of my mission while I journey here on earth.

I acknowledge and give thanks to the still, small voice within me that urged me to write and channeled words and insights for this manuscript one sentence and paragraph at a time.

Special thanks to Donna Buiso, Sonia Claudio, Danelle Givner and Johnette Hessburg for their kindness and assistance with the review and final edits of **BONSHEÁ *Making Light of the Dark.***

I also want to thank my friends, who, throughout the years, extended acts of compassion and kindness, and "literally stood in the fire" with me.

And finally, I want to thank the women in my life, Addie Archer, Julie Caraway, Annie Bell Lee, Dawn Thom and Shirley Walsh, who have served as mothers and mentors, and who, have encouraged and supported me in my journey back to <u>self</u>.

Coral Anika Theill, Battered Mother's Custody Conference, The George Washington University Law School, May 2013

"Writing is dangerous because we are afraid of what the writing reveals: the fears, the angers, the strengths of a woman under triple or quadruple oppression. Yet in that very act lies our survival because a woman who writes has power. And a woman with power is feared." - *Gloria Anzaldua*

Introduction

Christian Fundamentalism and Patriarchy
vs. Freedom, Justice and Equality
by Christophe Difo, J.D., and Sean Prophet
AUGUST 2021

Among some members of Native American communities Ms. Coral Anika Theill is said to be a "good medicine woman." Having gotten to know Coral over the last year - having heard her story, having witnessed the conviction with which she tells it, having experienced her story's capacity to inspire, having felt the healing warmth Coral exudes despite the crushing trauma her story entails - there is no doubt in our minds that those tribal members and elders are correct.

Our relationship with Coral began in September of 2020, just days after Supreme Court Justice Ruth Bader Ginsburg passed away. It had become clear that Amy Coney Barrett would be then President Donald J. Trump's nominee to replace Justice Ginsberg on the bench. Coral was working fervently to derail Barrett's confirmation, expressing publicly and passionately, the harrowing story of her time in *People of Praise,* and sounding the alarm that Barrett had been a prominent member of the same organization.

People of Praise is a network of Christian fundamentalist communities whose worldview conforms strictly to the "covenant" philosophy as dictated by the Bible in general, and the Nicene Creed in particular. It operates 22 branches across the United States and Canada, as well as in the Caribbean. The group was founded in 1971 and it is headquartered in South Bend, Indiana. The *People of Praise's* estimated 1,700 members are mostly Catholic, though the group does admit believers from other Christian sects.

Submission to patriarchal power characterizes and pervades every aspect of a *People of Praise* member's life. At the organizational level, *People of Praise* is led by an all-male board of eleven governors the chairman of which is the overall coordinator. On the level of the family unit, women and children submit themselves completely to their "spiritual head," which is the man of the household in which they live. In the most granular and fundamental sense, the organization is built around individuals' - both men and women's - absolute, unquestioned submission to authority.

Coral's experiences at the hands of her tormentors, including members of the *People of Praise*, are heinous enough to disturb even the most seasoned social worker. The atrocities include serial rape, kidnapping, domestic assault, involuntary servitude, ritual humiliation, denial of medical care, financial exploitation, social ostracism, psychological torture, and disinheritance. For Coral, all of that immeasurable suffering pales in comparison to the agony she has endured as a result of her court-mandated separation and emotional alienation from her eight children. There is no language sufficient to express the extent of the physical and psychological suffering Coral has endured in the name of religion. The only thing that's more shocking than Coral's experience is that she survived it.

We were drawn to Coral's story with both fascination and outrage. Christophe Difo is an employment lawyer, writer, and editor, and Sean Prophet is a small business owner and television editor. We are committed to secularism and social justice, in significant part, due to the religious fundamentalism we experienced in a new-age religious organization called the Church Universal and Triumphant (CUT), also known as The Summit Lighthouse. Following the years of personal growth required to move on from the CUT experience, we emerged deeply committed to confronting the injustice that religious fundamentalism inevitably brings to whomever it touches. We are likewise advocates for public policy and philosophies of life calculated to maximize individual human flourishing.

CUT's doctrines have reverberated through both our lives in countless ways. Still, our experience pales in comparison to the visceral torture Coral suffered at the hands of the twin beasts of theocracy and patriarchy. We were grateful and humbled when she accepted our invitation to appear as a guest on our show, The Radical Secular Podcast. We found her to be unbroken, unbowed, and unapologetic. She shared her story with courage and conviction and each grotesque new revelation pushed our jaws ever-closer to the floor. We launched **The Radical Secular Podcast** in part to explore and expose the sorts of destructive hierarchies which animate Coral's story. Our conversations with Coral have hardened our resolve to sound the alarm about creeping theocracy, and they have reminded us to count our comparative blessings.

Our interview with Coral titled, *Raped for God: The People of Praise*, aired on February 15, 2021.

The frightening implications of Christian fundamentalism's infiltration of the highest court in the land motivated Coral to publish this new edition of her memoir. Every person who begins reading this defiant chronicle of Coral's experience under the lash of Christian fundamentalism will emerge deeply concerned for the future of justice, equality, and freedom, including religious freedom, under the United States Constitution.

Unearned Hierarchy is the Root Coral's Suffering

We are adamant that freedom of conscience, including freedom of religion, be sacrosanct in a free society. We also agree with the drafters of the United States Constitution in their conviction that secular government is the best way to ensure religious freedom for all members of society. We have found that at the core of the tension between church and state is a struggle between equality and accountability under the law on one hand, and unearned hierarchy and privilege on the other.

The United States Constitution, as originally written, is a blueprint for an unjust hierarchy: a society that privileges White, wealthy, heteronormative men. Sometimes explicitly, but always at least implicitly, America's founding documents excluded from its promises women, enslaved people, and indigenous people. The 14th, 16th, and 20th Amendments, as well as the Civil Rights Act of 1964 and the Voting Rights Act of 1965, marked substantial progress along the United States path toward living up to the promises of its creed. However, the chasm that remains in American society between the status of White men versus the status of everyone else is increasingly difficult to ignore.

Why? How is it that a nation founded on explicit, unprecedented guarantees of justice began reneging on those promises immediately after articulating them? How did "liberty and justice for all" so quickly metastasize into a social hierarchy that privileges wealthy, White, Christian, heteronormative men?

Our search for answers to these perplexing questions reveals that representative democracy is an aberration in the annals of human history. Healthy social democracies, which guarantee equal justice to all citizens, are rare even in the 21st century, and were practically non-existent in the tens of thousands of years that preceded it. Sharing power and sharing resources with individuals outside of one's tribe is deeply unnatural for human beings, and as such, systems which feature such rarely realized ideals are perishable. Those of us who advocate freedom, and justice, and equality must remain vigilant in our defense of civilization against the barbarism to which human beings so rapidly revert in the absence of robust systems of accountability. We share Coral's deep commitment to that critical work.

The American Christian Power Apparatus

There are perhaps no more dangerous and pervasive examples of human barbarism than those expressed in service of theocracy and its inevitable corollary, patriarchy. We do not presume that American religious communities are monolithic in their vision of what constitutes a just society. There certainly are religious organizations in the United States and elsewhere which preach genuine tolerance, which support universal justice, and which perform good works in their communities. Those congregations, such as the Unitarian Universalists, eschew patriarchy, discrimination, and dogma in favor of open-hearted community and open-minded search for meaning. We do not refer to those organizations here.

When we talk about theocracy and patriarchy in the United States, we refer to fundamentalist or evangelical Christianity as well as to conservative Catholicism. Our shorthand for this ubiquitous system of oppression is, The American Christian Power Apparatus (ACPA). To be clear, the ACPA is not necessarily a cabal of sinister Christian elders handing down deliberately oppressive edicts from behind tented fingers in dimly lit church conference rooms. We are not talking about comic-book villains. The ACPA concept is shorthand for a decentralized, amorphous system, perpetuated often unwittingly by well-meaning people, which results in pervasive and systematic oppression, especially of women and girls. (Fundamentalist Jewish and Muslim communities are no less problematic in principle. However, since there are far fewer such organizations in the United States than there are fundamentalist Christian churches, we focus here on the latter.)

The ACPA concept might seem unduly dramatic or sinister to some. Indeed, many people regard theocracy, secularism, and even patriarchy as abstract ideas, detached from their day-to-day lives. Court battles over whether churches may engage in particular political activities, whether public monies may fund private religious schools, whether same-sex couples may adopt children, whether one's sincerely-held religious beliefs are tantamount to a license to discriminate, and whether the state may force a woman to remain pregnant against her will, can seem far away to those of us whose lives are not directly impacted by individual judicial verdicts.

Still, every weekend, from hundreds of thousands of pulpits across The United States, agents of the ACPA, draped in frocks of supernatural authority, reinforce a conservative moral and ethical worldview in the minds of tens of millions of Americans. It's a hierarchy which celebrates male superiority and "headship," disdains women's' independence, aspires to quash women's' bodily autonomy under the pretense of "protecting unborn life," and proffers charitable half-measures to deflect attention from its countless abuses of power even as it extracts resources from the very communities it ostensibly serves. It is an astonishing system of religious privilege that is woven tightly into the fabric of American life, both in law and in culture.

It is no longer possible for good-faith observers to dismiss this travesty of justice and equality as alarmist hand wringing. The American conservative movement's 40-plus-year-long lurch to the political right has drawn brazen theocracy and patriarchy back into the political mainstream. The popularity among Christians of the Trump movement's anti-democracy, pro-theocracy brand of White, Christian nationalism has laid bare the inordinately powerful and privileged position religious institutions occupy in American society, as well as their outright contempt for democratic institutions. During the Trump years, right-wing actors, even as they donned mantles of piety, demonstrated a galling lack of accountability and bad faith, as well as callous disdain for vulnerable members of society. That disgraceful circus revealed the American Christian movement for precisely what it is: a relentless drive to impose conservative social and moral hierarchies upon individuals, while slowing America's progress toward pluralistic humanism.

Coral's Honesty Challenges Us to Reflect

Coral has suffered under the ACPA's moral hierarchy in a manner so intimate and so cruel as to be nearly unfathomable. Her soul-baring story pierces the darkness of that theocracy, and illuminates the desperate place where millions of women and girls suffer every day, in conditions that can only be described as slavery. Coral's testimony gives those victims a voice. Her triumph and escape gives them hope.

The story you are about to read challenges each of us, especially those of us whose day-to-day lives are not obviously impacted by patriarchy and theocracy, to examine the role we play, perhaps unintentionally, in perpetuating the system of Christian privilege that inheres in patriarchy and theocracy. "American Christianity isn't a faith or religion," Coral confided to us in an interview, "it's a crime syndicate." "The Polk County Sheriffs were chasing me like I was an escaped slave. Society accepts this," she continued. "Society accepts what they did to me. I tell every woman who buys my book and likes my story, and who is still a Christian, I can't help you. [You] are a part of it. [You] are helping the Patriarchy. [You] women are my oppressors."

The roots of Christian privilege in the United States, as well as the horrors of Coral's story, are grounded firmly in the patriarchal construct that is the Judeo-Christian God, Yahweh. Most people have difficulty giving up the hope that some kind of benevolent force governs the universe. Many well-meaning, moderate Christians assure themselves, moreover, that "real" Christians are uninterested in theocracy or patriarchy. For them, faith entails a personal relationship with God which may even obviate the need for formal religious ceremonies, including church services. Their spiritual life transcends the gendered imperfections of church organizations, they believe, because God is above all human corruption. Or, in an adaptation of the "bad apples" theory, moderate religious folks may assuage themselves that religion is mostly a force for good, and that abusive patriarchs are the exception rather than the rule.

Though we are both atheists, we do not claim to have answers to unanswerable questions and we therefore do not deny the possibility that some kind of divine, omnipotent being might exist. And we do not here disparage the "personal relationship" believers experience with the gods of their understanding.

Still, such charitable interpretations of the Judeo-Christian God are the exception, not the rule, among American Christians, and certainly within the ACPA system.

The God spoken of from pulpits on Saturdays and Sundays, who is described in the pages of the Christian Bible, and whose voice admonishes daily in the minds of the faithful, is decidedly male. So much so that a Christian is likely hard pressed to conjure a mental image of a female supreme being, and might even be offended by the concept. The Virgin Mary is a beloved Christian icon, certainly. But Mary is not God. Mary is subservient to God and even to her son, Jesus, as is her entire lineage, and all women, from Eve in Genesis to the "Woman of the Apocalypse" in Revelation. These Christian doctrines are structurally oppressive to women because they instill in believers a ready acceptance of male-dominated hierarchy and female submission.

Coral's Courage Inspires Us to Act

Coral's story is a stark warning to all of us, like the beam from a lighthouse, piercing the fog of society's ignorance and indifference. The ACPA, especially as manifest in the sorts of small towns and insular religious communities that formed the settings for Coral's ordeal, is a system of oppression deeply hostile to women's equality and women's independence. It is indeed hostile to the very *ideas* of equality and independence. Coral's story illustrates, in heart-wrenching detail, the ubiquity of that system. Her words articulate the parameters of the physical, psychological, and financial prison that system constructs around the women it ensnares. It is a testament of just how far into the pits of depravity men are prepared to descend to enforce their dominion over women. And, it is a grisly description of what happens to women, like Coral, who summon the courage and daring to fight back.

The ACPA's system of aggressive subjugation does not end at the threshold of Christian men's homes. Expansionism and conquest - evangelism - is at the core of the ACPA's identity. It's not enough that American law and culture, under cover of "religious freedom," sanctions men's tyrannical, and frequently violent, dominion over their households. The ACPA is committed to converting *all men* into street-level enforcers of White, Christian, male, heteronormative hegemony.

The ACPA's survival depends on street-level enforcers because its premise is to compel human beings to exist in a fundamentally unnatural state. No one willingly embraces second class citizenship. No one asks to be subjugated. So, like other oppressive systems, patriarchy and theocracy succeed only where a privileged few wield social and political power over the disenfranchised many.

The ACPA is therefore intrinsically incompatible with socio-political systems premised on democracy, pluralism, and evidence-based public policy. It rejects all of the hallmarks of a just society that is committed to universal human flourishing.

Coral's story is also, therefore, a call to action for anyone whose ethical and moral outlook is rooted in humanistic progress. The Republican party in the United States, at least since the passage of the Civil Rights Act of 1964 and the Voting Rights Act of 1965, has been engaged in a concerted, reactionary reassertion in American society of White, Christian, heteronormative, male dominance. The Right responded to the explosive democratization of information in the late 20th and early 21st centuries with increasingly flagrant temper tantrums, beginning with AM talk radio in 1987 following the repeal of the FCC's fairness doctrine. The outbursts grew more intense following the 1994 Republican sweep of the House, Senate, and Gubernatorial midterm elections. The launch of Fox News in 1996 granted a megaphone to this growing spasm of reactionary grievance, which reached full flower during the George W. Bush years. President Barack Obama's two terms in office were a direct affront to the traditional social hierarchy the ACPA stands for, and they supercharged conservatives' reactionary movement, yet again, by presenting the highest-possible-profile target on which to focus its long-festering racial animus.

Conservatives' furious backlash to the demands of the diverse American plurality for an equal seat at the table of power, mirrors Coral's abusers' violent reaction to her drive for freedom and autonomy. Everyone who reads this memoir, and who, like Coral, is committed to universal human flourishing, will draw strength and inspiration from her courage, persistence, and strength of character. She reminds us that we each have a role to play in standing up for justice, and that it is up to each of us to determine what that role is. And to act.

Coral told us in an interview that she once lived next to a polygamist community involved in the Fundamentalist Church of Jesus Christ of Latter-Day Saints. She secretly shared an earlier edition of her memoir with the women in the community. After reading it, the women wept. The husbands eventually found the book, confiscated it, and forbade the wives from speaking to Coral again. Coral and her memoir were "banned" by their Mormon bishop.

That extreme reaction is indicative of the power this book holds to chip away at the patriarchal religious structure that pervades American society. Coral reminds us that our voices matter. She empowers us to "speak the truth, even if our voice shakes."

Speak the truth even if your voice shakes

I am a Handmaid Survivor and Former Member of U.S. Supreme Court Justice Amy Coney Barrett's People of Praise Community [Cult]

Coral Anika Theill's Letter to The Senate & Judiciary Committee: Judge Amy Coney Barrett

"There's really no such thing as the voiceless. There are only the deliberately SILENCED, or the preferably unheard." - Arundhati Roy

On October 26, 2020 Judge Amy Coney Barrett was confirmed as our U.S. Supreme Court Justice.

Senator Lindsay Graham would **NOT** allow me to testify at Judge Amy Coney Barrett's nomination hearings.

Crimes were committed against me while I was a "handmaid" & member of JUDGE AMY CONEY BARRETT'S PEOPLE OF PRAISE COMMUNITY (cult): marital rape, illegal detention, illegal interrogation, kidnapping. I also suffered from being shamed, humiliated, exorcised & shunned.

From September 2020 through June 2021, I participated in nearly 40 media, radio and TV interviews, including the *AP*, *Washington Post*, *Freedom of Mind* with Dr. Steven Hassan; *Freedom from Religion Foundation* with Annie Laurie Gaylor and Andrew L. Seidel; *The Radical Secular Podcast* with Christophe Difo, J.D. and Sean Prophet; *The Guardian*, *Reuters*, *Newsweek*, *Amy Goodman: Democracy Now*, *Inside Edition*, *Reforme* – Paris, France, as well as dozens of other media outlets. I appreciate the support I received from people nationally and internationally. I was surprised at the level of alarm the Judge Amy Coney Barrett nomination generated all over the world.

*Coral Anika Theill with her twin daughters, Sarah & Rachel, in
1984 when she was a "handmaid" and member of the PEOPLE
OF PRAISE COMMUNITY, Corvallis, Oregon*

October 8, 2020

Dear U. S. Senators,

My name is Coral Anika Theill, aka Kathryn Y. Warner (nee Hall). I legally
changed my name in 1999 to Coral Anika Theill when I entered a state address
confidentiality (protection) program for safety from my ex-husband, Marty
Warner, i.e., V. Martin Warner, Independence, Oregon.

I would like to testify at the confirmation hearing of Judge Amy Coney Barrett
as to the oppression, abuse and crimes that I and other women were victims of
in the People of Praise sect, to which Amy belongs. Although men have ultimate
authority in the sect, women leaders, like Amy, are complicit in the subordination
and mistreatment of lower status women like me.

I became a member of the Vine and Branches sect in 1979 in Corvallis, Oregon.
It was formally absorbed into People of Praise in 1982 and I escaped the group
in 1984. My abuse became more severe after we became a People of Praise
Community.

The entire time I was there, I was under the control of men and subjected to
psychological abuse, including undue influence, threats, shaming, and shunning
by leaders and my husband. Coercive persuasion was used on my children to turn
them against me. My husband and community leaders used coercive control,

isolation and intimidation to strip me of my personhood, safety and freedoms guaranteed to me as a United States citizen. They also launched a smear campaign when I finally got the courage to leave.

The actual crimes committed against me in the sect were: marital rape, false imprisonment, kidnapping, and illegal interrogation. I did not know these were crimes at the time. I believe these crimes are still occurring in People of Praise communities and need to be investigated.

The People of Praise Community that I was forced by my husband to join, was founded in South Bend, Indiana in 1971. I met and attended meetings with the founder, Paul DeCelles and attended a retreat which his wife, Jeanne DeCelles, led. They teach that men have total authority over their wives. Their policies are based on the domination of men and submission of women. They assert that men's power is absolute and instill fear in women that great harm will come to whoever questions and/or defies that power.

I was told I had to obey my husband, who was my "head". I was required to be a "helpmeet", which is a biblical term for a wife's duty to "help" her husband, i.e., do whatever he wants, whenever he wants. This was a main reason my husband wanted to join the group—to give him complete control over me. I had to ask my husband if I could leave the house, go to the store or anywhere else. I was not permitted to do anything without his permission, even go to the store or the doctor. My husband instructed me in what kind of clothes I could wear, how to style my hair, whether I could wear make-up or not, when and what I could eat or drink. Even bodily functions were monitored.

He told me what books I could read and destroyed books if he disapproved of them, including a favorite of mine, *Our Bodies Ourselves: A Book by and for Women*, by the Boston Women's Health Collective. His comments toward me were consistently insulting and demeaning. I couldn't do anything right in his eyes.

I was not allowed access to money or knowledge about our finances. I was forbidden to work outside the home or attend college classes. I was allowed to buy groceries and I purchased most of the children's and my clothes and household items at second-hand shops. My husband read my incoming and outgoing mail. I was not allowed to read a newspaper.

I was forbidden to take birth control and was even accompanied by my husband to OBGYN appointments. I was required to submit to my husband's demands for sex at any time - even immediately after giving birth. My husband could rape me at will and that was fine with the leadership. The most serious crime committed against me while in the People of Praise were continuous marital rapes.

I had to attend weekly meetings, retreats, mandated women's meetings and ministry meetings. Little time was left for family or self. The male "heads" of the sect, those in highest authority, were the main force in controlling members' actions and thoughts. "Headship" involved matters such as the discipline of children, how to deal with a wife, how to help one's wife see and deal with her problems, whether to have another baby, what kind of car or home to buy, etc. Husbands sometimes sought help by their own "heads," on how to get their wives to fall in line—obey.

Each week I was forced to endure a "headship" meeting with my husband who would "correct" me and the children. He would remind me that I set an example for the children by obeying him in all things, and this was a direct correlation to how they would respond and obey him. My husband reported to leaders in his own "headship" meeting any comments I had made that questioned his absolute authority. He kept a black book and listed each of my infractions.

When I tried to share my feelings with my husband and the leaders, my feelings were dismissed. I was told how I should feel. They were the authorities and that fact gave them the right to rule over my emotions. I was required to tell my innermost thoughts and emotions to a woman leader called a "handmaid", who reported what I said to the male leaders who then reported them to my husband, who could then "correct" me in our headship meeting.

When I dared to question or use my own reasoning processes, I was called a rebel and mentally ill and told I had to atone. The threat of being put in a mental institution was added to the litany of humiliations. I was subjected to exorcism and put in "special counseling" with Father Charles Harris, the People of Praise Community leader.

I was forced to attend a People of Praise Community women's retreat where the other women shunned me. They were not allowed to speak to me or look at me. I was often forced to sit on the floor, outside of Community meetings where members would pass by and shun me. I was an outcast, yet not allowed to leave the Community because my husband still was a member.

I was not permitted to see outside friends or relatives. My father died in 1984, during the beginning of my fourth pregnancy in 1984. My husband did not permit me to visit him in the I.C.U. at the hospital the night he died.

When my husband was out-of-town, he assigned other men in the community to "check-up" on me or leaders would enlist members from the Vancouver branch to "watch" me in my own home so I could not leave, call friends or escape.

I lived under the constant threat by my husband and the leaders that great harm would come to me if I didn't obey them, including taking my children away. After I left, Family Court did their bidding and took custody of my children away from me and allowed my husband to alienate them from me. I was threatened they would put me in a mental institution if I did not submit to their authority. I now understand this was a crime: false imprisonment.

One example of the oppression I endured is that after my second miscarriage and D & C surgery in the spring of 1984, I was required to attend the mandatory People of Praise women's meeting. I was still bleeding heavily and was weak from the surgery. The women wished to go on a shopping excursion that evening. I shared I would be unable to go shopping with them and walked out of the meeting. The "handmaid" of the women's group, Connie Hackenbruck, immediately called my husband and reported my disobedience. My husband called another member, Bruce Berning, to watch our three children and as soon as I arrived home, I was forced into a car and driven to the home of Ed Brown, my husband's "head." He told me that some people (like me) couldn't "cut the mustard"—the narrow walk with Jesus Christ. I told him I was tired and wanted to go home but it was only after several more hours of interrogation, I was finally allowed to leave.

Because I was brought and kept at Ed's house against my will and he used insults and threats during the interrogation, I believe this fits the crimes of kidnapping and illegal interrogation. The next day the members in the community were instructed to shun me – not to speak to me. I was considered "poisonous" and a danger to the community's well-being, but still forced to attend meetings and women's retreats. Shunning is a cruel and inhumane practice within many church groups and cults, a form of silent ridicule. My crime: I was in disobedience to the leaders.

I experienced much depression and anxiety as a result of all of this abuse. I still suffer from PTSD.

Head coordinators and their wives from South Bend, Indiana, Amy's group, would visit our community periodically presenting at retreats. Paul and Jeannie DeCelles and Bud and Sharon Rose were frequent speakers. Bud and Sharon Rose eventually moved from South Bend to live in Corvallis for a year, so there was much coordination and interaction between the two communities.

One of People of Praise's first leaders, Notre Dame professor Adrian Reimers, confirms that the husband is always the "head of his wife" and the wife must "submit in all things". In his book, *Not Reliable Guides*, Reimers describes how a married woman in the People of Praise is "expected always to reflect the fact that she is under her husband's authority...This goes beyond an acknowledgment that the husband is 'head of the home' or head of the family; he is, in fact, her personal pastoral head. Whatever she does requires at least his tacit approval. The wife, as a good member of the community, has a *prima facie* obligation to obey her husband as the bearer of God's will. In practice, this means that the two do not—indeed, cannot—relate as equals." The "subordinate role of women to men is a fundamental cultural premise" for the group, he wrote.

People of Praise has released a statement to the media saying they were unaware of any abuse, but that is not true. They were actors in the abuse I suffered. There are numerous individuals who witnessed the abuse I have reported, some of whom are willing to testify. I documented the abuse I suffered in my published memoir, *BONSHEA Making Light of the Dark*, in 2003 and 2013. No one has refuted my claims or sued me for defamation. My memoir has been used as a college text for nursing students at Linfield College, Portland, Oregon and has been cited in many articles and books.

At her nomination party at the White House, Amy deflected from accusations of the gender discrimination in her sect by saying she and her husband share domestic tasks. First of all, she is a leader in the community, so she has a much better life than most women who are expected to stay home, keep having babies, even when it is unhealthy or dangerous, and take care of children themselves, as I was forced to do. But the more important point is that there is not equality or autonomy for women in the sect, instead a serious imbalance of power between men and women.

It should be concerning to members of Congress that Amy did not disclose her membership in the sect to the Senate, while information about her involvement and leadership in the People of Praise Community has been scrubbed from the internet. It appears that she—and the male leaders she is beholden to—are trying to hide her leadership in the community; however, a Washington Post source has provided documentation supporting she is (or was) a handmaid and a top woman leader. The public has a right to hear about her sect's commission of crimes and abuse of women.

I believe crimes and abuse against women are being committed systematically and methodically by People of Praise under the cover of religion. But this is not about religion. It is about power men are given to keep women under their control

I have witnesses who can corroborate my abuse and know former members who can give written testimony (and perhaps in person) as to the abuse and subjugation of women in the People of Praise sect. The confirmation hearings should include this testimony.

I would very much like to testify to the Senate in person as I believe the public should hear first-hand about Amy Coney Barrett's support of patriarchal ideology and resulting oppression of women. This should be a disqualifier for the highest court in the land.

Respectfully,

Coral Anika Theill
Aka Kathryn Y. Warner (nee Hall)
Author, Advocate & Military Reporter
Memoir: *BONSHEA Making Light of the Dark*
Contributing Writer for Leatherneck Magazine,
"Short Rations For Marines" &
"RECLAMATION: A Survivor's Anthology"

*Author's note: In October 2020 Dr. Paul Hessburg, Sr., a former member of the People of Praise Community in Corvallis, Oregon and Vancouver, Washington, spoke to me and also with Dr. Steven Hassan, America's cult expert, at Freedom of Mind. Dr. Hessburg's testimony was recorded by video with Dr. Steven Hassan in October 2020. He testified that he had witnessed the abuse I suffered by my husband and community leaders as well as seeing me sitting on the floor outside of People of Praise Community Meetings at St. Mary's Catholic Church, Corvallis, Oregon. Dr. Hessburg was a former best friend of my husband, Mr. Marty Warner, and belonged to the same men's group. He had the same "head" – Ed Brown, as my husband. In his October 2020 interview with Dr. Steven Hassan, Dr. Hessburg stated that he believed the People of Praise Community leaders enabled my husband to be a "predator" in his own home.

The Questions I Would Have Asked Judge Amy Coney Barrett Before Voting for Her to Ascend to the United States Supreme Court

Published 19 October 2020 at "VERDICT"
by Marci A. Hamilton

As soon as Judge Amy Coney Barrett's name surfaced as the next Supreme Court nominee, a slew of right and left opinion writers warned against the political dangers of criticizing or even asking about her religious affiliation. Barrett has been a member and leader in the little-known People of Praise, which is related to Roman Catholicism. The small size of the group alone would justify some explanation, but senators took the pundits at their word, and nary a word was spoken about her faith during the hearings. Now a vote is scheduled for Thursday, October 22, and I have to say that I am left wanting answers to important questions senators did not pose.

While the political elite knowingly clucked about the futility or supposed inappropriateness of asking Barrett to be more forthcoming about her religious affiliation, the #MeToo movement spurred yet another set of victims to tell us about their suffering. These victims say People of Praise has condoned and perpetuated domestic violence against women and children. As recent history proves again and again, ignoring the victims may result in delay, but it won't avoid an eventual reckoning.

I presume the senators would have been outspoken had she been a member of a white supremacist organization. But God forbid they question religious affiliation. They are so fearful of being falsely called "anti-Catholic"—even when seeking the truth on behalf of victims of domestic violence—that they are publicly perpetuating this culture's systemic and silent acquiescence in the oppression of women and children in some religious settings.

The loudest, brave voice is that of Coral Theill, who published a memoir of her suffering at the hands of this organization in 2003, *Bonshea Making Light of the Dark*. The media has been covering her, but you'd never know that she exists if you only watched Barrett's hearings, where Senator Lindsey Graham sang her praises for being pro-life, but said nothing about the troubling facts that have been emerging about this organization that has been such a significant element of her life.

Theill has sent letters to senators asking to testify about the truth of her experience in the People of Praise, but has received no answer, which is why I am writing this column. The following are the unanswered questions that I feel the American people have a right to ask and have answered. They are also the issues the senators should understand before they rush to confirm Barrett.

1. Am I correct in assuming that you are aware of the #MeToo movement, the movement to end child sex abuse, and the movement against domestic violence that have encouraged victims to come forward to the public to unmask oppressive practices in numerous contexts? How have these movements affected the organizations with which you are affiliated?

2. You are a lifelong member and apparently leader of a religious organization, the People of Praise, which is credibly accused of domestic violence by numerous women. What have you done to investigate or end these practices?

3. There is an epidemic of domestic violence, and, as a matter of fact, it is not uncommon for it to be inflicted for religiously motivated reasons. Do you agree?

4. Would you apply a less strict legal standard to religiously-motivated domestic violence and child abuse than other instances? For example, how will you interpret the Religious Freedom Restoration Act when it is invoked as a defense in federal sex trafficking cases involving religious actors?

5. In addition to being a member of the People of Praise, you also describe yourself as a "devout Catholic." The Catholic Church has experienced a global crisis involving the sexual abuse of children by clergy, a problem that continues to this day. What have you done or written in response to this human rights crisis?

6. There are numerous clergy sex abuse lawsuits in the United States, many of them involving the Catholic Church, and issues arising from them are likely to land at the Supreme Court. Will you recuse yourself in those cases, given your tight relationship and avowed allegiance to the Catholic Church?

7. You have endorsed an originalist approach to the Constitution. At the time of the framing, women were the property of their husbands. How does that historical fact affect your interpretation of the civil rights of women?

8. Children were also property at the time of the framing. How does that historical fact shape your views on children's rights against abuse and neglect?

It is taboo to publicly criticize religion, because there is a false, public mythology in the United States that religion is always good and pure; and, of course, the religious right has turned its culture war losses into the stigmata of victimization. I would agree with the pundits and political strategists who counseled ignoring Barrett's religious affiliations if religion were nothing but a good and benevolent God. In fact, here on earth, it's run by humans, and humans can and do bend religion to oppress and harm others.

For the sake of the vulnerable, let's stop pretending religious affiliation is irrelevant at the highest court in the United States.

Marci A. Hamilton is the Fels Institute of Government Professor of Practice, and Fox Family Pavilion Resident Senior Fellow in the Program for Research on Religion at the University of Pennsylvania; the founder, CEO, and Academic Director of the nonprofit think tank to prevent child abuse and neglect, CHILD USA, and author of *God vs. the Gavel: The Perils of Extreme Religious Liberty* and *Justice Denied: What America Must Do to Protect Its Children*

Christmas Letter to Coral Anika Theill's Eight Children

from Donna Buiso

December 2020

To Coral's children,

My name is Donna Buiso and I am the Author of *NOTHING BUT MY VOICE*.

I am also a mother grieving the loss of live children.

I am also a grandmother grieving the loss of live grandchildren.

I was sentenced to a life sentence by Family Court almost 20 years ago. I have been erased, I have been shunned, I have been libeled and I have been financially annihilated. My crime? Unknown.

The worst thing that was ever said about me was that I was "mentally ill". It was a diagnosis given to me by no one but my abuser. No professional ever substantiated it but many refuted it in the many letters written to the court.

My abuser is a disturbed individual. What is even more disturbing is the courts that are supposed to uphold the law and protect the innocent and in fact, often do the opposite. No one can give me back all the birthdays, holidays and milestones that I should have had with my family. There are no reparations. My children and grandchildren have also lost greatly. My children lost a mother who loves them dearly and wanted nothing more than to protect them, encourage them and be there for them. My grandchildren lost having a grandmother who would have doted on them and been one of their fiercest allies.

Who has won in all of this? My abuser certainly feels victorious. He was able to murder me as a mother and not have to lay a hand on me. The courts are able to continue their misogyny and their corruption to greed and power.

I am in my late sixties with 70 on the horizon. I will most certainly die of a broken heart but in that broken heart I have made peace with myself. Through all of these years no one has been able to stop me from loving, from honoring my truth, or from speaking my voice.

I pray for every parent who has ever suffered separation from their child and for every poor child who was forced to not be able to receive the protective love of their mothers.

Abuse needs to be called out in both the people who abuse and the systems who abuse. I believe it's putting a purpose to the pain and is probably the reason I am still alive to talk about it.

I will go to my grave speaking out. I may never see change in my lifetime either personally or nationally but it will not stop me. Our voices matter.

This letter was read for me at a Conference for Alienated Mothers. It's my story but it's also the story of so many, many others; among them, your mother, Coral Anika Theill, aka, Kathy Warner.

In the many years that I have lived this nightmare it never ceases to amaze me that so many of the women targeted are the most loving, kindest and smartest people that I've met in my long life. Certainly, your mother stands out as one of the strongest examples.

Coral is loving. Coral is kind. Coral is incredibly strong and brave. Coral is also one of the smartest people I've ever known. Rather than be brought down by the pain in her life, she has committed to living her life in truth and valiancy. She is one of the most remarkable people I have ever known and I am so proud to have become her friend.

I'm not writing this to try and convince you of anything or to try to make you feel guilty. I'm writing because I feel you need to hear how others view your mother. I'm also writing because I feel sorrow for what you've missed as well as what she's missed. Things aren't always as they seem. We can grow up with certain beliefs but sometimes challenging our beliefs, as painful as that can be, can lead to an amazing inner peace. I know this from experience.

Your mother did not ask me to write this; nor would she ever. I'm doing it of my own accord. We are moving into the last parts of our lives and words need to be spoken. It's all we have left.

If there is any good that has come of our situations, it is that we have found each other as well as other like- minded souls. One of my dear friends, who is also an estranged mother, refers to certain people as lighthouses along our journey. Your mom has not only been a lighthouse for me but for so many others as she continues to speak truth to power even when it is dangerous to do so

This is what I told my children in a letter. **"You can deny me with your words and with your actions, but you can never deny that I live within each of you. I am a part of you and you of me until the day we die. The invisible umbilical cord can never be broken. I live inside of you."**

I pray that if nothing else you give this letter some thought. It is never too late to change our paradigm.

With love,

Donna Buiso
Author, *NOTHING BUT MY VOICE*

*Author's note: Thankfully there are many advocates and survivors who are giving voice to the violence and demanding change: *Mothers on Trial*, by Phyllis Chesler, *Crisis In The Family Courts: Batterer Manipulation and Retaliation Denial and Complicity In the Family Courts* by Joan Zorza, Esq., *What is Fair for Children of Abusive Men?* by Jack C. Straton, Ph.D, Portland State University, *Justice Denied* by Marci A. Hamilton, *Child Custody Justice* by Lundy Bancroft, *The Motherless Project* by Robin Karr and Janie McQueen, *No Way Out but One* by Garland Waller, *Prosecuted but not Silenced* by Maralee McLean, *The Story of Naming Maternal Alienation* by Anne Morris, *Beware Family Court: What Victims and Advocates Should Know Cracking the Code of the Family Court Cult: ADA Remedies for Women Accused of "PAS"* by Karin Wolf, *Nothing but My Voice* by Donna Buiso, *Writings in the Sand* by Ruth Colllins and *Why Doesn't She Leave?* by Marie De Santis.

Coral Anika Theill, Quantico Marine Corps Base,
Quantico, Virginia, Christmas 2018

Bearing Witness

BONSHEA *pierces through the darkness that hides the legal system's routine abuse of mothers and children.*

BONSHEA is a work of immense courage, a true tale of heartbreak and salvation. By exposing what was done to her by the court system, by the religious authorities and by their enabling cronies as she took the moral high ground by leaving an abusive husband, the author gives readers the tremendous gift of her hard-won insight and spiritual awakening. As shocking as it may be, Coral's story resonates with the truth. I hear pleas for help from protective mothers like Coral every day, week after week, year after year—all of them pleading for their very birthright, their greatest right, which is to be a mother.

She pinpoints, with heart-piercing accuracy, the historical hatred of females and of the feminine that has permeated societies, including our present one, for eons. Her personal story of living with and divorcing an abusive "religious" man who was cheered on by the community's religious, governmental, and legal authorities mirrors the persecution of all women who, like Coral, choose to say "no" to male dominance and power. These include Middle Age "witches," midwives, mothers who protect their children from a father's abuse, mothers who dare to have careers and mothers who elect to stay home with their children. Coral also calls out for the only true cure for the dark side of human nature, and that is *to live in the light*.

Coral's work is a special blessing for me and for my sisters throughout this country. Not a single particle of the wisdom Coral shares misses the mark. - *Maureen T. Hannah*, Ph.D., Chair, Battered Mother's Custody Conference, Albany, New York, Co-editor of *Domestic Violence, Abuse, and Child Custody: Legal Strategies and Policy Issues*

"And the time came when the pain to remain tight in the bud became greater than the risk it took to blossom." *–Anais Nin*

Preface

BONSHEÁ
Making Light of the Dark
by Coral Anika Theill

I have spent long hours trying to make some sense of my life and have come to the conclusion that when horror overcomes us the only response possible is to remember what happened and tell the story.

> "When the content of the story cannot resolve the irrationality of such suffering of any suffering, the act of telling the story can be the one valid moral response, the sole way to give what happened a meaning. Hopefully in writing, telling the story, it can give the suffering ultimate significance and meaning to an experience of a destruction of meaning." –Robert H. Hopcke, *There Are No Accidents*

Once on the other side, (of our crisis), one must look back and throw down a footbridge, for followers to use. When you have "jumped outside of the given", there is an obligation to share with others what you learned. You must not only tell how you got there, but the process of survival as well. Someone must have the wisdom, courage and strength to live their truth fearlessly. That someone becomes "the living bridge."

I have a personal story to tell of a lifetime of abuse: childhood abuse, marital abuse, mental and physical abuse, sexual abuse, ritual abuse and now finally judicial abuse, condoned first within some of the fundamental, evangelical Christian movements (cults) that thrive today, and now within the very court system of my own country. My story is about the overwhelming stigma that comes with abuse. My story is also about survival and overcoming, truly 'Making Light of the Dark.'

The world I describe of far-right religious cults is extreme, but many aspects of these groups have seeped into our national political scene and fostered a great divide that is increasingly hard to bridge. Presidential candidates Rick Santorum, Sarah Palin and Michelle Bachman and other political leaders have been adherents at least in part to the Dominist, homeschool, 'quiverfull,' and Right-to-Life movements.

One characteristic of all of these movements is that there is no room for compromise. It is a toxic brand of extremism that is expending a lot of money to influence and pervert our political process. Even more 'mainstream' conservative Christian groups, when their core beliefs are examined, believe divorce is a cardinal sin, a wife must submit to her husband in all things, and under no circumstance (health of a mother, incest or rape) should abortion be allowed.

A few years ago, I believed by sharing my truth and breaking my silence, my very life would be threatened. Breaking the silence and 'telling secrets' takes courage. But I have discovered there is more danger in keeping secrets. If violence cannot be talked about, it cannot be stopped. I truly believe more victims would be willing to share their pain, fear and shame if they could expect to be believed, respected and vindicated.

I do not blame my childhood or my marriage for my unfortunate life experiences. I take full responsibility for my life and my emotional, spiritual, physical and financial well-being. I believe that our dark experiences in life push us to the light. Although this fact does not take away or lessen the raw pain—what these experiences can do for the soul is a good thing. I am grateful.

The day you embrace your triumphs *and defeats* is the day you find your sacred ground. No one can take your sacred ground from you because it is yours. You own it. It is embedded within your spirit. I have embraced my memories, and by doing so, made them my sacred ground. They are who I am. What I have experienced, no power on earth can take away from me.

I believe to heal from our trauma, we must be able to tell the absolute truth and face it squarely. Alienation from our memories dooms us to live in a constant present, cut off from the past and the future. I have remembered and am ready now to share my memories, my healing, and my process of "making light of the dark." I remember so I can help others see that they can help themselves.

1

Holocaust survivor Elie Wiesel writes, "What does it mean to remember? It is to live in more than one world, to prevent the past from fading and to call upon the future to illuminate it. It is to revive fragments of existence, to rescue lost beings, to cast harsh light on faces and events, to drive back the sands that cover the surface of things, to combat oblivion and to reject death."

I am sharing intimate details of my life because a grave injustice has been committed. My situation begs for resolution and justice. Unlawful, malicious, and criminal acts have been committed against me and my children by judges, attorneys and religious, hostile witnesses in a courtroom of law. My story and transcripts not only reveal a lifetime of child abuse, marital abuse, and the ritual abuse of religion, it exposes the physical and mental abuse a woman is subjected to in our "judicial system." This case remains unchallenged.

Domestic violence is a huge problem in the United States. In 1999, Governor Kitzhaber reported that domestic violence is at epidemic proportions in Oregon – *and nothing substantive has changed in the years since he made that statement.* New legislation is needed that would promote safety, wellness, and wholeness for women, children and families involved in domestic violence and abuse incidents in Oregon.

In January 1995, my physician, Dr. Charles South, confirmed the pregnancy of my eighth child. Dr. South appeared disturbed to see me pregnant and was also aware I was still recovering from the two-year period of my breakdown. He told me, "Go get the best attorney you can find and divorce the son of a b-tch."

I went to the judicial system for help and was not prepared for the horrors I experienced within our legal system. I found a system which treated me as deplorably as my former husband and his religious supporters. I have extensive documentation, including affidavits, court transcripts, tapes and videos, medical and mental reports, and witnesses to substantiate and elaborate on this story. I believe that when this case comes to light, someone will have to answer for the abuse and *silent violence* I have suffered in the Polk, Marion, and Wasco County courts. Marital and ritual abuse evolved into legal abuse.

The abuse I suffered from my family, ex-husband, his religious supporters, and the judicial system in Oregon cut deep wounds in me. Although my wounds have mostly healed, I am still haunted by the cruelty and injustices.

There is a dark side of human nature when all people are not valued. My intent in sharing my story with you is an effort to reclaim dignity, equality and honor, not only for myself, but for everyone. I envision a world that values freedom, and diversity, and humanity.

The important lesson to be understood from the horror I, and others, have survived is not so much that it is happening, but that it is being *allowed*–not only on an individual level, but under the disguise of church and state.

In her book, *The Dark Side of Christian History*, Helen Ellerbe writes, "The Christian *(and Catholic)* Church has left a legacy that fosters sexism, racism, and the intolerance of difference. The Church, throughout much of its history, has demonstrated a disregard for human freedom and dignity. The Church's control of people through dictating and containing their spirituality has been the most devastating slavery throughout the history of mankind. We must recognize the fact that ideas and beliefs which foster the denigration of human rights and the intolerance of differences must be examined and brought to light."

As long as we have stories that praise those who rape–like too many of the favorite heroes in the Old Testament (like Lot who wanted to hand his virgin daughters over to the men of Sodom) and gods in Greek and Roman mythology, victims must continue sharing their stories to help eradicate the toxic effects of religion to individuals and society.

My case speaks loudly of the insidious crimes that are legally permitted and condoned under the guise of church and state-sanctioned domination of males in marriage. The message that the current judicial system gives to many domestic violence and rape victims is that they are not worthy, and that no one cares. This needs to change.

In our society, domestic violence is encouraged and condoned by patriarchal based religious organizations. The fundamental evangelical Christian movements (cults) that thrive today refuse to speak out against domestic violence, rape, incest and abuse because their doctrines are the foundation for conditioning women and children to accept abuse.

Women and children are taught shame, fear and guilt and that patriarchal hierarchy must be lived out in the homes. Patriarchal religion has proven to be devastating for women around the world. External oppression of a people leads to internal oppression.

The courts are an extension of our patriarchal heritage that views women as less value than men. By ignoring these facts, we perpetuate the cycle of violence. The religious organizations and the courts have closed their ears to my cry for help. My task is to "make known the unknown."

Wealthy perpetrators, supported by Oregon's judicial system and attorneys, can continue to commit crimes of violence against their victims by harassing them and stalking them through the courts. My case history supports this fact. When you do not have monies for your own legal defense, you can be victimized indefinitely. Oregon's legal system has given numerous individuals the legal right to commit criminal, depraved and inhumane acts against me.

"When courts blame victims and fail to hold abusers accountable, they reinforce abuser behavior, subvert justice, disempower the victims, teach children that abusive behavior is permissible and may even be rewarded, and reinforce the cycle of violence. Most batterers know they can bring criminal and contempt charges at no expense to the abusers, but they take an enormous financial and emotional cost on their victims. The result is that many abusive men drag on the litigation and file spurious claims openly acknowledging they are trying to drive their victims onto welfare or into homelessness; half of all homeless women and children in the U.S. are homeless because of domestic violence." - Joan Zorza, Esq.

The judicial system acts as the conscience of this country but we know, in most cases, that is not what happens.

Everyone was shocked by Jaycee Dugard's life and story, *Stolen Years*. She was kidnapped, raped and kept enslaved for years. I am thankful she was found and that she and her daughters are safe. I identify with her ordeal, but see one difference in our stories. Oregon Circuit Court Judge Albin Norblad removed my children and nursing infant and awarded custody to my abuser after I sought safety. Oregon Circuit Court judges ordered me, a disabled woman, to pay my abuser/rapist/kidnapper child support.

My court ordered child support ended in 2003 due to being homeless, disabled and destitute but I am required to pay the support that accrued before the child support was suspended. Presently, my passport has been revoked; the courts could punish me with jail time and/or revoke my driver's license because of unpaid child support which was calculated at twice the amount I now receive on disability. I cannot afford to pay the back child support of $5,815.74 plus 12% interest. My ex-husband has stated, "I will never dismiss the judgment." I understand that I am being punished for leaving my abuser.

In my quiet times, I still feel moments of raw pain from my past. I look at it for what it is: a catalyst for me to find the sacredness of my inner being—to realize more of myself and who I truly am. I believe how we think and act and how beautifully our spirit responds to our challenges is all that matters. My counselors and friends agree with this truth *"that the only thing man cannot take from you is your attitude in any given set of circumstances."*

My hope is to shed light on the unknown so my readers may understand the answer to the most often asked question, "Why did you stay so long?" After reading my story and documentation, I pray this question will cease to be asked, and instead the question will be, "Why did we allow this man, the religious organizations, and the law and judicial system to abuse, harass and enslave this woman and her children?"

I believe the judicial and religious systems in America are archaic. I believe our country is in need of changes. I believe that the only way to move things is to speak the truth in the face of fear. I have been threatened to stop all contacts with the media and to stop my writing. I refuse to be silenced. Why? I do not want anyone, including you or members of your family, to experience what has happened to me. If one woman, man or child's life is helped by my story, then I have accomplished my goal.

By writing I have created what is called a *healing crisis*. I have a lightened spirit knowing I have aired my past and my memories, have visited the ghosts and faced the demons.

I also believe I have an obligation to share with others what I have learned. Truth spoken in the absence of fear is a catalyst for healing and enlightenment.

Since I am only a name and not a face, I ask you to imagine yourself, or your own daughter, sister or mother as the woman in this story. I also ask you to respect my courage for sharing my personal holocaust. Today, I believe people are finding the courage to break through the silence - releasing secrets that have kept all of us trapped. People are saying "no more" to the shame, fear and pain.

If this story has fallen into your hands, I say, "Shalom". There are no accidents in life.

I hope by reading this account of my life, you will be encouraged to "remember who you truly are". Please join me on my journey in life of "remembering who I truly am."

Although my story addresses my own plight and survival through years of sexual abuse, domestic violence, ritual abuse and judicial injustice, I acknowledge that many men have experienced and survived similar horrors, including the loss of their children. I believe they have been harmed by the same rigid and perverse societal construct where money means power and power makes right.

I believe that the extremely patriarchal view of the roles of men and women in our society harm everyone and hinder our human evolution and ability to live fulfilling and mentally healthy lives - both for men and women. It alienates us from each other and isolates us from the divine.

> While my story addresses the ideological rigidity within our
> religious and judicial organizations, it does not discount the
> acts of kindness and compassion extended by men and women
> with various religious backgrounds and philosophies.
> For these people and their generosity, I am eternally grateful.

> Darkness is to be brought to light, and not the other way around.
> It is terrible for everybody when the truth does not come out.
> It is terrible for SOME when it does.

> *Some people may be pained by having their names appear in print, but I*
> *ask you, if one hides truth behind anonymity, can it really be truth?*
> *I felt compelled to honestly tell my story because for too long, crimes*
> *of abuse have been hidden behind walls and curtains and even the*
> *victims have pretended that nothing is wrong, nothing happened.*

The Cave

"Plato spoke to the relative inability of people
to take in information outside their usual belief
systems in his enduring classic *The Republic.*
There were a people who lived in chains, facing
the back of a dark cave. The only reality they
knew consisted of shadows cast by the activity
from the outside world. Finally, one of them
became bold enough to try to escape. He
returned to set the people in the cave free from
the prison of their illusions, reporting on a miraculous
outside world of light, color and substance. The
others could not believe him. They thought he was
crazy because the new information could not be
integrated into their previous experience."

–Joan Borysenko, Ph.D., *Fire in the Soul*

"To judge how much our acts will influence the future, we must look back and see what influence the past has had upon us." - *Matilda Joslyn Gage*

The Gift of Healing is Our Birthright

by Coral Anika Theill

In America there are many victims of childhood molestation and abuse, rape and domestic violence! But guess what: *There are relatively few batterers and perpetrators.*

In their efforts to seek safety, justice and vindication, victims often become further victimized by our judicial system. Why? The batterers and abusers are "innocent" and protected by family, friends, co-workers and church members. Often family and friends turn against the victim in order to protect the abuser and their own reputations.

Victims suffer not only from the abuse they experienced but also from the threat of meaninglessness and powerlessness that comes with it. People who experience the trauma of violence at the hand of someone they know, (i.e., a partner, parent, relative, therapist, teacher, pastor, or priest) - struggle to make meaning, usually in a context of isolation, if not moral condemnation and victim blaming.

Meanwhile, as the years pass, many victims become progressively more mentally, physically and emotionally sick because the victim has been rejected and betrayed all over again by those close to them who refuse to deal with the truth and by those who find denial an easy alternative. The burden placed on the victim's shoulders becomes unbearable. Finally, family and friends who "knew the truth" dismiss the crimes of molestation, rape and violence because "it happened a long time ago."

The victim's worst nightmare has come true. If the perpetrator is "innocent," then the victim must be guilty by default. It was their fault to begin with (they were told by their abuser). In the victim's mind, they must be both the criminal and the victim. The victim has a hard time finding where "they" are inside themselves. Finally, the victim becomes so physically sick and unnerved that he/she has a breakdown.

My married life continued the pattern of my childhood. After experiencing twenty years of violence and abuse in my marriage, I intuitively knew that continuing this way of life would eventually kill me. I went to Oregon's courts for help and protection for myself and my children. Nothing had prepared me for the horrors that I would experience in what we call 'Oregon's justice and legal system.' Marital and ritual abuse evolved into legal abuse.

As long as we continue to condone those in power who harm and victimize innocent people, then we will continue to witness injustices against those who are vulnerable and unable to protect and defend themselves. I believe my own life and experiences these past years reveal a moral dilemma for the religious organizations and judicial systems that exists today.

For recovery to begin, abuse victims must create a safe environment. Without freedom, there is no safety or recovery. Safety for many survivors is often at a great cost. Battered women may lose their babies and children, their homes, their friends and their livelihood. Survivors of childhood abuse will often even lose their families. Rarely does society recognize the dimensions and long-lasting effects of this reality for the victim.

After over a decade of personally seeking assistance from advocacy groups on a local, state and national level, **the advocacy system, as is, has offered me nothing.**

I met pseudo advocates these past years, who could not counsel with me, as my traumas were too "over the top" they said. Some advocates had their own "baggage" which prevented them from healthy thinking and viewpoints, other counselor/advocates projected their own judgments on me, because my traumas did not fit into their own religious perspective and beliefs. *Some advocates were as abusive, non-ethical, disrespectful and dismissive as my abusers.* And sadly, I met a few advocates who wish to keep their clients as "victims."

Not all individuals who offer help as counselors, therapists and advocates have good intentions. Some of the people who get involved in advocacy groups have their own narcissistic tendencies that turns their good intentions into something that can hurt and further victimize the people they say they want to represent.

Susan B. Anthony knew the definition of advocates and wrote, "Cautious, careful people, always casting about to preserve their reputation and social standing, never can bring about a reform. Those who are really in earnest must be willing to be anything or nothing in the world's estimation, and publicly and privately, in season and out, avow their sympathy with despised and persecuted ideas and their advocates, and bear the consequences."

The past seventeen years has been an incredible journey from darkness to light. Through my journey of "making light of the dark," I have had the privilege of meeting extraordinary individuals, who, like me, are human, flawed, spectacular and deeply compassionate. I am thankful for their assistance in my survival these past many years. Most importantly, they helped me heal the imbalances created from past wounds and see my past from a new perspective.

"When the pupil is ready, the teacher arrives."

In 1997, I was in shock and numb from decades of trauma, abuse and horror. At that time, Dr. Barbara May, Professor of Nursing at Linfield College, Portland, Oregon, came into my life as my long-term mentor and counselor. Among the many truths she imparted to me, these were the ones that literally set me free: *Keeping secrets only protects the abuser. Abuse does not deserve privacy. If violence cannot be talked about, it cannot be stopped.*

I truly believe more victims would be willing to share their pain, fear and shame if they could expect to be believed, respected and vindicated.

When I met Dr. May, I did not know the extent of my traumas, as abuse was the only life I had known. I had not heard of the term "domestic violence" or "Stockholm Syndrome" in my years of marriage. Divorce was never an option in the legalistic, fundamental Christian world that I had escaped. Wholeness, wellness and joy had not been an option in my previous years of marriage.

As I began to seek the Truth that would create wholeness for me, mentors and friends assisted me in remembering who I truly was apart from my trauma. They taught me how to respect and honor the sacredness of my being. They helped guide me from a devastating past to wholeness. Through their assistance, I am in touch with the wildish and sacred part of my soul, again. Most of all, they helped me understand Dr. Viktor Frankl's wise words, "To live is to suffer, to survive is to find meaning in the suffering."

Healing is the process of rounding up all the fragments of our shattered self and reconciling them. The traumatized person who accomplishes the work of recovery and healing has the potential of becoming more integrated and more aware and conscious than the person who has endured no blatant trauma and has never had to piece together a shattered psyche. Throughout the years, I learned to value the horrifying scars of my childhood and past adult life as valuable raw material for soul work, that I was responsible for my life and could be a part of "creating my reality."

My counselors assisted me in regaining my spiritual and emotional wellness by meeting me in the place of chaos and aiding me in regaining my spiritual center—our inner knowing and sacred power. I believe our emotional wellness is balanced and strong when we are operating from our place of inner knowing and that individuals heal themselves, counselors simply offer support.

They always encouraged me to listen and follow my own intuition and integrity, my own commitment to truth. I learned that when I listen inside, I discover who I truly am apart from the conditioning and brainwashing so prevalent in our society, culture, politics and religion.

My greatest coping tool and gift I possessed was my own still quiet voice, my intuition. As I began to listen to my own inner voice, lights within me turned back on and I became more aware of myself and the world around me. Intuition is like hearing a song played only once—you must respond to it when it offers itself, for it seldom plays the same song twice. I value this gift—intuition. It has never never failed me.

Counselors and friends, throughout the years, introduced me to great thinkers, authors and writings that led me in my own research to help me understand "what had happened and why," i.e., *Women Who Run with the Wolves*, by Clarissa Pinkola Estes, Ph.D., *Women, Church and State* by Matilda Joslyn Gage, *Trauma and Recovery* by Judith Herman and *Man's Search for Meaning*, by Dr. Viktor Frankl.

My mentors helped me understand the importance of finding my voice and "giving voice to the violence." They also encouraged me to write my life story.

At first, I found that many chapters of my life were too difficult to discuss or talk about. By writing, I created what is called a "healing crisis." To heal from our trauma, we must face it squarely. Alienation from our memories dooms us to live in a constant present, cut off from the past and the future. By remembering, I am a "healed healer" prepared to help others see that they can also help themselves.

My mentors encouraged me to "go to the edge of the light, listen deeply and feel my own inner guidance." They helped me realize the truth that we all possess, that each one of us has a right to live without fear, to be treated with respect, to have and express our own feelings and opinions, to be listened to and taken seriously, to set our own priorities, to say "no" without feeling guilty, to ask for what we want without reprisal, to ask for information from others, to have our own needs met, to have privacy and support and friendship.

As I healed, I began to understand that my personal losses could be a vehicle to experiencing a greater good. Surrendering lost dreams helped me prepare for new dreams. My mentors never told me what to do, but instead equipped me by helping me become aware of a wide range of self-care and self-help books, alternative health literature, spiritual history and delight directed activities that strengthened me physically, mentally, emotionally and spiritually.

I learned that true freedom begins the day we walk away from fear, scarcity, blame and guilt.

We must take responsibility for our own life, to the best of our ability and serve as beacons along the way. As I healed, I understood that the greatest gift I could offer to those around me was my own inner joy and wholeness. Once healed, all that is left is compassion and inner joy.

"To stay with one's joy, we sometimes have to fight for it, we have to strengthen ourselves and go full-bore, doing battle in whatever way we deem most shrewd. To prepare for siege, we may have to go without many comforts for the duration. We can go without most things for long periods of time, anything almost, but not our joy...... "- Clarissa Estes, Ph.D., *Women Who Run with the Wolves*

Many of my friends and counselors possessed the rare gift of being able to sit with another's raw pain, without having to move it, change, it, shift it, or judge it. Their compassion and empathy, along with resonating respect, gave me the support I needed to not only heal, but become an empowered and intuitive woman. Often no words were needed, but in these moments, I knew I was with someone I could trust for life who would never betray me, and who literally stood in the fire with me month after month and who encouraged me through many dark nights of the soul.

Another positive component involving my counselors and friends was the fact that they "believed me and believed in me." They had a profound gift of gently walking me through some of the unexplored territory of my life, when it was correct for me, and help draw out unspoken pieces of me. They allowed me to see more of myself. Even though I was in such a broken state, my counselors and friends envisioned me as "whole." And that was their gift to me, someone who not only believed in me but could envision me "all anew."

To heal and become empowered we need to "go home." Home was a place I was not familiar with. Up to this point, I had only known how to obey to avoid further cruelty and harm.

Many people are living like this. Their soul has gone off and left them without feeling. Many people have been conditioned to give their *power* away and feel helpless in the face of conflict, illness, disease and overwhelming emotion. I have learned that when we go home we weep when we first step on that wonderful sacred ground again.

When we never go home, we enter a zombie zone. I've been there.

"The most cruel part of this lifeless state is that the woman functions, walks, speaks, acts and even accomplishes many things, but she no longer feels the effects of what has gone wrong—if she did, her pain would make her immediately turn to the fixing of it."

"Home is the pristine instinctual life that works as easily as a joint sliding upon its greased bearing, where all is as it should be, where all the noises sound right, and the light is good, and the smells make us feel calm rather than alarmed. Home is whatever revives balance. Home is where we can imagine the future and also pour over the scar maps of the psyche, learning what led to what, and where we will go next." - Clarissa Estes, Ph.D., *Women Who Run with the Wolves*

In the words of Alice Miller,

"To live with one's own truth is to be at home with oneself. That is the opposite of isolation."

Throughout the years, I discussed with my mentors my longing to be safe. Through their spiritual and personal reflection with me, I found safety not in a physical sense, but more in a spiritual sense.

Making a safe place begins with each individual creating a safe place within themselves. When we can experience and realize ourselves on the inside, the condition of our lives and our world will change and improve on the outside. **We become the light we radiate.** I have come to understand that "true spiritual courage is more than faith that the universe is friendly and that, despite all earthly appearance to the contrary, we are ultimately safe. It is the *inner knowing* that this is so."–Dr. Joan Borysenko, *Fire in the Soul*

My counselors never treated me as a victim, or that I was "less than" even though my traumas had left me shaken in a world I did not know or understand. They treated me as an equal, always, and it was with the respect they resonated toward me, that I was nurtured, not just back to health, but to an evolved and spiritual woman.

My breakdown and collapse in 1993 was truly a "reset button." This painful time was a catalyst to my spirit waking up and learning how to function beautifully. I learned to love, respect and honor myself. I found the center of my universe— my own balance and harmony. Relationships based on respect create a sacred place for the unhealed places of our hearts and souls to heal. I understood and trusted that this place would be protected, not violated, in my association with my trusted counselors, mentors and friends. This fact was the foundation of my healing and is a RARE find.

Many victims move on without realizing that a part of them is missing. They compensate or cover for the part that's gone. They know something is wrong but they don't know what. To heal properly, I discovered it was important to pick up the pieces I had left behind. This process is different for everyone, but the result is the same: you will once again, discover your true essence.

Your trauma is not who you are, it is just what happened to you.

In his book, *Five things We Cannot Change*, Dr. David Richo writes about the unfairness of life as a given and that is certainly true. He also has a lengthy comment about victims.

"To be human is to be vulnerable, and an ego that cannot accommodate that and move through it is a hazard to spiritual development. If everything collapses, I will deal with it by staying with the pieces and then picking up the pieces. That piecework practice helps us distinguish two kinds of victims:

"Some victims lay themselves open for pain and contempt. They may wait for someone to come along and set them free. They become more and more open to being preyed upon as they lose their boundaries.

"Other victims however are simply vulnerable in an open, healthy way and let themselves experience the betrayals that life and relationship sometimes bring. They are hurt, but they have a spiritual technology to deal with their hurt. They do not hurt back. They do not let themselves be hurt more.

"They stand up for themselves and wish enlightenment for those who hurt them. This is how they let their hearts open more than ever and become strong against predators while still penetrable to the slings and arrows of love. They may be victims but they are not casualties.

"Thus, the adult challenge is to believe that there is a design that wants to come through in our lives despite the random and untidy display."

If you think of yourself as a victim and are unable to move past that view, you won't recover. If you see the violence only as a horrible event that happened to you, and not allow it to define you or prevent you from redefining your experiences with a new spiritual outlook, you will recover, choose life; move forward—with or without justice. Most victims have to recover without the conscience of this country validating their story, without justice and without restitution. I truly believe, though, that we are victimized twice if we do not seek "justice."

In her book, *Fire in the Soul*, Dr. Joan Borysenko writes, "Freedom is the destiny of every living being. We become free by waking from our dreams of fear, scarcity, blame and guilt, by taking responsibility for acting, to the best of our knowledge, with care and loving-kindness that we may kindle the light of love within and by that light see our way home and serve as beacons for others along the way. It is most often suffering that kindles love, loss that deepens understanding, hurt that opens the eyes of the heart that see forgiveness as a way of life and peace of mind as our birthright."

In so many cases, and this is not to be judged, many people will not or cannot "arrive on the other side." This is the place I use to refer to as "living in the present moment, our now," apart from our traumas.

As we live on the "other side" of our traumas, we can, for the most part, function well in society. The chains and haunting of our past, which often rob us of our present joys, our very life, do not control us. I believe our task in life is to live with all that is hard in our lives without being able to know why it happens and still find a way to fully choose life, every day.

It is my hope and prayer that individuals facing insurmountable crisis and tragedies will be blessed with compassionate friends and advocates extraordinaire such as the individuals who have shown up in my life. Their compassion was always equally balanced by a healthy sense of humor, which to this day, I appreciate.

Bearing Witness

April 2010

Dear Coral,

Even if your children choose not to have further contact with you (that is always our greatest fear as estranged parents); it doesn't mean that our children won't know -unconsciously at the minimum - that they are cherished and loved by someone outside their lives with the perpetrators. They may not be able to remember that we were the source of that love, but they will still have a strong sense that it's out there. They may equate the big, powerful outside with a god or goddess; that's okay. It still works to help them to feel truly loved, and protected, and cared about - in the most secret compartment of their soul, where it is not touched by any invader.

Even if our children are too young to remember when they're removed from us, or if they have been brainwashed by their new caregivers to think of us as other than who we really are - and criminal sociopaths are usually quite good at that - our children's earliest sensory memories of our love and nurturing will remain a mental/emotional protective factor for the rest of their lives.

I've learned enough about childhood neurobiological development and secure attachment to understand why it happens that way. Our conscious memories of our parents' love - if we experienced such love - may fade away completely or be suppressed out of necessity to conform with our new family system and keep them from turning on us in anger. Still, the neurobiological/sensory imprint of our parents' love is like a fossil imprinted deeply in a dense rock. The nonverbal neurological/sensory imprint remains for life and is a part of everything we are and do; even if we're completely aware of its influence.

Nobody can erase the imprint without killing us because the imprint of love is strong, more natural, and more resilient than the effects of human evil. And so, even if you are not able to connect with your children now; you've already given them their most important protective factor: "early-onset" love and nurturing." - *Kathleen A. Sullivan*, MSW, Chattanooga, Tennessee

"Out of suffering have emerged the strongest of souls; the most massive characters are seared with scars." - *Khalil Gibran*

Bonsheá

Making Light of the Dark
The True Account of the Life of Coral Anika Theill
Written by Coral Anika Theill

On March 10, 1996, I was forced, by an Order of the Court, and by my ex-husband, his attorney, his family and religious supporters, to do something that raged against my good conscience, my common sense and against all my motherly instincts. After a temporary custody hearing, a Court Order signed by Judge Norblad forcibly removed my nursing infant and two youngest children from me. I obeyed the Court Order and gave my children over to my ex-husband. I drove to the hospital, rented a breast-pump and later collapsed and went into shock. I could not understand what had happened and why. I have not yet recovered from the shock, perhaps I never will.

For nearly twenty years, I was married to a man who ruled his household with absolute authority. His personal justification for his behavior came from Biblical scripture. During the course of our marriage, I bore him eight children. My firstborn children were identical twin girls. I also suffered three miscarriages. I home schooled the oldest children for several years, renovated three houses, baked, canned, gardened, etc. I was treated as a possession (slave). In the course of my marriage I was drawn, against my will, into several extreme fundamental churches and cults which emphasized patriarchal authority and the obedience of women, i.e., Mr. Bill Gothard of Basic Youth Conflicts, Catholicism, People of Praise Catholic Charismatic Covenant Community, Corvallis Christian Center, Assembly of God and Pentecostal Churches, The Sacred Name Movement, "Quiverfull Movement," NW Hills Baptist Church, Bridgeport Community Church, Marion Church of God Seventh Day, and Mr. Warner's own "home church."

I met my former husband, Mr. V. Martin Warner, in January 1974. At that time, he was working in Portland, Oregon, as an engineer, and I was attending court reporter school. We were married two years later at St. Mary's Catholic Church in Corvallis, Oregon. My husband's cousin, Father Pat McNamee, performed the ceremony. Over nine hundred family and friends attended our wedding and reception. My parents arrived at the last minute. They had threatened not to attend because the wedding was being held in a Catholic Church. I vowed to love, honor, cherish, respect and <u>obey</u> my husband. We lived in Corvallis for the next fifteen years. In August 1991 we moved to Independence, Oregon.

Coral with her father at her wedding

Coral Anika Theill, aka Kathryn Y. (Hall) Warner with her
father, Bobby Ray Hall, at her wedding, April 10, 1976,
St. Mary's Catholic Church, Corvallis, Oregon

Mr. Warner was born in 1949 and raised in Ridgefield, Washington on a dairy farm. He was the second of nine children. His parents, Bernard and Helen Warner were devout Catholics. After high school, Marty Warner attended Washington State University and received a degree in engineering. While attending college he was very involved in fraternities and college government.

Although his family was respected within their religious community, there were numerous horrors experienced in the Warner household. Two children, one son and one daughter, were sexually molested by outsiders who were welcomed into the home. One fourteen-year-old son was crushed and killed by a bull while the parents were away from the farm. One son impregnated a young girl when he was sixteen, and Marty's father divorced his wife, Helen, in the 1970's. Marty Warner never acknowledged his parent's divorce, even though his father had another child with his new wife. As Marty entered his twenties, he often returned to the family farm on weekends. Marty was known to use physical violence on his younger brothers to keep them in line and he often abused alcohol.

People will question how it is possible to know someone for two years and not see the signs that something is wrong. Looking back, I can say, "I brought this on myself because I didn't want to know the truth," but nothing had prepared me to be able to *see* the truth.

The signs I should have recognized were two recurrent themes in Marty's decision to propose to me–he repeatedly asked if I would be a submissive wife. He also made me promise to *never* refuse him sexually. But I had been trained to try to please so these requests did not set off any internal alarms. Then, after he raped me prior to our marriage, I felt I had no escape. Society's rule was if a *woman* had sex you *must* marry.

Marty drove up to Longview, Washington, to visit me at my apartment after a long day of work at his family's farm. He knocked on my door late one night, came inside and brutally raped me. He later continued to stalk me while I was working in Longview. I was 19, he was six years older. There was no one to tell, nowhere to go.

> Marty Warner was sexually very aggressive. I believe this incident, along with others throughout the years, was why I felt controlled by Mr. Warner. Assaults of this nature produces guilt, fear, shame and embarrassment. They also create an element of fear. Some people fall in love. I believe, in my relationship with Marty Warner, I fell into bondage.

After we were married, I did realize his ideological rigidity was going to create my personal hell on earth. But I had made a vow and I learned to live with it the best I could. The word divorce couldn't even be mentioned in the circles of people we were associated with (mainly extremist religious churches, cults, fundamentalist, etc.) My children were my only source of joy in my life and home.

Today, I believe that commitment to someone doesn't mean staying with someone if it becomes destructive or devitalizing. Commitment means being direct about one's intentions and, if the situation changes, communicating honestly with the other person. Commitment is to follow one's own integrity.

Mr. Warner ruled our marriage by certain scriptural principles (isolated verses from the Bible). He believed these verses are irrefutable principles that govern the marriage of a righteous Christian man and woman.

> *"Wives, be subject to your own husbands, as to the Lord. For the husband is the head of the wife, as Christ also is the head of the church, He Himself being the Savior of the body. But as the church is subject to Christ, so also the wives ought to be subject to their husbands in all things."* Ephesians 5:22-24

> *"But I want you to understand that Christ is the head of every man, and the man is the head of a woman..."* I Corinthians 11:3

> *"For a man does not originate from woman, but woman from man; for indeed man was not created for woman's sake, but woman for the man's sake."* I Corinthians 11:8-9

> *"Husbands, love your wives, just as Christ also loved the church and gave Himself up for her, that He might sanctify her, having cleansed her by the washing of water with the word, that he might present to Himself the church in all her glory, having no spot or wrinkle or any such thing; but that she should be holy and blameless.* Ephesians 5: 25-27

Marty took these principles and interpreted them to mean that any disagreement with his wishes or beliefs was ungodly rebellion against himself and God. He interpreted them to mean that I (his wife) needed constant correcting and punishment to make me pure before God and that he was the husband that God had given me in order to make me "spot free."

My husband believed that women were created solely for the pleasure of man, and from his biblical perspective and conviction, were to obey and submit to their husbands "in all things." (I Cor. 11:3-9 and Eph. 5:22-24) He believed that women in our society were all feminists and were in rebellion to the Word of God. Within the context of my marriage, I soon became a "Stepford Wife," a glassed over robot to meet my husband's every demand. I learned quickly how to obey in all things, or else.

> I remember being shaken violently by Marty at the beginning of our marriage when I asked why he would not let me call my father or mother. The stage was set. I had a good memory. I learned quickly.

Marty Warner is a man of intense religious zeal. Keeping up with his ever-changing and extreme convictions took an enormous amount of energy. He was sometimes involved in several church organizations at one time. He led our family through eight cults including his "own personal cult" which he created within our home. I did not realize the long-term cost and effect my marriage would have on my spiritual, mental, emotional and physical well-being.

I was required to be a "helpmeet" in a world not unlike the one from Margaret Atwood's dystopian novel "*The Handmaid's Tale*." My husband, Marty Warner, used coercive control, isolation and intimidation tactics to strip me of my personhood, safety and freedoms as a United States citizen.

In Atwood's novel, a "handmaid" - a woman designated to be a breeder - is treated as property, with no rights. Her only value to society is to make children for officials and their barren wives.

In this society, the rights of women and children were reconfigured while being told they were the ones in charge, and the patriarchy was solidified through strict, subversive control of women's status and roles.

Bearing Witness

BONSHEA provides incredibility disconcerting insights into the labyrinth of self-proclaimed morally self-righteous communities within our society. No article about Coral's crusade to correct the injustices she has suffered can truly capture the personal strengths which Coral demonstrates on every page of her book. It is very difficult to feel Ms. Theill's pain without actually reading her story, although many of us can empathize with people in abusive relationships. Very little occurs which does not provide insights into other conflicts. Gang violence, the death and destruction Sunnis and Shiites perpetrate upon each other daily around the world, the hate between Protestants and Catholics in Northern Ireland, are all variations on the "cultism" which has caused Coral so much pain. Without this understanding, some could say Coral is the victim of isolated acts of violence by one person. That is not the case. She is the victim of a morally tainted community within an uncaring broader society.

Regardless of the future, nothing will allow Coral to recapture the past. Yes, she can pray for having some of the burden taken from her shoulders, and indeed, she has lost much, but clearly Coral is not saying "stop my suffering" because stopping the pain is something only she alone can do. Ms. Theill is asking for others to understand how she has suffered, and the truth of why she has suffered.

The power of her life is not that she escaped from a "cult", but that she continues to serve as an agent of change. This is not a "she said/he said" tale of abuse, but rather a self-damning expose of her struggle to survive. She is not a martyr. She is a victim of the too frequent chasm between a blind adherence to an interpretation of laws and a true understanding of justice.

The question which may be too painful for us to answer, "Is religiously justified domestic violence the reality which our society cannot face?" Making truths inaccessible does not change the truth. - *Bruce McLelland, Washington, D.C.*

"The problem's not that the truth is harsh but that liberation from ignorance is as painful as being born. Run after truth until you're breathless. Accept the pain involved in re-creating yourself afresh." – *Naguib Mahpouz*

I

Childhood, "Soul Murder," Marriage, Children, Religious Cults, People of Praise Cult, Quiverfull Movement

I believe life is a series of rooms. Who we get stuck in the room with is what our lives are.

I was born in Tawas City, Michigan, to Bobby Ray and Carolyn Jean (Karstensen) Hall. My father was serving in the Air Force at Lansing Air Force Base. My birth name was Kathryn Yvonne Hall. I grew up in Washington State. I was a straight 'A' student, president of Honor Society, co-valedictorian of my high school class and voted most likely to succeed and most academic. I had received my solo pilot's license by the time I was seventeen years old at Pearson Field Airport in Vancouver, Washington. I volunteered in nursing homes, at schools for the blind and deaf. During my childhood, I suffered years of sexual molestation, physical, mental, verbal and emotional abuse. I do not blame my parents or my childhood for the way my life unfolded.

My father was transferred to McChord Air Force base, so we moved to Washington State when I was five years old. I took care of my mother who was ill during most of my childhood. I also helped my father renovate our homes, old classic cars and wrecked helicopters. (Instead of cars in our garages, we had helicopters.) I also cut and delivered cord wood to help assist the family's income. I baby-sat, worked in orchards and picked berries and cut berry canes for extra money. I had one brother, Donald, who was two years younger.

1

My father served in the Air Force for fifteen years and later worked as a pilot for the federal government until his death in 1984. His job assignments were mostly out-of-town. In the mid 1960's, my brother and I crashed in a Bell Helicopter with my father in Libby, Montana due to the altimeter failing. My father was demonstrating aeronautical stunts over the runway to amuse my brother and me. We all walked away from the crash fine, but the helicopter was quite crippled. Prior to my senior year in high school, my father encouraged me to pursue a career in aviation. I enrolled in ground school and completed two years of flight training. I passed my FAA exams at the Portland International Airport.

I spent most of my growing up years in Kennewick, Federal Way and Vancouver, Washington. My childhood was filled with many experiences, some of which I was not prepared for, including several years of sexual molestation by my great-uncle, and physical, mental, verbal and emotional abuse from members of my family.

On occasion my brother and I would visit my paternal grandmother and step-grandfather, Odis and Fern Hall, in the summers. I have memories of severe beatings with belts from my step-grandfather from the time I was five years old. He had done the same to his step-son (my father) but used whips and chains. This type of punishment seemed normal to him and he often hit me in public. After one beating when I was five, I could barely walk and became very ill with the German measles. My mother watched the beatings and appeared pleased to see me suffer. During this illness I remember feeling weak in body and spirit for a long time. My grandparents were very occupied with their foster children during these visits and throughout my childhood and therefore had little time to give attention to their own grandchildren.

I was taught by my family to submit and to obey my parents, teachers and elders. Approval and security centered on how well I pleased my parents and those placed in authority over me. My parents did not consider my feelings as a person because I was their "property". By my birth, my parents claimed "ownership" of me and my life. I was used as a possession and an extension of my parent's ego and identity.

My mother was a sociopath and narcissist. I was not allowed to speak, feel, and show emotion or cry while living under the rule of my mother. My job was to serve her and make her happy. My life as her daughter was a cross between the *Mommy Dearest* and *Carrie* movie.

2

My mother's personality was ego-centric, narcissistic and hypochondriacal. She was cold and demanding. For years she abused me verbally, emotionally, physically, sexually, financially and spiritually. I lived in fear of her rage and mood swings every day of my life. During the night she would walk in my bedroom and throw Bibles at me. She also appeared to derive pleasure from publicly humiliating me. From the age of fifteen I was her personal chauffeur, beautician, marriage counselor, nurse, cook and maid. My mother viewed me as someone who should be in service to meet her every need. She viewed herself as privileged and superior.

Narcissistic parents do not respect and value their children's feelings or see them as independent from them in a positive way. They do not feel that their children's thoughts and feelings are as important as theirs. Children under these circumstances often grow up feeling 'voiceless.'

To raise emotionally healthy children, you must give them the gift of 'voice.'

During my teenage years, I longed for safety away from my mother and I thought of running away, but there was nowhere to go, no one to tell. I was isolated from family and friends. My mother said I had no time for other people. Outings with friends were a rare occasion. When I did enjoy an occasion away from the home, my mother verbally abused me for weeks afterwards. I learned at an early age the lack of equality of men and woman. My family favored my brother and other male relatives. Male-privileged entitlement was the norm in our home.

My mother exhibited extreme prejudice by her speech and actions. I did not relate to her feelings against people from other ethnic backgrounds or religions. I was greatly disturbed to hear her projections of hate toward men and all those she did not care to understand or tolerate. I could not understand why she felt this way. Her beliefs were foreign to me as I felt acceptance towards all people.

My father was a loner. Although successful as a pilot, mechanic and carpenter, he suffered an emotional numbness as a result of his own childhood. He was severely beaten by his step-father with chains and whips from the age of four until he left home and enlisted in the Air Force.

He became a pilot and captain in the Air Force and flew secret missions during the Korean War. I remember the thrill during my elementary years of riding in helicopters with my father as he traveled to job assignments. I was closest to my father, but my mother forbade me to spend time with him when I reached my high school years and adult life. My father told me that my mother lied to him about being pregnant, so that is why he married her. I witnessed years of my mother abusing my father. They suffered an unhealthy marriage, infidelities, and serious health problems until my father's death in 1984.

Coral Anika Theill, aka Kathryn Yvonne Hall with her father, Bobby Ray Hall, Lansing, Michigan, 1957

Soul Murder

As a young girl, age six, I have memories of visiting my great-uncle, Herschel Stonebraker, on several occasions. He lived in a compound of buildings with surrounding walls, fences and wires. I was told that this was where my great-uncle "worked". While sitting in the "visiting room" at this facility, I remember feeling very uncomfortable–there was no privacy for the couples. My great-uncle was serving time at the Walla Walla State Penitentiary. My parents and grandparents were trying to show support to get him paroled early. Many years later, as I pieced my life back together, I would discover the *truth*.

My great-uncle, Herschel Stonebraker, murdered his sixteen-year-old daughter, Patricia, in a drunken rage in 1956. At his court trial my uncle is quoted as saying his "daughter had it coming to her," after he shot her. He was not remorseful. Testimony at his court hearings state he was angry with his wife for cheating on him. He had also assaulted his wife with a pistol and threatened to kill her after he murdered his daughter.

4

He served a few years in prison and was released with the understanding that he was to live with my grandparents in the Tacoma area and not in the Kennewick area where his ex-wife and two remaining daughters lived. But he moved in with *our* family in Kennewick, Washington, the same town as his ex-wife. His probation conditions also stated that he was not to live in our city or have contact with young girls because he had formerly sexually molested his daughters. (Hershel's ex-wife, Pauline, died in a house fire shortly after he was released from prison.)

My great-uncle's probation office was "missing in action."

My father once shared with me that while he was being severely beaten by his step-father, his uncle, (Herschel), came to his aid. My father's gratitude toward his uncle for this incident would blind him from protecting me, his daughter, from this man.

As a child, I deserved to feel safe in my own home, be respected, be responded to with courtesy, live free from emotional and physical outburst and rage of others, manipulation, intimidation and trickery and not be subjected to sexual molestation and human trafficking. Safety was not my mother's concern for me – destroying my very being, spirit and soul was her goal.

> To this day, I cannot understand why my parents and grandparents had my father's uncle come to live with our family after his release from prison.

During my elementary years, my mother sent me to an upstairs apartment each night to sleep with my alcoholic great-uncle, Herschel Stonebraker, although I had my own bed and separate room on the main floor of the house. I was also severely beaten by my step-grandfather during these years.

> I was fondled and caressed in very explicit and sexual ways and forced to touch and do things no child should have to do. My own sexuality, which hadn't even developed at that age, was forced upon me and twisted. I was forced to be the object of my great-uncle's desire. Family members taught me to obey and be "seen and not heard."

Sometimes on weekends and Christmas Eve when my father was home, I was allowed to sleep in my own bed.

Physicians and counselors have commented about my childhood. They believe my family members offered me to my great-uncle "to keep him home" so he would not be arrested for molesting other young girls in our community. But if that was their plan, it did not work well.

After my uncle was released from prison, he was caught molesting another young girl. My grandparents paid large sums of monies for attorneys to keep my great-uncle from being sent back to prison. After the trial, I was again handed over to my great-uncle to meet his sexual needs. I begged for help, but no help came.

Coral Anika Theill, aka Kathryn Y. Hall, with her brother, Donald Hall 1961

They dismissed my calls for help and I did not have a vocabulary to make them understand.

> The message I got from my parents was that if I told the truth,
> I would be rejected and my abuser embraced.

> Instead of my protectors, my parents exploited me for reasons
> that only they will have to answer for.

People, even my former psychiatrist, Dr. Charles H. Kuttner, have asked why I did not try to get help from someone outside the family while this was happening.

I think adults asking a question like that forget how small and vulnerable a child is. And when all of the people that you expect to be good and trustworthy - the people you have looked to for protection and comfort your whole life - betray you and tell you nothing is wrong or its all your fault, as a child you don't have a lot of power to change your circumstances. I tried to please my family and suppress the feeling that everything was wrong. I could escape into my imagination and numb my feelings. Add to that the fact that you've been told to keep a secret or you are afraid of punishment if you tell someone, it's rare that an abused child is able to reach outside of their world to seek help.

Uncle Herschel lived with us throughout my junior high and early high school years. I was required to be his caretaker when he was ill due to his alcoholism. He left only after his drinking problems became too difficult for my father to manage and tolerate.

My mother received great satisfaction observing the abuse I suffered. She was cold and demanding until the day she died in 2010. Some details of my mother's abuse of me are too humiliating and shameful to articulate.

Before her death, my mother (like my ex-husband) had friends whose consciousness was aligned symbolically and in terms of beliefs of their own selfishness, fear and corruption.

While speaking to my mother by phone, she spoke to me about my childhood and acknowledged the abuse I suffered, but she expressed no remorse for what she had done to me. Just hearing her voice re-traumatized me. In her letters, she admitted what she did to me, but felt no responsibility. She would ask me if I was reading my Bible and if I Jesus was my Lord and Savior.

My mother's hate of me did not stop me from loving her. Since I was her target, later in life, I stepped aside to heal because of the ongoing atrocities and crimes she committed against me. In short, my mother was my pimp and trafficked me throughout my childhood. Love was and is still stronger than her hate of me.

Because I confronted my mother about the abuse I suffered several years ago, she disinherited me and left her and my brother's sizeable estate to my well-to-do cousin, Mrs. Beverly Ann (Stallings) Moerke, Walla Walla, WA, and me, $1.00.

Beverly's relationship with my mother was not conflicted – my mother's rules for me did not apply to her. Beverly, a devout Catholic, sent me a $1.00 check through her attorney, Mr. Bradley V. Timmons, just in time for Christmas 2011. Even though I live under poverty level due to disabilities, I never cashed the check. Friends confronted Ms. Moerke, but there was no response from her. **In short, my cousin made me into a *"bastard child."***

I know my father is rolling in his grave over the fact that I was disinherited. No matter – I am still my father's daughter.

Mentors and friends wonder what price my cousin, Mrs. Moerke, would put on the sexual service I was forced into by my mother and great-uncle during my young childhood years. I received no compensation or restitution for the many years of torture and for the crimes my mother committed against me. Under the *Child Abuse Accountability Act* adult children can sue their abusive parents.

> **Childhood sexual abuse and rape is "soul murder" and child homicide.** The effects of these types of crimes reverberate through a child's life and extend into adulthood. Survivors become the walking wounded.

Coral Anika Theill, aka Kathryn Y. Hall, 1965

Besides the years of my uncle's molestation, I was also attacked by a man while I was baby-sitting for my neighbors. I resisted and thankfully he did not rape me. I was fifteen years old and was terrified from the incident. He was in his 30's and married. I did tell my mother and the woman I baby-sat for, but no one responded. I remember going home and showering to try to feel clean again.

As a young girl, connecting with nature, rock hunting and spending time in the forest was restorative and relaxing for me. Anorexia became a coping tool for me throughout my teenage years. I also suffered hormonal imbalances because I wasn't eating and I was under a lot of stress. My mother took me to an OB/Gyn because my menstrual cycles had ceased for several years. He sent me to a specialist at Providence Hospital in Portland, Oregon. After a short visit with the specialist, he required me to strip naked in a room full of young male medical students. I remember him touching parts of my body with a pointing stick. My mother was also present in the room. I was mortified.

My mother made another appointment for us to return. When I got home, I begged my father not to send me back to the hospital again. He said to obey my mother. Again, I was taken back to the specialist. I was given hormone shots each week for a couple months. I did not feel well, my hair began to fall out and I bled for most of this period of time. The physicians finally stopped their experimentation with my hormones.

In the circles I lived in, women would demonstrate their "love" for their husband and/or father by appeasing him and keeping him happy—no matter the cost to their personal well-being. Sexuality was not spoken about in our home, but there were underlying messages given by both parents that were unspoken. My father appeared uncomfortable with my becoming a young woman, and somewhat disapproving. My mother became jealous. Teachers had similar projections.

But the view the world saw of me was much different than how my family saw me. During my adolescence I demonstrated maturity and responsibility beyond my years.

During my senior year at Columbia River High School, Vancouver, Washington, I received a "Daughter of the American Revolution," D.A.R. citizenship award, an Outstanding Business Education Award, and was co-valedictorian of my class (almost 300 students). I was well respected by my teachers, fellow classmates and the community.

Coral Anika Theill, aka Kathryn Y. Hall, high school graduation,
Columbia River H.S., Vancouver, Washington, 1973, Co-Valedictorian

For many years, I blocked the unpleasant memories of my childhood. Although I did not harbor feelings of resentment or bitterness toward my abusers, inside

I knew that my soul had been violated. I knew someone, somehow, had taken something very sacred of mine. Feelings of shame, uncertainty and chaos would haunt me in the years to come as a result of living in a home where no one listened and boundaries were seldom honored. The memories of childhood were painful because those I looked to for guidance and protection never "showed up". My parents and family not only betrayed me; they sabotaged me.

> In her book, *Fire in the Soul*, Dr. Joan Borysenko writes, "When we suffer a trauma, we lose part of our soul. It stays stuck to the trauma, lost in the imaginal realm beyond space and time. We cannot move on and experience newness in this world because invisible cords keep us tethered to pain and sorrow in another time and place. Many cultures believe that this soul loss is directly responsible for mental and physical illness, a point of view that I share at least in part. It is the shaman's job to enter the imaginable realm and free the part of the soul that is bound."

When I was nineteen, I tried to confide in my mother so she would know the truth about my childhood. She glared at me and called me a "slut." That was the end of me attempting to have a conversation with her that had anything to do with reality. I couldn't deal with the pain and horror of my childhood years until after my divorce. I was conditioned by my parents, religion and my ex-husband that I must always compromise, deny the truth, and give away my soul to avoid further harm, pain and terror.

After I sought safety from my husband, I realized that my parents and grandparents were also predators in my life. I asked myself these questions, when considering contact with my family. Do we send flowers, cards and presents to rapists and people who would assault us? Do we socialize with those who rape us or assault us? The answer, of course, is "no." So, why do many of us allow our abusive family members to further harm us? I believe it is because of societal and religious conditioning....it is definitely not a directive from God. I believe in a God who does not want us to be subjected to cruelty.

Sadly, many adults are unable to escape relationships with the very people who have abused, tortured and/or molested them, just because they are "family." I believe people can develop 'trauma blindness' and either deny their pain or become so accustomed to it that they are afraid to relinquish it. 'Trauma blindness' is the mental scarring that somehow prevents you from accurately 'seeing' trauma around you and being able to avoid it.

> Today, the mentors in my life are assisting me as I bring the pieces of my soul and self back. As a young girl, I prayed to the Universe to please help me. My prayers are being answered. I feel whole, well and safe.

> My mother and family have never apologized for or even admitted their negligence and their exploitation of my mind, body and soul. I have learned in life that much of the population is asleep, dead, or "missing in action". There appear to be two types of people populating the earth– those who are awake and who walk in the ways of compassion and those who are the walking dead, who are asleep and who know compassion not.

During my high school years, I was occupied with studies and caring for my mother. I did not become involved with drugs or alcohol. I had several buddy friends, but no boyfriends. I dated my flight instructor for two months. We were never intimate. During my high school years, I did not feel emotionally, physically or mentally prepared for intimate relationships. I wanted to attend college and start a career. I did not have plans to marry or raise a family. I longed to get acquainted with myself–I longed for wholeness–for the <u>solitude of self</u>.

After graduation from high school, I enrolled in court reporter school in Portland, Oregon, and within twelve months was working for the Superior Court in Washington State as a secretary to two Superior Court judges, as a bailiff clerk and as a juvenile court reporter. My job gave me experience and exposure to our judicial system and to sheriffs, crisis care teams, district attorneys, etc. I worked for the Superior Court for two years prior to my marriage, and for a short time, I worked as a legal assistant for a district attorney after my marriage.

Although I was working a full-time job, sometimes eighteen to twenty-four hours at a time, and was living out-of-town, my father continued to demand that I travel to Vancouver, Washington, to stay with my mother on my off hours. This was very exhausting for me. They had the money to hire help, but expected me to work two jobs. During this time, my mother often called me at work to verbally abuse me. This made my life and job more difficult. I had not learned, yet, how to create the healthy boundaries I so desperately needed.

In 1979 Alice Miller's first book, *The Drama of the Gifted Child,* was published in Germany. First titled *Prisoners of Childhood,* described how parents project their feelings, ideas, and dreams upon their children. To survive and be loved, a child learns to obey. In repressing his or her feelings, the child stifles attempts to be herself or himself. The result, said Miller, is all too often depression, ebbing of vitality, the loss of self. We instill humiliation, shame, fear, and guilt as we are "training" children. By encouraging conformity, suppressing curiosity and emotions, a parent reduces a child's ability to make crucial perceptions in later life. Children are tolerant. They learn intolerance from us."

Although raised and educated in America, I knew very little about my rights and personal boundaries. From what I was experiencing, I had none. My parents and grandparents abused prescription drugs. My father was absent on out-of-town jobs most of my childhood. Although I had some extended family, those ties were strained. I recall my mother breaking off relationships with her own family and in-laws.

Dr. Clarissa Estes' profound book, *Women Who Run with the Wolves,* has assisted me in my healing. Many of the stories in her book are about how to sharpen your awareness, your instincts, how to live the "instinctual life." I relate to her story *"Red Shoes."* The story is about how someone fashioned "Red Shoes" for a young girl, but the shoes controlled her. That was the cost of someone giving her the shoes and her wearing them. Eventually, someone had to cut off her feet for her to be free of the Red Shoes. Her feet, in the story, eventually grew back. "Red Shoes" is an insightful story with wisdom for all.

My parents were my first shoemaker. The shoes they fashioned for me almost killed me. My ex-husband's Red Shoes fit very similar to the shoes my parents fashioned for me and those shoes almost killed me too. I only wear shoes I have fashioned for myself now. It is more safe, sane and spiritual.

"Yes, there is pain in being severed from the red shoes. But it is our only hope. It is a severing that is filled with absolute blessing. The feet will grow back, we will find out way, we will recover, we will run and jump and skip again some day. By then our handmade life will be ready. We'll slip into it and marvel that **we could be so lucky to have another chance.**

"A feral woman cannot afford to be naive. As she returns to her innate life, she must consider excesses with a skeptical eye and be aware of those costs to soul, psyche, instinct. Like the wolf pups, we memorize the traps, how they are made, and how they are laid. That is the way we remain free.......Even those in worst circumstances as portrayed in *"The Red Shoes,"* **even the most injured instincts can be healed."**

"If you want to re-summon Wild Woman, refuse to be captured. With instincts sharpened for balance—jump anywhere you like, howl at will, take what there is, find out all about it, let your eyes show your feelings, look into everything, see what you can see. Dance in red shoes, but make sure they're the ones you've made by hand. You will be one vital woman." - Clarissa Estes, Ph.D., *Women Who Run with the Wolves*

Before I was able to recover from childhood abuse, my mind was filled with more lies. I was proselytized by a fellow high school student, Cindy (Fowler) Haugland. She witnessed to me about salvation and my lack of spirituality in homeroom class every day. Again, I was put in a place of inferiority and bondage and made to feel that I was somehow *less than.*

I opened myself to her ideology and attended some religious retreats and Bill Gothard's Basic Youth Seminars in 1971. The preaching had familiar tones: shame, fear and guilt. The religious leaders used their authority over me, reminding me constantly of my duties as a woman of God - submission, obedience and silence. The brainwashing from these meetings further eroded my self respect. In the years to follow, I was to learn that "love" was people's need to control me, not their concern for my welfare; or my value as a human being.

While I attended the Basic Life Conflicts Seminars by Bill Gothard, we were instructed not to share any of the "Basic Life Conflicts" materials or literature that we had purchased with anyone who had not attended the seminars. Today, I am aware that their secrecy smacks of cultism. When I was sixteen and vulnerable, I was not able to discern why they were making this request and honored their wishes.

It is a sad fact to discover that much of my abuse throughout my life stemmed from other's twisted religious viewpoints, biblical interpretations and theology. There has been little, if any, compassion or love among these religious people. They are, in my opinion, a group of people in "huddled fear." Organized religion has conditioned them to lie to themselves and others. They are taught not to listen to their own inner voice–their truth. If you step out of the group to obey your own intuition and be true to yourself, they seek to destroy or kill you. Historically, religion has been a convenient tool and method to control the masses.

My brother, Don, was also affected by my mother's control in our home. He found legalism and fundamental Christianity as a tool to cope with his feelings of hate toward his mother and women in general. My brother believed he was a "prophet" and worked in church ministries that emphasized exorcism and "casting out demons."

> I believe when we realize that we are all interconnected and that we have a right to create safe boundaries to protect us from those who have harmed us, there is no need to be involved with religious ideaism that creates walls and barriers between family and friends. I believe the more spiritually enlightened women and men become, the less need there will be of patriarchal religions in our society. Self- loathing often perpetuates fanaticism. People who are insecure often embrace religions that emulate control and power over others.

I met Marty Warner on the Vancouver/Portland bus during the fuel crisis in January 1974. He asked me general questions about my family and asked my father's name. I told him.

I did not give him my phone number, but in a few days he called me at my parent's home and told me he was coming over to meet my family. He was much older and experienced in the world. I felt alarmed and uncomfortable around him, but did not have the tools or skills to protect myself. No one had spoken to me about boundaries or power and control issues. Marty arrived shortly after his call and spent the afternoon visiting with my parents. My father commented that he found him odd.

> My feelings were trying to speak to me, but my response to those feelings had been severed years ago. I had no healthy reference point or role model. Although I sensed "red flags," I had been desensitized throughout my childhood through abuse.

Later in life I would understand the words of Jamie Sams, "As human beings, we have Sacred Space, which encompasses our bodies our thoughts, our feelings, our possessions, and our creative energy." *Dancing the Dream: The Seven Sacred Paths of Human Transformation*

On one of my first dates with Marty Warner, he asked me, "Kathy, has someone violated you?" I was surprised with his question and answered, "Yes, my great-uncle, when I was a child." Marty Warner would learn in the weeks and months ahead that I had never talked with anyone or received any help. He asked me to marry him six months after we had met.

Although, Marty Warner acted as though he was interested in me as a person, I would find out later that the information he was collecting from me was going to be used for other means. He now had the facts he needed. He had found what he had been waiting and looking for, "the perfect victim."

"The predator can always tell who is without protection." – Dr. Gabor Mate

When I met and married Marty Warner, his religious belief system and controlling personality was a continuation of all that I knew and was familiar with from my childhood–destructive and devitalizing from religious brainwashing. Like my mother, my husband was narcissistic. They see themselves as "martyrs." In their minds, they are superior to everyone.

I believe, until healed from our past, we continue to attract the lessons into our lives that will some day bring us wholeness.

Physically, I stayed in the marriage for almost twenty years. Mentally, my bags were packed. No one ever becomes accustomed to abuse and emotional blackmail.

During our engagement I recall a long conversation I had with Marty's cousin, Jo Robinson. She knew both of us and was concerned with our upcoming marriage. She pointed out to me her observations and believed it would be difficult, if not impossible, for me to have any identity as a woman and be married to Marty. I felt the same concerns, also, but had very few assertive or confrontational skills to voice my opinions. I spoke with Marty a month before our wedding date about calling off the wedding and expressed my concerns. He dismissed my concerns as exaggerations and "cold feet."

> I had not yet learned the spiritual principles of following your own intuition, your life force, and creating harmony and balance in one's daily life. I was caught up in a web of those who had assumed a role of authority in my life. I allowed others to bring their chaos into my life.

In our society, engagement is a time of joy and anticipation. For me, it was a time of threats and betrayals by my fiancé, Marty Warner. Before I met Marty Warner, I was still a virgin and was very naive. He continually threatened me that if I did not submit to his sexual needs; he would go have a "one night stand." By this time, he had already contracted venereal disease from his escapades and was afflicted with several infections during the early years of our marriage. He used no precautions to protect me.

Soon after our marriage in 1976, I joined the Catholic Church to appease my husband. I didn't understand or feel comfortable with many of its teachings and doctrines, but thought that I could attend church with my husband and keep my own beliefs intact. I was unaware, at that time, that my marriage was more or less a relationship of mind control.

My husband was often out-of-town on business trips for the first six years of our marriage. While away on trips, I would not hear from him for several weeks. The fact that I had made a vow before God and man, (which I had been taught was to be kept until "I die"), was the only reason for staying in this loveless marriage.

My father understood that I couldn't talk to him when my husband was home. He would call me when he was refueling his helicopter at the Corvallis Airport. We often met in Eugene, Oregon, when my husband was out-of-town. It allowed us to visit and spend time together that would not be permitted in the presence of his wife, my mother.

Early in the marriage, I worked for a district attorney for a few months, but my husband felt it would be better if I were at home and available to join him occasionally while he worked out-of-town. He told me to quit my job.

A year after we were married, my husband's brother and wife invited Marty to a Full Gospel Businessmen's Meeting in Vancouver, Washington. The speaker encouraged people from all faiths to be "baptized in the Holy Spirit" according to the bible references in the New Testament. Marty was prayed over and felt he had experienced the "baptism of the Holy Spirit." This began a new chapter in his life of spiritual exploration outside of his Catholic beliefs. Marty also insisted we become involved in the "Marriage Encounter" movement. I was uncomfortable with their program, but had no choice but to follow Marty's decisions.

In January of 1979, my twins, Sarah and Rachel, arrived. Sarah and Rachel brought joy into my life, although the pregnancy had been difficult. My physicians had ordered bed rest for the final four months of the pregnancy. I experienced toxemia. After the birth, my body slowly healed. My husband had the same obsession as my parents with my body size and weight. He required that I keep fit and in shape and demanded me to start exercising within days after my babies were born.

Although married, I lived as a single parent because of my husband's out-of-town business trips. Exhaustion and sleep deprivation were crucial factors as the months and years passed by. Mrs. Shirley Walsh, a friend and mother of seven children, was a continual support to me during these early years. Shirley encouraged me to "listen to the intuition you have been given as a mother." We both embraced natural mothering views in a society that had long forgotten mother/child bonding and natural birthing.

In the spring of 1981, my son, Aaron was born. I was thrilled with my new baby. I now had three children two years old and under. Although I experienced much joy as a mother, raising children with a husband that was gone for long periods had its drawbacks. At this time, I was not allowed to question the way our family was structured. In 1981, Mr. Warner changed jobs and started working as an engineer for another company in town. Although he didn't travel as much, he found other opportunities in town to be away from home.

The summer of 1979, my husband was invited to join "The People of Praise Ecumenical Covenant Christian Community" in Corvallis, Oregon. I felt uncomfortable and I told my husband that I wanted no part of this cult. Mr. Warner told me that I was a maladjusted individual and dismissed my feelings. He told me I had no choice. I was his wife and I would have to submit to his decisions and to the leaders of the community. The following four years were a nightmare.

In the beginning we attended weekly meetings. They were called "formation meetings." These meetings were used to instruct us in "the rules" of the community and were an informal way of controlling the people who attended. The main rule was that we had to agree to have limited outside contact with family and friends. Their "teachings" were the "living water" and outside influences would poison the water. We were to "put on the mind of community" in all things. I soon learned that lack of conformity meant sessions of open humiliation by the community leaders and members, threats, shunning, etc.

Community teachings included weekly instruction in our duties as men and women as interpreted by the "People of Praise" leaders of South Bend, Indiana. A woman must live in total submission to the will of her husband and the various heads of the community. Every personal decision went through the hierarchy of leadership. There was no privacy - intrusion into your thoughts and emotions by the leaders was to be expected and tolerated.

> "The teachings of cults are often fully presented half-truths and cleverly disguised lies mixed in with a good helping of people's hopes and dreams."–Author Unknown

Head coordinators and their wives from South Bend would visit periodically presenting teachings at retreats. Paul and Jeannie DeCelles and Bud and Sharon Rose were frequent speakers. Bud and Sharon Rose eventually moved from South Bend to live in Corvallis for a year. Paul DeCelles taught that the covenant relationship one shares with another member of the People of Praise is more important than any relationship with any other person. They likened the covenant of the People of Praise to the marriage vow. *(I felt that my husband shared a deeper relationship and commitment to the "community" than he did to our marriage.)*

We were expected to tithe at least ten percent of our gross income each month to the leaders of the People of Praise Community. Father Harris, a retired Catholic priest and former professor at Notre Dame, required each member to "recruit" a certain number of new members by specific dates. In 1984, community members participated in a ceremony similar to a marriage where they vowed to keep the "covenant of the community."

This is the "covenant" we lived by: "We covenant ourselves to live our lives together in Christ our Lord, by the power of His Spirit...We agree to become a basic Christian community, to find within our fellowship the essential core of our life in the Spirit: in worship and the sacraments, spiritual and moral guidance, service and apostolic activity...We accept the order of this community which the Lord is establishing with all the ministry gifts of the Holy Spirit, especially with the foundational ministry gifts of apostles, pastors, prophets, teachers and evangelists. We agree to obey the direction of the Holy Spirit manifested in and through these ministries in full harmony with the Church...We recognize in the covenant a unique relationship one to another and between the individual and the community. We accept the responsibility for mutual care, concern, and ministry among ourselves. We will serve each other and the community as a whole in all needs; spiritual, material, financial...We agree that the weekly meeting of the community is primary among our commitments and not to be absent except for a serious reason."

In community meetings, during the time for prayer and praise, people would speak in tongues and share "prophesies from the Lord." The prophecies were interpreted by other members and they would share the message. Many of the messages consisted of these words, "Obey your leaders, trust them, submit to them..."

On one occasion, in May of 1981, my husband was asked to give a teaching to the community. His teaching was entitled, "God as the Center of Our Life–Our First Love." His teaching ended with these words, "God has spoken to us through the prophets and through His Holy Word. We can no longer claim ignorance as an excuse or act as though we do not know. We are responsible for the instruction which God has given and continues to give us and we must be obedient. We must pay much closer attention to what we have heard, lest we drift away from it and fall short of the mark, which is salvation.

For only by fixing our thoughts on the Living Christ and by faithful and committed obedience to His purpose, not deviating from it no matter what; will we be welcomed into His Kingdom."

> After a large group of individuals, including an influential member left the community, Head Coordinator, Kevin Ranaghan in 1978 addressed the "People of Praise Community" in South Bend. He interpreted what happened and commented that one should see fidelity to the covenant as a similar kind of obligation. He attributed the loss of members to an evil spirit, specifically a "quitting spirit."

In a charismatic dictatorship, the leaders are appointed in a fashion much the same as other hierarchies, with one submitting to the next higher in the chain of command. Total discipline is imposed upon those who submit themselves to their "head." This includes submissions of self-will, desire, actions, putting self and family under not just the guidance of, but the imposed will of the "head" or leader. Tithes and offerings are expected and collected by appointed members.

Spiritual and mental bondage is often soon realized by those who are under submission. Invasion of privacy is a signature feature of cults. (Additional information on cults and their adverse effects on individuals and society can be found in the section entitled "Spiritual History")

We proceeded to attend weekly meetings, retreats, mandated women and men's meetings and ministry meetings. Little time was left for family or self. We all reported to someone in authority. They were our shepherds. The "heads", those in authority, were the main force in controlling the group's actions and thoughts.

Headship involved matters such as the discipline of children, how to deal with a wife, how to help one's wife see and deal with her own problems, whether to accept a promotion at work, whether to have another baby, what kind of car or home to buy, etc. Wives sometimes resented the relationship between their husband and his "head." The husbands were confused by this and sought help by their "heads," wondering how to get their wives to fall in line–obey.

Community leaders and members often referred to Christian authorities and ministries such as Dr. James Dobson and Bill Gothard's teachings because of the belief in the "corporal punishment of children." Bill Gothard's teachings about the "chain of command" and "submission of women" supported community's teachings. Pat Robertson also taught beliefs similar to the community's in regard to "speaking in tongues, prophecies and miracles."

A former leader, Adrian J. Reimers, within the People of Praise Community wrote an article entitled: "Charismatic Covenant Community: A Failed Promise" printed May 1986 in "Fidelity." He writes: "One of the teachings within the community taught that women were manipulative by nature. This is one of the effects of Original Sin on them. The wise husband will factor this into his relationship with his wife, recognizing that much of what she does is insincere. To deal with this, the husband should mistrust her motives and instead draw closer to this head and the men in his men's group."

When I tried to share my feelings with my husband and his religious authorities, my feelings were dismissed. I was **told** how I should feel. They believed they were the "authorities" God had placed over me and that fact gave them the right to rule over my emotions.

Mr. Reimers further writes, "At a men's retreat in 1984, we learned that unwillingness to submit one's budget to a head is one good sign of the capital sin of greed. At one women's retreat, one handmaid taught (with the approval of the coordinators) that one manifestation of pride is the failure to submit one's *thoughts and opinions* to the heads of the community for correction." Individuals within the community believed, "What is good for the community is good for me: the coordinator's plan for the community is the surest sign of God's will for my life."

When I left the community in 1984, I was threatened and told that they would put me in a mental institution if I did not submit to the "authorities God had placed over me." "Father" Charles Harris, provided leadership and "headship" for the "People of Praise Community" in Corvallis, Oregon, for several years.

Everyone tried to avoid the repercussions of disobedience within the group. When I did dare to question or use my own reasoning processes, I was exorcised and put in "special counseling" with Father Charles Harris. I was called a rebel, and this, of course, was a disgrace to my husband for which I had to atone. My questioning disturbed them, so my husband and others accused me of being mentally ill. This conclusion for my lack of conformity comforted them. The threat of being put in a mental institution was added to the litany of humiliations.

Each week I was forced to endure my husband's "headship" meeting. These were meetings that he used to "correct" me and the children. He reminded me that the example I set for the children, by obeying him in all things, was a direct correlation to how they would respond and obey him. Mr. Warner reported to his leaders in the "People of Praise Community," any comments I made that questioned the absolute authority my husband and his "cult" leaders had over me. He kept a black book and listed each of my infractions. When Mr. Warner was out-of-town, he assigned other men in the community to "check up" on me. (Please see report on "Shunning in the Charismatic Community" by Robert L. Walsh included in documentation.)

In the "headship" meetings, Mr. Warner would give me instructions; duties and obligations that I was to perform for him before the week was over. My daily schedule was divided into thirty-minute segments. My responsibilities as wife and mother consisted of taking care of the children, feeding, bathing, dressing the younger children, changing diapers, breast-feeding and caring for my infant child, two to four loads of laundry each day, and cleaning the home and keeping it immaculate. Mr. Warner expected me to hang out all our laundry outside from May to October to save money. I also was responsible for cutting everyone's hair. I was to run errands, buy all the groceries and cook our meals and desserts from scratch.

I took the children to doctor and dentist appointments and as they got older, dropped them off at school and picked them up each day. I bought all the children's toys, educational and craft supplies and helped them with craft and hobby projects. I took the children to parks and museums often, and visited the library about once or twice a week. I read to the children during the day and for long lengths of time in the evening before their bed time. I also arranged for their friends to visit and organized their birthday parties. As Sarah, Rachel and Aaron got older and there were more children, I also drove them to their piano and swim lessons, ballet, violin, flute and softball practices and games.

I also felt a responsibility to protect my children from harm and was selective of who they spent time with. I taught my children that their bodies were sacred and that no one was to violate or touch them inappropriately. I taught them that they would be safe to confide in me. I wanted them to know that I was a champion for their safety and well-being.

I had small vegetable and flower gardens and was also expected to can enough fruit, jam and vegetables for the coming winter. When Mr. Warner required, I was to cook large dinners to entertain his guests. During the nights I took care of the children when they were ill and breast-fed my infant. I made meals for families who were experiencing illness or grief. I decorated our homes and helped in the selling of each home. My husband expected me to perform any and all secretarial duties.

During our involvement in this cult, the group's leaders asked us to give them the deed to our home so they could purchase an apartment complex south of Corvallis. This was not something I wanted to be involved in, but I had no choice. My husband gladly handed the deed to our home to the cult leaders. Eventually the deal fell through. I was relieved.

> During the years of our marriage, fear of my husband, his religious leaders and religious authorities were branded in my mind. The quiet still voice inside of me reminded me that something was very wrong. I felt alarmed, but there was nowhere to go and no one to tell. Several years of severe mental and physical abuse left my senses blunted; everything became blurred. The instincts of self-preservation, of self-defense, of pride, deserted me. *And I loved and cherished my children.*

My health began to deteriorate at a rapid rate while involved in this community. My body and mind were showing signs of stress—weight loss, panic attacks, nightmares, confusion, migraine headaches, etc. In a six-month period of time (1983 - 1984), I suffered two miscarriages. After the second D & C surgery, my husband picked me up from the hospital and dropped me off at my home with our three young children. He had a community men's meeting to attend.

My abusive husband used coercive control, isolation and intimidation tactics to strip me of my personhood, safety and freedoms as a United States citizen.

"Coercive control shares general elements with other capture or course-of-conduct crimes such as kidnapping, stalking, and harassment, including the facts that it is ongoing and its perpetrators use various means to hurt, humiliate, intimidate, exploit, isolate, and dominate their victims. Like hostages, victims of coercive control are frequently deprived of money, food, access to communication or transportation, and other survival resources even as they are cut off from family, friends, and other supports through the process of "isolation." But unlike other capture crimes, coercive control is personalized, extends through social space as well as over time, and is gendered in that it relies for its impact on women's vulnerability as women due to sexual inequality. Another difference is its aim.

"Men deploy coercive control to secure privileges that involve the use of time, control over material resources, access to sex, and personal service. A main means men use to establish control is the microregulation of everyday behaviors associated with stereotypic female roles, such as how women dress, cook, clean, socialize, care for their children, or perform sexually. These dynamics give coercive control a role in sexual politics that distinguishes it from all other crimes." - Dr. Evan Stark, Coercive Control: How Men Entrap Women in Personal Life

My obstetrician, Dr. Charles South, told me after my second D & C surgery, "Kathy, *(Coral)* when deer are hunted, they lose their young." He had no idea how isolated I was and the profound impact his statement made on my life. He is a perceptive man.

> The most powerful emotional control tool cult leaders use on its members is fear. The leaders create a phobia indoctrination. A member will have a panic reaction at the very thought of leaving the group (cult). A member will perceive that it is almost impossible to conceive that there is any life or spirituality outside of the group. There is no physical gun held to the member's head, but the psychological gun is just as, if not more, powerful.

Spiritual abuse is the use of spiritual knowledge to deprive, torture, degrade, isolate, control, or (in rare and extreme cases) even kill others. It is used by evil-minded church and cult leaders, to gain advantage, dominate, or exercise control over others

A week after the second miscarriage and D & C surgery, in the spring of 1984, I was required to attend the mandatory women's meeting. I was still bleeding heavily. The women wished to go on a shopping excursion that evening. I was still healing from the D & C and was weak. I walked out of the meeting and went home. The leader of the women's group, Mrs. Connie Hackenbruck, immediately called my husband and reported my disobedience. My husband called another cult member to watch our three children and as soon as I arrived home, I was greeted by my husband, forced into a car and driven to the home of Mr. Ed Brown, my husband's "head."

I was interrogated for several hours with such questions as, "what is truth, what is false, etc." I was spoken to in a disciplinary and condescending manner. I could not give him the answers he expected. Truth, for me, did not mean absolute obedience to the community or my husband. The teachings of the community disturbed and alarmed me. I did not believe in the "us" and "them" mentality that permeated the community's thoughts, actions and teachings. My beliefs were more universal. I felt interconnected to all people, not just those in the community. The leader told me that some people (like me) couldn't "cut the mustard"–the narrow walk with Jesus Christ. I told my husband's "head" I was tired and wanted to go home. After several hours, I was finally allowed to leave.

The next day the members in the community were called and instructed not to speak to me. I was considered "poisonous" and a danger to the community's well-being, but I was still forced to attend People of Praise Community meetings and women's retreats where the members shunned me. They were not allowed to speak to me or look at me. I was an outcast, yet not allowed to leave the Community because my husband still was a member.

"The most potent weapon in the hands of the oppressor is the mind of the oppressed."— *Steve Biko*

While Mr. Warner was a member of this Catholic/Charismatic cult, he and his religious "head" forced me to sit on the floor in hallways as a shunning practice during their meetings at St. Mary's Catholic Church. Their efforts to brainwash and break me were futile. I could not conform because I could not allow my spirit to be corrupted or live a lie. While our family was involved in this cult, I made meals and gifts for the women and helped take care of their children as an act of love. I could feel affection for the members of this cult, but I could not accept their beliefs or authority over me.

St. Mary's Catholic Church Hallway, Corvallis, Oregon, where Coral Anika Theill, aka Kathryn Y. Warner, was forced to sit on the floor outside of People of Praise Community Meetings

26

In an honestly motivated spiritual group or organization the individual is always encouraged to exercise free will and arrive at their own conclusions. If someone genuinely cares about your well-being, they will not try to control, manipulate, exhort, threaten or convince you to adopt their way of thinking. (For more information, please refer to *Mastery of Love*, by Don Miguel Ruiz.)

To this day individuals from the cult are involved in the practice of shunning me. Although healed, for the most part, from the devastating effects of this cult, the experience of being shunned had long-term psychological repercussions in the years to come.

I had learned as a child that if I didn't do as I was told, my personal safety would be endangered. My experiences in this cult reinforced these experiences–isolation and emotional and mental pain would follow any questioning of others' motives, power and control of me. Shunning is a cruel and inhumane practice within many church groups and cults, a form of silent ridicule.

My husband continued attending the cult's meetings and participated in the cult's practice of shunning me, but after several months of my refusal to conform and obey the community's teachings and leaders, he was asked to leave. This was devastating for my husband. He lost face because he could not control his wife. I was thankful that my children and I no longer had to be a part of this group and their threatening behaviors. I didn't perceive that things could get worse.

In the years that followed my husband expected me to speak, represent and teach "his truths" while in his presence and his absence. I was not allowed to express my own beliefs and spiritual truths. Mr. Warner would become violent when I did not conform to all his wishes. I often would share with my children, "I am only doing this because I must obey your father."

One Christmas holiday while visiting his family in Ridgefield, Washington, the road conditions were hazardous and the State Police recommended individuals stay home. The black ice had caused numerous accidents. Mr. Warner did not want to miss out on visiting his uncle and aunt in Portland, so we were forced into the car while he drove us to a holiday dinner at his uncle's. His family was alarmed that Mr. Warner was so insistent. I did not want to go or endanger my children or my life. We had no choice. We had to obey.

During the years of our marriage Mr. Warner instructed me in what kind of clothes I could wear, how to style my hair, whether I could wear make-up or not, when and what I could eat or drink. Even body functions were monitored. His comments toward me were insulting and demeaning. I couldn't do anything right, in his eyes.

If I shared with Mr. Warner that I felt uncomfortable around specific individuals or places, he would dismiss my comments. I had no right to protect myself from situations that were re traumatizing for me. With no regard for my feelings, Mr. Warner continued to open our home to individuals I was not comfortable being around.

I was not allowed access to money or knowledge about our finances. I was forbidden to work outside the home or attend college classes. I was allowed to buy groceries and I purchased most of the children's and my clothes and household items at second-hand shops. I was not free to talk to friends or family members. My husband read my incoming and outgoing mail. I was not allowed to read a newspaper. He told me what books I could read and burned books of mine if he disapproved.

Throughout our marriage, Mr. Warner was an avid supporter of Phyllis Schlafly, Mary Pride, Dave Hunt, and Concerned Women of America. He presently supports the ministry of Brannon Howse.

In the early 1990's, Mr. Warner forced me to watch the Rush Limbaugh program, which I found repulsive and oppressive. Limbaugh's anti-women rhetoric and style of superiority, dark anger, resentment, jealousy and vindictiveness was similar to my husband's beliefs and characteristics.

Another stress during the beginning of my fourth pregnancy in 1984 was the death of my father. Mr. Warner did not permit me to visit my father in the I.C.U. at the hospital the night he died, in November 1984. Mr. Warner was obsessed with control and could not release me of my duties to the family nor could he accept the feelings of affection and love I had for my father. Mr. Warner expected total allegiance.

During the years after our involvement in the cult, Mr. Warner kept busy attending Knights of Columbus and Social Action Committee meetings for St. Mary's Catholic Church in Corvallis, Oregon. Mr. Warner was also very active in the "Right to Life" movement. He was the state representative for Oregon Right to Life. Through the "Right to Life" organization, he became friends with Betsy and Chris Close in Corvallis, Oregon. (Betsy Close served as an Oregon State Representative in 1998-2004. Fr. Oregon State House Representative Betsy Close was appointed to serve as Oregon State District 8 Senator in 2012.)

Jean Weisensee, a woman I met at St. Mary's Catholic Church, befriended me during 1984. She had divorced her husband, who had been abusive toward her for years. Jean had worked as a nurse and raised her children. She suggested a wonderful counselor to me, Gertrude Branthover, in Corvallis. I saw her a couple times and was encouraged by her insights. I really liked her. My husband forbids my seeing her again because Ms. Branthover was not a Catholic or a Christian. My husband also restricted my contact with Jean Weisensee because she was "a divorced woman." This saddened me because I related to Jean and was encouraged by her.

I visited the priest at St. Mary's Catholic Church and shared some of the things I was struggling with, i.e., the community, my father's death, my marriage. He suggested I go to the pastoral counseling center. I briefly saw a woman counselor there, but I stopped seeing her because I do not think she believed me when I spoke about the abuse issues in the community, I had been involved in. She also was a part of a counseling service that was connected to some of the people I was speaking about. Attending St. Mary's Catholic Church was a painful experience because many of the cult leaders and members of the "People of Praise Community/cult" shunned me at church due to me leaving their community.

In the summer of 1985, my fourth child, Theresa, was born. Mr. Warner was still very involved in outside activities, specifically, "Right to Life." While I was in hard labor at our home, I continued to ask Mr. Warner if he would take me to the hospital, (a half hour drive), he kept talking on the phone for an hour with other "Right to Life" committee members. I finally was taken to the hospital and birthed my baby soon after my arrival. Betsy and Chris Close gave me a baby shower at their home after the birth of Theresa.

I fully realized after four children that my plate was full time and energy wise. Shortly after Theresa was born, I began to experience tearing of the membranes of my eyes. I did not want to get pregnant again at the time, so I also visited my obstetrician, Dr. South, and was fitted for a diaphragm. Mr. Warner made me throw it away. He would not allow me to use contraceptives. His second "bible" was Mary Pride's book, *The Way Home - Beyond Feminism Back to Reality*. *A Full Quiver* by Rick & Jan Hess and the Catholic Church was Mr. Warner's authority regarding "family planning."

My husband's Christian beliefs were pro-birth – in other words, **Christian competitive breeding.** This is a strategy for increasing church membership and is at the core of the Catholic anti-contraceptive stance and the Protestant Quiverfull movement - *Women will be saved through childbearing.* (1 Timothy 2:15) and *be fruitful and multiply.* (Genesis 1:28)

Quiverfull is a conservative fundamentalist Christian movement that promotes procreation, condemns all forms of birth control including natural family planning, and views all sexual activity that does not have conception as its goal as an abomination. The movement derives its name from Psalms 127:3-5, where many children are metaphorically referred to as the arrows in a full quiver.

Quiverfull authors and adherents cite God's commandment to "be fruitful and multiply" and model a return to Biblical Patriarchy.

Martin Luther, leader of the Protestant reformation in the 1500's, stated: "If a woman grows weary and at last dies from childbearing, it matters not. Let her only die from bearing; she is there to do it."

Mary Pride, author of *The Way Home*, a book that was a much prized and often quoted by my husband, was a self-proclaimed radical feminist before embracing a fanatical brand of fundamental Christianity. She states, "woman shall be *saved* through child bearing" and Christian women should be "homeworkers," not employed outside the home. Many Christians have read Pride's writings and taken her interpretations of Scripture literally and embraced her message.

In *The Way Home*, she tells her story of walking away from "feminist" beliefs and finding "true happiness" in the **"biblically mandated role of wives and mothers as bearers of children."** She believes that "the church's sin, which has caused us [women] to become *unsavory salt* incapable of uplifting the society around us, is the selfishness of refusing to consider children an unmitigated blessing."

Pride wants more than women to just stay home and have babies. She wants the babies indoctrinated, and calls for a new generation of godly homeschooled children as the only way to change America and bring it back to its Christian foundation. Pride's overnight success in the 1980's occurred for several reasons. She was a capable writer and was speaking to legalistic Christians who could be swayed by "the Bible says" argument. Her "quiverfull message" also spoke to the anti-abortion fundamentalists who were organized against *Roe v. Wade*.

In "Help," Mary Pride's monthly newsletter, she printed an article written by Alida Gookin entitled, *Witches and Housework.* Ms. Gookin writes, "In ancient Rome, spinning so symbolized feminine devotion to the home that in the Roman marriage ceremony, the bride carried a spindle and distaff. Girls in ancient Rome, as well as in other cultures until the Industrial Revolution, were taught to spin and weave. Hebrew and Christian cultures saw the virtuous woman in Proverbs 31 as one who "stretches out her hands to the distaff and her hands grasp the spindle. Not all women accepted spinning as dutifully. Some women, notably witches and prostitutes (both of whom the Bible explicitly calls "rebellious") sought to be "liberated" from childbearing and women's work." Gookin's final paragraphs state, "The Bible tells women to reject witches and their lifestyle; "bear children, guide the house" less one be "turned aside after Satan." (I Timothy 5:13-15) No, feminism is not new. It's been here ever since Eve decided she'd rather socialize with a serpent than work on her garden."

I was beginning to wish for a separation from Mr. Warner, but he threatened me that I would not be able to leave with the children. We visited two counselors as a couple, but they turned out to be oppressive and legalistic in their beliefs. Because I believed my husband would carry out his threats, I stayed in the marriage for ten more years. Every day I wished I could escape Mr. Warner with my children and start a new life–free of tyranny and abuse.

About six months after the birth of Theresa, I enrolled in a jazzercise class held at a gym a few minutes from our home. I went to the class a few times in the evening after I had put the children to bed. The class was refreshing for me and fun. After a few weeks, Mr. Warner forced me to quit. I shared with him how important the class was for my health and fitness. His mind was made up. During the years of our marriage, Mr. Warner often worked out in gyms and made sure his work out time was protected.

The inner struggle throughout the years of being forced to obey a man who did not love me or care for my well-being became increasingly confusing for me as I tried to honor my marriage vows. Although, I was encouraged by many well-meaning men and women that this was "God's will" for me, and that obeying my husband was pleasing to God, I could not understand why I felt so miserable. I felt like I was dying. I couldn't understand why God would orchestrate a system (marriage) that would oppress an individual and strip them of their rights. Inwardly, I despised being treated like a second-class citizen while being told that this was "love."

Mr. Warner seemed obsessed throughout our marriage with the evils of the feminist movement and women's rights in our society and often required me to send books he approved, i.e., Mary Pride's book, *The Way Home*, to women friends and acquaintances. I later realized this was just another way of him isolating me from women who had been a part of my life. Most women were repulsed by this book and sent it back. I remember the two things I felt most strongly during this time were loneliness and determination to stay safe by appeasing the man I lived with.

Mr. Warner would often comment that working under a woman at work was in direct violation of his Scriptural convictions. He also had problems with the fact that his fellow co-workers were women. He believed that women belonged *at home*. Florence Howe, Publisher/Director of The Feminist Press wrote this definition of feminism: "*Feminism means the action by women and men to establish equality and justice for women.*" I embrace and honor the efforts of feminism.

In April of 1986, I left the Catholic Church. This was the beginning of five to six months of emotional and verbal threats from my husband. Many friends and a family member were aware of my husband's violence and rage toward me. Mr. Warner badgered me daily and asked me, "Whose church authority are you going to be under?" I simply stated, "no one" that I just wanted the right to 'be.'" This was an unsatisfactory answer for Mr. Warner.

Betsy and Chris Close were aware of Mr. Warner's rage and violent behavior towards me because I was no longer attending the Catholic Church with him. They offered a room in their house should the children and I ever need to escape for safety reasons. I kept diapers for my baby and clothes for the children in the tire compartment of our station wagon for a period of six months or more. Many friends and a family member were also aware of my husband's violence and rage toward me over the fact I left the Catholic Church.

Peggy Stephens and my brother, Don Hall, also offered their homes as a "safe place" to the children and me, should I ever need to escape my husband's rage and violent behavior.

In the early years of our marriage, my husband had made it very clear to me, that if I ever tried to leave, his "empire" would remain intact. The estate was his, and in his opinion, the children were a part of his estate. Whatever I had brought into the marriage was his.

After our marriage in 1976, he took over my accounts and my car and cashed the life insurance policy I bought when I was twelve years old. My properties became his properties. I wasn't aware of how I was becoming enslaved one day at a time.

During this difficult time, in the spring of 1986, my husband required me to go on a pre-scheduled beach trip with some friends of his from the community we had belonged to in Corvallis. This sounded disastrous to me because I did not embrace the same beliefs as my husband and this couple. One evening after the children were all in bed, we began talking about our lives and experiences. I began to honestly share my feelings about the community they belonged to and my reasons for leaving both the Catholic Church and this community.

I also confronted the man about his physical abuse toward one of the women members of the community and how I felt this was inappropriate for people who claimed they were living "as the remnant of God." This was a mistake. The man became very hostile toward me and said that he had every right to do what he did. I remember his wife telling me how he would wake her in the middle of the night to tell her to clean up the coffee grounds that were spilled near the garbage in the kitchen.

My husband was outraged that I would confront his friend. (Women do not do such things!) The man I confronted had often been left in charge of me as my "head" in the community when my husband was out of town on business. The men embraced the teachings of "headship" and "chain of command" because it was the only way they could get respect, by force. I also believe it was because the men didn't believe women could make decisions on their own.

I called my brother, Don Hall, Betsy and Chris Close and another friend in Seattle for help and emotional encouragement for the duration of this weekend. Betsy and Chris Close offered to come and get me, but I survived the weekend. When we returned home, my husband forced me to write an apology letter to this couple and ask for their forgiveness.

Our marriage continued to deteriorate. Betsy Close recommended we see her pastor at a charismatic church she and her husband attended in Corvallis. My husband and I met with the pastor and agreed to eight sessions, once a week for Scriptural marriage counseling. From the beginning, this pastor was oppressive toward me. I shared with my husband that I could no longer counsel with this pastor. He reminded me of the leaders of the cult I had left. My husband said, "No, Kathy, we will finish the course." The pastor made me write down a list of every sin I had every committed. He kept it on file. Later I asked for the list to be returned to me. He finally conceded.

My husband related well with this pastor. During this time of counseling my grandfather died. I told the pastor that I would be missing one of the counseling meetings to attend my grandfather's funeral out of state. The pastor said, "No, you made a commitment to me and to this counseling program." My husband agreed with the pastor. As the weeks went on I experienced the ramifications of heavy oppression, a condescending attitude, humiliations and all the "outward appearances" of a cult leader. I warned Betsy Close and her husband about their pastor and the church they were attending. They dismissed my warnings.

While managing a pregnancy counseling center in Corvallis, Ms. Close carried several of her pastor's audio teaching tapes on raising children, which included teachings on severe corporal punishment for toddlers. The pastors and elders of this church expected absolute obedience of the congregation. Later on, this pastor was confronted by his congregation about his adulterous lifestyle with women in his congregation. He confessed it was true. He and his family left Corvallis and started a new church in Portland, Oregon.

> As I have watched the lifestyle and beliefs of many Christian leaders, many of them have one thing in common–adultery. I

believe that spiritual pride is a common denominator in many of them. Proverbs says that "Pride comes before the fall."

In 1987, my husband began to spend time with Rich Vasquez in a disciplining relationship. This added some help in our marriage because Rich confronted my husband about abuse issues, but there was too much similarity between them. It became more a struggle for power than a place for growth. My husband then created his "own church" in our home. He informed me I did not need friends in my life and that all decisions were to go through him and him alone.

> Some friends and family members have commented that they did not feel welcome in our home. I reply that even I did not feel welcome in my own home. I was told what to say and what to do. My words, thoughts and actions were monitored at all times by my husband.

Before my fifth pregnancy in 1987, I was having problems with my eyes and was diagnosed with anterior membrane dystrophy, a rare disease of the eyes. My eyes were patched for several weeks. A surgery was performed on my eyes in Corvallis. The doctor removed the membrane from my eyes in hopes that it would grow back normally. I had no household help and did the best I could to get my chores accomplished. Because of the gauze bandages covering my eyes, I could not drive and had to walk to stores and schools with the younger children in wagons or strollers. The surgery and recovery was painful. Mr. Warner impregnated me during this time, while my eyes were bandaged. I was under a great deal of stress at the time with four children and bandaged eyes. My husband simply told me to "trust God."

The surgery was unsuccessful and I was referred to the Casey Eye Institute in Portland, Oregon. My physician there, Dr. Larry Rich, recommended I wear bandage lenses (large contact lenses) to help heal the scar tissue on my eyes. If this did not work, they suggested another surgery. Mr. Warner asked Dr. Larry Rich what might be aggravating my condition. Dr. Larry Rich explained that the numerous pregnancies were a stress to my condition.

Mr. Warner assumed the role of teacher, doctor and mentor in our home. He also believed he was the "priest" of our family. I had no right to think and make decisions for myself. I was not allowed to express my emotions, feelings or beliefs. But even though he considered himself the absolute master of home and family, he was often absent for weeks at a time throughout the years of our marriage.

35

He would work long hours, spend weekends at spiritual retreats or with church/community members, be involved in religious committee work, or visit his family at their dairy farm in Washington.

In 1988 I birthed our fifth child, Joshua, at the Albany General Hospital in Albany, Oregon. That same year I began homeschooling our four youngest children. Mr. Warner decided it would be less expensive than the private schools and we did not want to send the children to public schools. Although, Mr. Warner was very enthusiastic about home-schooling he was not supportive with his time. Although homeschooling has its positive aspects, exhaustion for the teaching parent is the negative side of the equation.

Another stress to our marriage and family, at this time, was the fact that Mr. Warner had left the Catholic Church. His family blamed me for this, but I had nothing to do with his beliefs. He did what he wanted to do throughout our marriage with no regard to my needs or wishes.

His mother, Helen Warner, told others I had "poisoned" her son. Whenever she visited our home she would stay up throughout the night ranting and raving to her son that I was a "bigot," and a horrible mother and wife. He would let her go on and on and say nothing. She would degrade me in front of my husband and children. When she spoke to me, it was in a condescending manner. Her presence in my home and life created stresses on an already stressful situation. I now had "two Marty Warner's" to answer to and one was I all I could manage in my daily life. Although I tried my best to treat Helen Warner with respect, my health could not tolerate her visits and hostility.

Throughout our marriage, Mr. Warner continually compared me, in my domestic capacity, to his mother. In his eyes, she was "domestically perfect," except for the fact that, in his words, "she was worshipping in the 'Whore of Babylon' (his term for the Catholic Church) and worshipping demons."

I told my husband that he could see his family anytime he wanted. I did not want to go with him or have my children exposed to the disrespectful manner in which I was treated by his mother and family members. I also did not want my younger children exposed to the heavy drinking and extreme "negative humor" their family displayed toward everyone around them. Because my husband did not have a history of supervising our children while visiting, I asked him to leave the children with me, if he should ever take trips to visit his family.

I was never able to feel comfortable around Mr. Warner's mother. She talked to me in ways that were critical, insulting and demeaning. I did not relate to her belief system and fanatical Catholic viewpoints.

When she visited me, she was critical of my natural mothering beliefs, such as nursing my infants, etc. She had adopted many beliefs that were taught by Dr. Spock that I felt had a detrimental effect on children. Although I was well-read and schooled in natural mothering and birthing methods, Helen Warner always presented herself as an "authority" on mothering when I was around. I did not agree with her methods. I believe several of her children experienced psychological trauma from her neglect.

Her pro-life viewpoints included supporting a woman in prison who had killed an abortionist. Mrs. Helen Warner also did not seem to be moved when confronted with her church's history and doctrines that have often been fatal to millions of innocent people who have not submitted to "papal worship."

I continue to be grieved that well-meaning individuals can submit to a church system that spends millions of dollars every year in lawsuits involving Catholic priests who have sexually molested children. The priests are seldom punished within our judicial system. They are recycled into another parish. I would be uncomfortable with my tithe monies being used to allow a priest to hide behind the "skirts of the Catholic Church" or to be spent for decadent displays of opulent excesses considered necessary by Catholics for proper religious worship. I suppose that is why Buddha stated, "Ignorance is the only sin."

For a brief period, Mr. Warner attended the local Baptist Church, which supported many of his views. I usually did not attend. When acquaintances at church would ask about me, Mr. Warner told them that women did not belong in the church; they belonged at home with the children. When Mr. Warner did talk with me, most of his comments involved his criticism of the entire Christian population. In his opinion, they did not know or understand the "truth" like he did. His other comments were critical statements against fellow co-workers and the company he worked for.

Mr. Warner soon adopted another cult to follow–The Sacred Name Movement. A couple approached him at a homeschool meeting he was leading. They wished to meet with him and share "truths" they had discovered. I shared with my husband that it was his right to believe how he wanted, but to not bring these people into our home.

He embraced these new truths, and I, as his wife and helpmate, was to embrace the truths and his fellow "believers" in my home. These truths involved using the Hebrew name of God and Jesus only, keeping the Sabbath and Old Testaments Feast Days and clean food laws. The belief in the "absolute submission of women" was supported by their doctrines and literature. We were also not to participate in any of the pagan holidays and Mr. Warner insisted we downplay birthdays in our home, also.

Mr. Warner expected the children and I to "keep the Sabbath," although he often went to work on the Sabbath. He would sometimes take naps on the Sabbath, and expect me to keep the house quiet, peaceful and orderly for him to get his rest.

I did not understand these beliefs. They were foreign to me. Although I understood and honored the symbolism of Hebrew Feast Days, we were not Jews. Mr. Warner spent long hours in the evening and on the weekends studying these "new truths." I did not have the time to study, but was forced to submit to his beliefs. Mr. Warner soon ordered Hebrew teaching materials and began to teach the children Hebrew classes on Saturdays. These classes would run several hours. The children tried to learn Hebrew under Mr. Warner's tutelage, but were frustrated to the point of tears from the difficulty of the language and their father's demands.

Mr. Warner bought a Hewlett Packard computer and shipped it to one of the leaders of this movement in Africa. They used the computer to print a new Bible for the world omitting the words, God, Lord and Jesus, and printing the Hebrew tetragrammaton instead.

My husband also spent time "discipling" young men in our home in the "truth." He would teach them the importance of "the obedience of woman" and the Sacred Name. There was no talk of compassion and unconditional love in his example or instruction to these men. He would also exhort his brothers from the Warner family whose wives had divorced them about the mistakes they had made. He told them that they were guilty of not protecting their wives from Helen Warner, their mother, and to be wise in protecting their children from her because of her idol worship and demonic practices (i.e., beliefs in the apparitions of the Virgin Mary in Medjugorje).

As Mr. Warner became more involved within the homeschool movement, he met a man named Karl Reed, a homeschooling father and speaker. He and his wife, Virginia, stayed at our home a few times. Karl Reed convinced my husband through scriptural studies that the social security number was the "mark of the beast." Mr. Warner encouraged me to have our next child at home for a variety of reasons—one being his conviction about social security numbers.

Also, during 1990, my husband ordered the "Financial Freedom Seminar" videos from Basic Youth Conflicts by Bill Gothard. He invited friends and acquaintances to view the film in our home. The films supported Mr. Warner's beliefs in headship, living a debt-free life, women's submission, homeschooling and the willingness to have a large family, in other words, no contraceptives.

In 1990 our sixth child, Rebekah, was born at home. Within a couple weeks I was expected to cook and pack for camping trips throughout the summer. If the tent trailer wasn't packed and all the children ready by the time my husband would arrive after work for these trips, he would become a rageaholic. My schedule in 1990 - 1991 included homeschooling four children, taking care of our toddler and an infant, cleaning the home and cooking the meals, and showing and selling our home in Corvallis. I was also responsible for packing our home in preparation for our move to Independence, Oregon. I was responsible for unpacking, homeschooling and organizing our new home in the country. Mr. Warner was working fourteen-to-eighteen-hour days. I assumed, during this time, he was at work. Except for errands to town for grocery supplies, the children and I lived in isolation.

> During these years, I became uncomfortable talking to anyone without Mr. Warner present. He told me others would be trying to confuse me, and would disrespect the headship of our home, (Mr. Warner) and try to deceive me. I was fearful of Mr. Warner. I was also fearful that someone might learn the truth. I was required to support my husband in his spiritual pursuits.

In 1991 I became pregnant with my seventh child. After the move, I had asked Mr. Warner if I could be allowed time for my body to recover from the exhaustion of the move, Mr. Warner said, "No, Kathy, you should have faith." My body was showing signs of severe exhaustion during this pregnancy. When things were not going well in our home, Mr. Warner's response would be that I needed to learn how to submit. I resorted to more and more books and videos that would aid me in organizational skills. No matter how well organized I was or how fast I worked, I couldn't keep up with the ever-growing demands of our large family.

On one occasion, while in the final month of my pregnancy with my seventh child, my husband forced me to stay up all night and finish a wallpapering project in my son's room. Mr. Warner's reasoning for "my punishment" was because he did not want to see the dresser from the bedroom in the living room one more day. I finished the project and collapsed into bed before he went to work. My body was in distress. As Mr. Warner's wife, I became a "human doing, not a human being."

> A friend sent this verse to me. They said it described Marty's treatment of me: Matthew 23:4 "And they lay up heavy loads and lay them on man's shoulders, but they themselves are unwilling to move them with so much as a finger." (Please see movie "Pharlap).

Before my baby's birth, I took some time to read pamphlets and religious material my husband had around the home regarding the "Sacred Name Movement" that he was involved with. I was grieved and sickened by the white supremacist and anti-Semitic mentality that was woven throughout the articles. I approached my husband about this and he dismissed my concerns. I asked him to remove the material from our home. He ignored me. I believe the shock of discovering the truth behind this new movement was another brick added to an already too heavy load.

Hannah Rose was born in July of 1992 at home. Mr. Warner left me alone after the birth. I was bleeding heavily, was feverish and my blood pressure was elevated. Mr. Warner told me, as he was leaving, to clean up my bloody sheets. That evening the children came down with the flu. I was up with my newborn infant and the younger children throughout the night. By the fifth day after my baby was born, the children and I went to Corvallis, for our weekly errands and groceries. Friends were shocked to see me in the store shopping, but there was no one else to help.

In the years I raised my children, I rarely left them in Mr. Warner's care. I did not trust him. He was not a patient or compassionate man, and he often took out his personal frustrations, rage and anger on the younger children for the slightest infractions (spilled milk, crying, etc.) I also did not enlist the older ones to baby-sit the younger children. I felt it was my job to take care of and nurture my children.

In August, three weeks after Hannah was born, my husband made plans to go to his family reunion in Tigard, Oregon. I shared with him that I wanted to stay home with the baby and rest. Mr. Warner said, "No, Kathy, we are going as a family." Although I did not feel strong enough for the trip, I obeyed and went along with the family.

After returning from his family reunion, my husband took me to the bedroom to satisfy his sexual needs. Afterwards, he told me to go can the peaches that were in the carport. I told him that I was exhausted from the day's activities and that I was still bleeding heavily from the birth. However, I obeyed telling him at this rate, "I am going to be dead by next summer." I recall scalding my arm that night while canning and being too numb and exhausted to care for the wound. In the next few months, I canned over four hundred quarts of fruit.

During that summer Hannah was born, I often felt weak, shaky and sweaty during the night and day. I asked my husband if I could see my obstetrician. Mr. Warner said we didn't have enough money. Several months later, I asked Mr. Warner if I could see a physician. I believe, at that time I was suffering from exhaustion and post-partum depression. When I had doctor appointments, Mr. Warner insisted on accompanying me, however, if my appointment conflicted with his schedule, he said it would have to wait. He was too busy at work.

I was in phone contact with my midwife, Mabel Dzata, and my OB/Gyn, Dr. Charles South, during the next few months. I knew something was very wrong. I was only getting a few hours of broken sleep each night and I felt weaker each day. In December, I told Marty "I am falling apart." He told me to "Have faith, this is God's will for you."

To add to the tension in our home, Mr. Warner had enlisted the help of our eldest twin daughters in the process of supervising my responsibilities as a godly woman and reporting to their father all of my "infractions." As the years passed, my daughters became as demanding and critical of me as their father. Slowly, they gained more and more authority over my life. By the time the twins reached sixteen, they had many more rights and privileges than I did. (Car, phone, money, friends, personal decisions—such as hair, jewelry, clothing, etc.)

> This was just another safety precaution in our home that Mr. Warner orchestrated to feed his need for power and control. I was unaware, at the time, of how this would deteriorate the girls' respect for me. It was a task that proved devastating to their psychological well-being. Although I have offered Sarah and Rachel professional help, they have refused any outside intervention in their lives.

In March 1993, eight months after the birth of Hannah, I suffered a severe infection in my left eye one night. I was still wearing bandage lenses to assist my eyes in healing from the anterior membrane dystrophy. I could not remove the bandage lenses by myself. Each month I went to the Casey Eye Institute and my doctors removed and cleaned them. I was in severe pain all night from the infection.

My husband said we would call the doctors in the morning before attending his grandmother's birthday party in Portland. We loaded all seven children in the car in the morning and stopped by the Casey Eye Institute in Portland before attending the party at 11:00 am. The doctors looked at my eye, removed the bandage lens and took a lab test. After seeing the lab report, they told us that if we had arrived even a few minutes later, I could have lost the sight in my left eye because of the severe infection. I was given medication for the infection and two sets of dark sunglasses to wear to protect my eyes and told to get some rest.

Instead of rest, my husband insisted on continuing his planned events. We then drove to the nursing home and attended his grandmother's birthday party. She was pleased to see Mr. Warner, but was indifferent to me. I was not a "Catholic" so, in her eyes, I didn't belong. I had lived around cult mentality a long time by now and was beginning to get used to the shunning, coldness and lack of acceptance.

After the birthday party, we attended a wedding reception for one of Mr. Warner's relatives. Afterwards, he took us to Vancouver, Washington to buy some beekeeping equipment. I was exhausted and was experiencing a lot of pain in my eye, but knew I had to quietly endure until Mr. Warner was ready to return home.

We arrived back in Independence at 1:00 am. I nursed my baby, Hannah, and put her to bed and helped the rest of the younger children to bed. I collapsed after being up for forty-eight hours and wondered if I would be alive the next morning. Mr. Warner commented to me that night, "Kathy, you are beginning to mature and are learning how to handle yourself like a trooper."

Our home in Independence, Oregon, with above ground swimming pool. I was very isolated.

During the next few weeks my health deteriorated rapidly–loss of weight (thirty pounds below normal weight), exhaustion, TMJ, severe head ringing, insomnia, etc. The children had the flu, the baby was teething, and one child was experiencing hives. In April 1993, I mentally and physically hit the wall.

> The following is the repercussion of thirty-eight years of abuse. My illness (mental/nervous breakdown) was my reset button. Two years later I landed on my feet sunny side up with my eyes wide open.
>
> Through it all, I learned to love and honor myself. This painful time was a catalyst to my spirit waking up and learning how to function beautifully. In the past few years I have found the center of my universe–my balance and harmony.

"Beyond a certain point there is no return. This point has to be reached." – Frantz Kafka

Bearing Witness

The most important lesson learned from *BONSHEÁ - Making Light of the Dark* is that it is urgent and imperative that we teach our daughters (and our sons) a different reality than the one Coral lived. Our daughters must be strong and hold up their heads–they must look themselves, as well as husbands, bosses, judges and even God in the eye and know their own worth and the strength of their own Spirit. This book is not joyful because it recounts real tragedy–but the fact the story is told by the one who survived makes it a very hopeful book. *–Judy Bennett*, Editor, Oregon

Every so often a book is written that touches the heart. This is such a book. **BONSHEÁ** is an unforgettable story that will leave an indelible mark on your psyche. This is a story of an incredible journey of escape from bondage. Coral Theill's struggles and successes are heartrending as she reveals her attempts to build a new life–a story of courage and fortitude. **BONSHEÁ** is a must read!" *– Adaline 'Addie' Archer*, Court reporter (Ret), Washington

"The object of life is not to be on the side of the majority, but to escape finding oneself in the ranks of the insane." – *Marcus Aurelius*

II

Mental/Nervous Breakdown, Marital Rape, Witch Hunts, Post-Partum Depression, Wings of Love Half-Way House, Bill Gothard Institute

In the spring of 1993, at the age of thirty-eight, I suffered what many call a nervous breakdown–mental and physical collapse. Eight months prior, I had birthed our seventh child at our home and hemorrhaged severely. I felt alarmed after the birth because I could not sense any reserve of strength left within me. I told the midwife I felt like I was dying. Everyone dismissed my cries for help and said, "You will be feeling fine soon." However, a woman knows when her body is in trouble. In medical terms I was suffering from severe exhaustion and post-partum depression. My husband would not permit me to arrange an office visit with Dr. Charles South, my obstetrician of almost sixteen years. He said it would be too expensive (although he bought a tractor and donated a large sum of money to a religious couple that same month). I had no household help and was isolated on a small farm. Physical exhaustion (I was still nursing Hannah and expected to maintain a perfect house), birth trauma and a home environment that gave no support, contributed to my collapse.

One night, I experienced a sensation as though someone had hit me with a sharp instrument on the back of my head. I felt blood rush up the back of my head, a flooding sensation. I looked in the mirror and noticed the whites of my eyes were red. The sensation was something I had never experienced before. My husband took me to our family physician the next day. He said I was just experiencing a panic attack. He encouraged me to see a counselor. I had experienced panic attacks for the duration of my marriage. I knew this was different. I went home to rest. I believe my brain had hemorrhaged. I felt that whatever had happened, it could take a long time to recover from. After this incident, I could not even accomplish simple tasks well. My memory was clouded and thinking processes were slow.

Mr. Warner bluntly said to me, if you don't get well this weekend, I will have to commit you to a mental hospital or bring in my mom. (The latter was the worst threat.) The following week my husband's mother, Helen Warner, came to "help" with the chores and the children. I was told by her continually, that if I had stayed in the Catholic Church and been a good Catholic and wife like her, this would have never happened to me. Her animosity towards me, especially in my fragile state, threatened my feelings of safety and I could not relax while in her care.

With the stresses of my husband and his mother, I became increasingly suicidal. I thought of the children often and realized that I was no longer capable of taking care of them or myself. I left a note once, with a friend, Kristi Gilsdorf, listing the names of people I wanted to help in the raising of my children in case something should happen to me. My husband, his mother and family were not included in the note.

> Even during these times of great desperation, I continued to
> protect the children from their father–the man who had been
> so harmful to the children and me.

In July of 1993, the Gilsdorf family came to our home for my daughter's eighth birthday. On this occasion they observed my husband order me to pick up some hazel nut shells that were left on the back porch and carport area. Mr. Warner was standing right there but made no move himself to clean up the mess. I got down on my hands and knees and meekly began to pick up the shells, apologizing to Mr. Warner and explaining that the children had just left them and I thought it was okay to have brushed them off the porch. Mike and Kristi Gilsdorf, in a gesture of support, bent over and started helping me until the issue blew over.

During the two-year episode of my breakdown (1993-1995), I was mentally, emotionally and physically incapacitated. Mr. Warner refused to acknowledge that I was experiencing serious problems. Instead, he and his religious counselors told me and my children that I had a "spiritual problem" and God was punishing me because I had not learned how to submit to my husband and the religious authorities God had placed over me. I looked within my soul and couldn't remember when I had not obeyed except for times I intervened when Mr. Warner was verbally, emotionally or physically harming my children.

While I was ill, I learned that most of the Christian community we were involved with did not believe that a Christian could have a mental breakdown. Mr. Warner took me to several fundamentalist groups and counselors during my illness. (He and his religious supporters believed that psychology was in error to the Word of God.) They exorcised me for being a witch and said I had a jezebel spirit. Mr. Warner's counselors could not understand or help me. I recall when I was ill, I told Mr. Warner's counselors that I was a whore and that I wanted to live on the streets. My breakdown was a place of honesty. My mind was voicing how I felt about myself based on how I had been treated by my husband. We met with many Christian "counselors" and they believed my husband because he is so convincing. I came to I understand the saying, "knee deep in water and dying of thirst."

> Psychiatrist R.D. Laing believes that when we invalidate people or deny their perceptions and personal experiences, we make mental invalids of them. He found that when one's feelings are denied a person can be made to feel crazy even when they are perfectly mentally healthy. There is significant research to support the idea that emotional invalidation significantly predicted psychological distress, including depression and anxiety symptoms.

Throughout my marriage I understood the unspoken rule which governed the whole Warner family. Helen Warner, my husband's mother, expected and demanded total allegiance from her sons and daughters and their marriage partners. Mr. Warner continued this tradition in our marriage and family. He demanded total allegiance from his wife and children.

More than anything, I wanted to be safe and permanently free from my husband, his mother and his religious supporters. It was hard to be "helped" because I was not allowed to tell the truth. It was difficult to "act right" during this time because my basic instincts and intuition had been forcibly cut away through years of abuse. I was frightened while I was ill because I did not have the strength or stamina to work harder and faster for my husband. The juggling act and the mask I had worn to get by my whole life was slipping.

> When you live with people who are existential vacuums, they use you up. I tried to draw from the place I went to when I was exhausted, but there was nothing left. I felt like an empty cistern in great need of refilling. While living with an abusive partner or parent you carry an enormous amount of guilt

because you can never get it "right" or perfect for them. You run faster, but it is never fast enough.

I longed to talk to someone who could truly understand or help me. I didn't know yet what it felt like, but what I truly longed for was humane treatment and compassion.

Emotionally and physically, I was numb, like coming out of anesthesia after surgery. You can see and hear everyone, but you are under a blanket or a fog, not quite here. I hated the feeling. During this time, I prayed that God would use me to help those who are broken from life's tragedies and traumas and that I would make a "difference in this life."

I didn't feel like myself and couldn't "think right"—the way everyone wanted me to think. My head literally felt detached from my body as if, lying on the bed, my head was on the next pillow. I continually felt electric shocks in my brain. It was almost impossible to sleep in the two-year period of my illness. The twisted projections, condemnation and judgment I felt from Mr. Warner, his counselors, the religious community, and his mother, increased my level of anxiety. It was a frightening experience knowing that my "recovery program" was in the hands of my husband and his mother.

My twelve-year-old son, Aaron, was very upset by my breakdown. He showed compassion toward me during the beginning, but like the other children, he was being told by his father and the religious counselors, that there was nothing wrong with me, it was all an act, and that I could be "well" if I would just repent. Aaron began to lose hope seeing me well again. There was no healthy person in the home to relate to, and this left the children in a very vulnerable state. My husband related to any of Aaron's questionings, confrontation, and needs by beating and assaulting him after work. Aaron was repeatedly victimized by his father during the two-year period of my breakdown.

During this time, my husband became involved with yet another religious group in Marion County, a Sabbath keeping church that practiced many of the doctrines of the Worldwide Church of God founded by Herbert W. Armstrong.

During July and August of 1993, I briefly saw Dr. Roger Jacobson and Dr. Michael May, psychiatrists in Corvallis, Oregon. They were both helpful and kind. Dr. May's diagnoses reads, "Major Affective Disorder, Depressed, single episode without psychotic features, panic disorder." He notes that I have tinnitus and also what sounds like Paroxysmal Atrial Tachycardia. Regarding a conversation with Mr. Warner, Dr. May's evaluation states, "I share with him some of Kathryn's concerns about discord in their relationship." Dr. Jacobson diagnosed me as having Generalized Anxiety Disorder. Both physicians prescribed me medications.

Dr. Jacobson's records on 9/10/93 indicate a call from Karen (Heintz) Lague, a former neighbor. His report states, "Ms. Lague was feeling helpless in the face of the Warners' shared beliefs that, Ms. Lague in turn believes, prevents them from getting appropriate care for Kathy." Ms. Lague stated to Dr. Jacobson that I had stopped taking medications, was no longer sleeping and was unwilling to work with psychiatrists. Ms. Lague was concerned because I had made comments in the past (last few months) about suicide. She commented to Dr. Jacobson that I was trying to deal with my difficulty by controlling my thoughts and working with some Christian counselors. *(Note: At this time, my husband, my friend Betsy Close, my husband's mother and my husband's friends and counselors convinced me, while in my weakened mental state, that I had a "sin" problem and that going to psychiatrists and taking medications was "evil.")*

In September 1993, I felt hopeless and suicidal. I tried to cut my wrists with an electric grinding wheel. After the incident, my husband took me to a religious counselor and author he respected, Mr. Tom McMahon, in Bend, Oregon. With my wrists bandaged from this attempt at suicide, my husband took me to a motel and used me sexually. *(No contraceptives were used. I soon discovered I was pregnant again.)* The next day we met with Mr. McMahon and I was again admonished that I had not learned how to "obey and submit to my husband" and God was punishing me.

In addition to these Christian "counselors," Mr. Warner took me to a number of psychiatrists, psychologists, and numerous doctors during 1993 to 1995, but I was always interviewed under the watchful and oppressive eye of my "concerned" husband. The one and only time I asked to speak to a psychiatrist alone was followed by such rage and abuse from Mr. Warner that I didn't try again.

> As my breakdown progressed, I felt a deep need to go back to past people and places. I wanted to find out what road I had turned on to end up here. I asked myself many questions, but had no answers–*yet*. I felt guilty, hopeless and worthless. How had I ended up feeling this way? I was at a loss to understand why. In frustration I would sometimes throw my Bible on the

floor and cry out to God, "I hate you." Although not a healthy sign for those around me, this was the beginning of my healing.

My true self was acknowledging that the male- patriarchal based religion that I had been indoctrinated into as a young girl had **not served me well; physically, mentally, emotionally or spiritually.**

I discovered later that when we deny our own true feelings and commitment to truth, we become victims to our guilt and shame. "Guilt is created when we adopt what others expect of us as our guideline, denying our own integrity and self-directed will." Jamie Sams, *Dancing the Dream: Seven Sacred Paths of Human Transformation*

Allowing others to make choices for you allows them to create your worth, and when they do, *they always make it too small.*

Also, in September 1993, I was forced by Mr. Warner, to attend a Basic Youth Conflicts Seminar by Bill Gothard being held in Portland. The theme of these seminars was "submission of women to their husbands." Dan and Penny O'Halloran, Mr. Warner's cousin and wife, attended, also, and prayed that I might learn how to submit and obey. My repentance, in their eyes, was the key to my healing and becoming whole again. (Dan and Penny O'Halloran were once participants in the Keith and Melody Green Christian community/cult in Texas). I quit all medications, wasn't sleeping well, and was doing my best to submit to the Christian counselors that my husband took me to.

My mental and physical health continued to deteriorate.

I have noticed one underlying theme for many individuals who become involved in extreme fundamentalist and legalistic groups and cults. They have been involved in one of many life's scenarios, whether it be as the abused or the abuser, infidelity, unwed mother, runaways, loss of job or loss of a loved one, etc. Instead of forgiving themselves and others, healing, and moving on, cults appear to attract these people at vulnerable times in their lives and project shame, guilt and fear.

In other words, cults capitalize on an individuals' experience of crisis, shock and trauma. They are proselytized by cult members, indoctrinated into rigid/legalistic thought patterns through covert induction. People seek affirmation from these cults and it never happens. Affirmation can only come from the Creator and yourself.

The type of trauma individuals experience from cults and their leaders is similar to that described by POW's. The trauma experienced by cult members results from being powerless and abused day after day, year after year, whether physically, emotionally, or spiritually – souls are literally emaciated. The Word of God is used like a thrust of a knife, constantly reminding the cult member (victim) of God's displeasure and eternal damnation.

Your dreams and relationships die and are replaced by daily obedience to the leaders. While spiritual abuse victims may or may not suffer physical abuse, their souls are battered and bleeding. Life inside a cult is death by a thousand cuts or what some experts call "metaphysical stoning."

In November of 1993, I saw Dr. Charles Kuttner, a psychiatrist. He diagnosed me as "adjustment disorder with mixed emotional features" and "Anxiety/Depression with obsessive-compulsive elements." Although he never "diagnosed" me as psychotic, on seeing how rigid I was in my self-criticism and guilt, he began to suspect I might be suffering from a psychotic depression. Dr. Kuttner explains "adjustment disorder" this way, "a person in a prison camp undergoes depression and anxiety in response to the situation. It means a fairly normal response to difficult to highly abnormal circumstances."

Dr. Kuttner had me admitted to the Woodland Park Mental Hospital, in Portland, for observation and evaluation. The doctor, Mr. Larson (a fundamentalist Christian), was abusive. He told me I had better learn to listen to my loving and caring husband. By now I was two months pregnant and it was humiliating and disturbing to be under lock and key. I felt so broken and traumatized that I did not believe I would ever be whole and well again.

I was given ink blot tests, which meant nothing to me. My mother-in-law, Helen Warner, brought my two youngest daughters, Hannah and Rebekah, ages 16 months and three and a half years old, to visit me at the mental hospital. Helen Warner appeared pleased with herself. I listened to her monologue of Catholic jargon then she left with my daughters.

During my breakdown I learned more about Mr. Warner's Irish Catholic mother and the hostility she felt toward several of her Protestant daughter-in-laws.

I longed for someone who could truly help me–someone who could acknowledge the "human spirit" that was within me. After undergoing several tests, I was released to the care of my husband.

During my breakdown, my greatest pain and grief was the fact that, besides being unable to care for myself, I was also unable to care for and protect my children. Since I could find no hope that I would be well again, I often thought suicide would be a solution to the family's emotional, physical and financial burden of me. But the love I carried for my children kept me hanging on. Emotionally, I could not stand the thought of leaving them alone and unprotected with their father and grandmother.

When my husband took me to Betsy Close's Pregnancy Crisis Care center in Corvallis for a pregnancy test during the period of my breakdown, I learned that Mrs. Close was promoting materials from her and her husband's pastor, Stan Houghton. Pastor Houghton, an abusive Pentecostal cult leader, encouraged parents to beat their children with thick boards. I asked Betsy Close to remove the materials from her center, as I found them repulsive. I tried to caution her of the dangers of this cult, but she dismissed my warnings.

My husband did not want my physician, Dr. Charles South, to learn of my pregnancy in 1993, so he put me under the care of Dr. Jess Hickerson, OBGyn in Corvallis, Oregon.

I suffered a miscarriage in December of 1993 and was admitted to Good Samaritan Hospital, in Corvallis, for a D & C.

Dr. Jess Hickerson, who performed the D & C after I miscarried, reports, **"This woman's medical history is significant for nervous breakdown. She has had a miscarriage and is scheduled for a D & C."** Dr. Kuttner prescribed me tranquilizers and Prozac etc...to cushion the shock of the surgery. Nothing seemed to help and the combinations of medication did not agree with me. I remember crying uncontrollably the night after my D & C. I didn't know who I was or what had happened. I felt so frightened. My body was shattered and I could not hide my pain, like I had before. The tough girl was all gone. My crying upset Mr. Warner so he beat me and put pillows over my face and smothered me until I stopped crying out loud. Any type of crying or emotional outburst was labeled as a weakness by Mr. Warner.

The next day I was forced to take a long trip. Mr. Warner wanted to be with his family in Snohomish, Washington for Christmas. The trip was difficult for me physically and emotionally. Being in the presence of his family, who were hostile to me, was not a prescription for health. In fact, it was like drinking poison. Thinking patterns towards another do not have to be spoken, they are felt. Einstein and other great thinkers and writers say our thoughts are things and I have experienced this to be true.

A few months afterwards Dr. Kuttner suggested to my husband and me that we add an antipsychotic drug to my medications. When a patient has a severe, agitated depression with delusions (e.g., that they're worthless or hopeless), antipsychotic drugs are sometimes used. He also said one of the possible side effects of the drug was tardive dyskinesia, a condition that can be permanent, specifically causing disfiguring and disabling movements of the face, hands, etc. I did not take the medication.

Concerned friends and family members called our home during my breakdown. Mr. Warner and my eldest daughters would not permit me to talk with them. Mr. Warner said it was because they would "confuse me." I was not allowed to call my family or friends. When I did, Mr. Warner would respond with violent outbursts and would yell and threaten me.

March 9, 1994, Dr. Kuttner wrote a letter to my husband and dismissed me as a patient because my husband was not cooperating with treatment. Mr. Warner would not bring me in for appointments and he was leaving me with unqualified and hostile people. Dr. Kuttner said Mr. Warner was endangering my life. (This letter is included in documentation.)

I was also counseled by a man named Bill Heard, from Roseburg, Oregon, early in 1994. My husband related to him well. Mr. Bill Heard is an assistant pastor of Covenant Life Fellowship in Roseburg, Oregon. Mr. Heard and Mr. Warner hold many similar viewpoints in common, i.e. oppression of women, patriarchal religion, etc.

Mr. Heard had served time in jail, his children had been in trouble with the law, and his wife, Linda, had all the outside appearances of an oppressed and abused woman. (She assisted him in his counseling.) He had no license to counsel, but was a member of the local church, who had ordained him as a pastor. He reminded me of my husband. He told me God used woman like me as a public and living example of what God does to women who are self-sufficient and disobedient. He told me that I was in spiritual confusion because I am in sin. He said, "If you would just repent, you could be well again."

Mr. Warner took notes from his conversations with Bill Heard. He wrote in January 1994: "Bill says Kathy is choosing her behavior, she is in rebellion and does not trust Yah, (Mr. Warner's word for God.) Kathy has a proud and critical spirit. Bill believes she should be in a residential treatment center or mental hospital. (I believe if we lived in a different era, they would have sentenced me to burn at the stake.) Bill Heard would later testify in court in support of my husband when I finally got the courage and strength to leave this marriage.

I spent many nights on my knees in front of this man repenting to him and my former husband. They made fun of my body and kept comparing me to a fearful horse. I was in shock and fear of these two very oppressive and sick men. They made sure I understood what my sins and shortcomings were by quoting Bible verses from a thick Christian Scriptural workbook that listed my sins in detail and the scripture verses. This book explained in great length all the things I had done wrong. Everything was my fault. I often felt suicidal after counseling sessions with this man.

On our drive home, I remember Mr. Warner singing "Praise the Lord," and "Hallelujah" after my counseling, interrogation and "repentance" sessions. "*Repent*, and you could be *well*," is what I heard from Mr. Warner all the way home and in the days, weeks and months that followed.

> Several physicians and counselors have told me that they believed my breakdown only would have lasted a few months, instead of almost two years, had I been spared of ritual, mental, verbal and physical abuse.

> I recently asked for copies of my records from Mr. Bill Heard. His wife replied on the phone and said they had been destroyed. She said that Bill Gothard's Institute agreed with her husband's counsel and treatment of me and they felt there was no reason to save my records.

On one occasion, I was allowed to visit the local library with the younger children and happened to hear a talk by, Alice Kern, author of *Tapestry of Hope*, a Jewish survivor of the Auschwitz Concentration Camp. After I became ill, I managed to call her and ask her what had helped her survive while living in the midst of hell. She said, "Kathy, you have to have something to hope for outside of the prison."

> I believe we all long for the freedom *to be*–that was what my spirit secretly longed for and hoped to experience. I believe we all long for freedom from oppression and bondage. I join the Jews each year at Passover and pray for deliverance from oppression and bondage for all mankind. I am grateful for each brand new day and the experience of *being*.

I was allowed to stay with Addie Archer, a friend in Longview, for a week. She was understanding and kind to me. When she first saw me, she noticed that my legs were both black and blue. She asked me what had happened and I told her simply that one of my older children had become angry and kicked me. Although, my mental health did not change, my soul was encouraged by her compassion. She left tender footprints across my heart. I felt ashamed to be in such poor mental, emotional and physical condition, but no matter how hard I tried to heal, I couldn't seem to find my way back.

> Post-partum depression is best described as a spider falling to the bottom of a hundred foot steel cylinder. The spider tries to climb back up to the top, but can't even climb a few inches without slipping back to the bottom. There is nothing to hold on to.

> It is reported that post-partum depression and post-partum psychosis was included in the Diagnostic and Statistical Manual, DSM, in 1994. Before then there has been little education on this type of depression.

> There are now support groups throughout the nation where women can turn to for help who believe they may be experiencing PPD.

During my breakdown, I felt that there was no hope for wellness and became increasingly suicidal as I realized Mr. Warner and his religious counselor's definition of wellness centered on my obedience and submission to my husband's power and control over me. Obedience meant submitting to his physical, emotional, financial, ritual and sexual abuse. The only choice, at that time, was more abuse or suicide. Suicide became more and more appealing as Mr. Warner's abuse toward me escalated.

> Dr. David Richo, author of *How to be an Adult in Relationships: The Five Keys to Mindful Loving,* writes, "Childhood forces influence present choices, for the past is on a continuum with the present. Early business that is still unfinished does not have to be a sign of immaturity; rather it can signal continuity. Recurrence of childhood themes in adult relationships gives our life depth in that we are not superficially passing over life events but inhabiting them fully as they evolve. Our past becomes a problem only when it leads to a compulsion to repeat our losses or **smuggles unconscious determinants into our decisions.** Our work, then, is not to abolish our connection to the past but to take it into account without being at its mercy. The question is how much the past interferes with our chances of healthy relating and living in accord with our deepest needs, value, and wishes."

Despite the pain of it, my breakdown was my escape. It was the way my body screamed to society of the terror and horror I had lived in under my husbands' rule in my own home, but no one heard. Dr. Clarissa Estés writes, *"When our lips don't speak it, our bodies will scream it."*

In the spring of 1994, a few months after my miscarriage and D & C, my husband and my midwife, Mabel Dzata's, pastor took me to "Wings of Love," a half-way house, on Killingsworth in Portland, Oregon. My husband threatened me that if I didn't shape up and start meeting my responsibilities, he would leave me at the half-way house. The house was filthy, rat-infested and broken down. It was run by a religious fanatic middle-aged black woman in one of the most dangerous parts of Portland.

My ex-husband's estate, at this time, was over a quarter-of-a million dollars and his monthly pay over $6,000 a month, as a facility engineer. He had numerous IRA accounts and stocks. We were totally debt-free.

A week later, my husband left me at the "Wings of Love" half-way house during the time of my illness, to "break me" (his words) to the will of God. We (i.e.

56

ex-cons, prostitutes, and street people) were forced to march and sing "Nothing but the Blood of Jesus" before we could eat. I went into shock and just wanted to die. In this place of horror, I had no hope of getting well. It depressed me to think of my future–continuing to serve a husband who believed it was his God given right to "break me." My husband said, "I love you, Kathy" as he left. The word "love" by now had a numbing effect on my soul.

I wondered what I had done to end up in a place like this. I thought about my father and what he would think if he were alive and could see me. The ex-cons kept busy killing the rats with shovels and axes. I remember bathing and dressing a 50-year-old woman who had been severely beaten and raped outside of the shelter. I also remember asking for a safety latch for the room I stayed in at night. It had a dirty, old couch. I don't remember lying down or sleeping. I just sat up all night. Mr. Warner, the pastor and the woman who ran the half-way house told me I would be staying there until I learned how to serve others. In their minds, I was a selfish woman.

Several weeks later, my brother, Don Hall, was granted "permission" by my husband, to pick me up from the shelter and take me home with him. I was subjected to my brother's and his pastor's interpretation of my sins and of what was "wrong." I was thankful though, for a safer and cleaner environment. My mind, at this time, was very tired and frayed. Although my brother cared about me, it was difficult for him to help me or show compassion because he embraced many of the same fundamentalist Christian doctrines as my husband. He took me to his church. I was very uncomfortable with the activities there. People were being slain in the spirit.

In my brother's opinion my breakdown was the result of being in sin, not holy, not under the right authority or church, not praying or fasting enough, etc. My brother's counsel was oppressive and devitalizing. I believe he thought I deserved what had happened to me. I slipped into a borderline catatonic-vegetative state–I couldn't eat or shower, stand or sit without someone commanding me or pushing me through the motions.

> A couple years ago, my brother and I were discussing childhood molestation and rape issues. He stated to me that if young children and women are under the blood of Jesus that they will not experience the sexual assaults that have become prevalent in our nation i.e., one woman is raped every two seconds and one in three children will be molested by age eighteen. I told him that his

words lacked compassion and were insulting to me. He escorted me out of his home. Throughout the years he told me I was going to hell and reminded me that he had the "truth" and I did not. I prayed that someday we could discuss spiritual wholeness apart from religiosity. Sadly, he did not wish to speak with me and shunned me for six years before his tragic death in 2009.

My husband counseled over the phone with Mr. Jim Logan, a man who specialized in counseling in matters regarding demon possession. He suggested my husband take me to the Bill Gothard Indianapolis training center in Indiana. A few months later, in September of 1994, my husband took me by plane to the training center for counseling and reprimand. This "Christian" training center is run by Mr. Bill Gothard of Basic Youth Conflicts.

> It has been widely reported in the mainstream press and in several Christian publications, including "The Bible for Today," and "Christianity Today," that the training center staff grossly abused their religious authoritarian positions and sexually molested and defrauded young women working for the Institute. It has also been documented that Bill Gothard and the Center are guilty of financial fraud and extravagantly misspend as much as $40 million in donations, and exerted extraordinary psychological control over institute employees. (Documentation can be obtained through "The Bible for Today," Collingswood, N.J., in "Bill Gothard's Sex Scandals– Watergate? or Waterloo? –An Evaluation of Some of the Primary Documentation" by Rev. D. A. Waite, Th.D., Ph.D. Rev. D. A. Waite's 140 pages of documentation include many newspaper articles, court documentation and letters.)

Bill Gothard became one of the most celebrated figures in the fundamentalist and conservative evangelical segments of American Christianity in the mid 1980's and packed auditoriums from coast to coast with a message of strict morality and biblical authority. His six-day, rally-like seminars were based in the belief god's divine authority is passed through a "chain of command"–conflicts can be solved "if employees obey their bosses, children obey their parents, wives obey their husbands and husbands answer to God."

Once again, at the Bill Gothard Training Institute, I was told how I had not learned to submit to my husband and religious "authorities" and that God was punishing me because of my rebellious spirit. I was accused of witchcraft and they tried, through prayer and exorcism, to cast demons out of me on a daily basis.

I was forced to listen to presentations by the institute every day on how to be a more submissive wife. The central theme message was from I Cor. 11:3-9, "But I want you to know that the head of every man is Christ, the head of woman is man, and the head of Christ is God. Every man praying or prophesying, having his head covered, dishonors his head. But every woman who prays or prophesies with her head uncovered dishonors her head, for that is one and the same as if her head were shaved. For if a woman is not covered, let her also be shorn. But if it is shameful for a woman to be shorn or shaved, let her be covered. For a man indeed ought not to cover his head, since he is the image and glory of God; but woman is the glory of man. Nor was man created for the woman, but woman for the man."

I was watched by 16- to 18-year-old girls who worked for the institute. During the day I scrubbed floors, cleaned toilets and made beds in their hotel. I remember looking at myself in the mirror, touching my reflection and saying, "Kathy all gone, Kathy all gone." She was.

I could not relate to the vindictive, punishing God they kept preaching at me. Listening to them preach shame, fear, and guilt was not healing to my fragile mind and body. I watched them humiliate teenage boys in front of large groups. Leaders at the institute encouraged these young men to repent of such acts as masturbation, holding hands with girls, etc. Young men were given pictures of Bill Gothard water-skiing at his resort in a full suit and tie for an example of how to dress properly.

Mr. Gothard is charismatic, just as Jim Jones was. His organization and ideology can be classified as a cult. He is well-respected and admired by millions of Christians in America and city and government officials, but he uses oppression, brainwashing and mind control tactics to deceive.

Many of the older women who lived there shared with me their horror stories of living under "Gothardism." I tried to tell them they were trapped in a cult and encouraged them to get out. They said they couldn't because their husbands worked for Mr. Gothard and the "institute" and would never leave. I realized that if I didn't get out, I would be in worse shape than when I arrived, and so I ran for my life.

I experienced horrendous abuses under Bill Gothard's "re-education" techniques which were thrust upon me by one of

Gothard's avid supporters and disciples, my husband, Marty Warner. Although Gothard is now yesterday's news, his victims languish on, sometimes taking years to recover from the ritual abuse and trauma inflicted on them.

I was watched constantly, but I did manage to escape. Even though my personal belongings, plane ticket and identification were locked up, I had enough money for a taxi ride to the Chicago Airport. I gave my name to the customer service employee at the airport. They looked up my ticket on the computer and I boarded a plane to Portland, Oregon. The plane ride was frightening because I feared repercussions from Mr. Warner as I returned to Portland. My brother picked me up at the airport and I stayed at his house in Washington State. My husband was disturbed that I left the Institute before they could "cure" me. He gave me "permission" to stay at my brother's home in Washington.

Throughout my illness, Mr. Warner's religious supporters and counselors exorcised me for being a witch.

> "Witch hunts" will continue to be very much a part of American history, as long as fundamentalist and religious institutions teach people to fear an oppressive, vindictive, ruthless, patriarchal god. Millions of women were burned as witches by the Catholic Church during the Middle Ages.

Beginning in the sixteenth century and peaking in the seventeenth century, the Christian church was similar to a terrorist organization, being the instigator of indescribable horrors of the infamous Inquisition. In France and, later, in other parts of Europe, tens of thousands of innocent men and women—even children—were persecuted, arrested, imprisoned, tried in secret, tortured, flayed, hanged, or burned at the staked due to the church's obsession with heretics, witches, herbalists, midwives, sorcerers, black magic and demon-possession.

> An excellent documentary film, *The Burning Times*, and the books, *The Dark Side of Christian History* by Helen Ellerbe and *Woman, Church and State*, by Matilda Joslyn Gage, exposes how the Christian and Catholic Church in cooperation with local governments instigated a reign of terror in the sixteenth century. Death by torture was the method of the church for the repression of women's intellect– knowledge being held as evil and dangerous in her hands. Those condemned as sorcerers

and witches, as "heretics," were in reality the most advanced thinkers of their ages.

False accusations and hysteria-driven trials led to torture, burnings at the stake, and ultimately to the destruction of what had been an organic and holistic way of life for women. *The Burning Times*, suggests that this widespread church and state-sanctioned torture and killing of "witches" set the stage for modern society's acceptance of violence against women. The crimes committed by these women were using herbs, performing the duties of a midwife, and refusing to "submit and conform" to the Papal Church. Men were instructed by priests of the Catholic Church to "beat their wives out of charity." Does any of this sound familiar?

Gage writes, "The Parliament of Toulouse burned 400 witches at one time. Four hundred women at one hour on the public square, dying the horrid death of fire for a crime which never existed save in the imagination of those persecutors and which grew in their imagination from a false belief in woman's extra- ordinary wickedness, based upon a false theory as to original sin."

Inga Muscio, author of *Cunt–A declaration of Independence,* writes, "The Inquisition justified the–usually sadistic–murder, enslavement or rape of every woman, child and man who practiced any form of spiritual belief which did not honor savior-centered phallic power worship. Women who owned anything more than the clothes on their back...were religiously targeted by the Inquisition because all of women's resources and possessions became property of the famously cunt fearing Catholic Church. Out of this, the practice of sending "missionaries" into societies bereft of savior-centered spiritualities evolved."

I agree with author James Redfield. He writes, "A group consciousness which speaks constantly of separation and superiority (our religious and legal systems) produces loss of compassion on a massive scale, and loss of compassion is inevitably followed by a loss of conscience."

Bearing Witness

You stand TALL amongst many. We're all wounded but some choose to heal so that they can heal others. Continue your incredible work. It shines the light across the seas… Even here in Africa, we tell your story… I am equally touched and indignant at the same time. Your story, because it's written from the heart, is so painful but very, very empowering because you saw the light. God bless you for this gift to all womenfolk.

Look at what it's doing for all of us in the world. It's reaching beyond the seas and cultural divides. I'm at a loss for words. Thank you, Coral, for your light…. - *Nana Ngobese-Nxumala*, Director, Woman Forward Political Party, South Africa

BONSHEÁ – coming out of the darkness and into the light is a lifelong journey as Coral illustrates in her own journey that she has so courageously shared with all mankind. She is among the deep and profound minds of our time; her story will provide you with enlightenment… or at the very least questions to ponder on your own journey. *Rebecca Leslie Weathers MS*, Counselor, Hamilton, New Zealand

> "We are caught in an inescapable network of mutuality, tied in a single garment of destiny. Whatever affects one directly affects all indirectly." – *Dr. Martin Luther King, Jr.*

III

Pregnancy and Birth of my Eighth Child, Evangelical Churches, No Divorce Policy, Stockholm Syndrome, Dark Night of the Soul

During my stay with my brother in October 1994, my husband visited me on one occasion. I was still suffering from my breakdown and was nearly catatonic. He brought me thyroid medication from an internal medicine doctor in Corvallis, Oregon. I had not seen this physician for a year and a half. During his overnight visit, Mr. Warner took me to a nearby motel and fulfilled his physical needs for the night. He did not use contraceptives. Once again, I was pregnant.

I stayed with my brother Don Hall, Hannah Humberd, and also with Stephanie Hawkinson, a former neighbor, during the early months of my pregnancy.

> Remembering my stay with her during this time, Hanna Humberd said, "You walked like a helpless child or a sleepwalker. Something had shut down inside you and I honestly thought you would never be normal again. You stayed with me a few weeks and I cared for you as a child. I made sure you ate your meals, propped you up on a couch with a breakfast tray, watching some old classic TV show. You just needed to feel safe and get lots of rest in a fairly healthy environment."

While I was ill, I took walks during the day and for safety purposes I placed post-it-notes inside my boots during this time that simply stated, "If you find this body, please call (503) 757-2069, Rich and Therese Vasquez. (In the summer of 1995, after Zachary was born, I threw these notes away.)

By January 1995 I was feeling better. My brother, Don, dropped me off at a former neighbor's home in Corvallis, Oregon. Stephanie Hawkinson had offered to let me stay as a guest in her home. My friend, Therese Vasquez picked me up at Stephanie's home and drove me to my doctor's appointment. Dr. South confirmed the pregnancy. Dr. South appeared disturbed to see me pregnant and was also aware I was still recovering from the two year period of my breakdown. He told me, "Kathy, go get the best attorney you can find and divorce the son of a b-tch."

One of the most life changing moments I had up to then was when Stephanie Hawkinson gave me information and a book about abuse. I had never been exposed to this kind of information before and found it very enlightening. The book answered questions about emotional or psychological abuse and stated that the sole purpose of the abuser's actions is to dominate, manipulate, and control another person.

The book listed abuser's tactics as name-calling or yelling, using angry expressions or gestures, humiliation (either in public or private), isolation of the victim from family and friends, accusations of infidelity, constant belittlement of another person, constant questioning of the other person's judgment or decision-making abilities, threatening to take the children away, accusations of insanity, and ignoring or minimizing the other person's feelings. Physical abuse could include, slapping, pushing, kicking, pulling hair, biting, choking, shaking or throwing someone around a room, twisting of any limbs, any form of restraint, and rape, i.e., forcing someone to have unwanted sex.

Other characteristics of an abuser included thinking there are no consequences for his behavior, depriving partner of money, making her beg for it or taking her money, restricting his partner's access to food, clothing, work, health care etc., destroying possessions belonging to his partner, believing in male supremacy, being pathologically jealous, being cruel to animals and children, being self-righteous and self-centered, denying or minimizing his abusive behavior, needing to be in control of every situation, and believing they are the "head of the household." Other signs of an abuser: prevent you from working or attending school and need to control all finances and force you to account in detail for what you spend."

> Psychological studies have determined that many individuals
> have Stockholm Syndrome to varying degrees. It has happened
> to concentration camp prisoners, cult members, pimp-procured
> prostitutes, incest victims, physically and/or emotionally

abused children, battered women, hostages and prisoners of war. Due to severe indoctrination, victims become prisoners of the twisted logic presented by their abusers.

"Victims have to concentrate on survival, requiring avoidance of direct, honest reaction to destructive treatment. Become highly attuned to pleasure and displeasure reactions of victimizers. As a result, victims know much about captors, less about themselves. Victims are encouraged to develop psychological characteristics pleasing to captors: dependency, lack of initiative, inability to act, decide, think, etc. Both actively develop strategies for staying alive, including denial, attentiveness to victimizer's wants, fondness for victimizer accompanied by fear, fear of interference by authorities, and adoption of victimizer's perspective. Hostages are overwhelmingly grateful to terrorists for giving them life. They focus on captor's kindnesses, not his acts of brutality. Battered women assume that the abuser is a good man whose actions stem from problems that she can help him solve. Both feel fear, as well as love, compassion and empathy toward a captor who has shown them any kindness. Any acts of kindness by the captors will help ease the emotional distress they have created and will set the stage for emotional dependency of Counterproductive Victim Responses." *The Stockholm Syndrome: Not Just for Hostages,* by Dee L.R. Graham, Edna Rawlings, and Nelly Rimini

Angelina Jolie's movie, *In the Land of Blood and Honey,* featured women who were sex slaves during the war or occupation and how they strived to please men - just for their safety. I resonated and related to the message in this film because that was all my marriage was based on - pleasing my husband - for my safety and well-being.

Evangelical Churches – No Divorce Policy

Battered wives who seek help or advice from clergy members are often told that they bring abuse on themselves by refusing to submit to their husband.

Rick Warren's Saddleback Church, through their doctrine, *"divorce is only permitted in cases of adultery or abandonment — as these are the only cases permitted in the Bible — and never for abuse,"* promotes the centrality of male authority. Mainstream evangelical culture believes **male authority can still be maintained in a controlled separation but is seriously threatened when a woman is given leeway of any kind, for whatever reason, in ceasing to submit to an abusive husband by divorcing him.**

Debi Pearl, half of a husband-and-wife fundamentalist child-training ministry as well as author of the bestselling submission manual, *Created to Be His Help Meet*, writes that submission is so essential to God's plan, **that it must be followed even to the point of allowing abuse.** "When God puts you in subjection to a man whom he knows is going to cause you to suffer," she writes, "it is with the understanding that you are obeying God by enduring the wrongful suffering."

Stephanie told me that when I could call the way I had been treated by Mr. Warner "abuse," then I would be on the road to recovery. I suffered from "Stockholm Syndrome," and was unwell at that time. I continued to explain to her that my husband was kind because "he let me plant flowers in our gardens." It would take me several months to be able to verbalize and articulate what was so obvious to the people around me. I began to have hope for the first time in my life. The brainwashing and conditioning that had left me numb was replaced with words of truth and empowerment.

My husband picked me up from Stephanie's and I returned to my home January 20 and resumed my expected duties. I took care of the children, cooked meals, cleaned the home and did the laundry and grocery shopping during this time. The four eldest children were attending a Christian school in Philomath, Oregon. I came down with severe toxemia and had difficulty sleeping because of the pain. Several weeks before my eighth child was born, all seven children came down with the chicken pox. One of my oldest daughters was also ill and had surgery.

Mr. Warner beat me twice during this pregnancy. His reason? I had asked him to please not send our younger children to his mother, Helen Warner. Our eight-year-old daughter witnessed these beatings. On one occasion, after Mr. Warner struck me on the head, I landed in the hallway outside of the kitchen. He stood over me and said in a threatening tone, "Kathy, look at what you are doing to the children." This was the second pregnancy that occurred during the two-year period of my mental/nervous breakdown. During this pregnancy, I was described by friends and relatives who took care of me, as a "glassed over, empty shell."

I could not eat or sleep. I was weak and disconnected from reality. (The first pregnancy ended in a miscarriage in December 1993.)

> During the two-year period of my psychiatric episode (brought on by post-partum depression after my seventh child's birth), I often feared the reality of being admitted to a mental hospital. I understood that I could be subjected to further abuse, rapes, etc. within the confines of a mental institution. My fears were misplaced. I didn't have to go far for further trauma to occur. My husband was truly my worst enemy.

Dr. Charles South was following my pregnancy. He told me that the birth of my eighth child would both be healing and stabilizing for me, or it may tip me over the edge (chemically) and I would end up in a mental hospital. Although hard words, they were truthful. Dr. South said he believed that mental abuse is far more dangerous and deadly than physical abuse. The brain can get bruised beyond human comprehension. Physical abuse is on the outside. You can see marks, but you cannot see the psychological hemorrhaging within the brain from mental and emotional abuse.

During the last several months of my pregnancy, my husband and I were counseling with a "Christian psychologist," Dr. Moynihan, in Corvallis. Although, he was an advocate for women and children, and exhibited more compassion than some of the previous Christian counselors, there was no help for my personal circumstances, home life or marriage. In a report written by Dr. Moynihan he states, "This patient has been run around the Pacific Northwest by her husband...trying to get her cured/fixed. While it is thought that this is not a chronic condition, much depends on the supportiveness of others and not looking for quick miracle cures. Given that the patient has been run around/down for the last two years (*including quackery*), I see this patient being in therapy for at least a year." He diagnosed me with having severe depression, no psychotic features, generalized anxiety disorder.

Although Mr. Warner acted like the supportive husband during my pregnancies, he was seldom at home. When I got close to my due date, Mr. Warner would schedule a spiritual retreat or fishing and camping trip out-of-state. Before Zachary was born, Chris and Betsy Close had offered to take me to the hospital, if needed. Mr. Warner was at Clear Lake on a fishing trip the week the baby was due, and he returned in time to attend the birth.

I birthed my eighth child, Zachary, on July 13, 1995, at the Albany General Hospital in Albany, Oregon. I went into labor after being violently pushed by an older child. I did not want my husband present at the birth, but knew if I had stated my wishes, more pain and trauma would await me. I remember calling Betsy Close from my birthing room while I was in labor.

I hemorrhaged again and my husband did not want the attending midwife, Linda Bishop, C.N.M. to treat me. She did, however, and I believe she saved my life against my husband's wishes. I was given Pitocin by shot and I.V. and stayed in the hospital for three days. I was released to go home after my hemorrhaging was under control.

Although physically frail, I experienced joy and mental and emotional wellness after the birth of my son, Zachary. Somehow, during the nine months of pregnancy I had managed to regain my sanity, and came to the conclusion that continuing in this way of life would eventually kill me.

The younger children were thrilled to have a mom back and a new baby brother. The older children were scarred from the previous two years and did not relate to me in a respectful manner. They had been well-schooled to please their father.

The fighting and screaming between my husband and my eldest twin daughters also became increasingly uncomfortable for me. I did not want my younger children and infant exposed to their rage.

I resumed homeschooling the children again in September 1995 with the help of a college student and tutor, Tashi Smith. I suggested to Sarah and Rachel if they did not want to participate in enrichment studies with the tutor I had hired, they could enroll in the local public school. They did not want to do either. I spoke to my husband about my concern for my twin daughters' education. He basically told me to leave them alone.

After the birth of my 8th child, Zachary, in July 1995, I refused to attend my husband's cults. Mr. Warner continued to bring his religious counselor, Mr. Bill Heard, in our home to work on my mind. After one counseling session, Mr. Warner became violent with me because I had mentioned to his counselor that I was often violated by Mr. Warner's lack of sexual restraint. My personal boundaries had never been respected in my home. As far as Mr. Warner was concerned, I had none.

Mr. Heard and my husband said I was in rebellion and threatened to put me in the state mental hospital. There was nothing wrong with me. I called my long-term friend and adopted mother, Addie Archer, in Longview, Washington. She worked as a court reporter for the Superior Court of Washington State for 25 years and personally assisted me in my efforts to seek safety in 1995. Her legal advice through the years of my court trauma was invaluable. Sadly, Addie passed away in 2010 at 81-years old.

I refused to submit to Mr. Bill Heard and my husband's brainwashing tactics. They were free to partake in "Kool-Aid drinking" together, but I did not want to participate. Although freedom of religion is a right each citizen has in this country, religious freedom was not a right I had in the confines of my own home. The accusations of not being a submissive wife continued and again I was being threatened.

> On one occasion, I was attempting to participate in a local craft fair to sell my beeswax ornaments and candles. I was loading the car one Saturday morning. My baby and young children were attending the fair with me. Mr. Warner became angry and ordered me not to go, that I would be "breaking the Sabbath." I told him that his beliefs were fine for him, but that I must follow what is right for me. He continued to harass and threaten me until I finally left.

> Mr. Warner often demanded I obey "rules" that he did not obey or keep himself. He often went to work on Saturday (his observed Sabbath), worked on projects around the home, and frequented stores when necessary. I found his lifestyle hypocritical.

In the summer of 1995, I met a few homeschooling mothers in the community. They invited me to the church they attended, Bridgeport Community Church in Dallas, Oregon. At first Mr. Warner would not allow me to go. He was attending a Sabbath Keeping church in Marion County near Turner. I finally was allowed to go by myself. I enjoyed meeting the people there. This marked the beginning of my spiritual exploration and my decision to leave organized religion. One Sunday Mr. Warner and the children attended the church with me. Mr. Warner and the children continued to attend Bridgeport Community Church with me while also attending and tithing monies to his Sabbath keeping church.

In her letter dated June 3, 1996, to Pastor Barnhart of Bridgeport Community Chapel, Mrs. Ellen Callen wrote of her observations and concerns regarding Mr. Warner and the impact he was having on the congregation and the way in which he successfully separated me from this community. (See Mrs. Callen's letter in documentation.)

I also became aware at this time that situations existed between some of the children that required outside help. Younger children were being threatened by some of the older ones. I wanted help for my children and knew the children and I needed healthy, outside intervention. Mr. Warner's only response was more beatings and exorcisms to vanquish the devil. The older girls were tyrannical and manipulative. My eldest son was subjected to his father's frequent beatings, needed protection and safety. As a result of his father's violence, my son redirected his anger as sexual abuse and aggression against the younger children. I realized that I needed to get help soon, for myself and for my children.

I spoke to the pastor briefly about my need for legal help and that I would be leaving because I did not want my situation to be a problem for their church. Events would soon turn for me. I would learn that I would not be welcome among the members at Bridgeport Community Church because, although I didn't know it yet, I was going to divorce my husband.

My ex-husband and his religious leaders and counselors threatened me, telling me that I could not seek help for my children or report the crimes that occurred in our home. The crimes would become a "family and church secret." One older sibling was being secretly counseled by Bill Heard, from Roseburg, Oregon, in the office of Pastor Ron Sutter, Bridgeport Community Church, Monmouth, Oregon.

Oregon law requires parents, pastors, teachers, physicians, counselors and professionals to report crimes of sexual abuse. Sadly, Pastor Ron Sutter and Bill Heard did not report the crimes of rape, child abuse and sex abuse. This church was above the law. I continue to hear from women who report that they have also been abused by Mr. Bill Heard to this day.

In 1995, I retained an attorney not only for protection against my husband, his friends, pastors and religious supporters, but also for the safety and well-being of all my eight children. My younger daughters needed protection as they had been sexually molested. They needed to be examined by their pediatrician and they needed professional counseling.

My older son needed safety, too, as he had been severely abused and assaulted by my Mr. Warner, for several years. I had also been raped and beaten during a period of time that I could not care for myself. I reported the documented crimes committed against me and my children. Even though the crimes against me were documented, Polk County District Attorney John Fisher dismissed the charges I filed against my ex-husband.

To this day, the individuals who have confessed the crimes committed against my children, including sexual abuse and physical abuse, are allowed full contact, while I, the mother who reported the crimes, am allowed no contact with my children per Court Order. I have also been banned from contact with my children due to the fact that I do not adhere to fundamental legalistic, cult Christian ideology.

Because of the abuse my oldest son suffered from his father and the deteriorating situation in our home, he left when he was 14-years old and lived with family and friends. The same fundamental Christian ideology ruled in these homes and I believe these experiences were also abusive and traumatic for my son. I was greatly concerned for him and knew he needed help, but had no means to intervene. His father made sure that all 'counseling' came from elders in the church.

Mr. Warner and his religious counselors only made the situation in our home worse. I understood that our children would receive no professional help. I did not want them to grow up without the help they so desperately needed. I understood that I needed an attorney not only for myself, but also for them.

> Physicians have commented on the turmoil the children must have been experiencing. They saw their own father abuse and threaten me all of their growing up years. There were no healthy role models. They were learning that power and threats win. The damage this was doing to the children was one of my main reasons for leaving Mr. Warner. I knew that they were witnessing violence against women and children and they were learning that men were given that right by church and religious leaders. Domination games were prevalent in our home.

When I told my husband that I was going to seek help from an attorney if he continued his abusive behavior towards me, he leaned back in his chair and glared at me. He replied, "You just try." He knew, along with his religious supporters and family, the judicial system was another weapon he could use against me, and it worked. I had stayed too long in the marriage. Mr. Warner, by this time, had what he needed to succeed in Oregon's Courts - my previous depression and mental/nervous breakdown.

In August of 1995, after a follow-up visit with my physician, Dr. South, I stopped by to visit Betsy Close at her home in Albany. I confided in her that I was having difficulties in my marriage. I didn't know how my health was going to hold out with the stresses I felt from my husband. She told me, "Wait until he commits adultery, and then divorce him." Although, well-meaning, this advice was not practical for my immediate situation. I continued to struggle about what to do. Divorce was still a "taboo" within the circles I lived.

Throughout our marriage, Mr. Warner donated monies to the Rutherford Institute. This is an organization founded on fundamental biblical principles. They will assist you legally should you have legal situations challenging your fundamental beliefs, such as male dominance, or other religious/and or abusive practices. I do not know for sure if his lawyer was paid through the Rutherford Institute, but it had a lot to do with Mr. Warner's confidence that he could break me if I went to court.

In the following months after Zachary was born, I experienced more bleeding. Soon after the birth of Zachary, just like after all my other births, Mr. Warner initiated sexual relations, (sometimes as soon as nine days following a birth.) In October, I had been bleeding off and on for two weeks. Dr. South, my obstetrician, believed my period was beginning (postpartum premenstrual). He recommended abstinence. He advised that any pregnancy would endanger my health in a serious manner.

I shared with Mr. Warner, at this time, my wishes—no sexual relations. I had been barring my bedroom door at night with furniture because he had never shown respect for my wishes or boundaries before. He didn't believe I had any. It was a terrifying time for me because I was so very frail from the two-year period of my breakdown. I did not want to become pregnant. I very much wanted to regain my health for myself and my children.

I spent a great deal of time meditating during the night. I prayed for the wisdom of when and how to let go. I did not want my children to repeat my life in their relationships and realized that my marriage was damaging them psychologically. I knew they would repeat this cycle of violence, if I did not stop it.

> During this time, I experienced, what many would call, my dark night of the soul. Deep down inside I knew the price would be high for my freedom. I wasn't quite sure I could emotionally, spiritually, and physically survive what I intuitually knew would transpire in the months and years ahead.

> Dark night of the soul is described by Jamie Sams as "Any period of time in a person's life when chaos and confusion continue without a break. Life will often present challenge after challenge, one heartache after another, or ongoing devastating experiences without any relief in sight. These periods force us to reevaluate what we think, how we feel, what is really important, which values give us strength, and what to let go of that no longer serves us. These Dark Nights create major reality adjustments that force us to reevaluate our priorities." *Dancing the Dream: The Seven Sacred Paths of Human Transformation*

> Joan Borysenko, Ph.D., writes in her book, *Fire in the Soul*, "Dark nights of the soul are extended periods of dwelling at the threshold when there is nothing familiar left to hold on to that can give us comfort. If we have a strong belief that our suffering is in the service of growth, dark night experiences can lead us to depths of psychological and spiritual healing and revelation that we literally could not have dreamed of and that are difficult to describe in words without sounding trite."

Mr. Warner did not respect my wishes and attempted to rape me one morning in October 1995. He came into my room pinned me down on the bed and said in a threatening tone of voice, "You get off your power trip, stop talking this attorney crap, and what you need is a screw." I asked him to get off me and he did not. Mr. Warner frightened me. I did not know whether he was going to rape me or not. He finally got off me and left.

Bearing Witness

Powerful Courageous Exposé of Spiritual Abuse
by Debra Wingfield, Ed.D., Author, *Her Eyes Wide Open: Help! with Control Freak Co-Parents* and Trainer in Interpersonal Violence Intervention/Treatment

In this excellent, first-hand portrayal of the extremes that spiritual abuse can take, Coral Theill shares the tragedy of her experience in her attempts to protect her children from their abusive father.

BONSHEÁ is an extraordinary account of the horrendous injustice to the Warner children and their mother. Coral Theill shares her overwhelming account of how the fundamentalist Church aided and abetted her ex-husband to do the unthinkable, remove her nursing infant from her along with her other children because she refused to submit to her ex-husband's abuse and control over her life.

Coral recounts in detail how the insidious spiritual and ritual abuse was compounded with a multitude of other abuses. These coercive control tactics were perpetrated in the home, the church, and the community by a power-hungry, greed-filled cast. People Coral Theill sought out for help from her abusive marriage used her cries against her to perpetrate one of the most heinous cases of abuse and coercive control I have come across in my work with survivors of domestic violence and coercive controlling abuse. A must-read for anyone impacted by abuse in marriage or relationships.

Coral prepares you to fight for your children's lives when you divorce in the current Family Court system. Advocates, attorneys, judges, and other professionals working in Family Court must read this account to understand the lengths abusers will go to continue to control and torture their abuse victims.

I applaud Coral Theill for the courage she shows making light of the dark secrets within the fundamental churches and the collusion of the family court system. Of note are other types of coercive control tactics used under the guise of acceptance by these groups. I noted emotional abuse, isolation, using children, economic abuse, male privilege, threats, intimidation, sexual abuse including marital rape, limited physical abuse due to fear induced control, litigation abuse, court-related professional abuse, and judicial abuse. Coral was stalked for more than 20 years by her ex-husband through the family court system. I highly recommend reading Theill's exposé of fundamentalist church groups' use of spiritual abuse.

Sgt Chadee Phillip, Coral Anika Theill and my special guest, 1st Sgt George Kidd, Montford Point Marine, Congressional Gold Medal Recipient, Marine Corps Birthday Ball, November 2011

Coral Theill Dancing at Marine Corps Ball, 2010

"I believe, as a wage-earning woman, that if I make the great
sacrifice of strength and health and even risk my life, to have a
child, I should certainly not do so if, on some future occasion,
the man can say that the child belongs to him by law and he
will take it from me and I shall see it only three times a year!"
- *Isadora Duncan* in her biography, *My Life* (1927)

IV

Meetings with Attorneys, Restraining Order and Marital Rape Hearing, Temporary Custody Hearings, Court Abuse, My Body Feels Like a Crime Scene

Despite his threats, I retained an attorney in the fall of 1995, initially for
intervention for my children, and secondly for my own safety. **During the
period of my illness/breakdown in 1993-1994, while I was nearly catatonic,
my husband used me sexually, raped, beat and impregnated me. According
to Oregon law, this is a criminal act.** (Extensive documentation is available
through many sources, physicians, witnesses, including my ex-husband's
admission in court of using me sexually and impregnating me while I was unable
to care for the children or myself).

Although I had no access to our finances, we did have one credit union account
that was in both of our names. I had been told not to touch it, but I took $2,000
from this account to retain an attorney. I knew Mr. Warner wouldn't know until
the statement came and I would be safe by then (I thought). Prior to going to the
credit union, I called two women co-workers of Mr. Warner's who had befriended
me. They met me at the credit union and gave me the number of CARDV,
Center Against Rape and Domestic Violence in Corvallis. They insisted I call
this number and throw away the note so Mr. Warner would not detect their
handwriting. I was unaware of women crisis centers until this time.

It took me many years to build up enough courage to leave him, knowing that his statements and threats to take away my children would come true in my life. I would have no children, unless I remained under his absolute authority and control, and if I left or escaped, I would no longer be able to protect my children from their father's rage.

I continue, to this day, to be concerned for my children's mental, physical, emotional and spiritual health. They are not aware of their rights and their father believes it is perfectly normal to assault and beat his children. He is their "father". (During my illness and in my absence from the home, my husband took out his anger and rage on the children.) I am well aware of what lies ahead for them in the home in which they are forced to live.

My first visit to the attorney was to seek assistance in getting help for my children. The advice I received was empathetic–I had to get safe first, before I could help them. I retained an attorney, Mr. Richard Alway, in the fall of 1995 and filed for a legal separation. Mr. Alway also suggested I get a restraining order. Friends of mine had called Mr. Alway about abuse issues in the home. My attorney asked me to submit to a psychological examination by Dr. Daryl Ruthven in Salem, Oregon to prove my mental wellness to the Court.

My attorney recommended I watch a film called, *"Broken Vows."* The film addresses the subject of domestic violence from a panel of priests, pastors and rabbis. The film was depressing to me. It did not accurately portray the abuse issues within a "Christian household." I did not feel the panel understood the problem or the origin of abuse. Also, the film did not portray accurately the horror of domestic violence and the violence that occurs behind closed doors, *"all in the name of God."*

Up until this point, I had no thought of divorce. All I wanted was help for my children, to not be pregnant again, and for a legal separation from my husband. I shared with my attorney that someday, when I die, I wanted to die with some dignity. Karen Heintz, a former neighbor, joined me at the attorney's office for support. Addie Archer, a friend from my court reporter days, watched my children during my appointments with the attorney. My eldest daughters, Sarah and Rachel, were staying with a great-aunt in Portland, assisting her at her store and were unaware of the actions I was taking, and so could not report me to their father.

Therese Vasquez and a woman from Bridgeport Community Church, Ellen Callen, drove to my home in December of 1995, and helped me leave with my five younger children before my husband returned from work. Ellen Callen had me follow her home. She wanted to go to the courthouse the next day with me as I sought a restraining order. After I arrived at her home, she called her pastor and elder to ask them for permission for me and my children to stay at her home. I waited many hours in her home for their return call. I do not believe she will ever understand the vulnerable and terrifying position she placed me in. I had no money and no where to go and could not return home to my husband that night. The next morning, I obtained a restraining order from the Polk County Court against my husband.

When an elder, Mr. Brian King, at Bridgeport Community Church, found out I was seeking a legal separation, he said, "Kathy, are you aware of the sexual temptation you will put your husband through if you go through with this?" His question traumatized me as I reflected on my role as Mr. Warner's wife for the past twenty years. It also aroused my fears for my daughters.

> During this time, I was counseled by an abuse counselor, Myra Phillips, in Salem, Oregon. She shared with me a tactic for survival in the months ahead. First, she instructed me in the importance of listening to my attorney and following his instructions. Also, she told me I would have to mentally put the painful memories, trauma, and Mr. Warner in a detached place and only refer to that place a limited amount of time each day. I took this to heart. Her advice became one of my best coping tools in the months and years that followed. As time passed, I learned that my trauma was separate from who I truly was. I learned that I was important, and that I was of value. I began to respect the sacredness of my being. I understood that a majority of the trauma from my past was because people did not value me or treat me humanely. Their (my parents and husband) "support" demanded absolute obedience and worship. My relationship with them was too great of price for my soul.

> My abusers hoped that they could "break me" throughout the court ordeal. They did not understand that their actions were pushing me farther into the light and to wholeness. Instead of feeling terror by Mr. Warner and his attorney's threats and legal abuse, I ended with only feeling pity for them.

78

I believe the reason why Christian religious leaders, counselors, and husbands fear women seeking help outside their religious supervision and structure is because counselors and shelters who assist battered women "will put ideas in her head." They will teach her that she doesn't deserve to be beaten, that she is a worthwhile person, that she is capable, competent and intelligent, that she can think for herself, that she can do things for herself, that she has the right to come and go as she pleases, that she has power over her own life, that she can use her power to take good care of herself, that she deserves to be happy and safe, that she should be able to visit with friends and relatives when she wishes to do so, that she is not the cause of another's violent and abusive behavior, and that she has the right to live a life that is free from violence and abuse.

These are not bad ideas. These ideas were truths she understood when she was born, they were already in her head, and they were just waiting until she was **safe enough to think them**.

Local church leaders from Bridgeport Community Church supported Mr. Warner while I had a restraining order against him. Mr. Warner actually lived with Pastor Ron Sutter and his wife during this time. He told them he was broke and had no money and nowhere to go, although his estate and accounts, at this time, were well over $500,000. My husband had contacted my brother's pastor and shared with him an assortment of twisted half-truths and lies about me. The pastor believed Mr. Warner.

Mr. Warner retained an attorney and contested the restraining order. A hearing was set on January 4, 1996, to be heard by a Polk County Circuit Court Judge. I had been told by my attorney that the hearing would be in the judge's chambers. It was held in the courtroom and evolved into an "attempted marital rape case." Mr. J. Mark Lawrence represented Mr. Warner.

Debbie Custis, a co-worker of Mr. Warner and Therese Vasquez, a long-time friend who had been briefly involved in the "People of Praise Community," testified in Court in regards to Mr. Warner's controlling and demeaning behavior towards women. Therese Vasquez testified that there was "an element of fear" in the marriage. Judge Collins acknowledged my fear, but overturned the restraining order.

Mr. Mark Lawrence, my husband's attorney, used the courtroom as an arena to humiliate me. He made unnecessarily crude statements to embarrass me and badgered me regarding my sexual relations with Mr. Warner. He delved into humiliating details regarding the episode of my breakdown three years previously. Mr. Warner's aunt, Mrs. Marilyn Schlabs, and an elder, Mr. Brian King, from Mr. Warner's church were present to support him. My seventeen-year-old twin daughters were present, in support of their father, but left the courtroom when the hearing began.

> I cannot, to this day, understand why Mr. Warner, Mr. Lawrence, my attorney, Mr. Alway and the Judge allowed me to be ridiculed and tormented in Court. My own attorney, Mr. Alway, did not defend me. Friends who came to support me were shocked by the proceedings.

> Legal advisors who have studied my transcripts since are appalled that Mr. Lawrence's degrading and abusive manner of questioning was allowed and that my own attorney did not stop it. After sharing with my physician, Dr. Kuttner, the abuse I was experiencing in the Courts, he commented, "Kathy, some men go so low that even the slugs have to salt them."

> I later learned that several Polk County staff employees were disturbed by the above court proceedings and believed I was victimized in the courtroom. In his Affidavit of Counsel and Points and Authorities in Support of Motion to Recuse Judge Horner by Mr. J. Mark Lawrence, Attorney at Law, January 1996, Mr. Lawrence states, "That Mr. Warner was told by a Polk County employee that the court staff thought Ms. Warner had been victimized at an earlier hearing before Judge Collins, that the court staff was characterizing Mr. Warner as a wrongdoer and that they wanted to see Ms. Warner prevail in this litigation."

Judge Collins stated in Court, "This Court does not have the power and ability to resolve these types of situations in this type of context. That is better left to professionals with more insight into relationships and psychology." He ordered me to go back into a home with a man I had learned never to say "no" to. I returned to the home with my younger children and nursing infant.

Since I had changed the locks, Mr. Warner, his family and attorney broke into the home before I arrived and set up their "fortress." They took pictures of each room. Plans were being made for Mr. Warner to "monitor" me for the two months until the temporary custody hearing.

> Mr. Warner's greatest fear was soon to become a reality. An abuser does well at fooling the entire world, but the wife he lives with knows him well, can see right through him and is aware of his fears. She lives each day under the constant threat and terror of his fears.
>
> For me to share my truths in a courtroom of law was unacceptable to Mr. Warner–his violence and rage escalated from this point forward. I did not have to say a word about my past with Mr. Warner to those around me. Mr. Warner proved who he truly was by his actions, words and demands in Court in the days, months and years that followed.
>
> Mr. Warner and his attorney believed they could silence me through their threats and continued court actions. They were wrong.

My mother-in-law, Helen Warner, and my seventeen-year-old twin daughters were very hostile toward me. Mr. Warner and his mother claimed that she was in our home to "help me" with the children, but she was focused on surveillance and control...and subjugating me. My daughters, who had been working for their great-aunt in Portland, were brought back to watch me...and protect their father's empire.

My attorney, Mr. Alway, first suggested I live behind my locked bedroom door until the temporary custody hearing. He also suggested I purchase a stun gun to protect myself from Mr. Warner. He told me to be encouraged by the stories of Daniel in the Old Testament. This way of living seemed unreasonable and not something I wanted my children to witness. After a few days of living like a prisoner in my own home, my attorney, a sheriff and a local safe home advised me to go into hiding with my nursing infant son, and my three-and five-year old daughters.

I did what was right. On January 7, 1996, I sacrificed a judge's ego and defied a court order in exchange for my safety and the safety and well-being of my young children. Addie Archer, Mike and Lynn Eisler and Karen and Richard Lague assisted me as I packed my van and left with my three youngest children and went into hiding for two and a half months. I left our home trusting that the Universe would meet our needs. It did.

I never have been more sure that the choice I made that day was a "sane" choice. Although I would be later described "as out of touch with reality," I knew now what reality was for me - safety, dignity, self-respect, hope. Even though my circumstances were traumatic, the longer I was away from Mr. Warner, the stronger I became in every way.

In January, after I left the home, Mr. Warner enrolled Sarah and Rachel in the local public high school and enrolled Theresa and Joshua in a small Christian school at the local church he was attending. (Bridgeport Community Chapel)

January 18, 1996, Mr. Warner, through his attorney, Mr. Lawrence, submitted an affidavit to the Court. It stated, "That in early 1993 Petitioner (Kathy Warner) had a psychological breakdown. That in March, 1994 Petitioner was seeing a psychiatrist named Charles Kuttner who diagnosed Petitioner as Psychotic Depressive and ordered drug therapy including prozac and trazodone. Petitioner stopped seeing Dr. Kuttner and her other doctors by April, 1994 and remains untreated to this day; that twice since Petitioner's breakdown Petitioner has tried to kill herself...That Petitioner's depression seems to have worsened during the last six months." Mr. Warner also mentions in this affidavit "that Petitioner has always been a good mother, cared fastidiously for her home and been attentive to the children's home-schooling needs." The rest of the affidavit supports Mr. Warner's twisted view of the truth.

Dr. Kuttner never made such a diagnosis. I was diagnosed by Dr. Kuttner in 1993 as suffering from anxiety and depression. I was dismissed by Dr. Kuttner as his patient in 1994 because my husband refused to bring me in for scheduled appointments and was endangering my health. I was not depressed the last six months in 1995. I had birthed my eighth child, Zachary, and had sought help from attorneys and other professionals and physicians to escape Mr. Warner and his religious supporter's abuse. I was exhibiting signs of health by honoring myself. This was foreign to Mr. Warner because he expected and demanded obedience. Because of his religious ideology, he translated my new found health as mental illness.

My physicians, counselors and friends were alarmed that any individual can submit untrue and unfounded information to a judge, and a judge would accept it as fact. My physicians, counselors, and friends were disturbed by the lies stated in Court and my husband's affidavits. My mental files make no record of a psychotic diagnosis. My physicians documented that I suffered from anxiety and depression.

While in hiding, I was told by my attorney that Polk County Sheriffs were searching for me and if I was found, I would be arrested. My crime - the need for mental and physical safety for myself, my baby and youngest daughters. The judicial system treated me as though I were a piece of Mr. Warner's property and would return me to Mr. Warner regardless of the consequences.

About this time, Mr. Alway, my attorney, began acting in a threatening manner toward me. He behaved as though he believed Mr. Warner and his attorney.

I was advised to talk with someone in the victim's program. I called and talked with one of their counselors. She instructed me to get back in the home and wait until I was assaulted by my husband and put in the hospital in order to have a formal record of physical abuse. She was quite emotional and said, "Your children will be taken from you by the Courts."

To add to the complexity of this case, Mr. Lawrence had several judges removed from this case in Polk County. I do not understand why my ex-husband and his attorneys have been allowed the privilege of "judge shopping." (Documentation available) This practice is viewed as highly unethical in other states. I was told by attorneys that Judge Norblad had a history of removing infants from mothers in divorce cases. Although my case was originally filed in Polk County, my case was heard by Judge Norblad in Marion County.

On the advice of Myrna Phillips, I sought another attorney who could deal with the bizarre nature of my case. Mr. David Gearing, an attorney from Portland, Oregon, became my lawyer in January 1996 until I dismissed him for financial reasons. I asked for my personal records and files from Mr. Alway and he sent a bill for an additional $5,000 before he would release my files. I borrowed the money so I could pay him. I had previously given Mr. Alway $2,000 in November. Mr. Alway's attorney fees amounted to $7,000 for him to represent me for two months and a two-hour hearing.

Mr. David Gearing initially required a $10,000 retainer fee and an additional $23,000 in cash the next month. Five thousand dollars was given to his private detective. I borrowed the money from my family and paid Mr. Gearing with a check. Debbie Dresler and Sharon Crouch joined me during my initial visit with Mr. Gearing. Mr. Gearing told me, "I am not a Christian. I do not embrace any belief in God." I told him I did not care. I needed help.

I lived in hiding with my infant son, Zachary, my three-year-old daughter, Hannah, and my five-year-old daughter, Rebekah, from the beginning of January until March 10, 1996. We lived briefly with friends, then stayed in several motels, and finally in a home offered to us by friends, for a month.

While hiding in motels, Debbie Custis and a few other friends brought food to the children and me and hid my van at night. My children believed we were "on vacation" and in the months and years that followed often shared with me that it was the most exciting and best time of their lives. My children often accompanied me to my attorney's office. I told them I was having business meetings.

These months spent in hiding were a very difficult time for me physically and emotionally. Deep down I understood that these were the last couple months I would have the honor of being a mother to my children. Several friends helped watch the children while I underwent approximately thirty-five hours of depositions by Mr. Lawrence, my husband's attorney. I hired two college graduates to tutor Hannah and Rebekah using their preschool and kindergarten schooling materials.

During the depositions, one of Mr. Gearing's partners came up to me during one of the recesses. While I was nursing my baby she told me, "Kathy, you will have to realize that depositions and court are similar to eating sh——. You are going to have to get used to it smeared on your face, you are going to have to get used to chewing it and swallowing it." Her words were true.

In February 1996 several of my friends and former neighbors submitted notarized affidavits to the court.

Mrs. Karen A. Heintz wrote these words in her affidavit signed February 13, 1996 to assist my attorneys in a hearing regarding my need to continue living in hiding with my children. Mr. Warner and his attorney, Mr. Lawrence, were of the opinion that the children and I belonged in the home. After a phone hearing with Judge Norblad, he agreed to allow me to continue living away from the home until the *pende lite* (temporary custody) hearing at the end of the month.

> "I have known Kathy *(Coral Theill)* and Marty Warner for over twelve years. For eight of these years, prior to their moving to Independence, they were my next door neighbors on Taylor Street in Corvallis. This situation gave me ample opportunity to observe Kathy's parenting skills, which in my opinion were exemplary. As a mother, and the primary caregiver to the children, (six at that time,) she was loving, calm and extremely responsible. The children were happy and content in her presence. I remember marveling not just at her organizational skills at managing that many children, but at the loving and gentle way she treated each one of them. After the birth of her seventh child, Kathy did experience a postpartum breakdown, but as far as I could observe, she was never a danger to any of her children. She continued to love them and worry about them to the best of her ability considering the circumstances. At present, Kathy seems completely recovered from her postpartum problem. I have had recent opportunities to observe her with her children, and she continues to treat them lovingly and responsibly.

> "At this time, I do have real concerns about Kathy (*Coral Theill*) returning to the residence with Marty. Throughout years of observing Marty as a neighbor, my husband and I both felt that he had a very strong need to control almost every aspect of his wife's life. He once told me in a backyard conversation that he would never allow Kathy to go to the doctor by herself. While my husband and I felt that it was not our business to pass judgment on how a neighbor conducted a marriage, we were made uncomfortable by the submissiveness Marty demanded from Kathy. While Marty and the older children sometimes took vacations, it often seemed that Kathy never left the house except to buy groceries.

> "After the Warner's moved to Independence, (Oregon), and after Kathy's post-partum depression had been going on for a while, I encountered Marty at a local Bi Mart Store. (I believe this was sometime during the summer of 1993.)

After describing Kathy's behavior in a very derogatory manner, and complaining about his own high blood pressure, he went on to tell me that Kathy "needed a spanking." I felt very uncomfortable about his statement, as it indicated to me that he had very little compassion for and/or understanding of the hormonal problem Kathy was facing.

"More recently, I accompanied Kathy to the Benton County Sheriff's Office on the day the restraining order against Marty was being served. Kathy was obviously terrified about what his response might be. The people at the sheriff's office front desk would be able to corroborate this, as Kathy told them she was afraid of her husband, and they offered her and baby Zachary sanctuary for the day if they needed it. Furthermore, although Kathy has the support of many people in the community, almost all of them have refused to accompany Kathy back home, or to stay with her in the Warner residence out of concern that Marty might resort to violence. I personally talked to five people who were afraid to go due to the volatility of the situation. Kathy also spoke to me about her very real fear of being made pregnant again by Marty if she returns to the home. Since she was made pregnant twice during the time of her breakdown, it seems to me a very realistic fear on her part. While Kathy is extremely concerned about the safety and welfare of her children who remain in the home, especially the two younger ones, her fear of returning home with the three youngest children to this uncontrolled and possibly dangerous situation seems understandable."

Mrs. Therese Vasquez also wrote an affidavit signed and notarized February 13, 1996. This affidavit was also presented to the Court.

"I, Therese Vasquez, being first duly deposed swear that the foregoing affidavit is true and accurate.

"I have been acquainted with Marty and Kathy (*Coral Theill*) since approximately 1979. Over the period of our relationship I have witnessed many instances of inappropriate/abusive behavior.

"Mr. Warner has treated Mrs. Warner with gross disregard, regularly through the course of our acquaintance. Upon the birth of their twin daughters in 1979, Mr. Warner abandoned his wife and children immediately after the birth. Mr. Warner displayed no interest in the delivery of care to the newborns or Mrs. Warner in her early post-partum state.

"Circumstances such as these occurred throughout the duration of our relationship, despite appeals by friends and other acquaintances to Mr. Warner.

"Mr. Warner regularly has degraded Mrs. Warner and the Warner children openly and without restraint. I believe the long-term abuse has been detrimental to the well-being of Mrs. Warner and the Warner children.

"Through the course of the relationship, Mrs. Warner complained regularly of psychological and sexual abuse on an extremely regular basis. On numerous occasions, my husband, Richard Vasquez made appeals to Mr. Warner asking that Mr. Warner consider how harmful his behavior was to Mrs. Warner and children.

"Mr. Warner has on numerous occasions replied to my husband that my husband must be mentally ill to suggest that treating Mrs. Warner in an abusive manner was somehow inappropriate.

"Mr. Warner has routinely objected and prevented Mrs. Warner from accessing medical attention in times of dire need with no regard for Mrs. Warner's health and well-being. I observed such denials of reasonable medical attention on not less than five occasions.

"Mr. Warner's extreme religious orientations have been imposed upon Mrs. Warner throughout their marriage. Mr. Warner makes no secret of his demands for female submission at all times, and on occasion would threaten to terminate relationships with friends and acquaintances if the male in friends' households did not subscribe to his religious beliefs to include, but not limited to female submission–socially, physically, psychologically and sexually.

"Mrs. Warner despite all the abuses continually attempted to meet the requirements of her husband. Mrs. Warner has displayed optimal parental skills, consistently throughout their marriage.

"Mrs. Warner suffered a breakdown after many years of abuse and unwanted extreme religious indoctrination. Since that time, Mrs. Warner has persevered and has recovered remarkably. The recovery seemed accelerated when they were separated.

"I pray the Court consider the actual cause and effects in this matter. As it is detrimental to Mrs. Warner and the Warner children to be exposed to any additional abuse by Mr. Warner."

How I Became a Brood Mare and Egg Donor for the Church and State: Rape is Torture

While preparing for my temporary child custody hearings, I asked my attorneys if they could present abuse and cult issues, regarding Mr. Warner, to the Court. They said, "No, we are going to center the case on your wellness and that you have been the primary care-giver for eighteen years." I also suggested to them that I only ask for custody of the younger children. I didn't want the home, either. They prepared the court case and stated to the Court that I wanted custody of all eight children (this included older children that would not talk with me) and that I wanted possession of the home.

Mr. John Benson, an attorney working on my case in Mr. Gearings' office, stated, "Kathy, (Coral) you need a criminal lawyer not a divorce attorney. By legal definition, Mr. Warner could be charged with ten counts of kidnapping." That was his view of my having been forced to go to all the cult meetings and "counseling" sessions against my will. (Mr. Benson was the only attorney who treated me with respect. I did not experience any abuse from him.)

In February 1996, I visited both Dr. Michael May and Dr. Roger Jacobson for psychological exams to be used in court as evidence of my mental health and well-being. They were relieved to hear I had survived my breakdown and were supportive of my decision to divorce my husband.

Dr. Michael May commented that he believed my previous breakdown would have only been a three-month episode with the proper help and the absence of ritual, mental and physical abuse. I also visited Dr. Charles Kuttner, Dr. Jean Furchner, Myrna Phillips, M.Ed. and Dr. Daryl Ruthven for evaluations. Patricia Cox, my husband's custody evaluator also interviewed me.

Before my temporary custody hearings, I instructed my attorneys to act in a civil and humane manner in court and to not unnecessarily harass my husband while on the witness stand. If they did, I would walk out. I did not want to be associated with anyone who conducted themselves like my husband's attorney, Mr. Lawrence.

I went through a three-day temporary custody hearing, February 28 - March 1, 1996. Judge Norblad heard the testimony of my physicians, custody evaluator and psychiatrists. Their testimony validated my recovery from my breakdown. Their recommendation, to the Court, was that the younger children and nursing infant remain in my custody and care because I had been the primary caregiver, was a nurturing mother and was fully recovered from my former depression.

In court, Judge Norblad stated his intent was to follow the recommendation of my physicians and leave the younger children with me. Dr. Kuttner was in attendance and heard him make this statement. However, the following week Judge Norblad signed a court order removing my younger children, including my nursing seven-month-old infant, Zachary, from me. In the letter from the Court, dated March 5, 1996, Judge Norblad states, "her experts (psychiatrists) testified that she is now well." Judge Norblad, nevertheless, awarded all eight of our children to my former husband. **No explanation for the judge's change of opinion was ever offered to me.** (Judge Albin Norblad has a long history of removing babies and young children from good, nurturing mothers.)

I was allowed to visit my children in the family home two weekends a month. Mr. Warner and his mother, who was living there at the time, were supposed to leave the house while I was there.

Mr. David Gearing, my own attorney, made me promise him in Court that I would never make any disparaging comments to my children about their father. I have tried to teach my children to respect everyone's right to their religious belief. However, when someone uses their religious beliefs to harm, hurt or abuse another human being, then I believe we should teach our children to protect themselves from that person. I am not allowed to tell my children the truth about their father "per Order of the Court." I am not allowed to say anything that would cause them to disrespect their father. The Court, society and my attorney have set my children up for abuse.

Although it is illegal to mentally abuse someone in court and in depositions, my former mental/nervous breakdown became the subject for ridicule in court. The judge didn't seem to mind Mr. Warner's attorney ridiculing me about my mental breakdown, or my physical shortcomings while I was on the witness stand. In court, Mr. Warner's attorney made numerous comments about my sexual abuse and molestation as a child. His questions were intrusive, inappropriate and abusive. I had not yet had the opportunity to seek professional help regarding my childhood sexual abuse issues and was traumatized by his questions. These issues did not pertain to my divorce or the temporary custody hearings. Each night my mother put me in a bedroom with a convicted murderer and sex offender during my elementary school years.

Several of my friends who attended my court trials were disturbed that Judge Norblad appeared to be asleep while court was in session and missed segments of testimony. (Judge Norblad had severe health problems soon after my final divorce trial.)

In depositions, Mr. Mark Lawrence also made light of my concern for my daughters' sexual safety in the home. My young daughters had sought help from me. They had been sexually abused by an older sibling. These crimes are documented. Sadly, my daughters never received professional help after my ex-husband was given sole custody. I was also concerned for my daughters because of the way my husband had treated me for twenty years. Mr. Warner had never exhibited any sexual restraint or self-control. There was no healthy-minded individual in the home to monitor the situation. (It is reported that one in three girls and one in four boys are sexually molested by the age of eighteen.)

Mr. Lawrence was aware of my frail health and that I was still nursing my infant. During one deposition, Mr. Lawrence and Mr. Warner were both aware that both the baby and I were very ill with the flu. They insisted on proceeding with depositions. That is harassment.

I was also questioned extensively on my personal interpretation of scripture while on the witness stand in court and in depositions by Mr. Lawrence. This was the first time my thoughts had been on trial.

Mr. Warner and his attorney were very aware of my limited physical stamina from my former breakdown and used it to their advantage during court hearings and depositions. Mr. Warner told my family and friends that he and his attorney were going to "break me." Professionals and mental health experts tell me this behavior is sadistic.

Mr. Lawrence also entered as evidence pictures of the family home that were taken after the restraining order hearing. I had followed my attorney's advice and put my husband's and twin daughter's personal belongings in the basement. The pictures reflected disorder. I found this humorous and sad after keeping Mr. Warner's home immaculate for almost twenty years.

Although mentally well at the birth of my eighth child and mentally well at my court hearings, the testimony introduced by Mr. Warner's attorney revolved around my mental/nervous breakdown that had occurred three years previously. Some of the witnesses he put on the witness stand had only brief encounters with me and some had never met me, but testified as experts on my seventeen years of mothering skills and my present mental condition!

Coral Anika Theill at Polk County Courthouse,
Dallas, Oregon, March 10, 2020

On several occasions Mr. Lawrence made comments about my body odor during the time of my breakdown and my inability to care for my personal hygiene at that time. I could not understand the relevancy this had during a child custody hearing. I was not ashamed of my breakdown, but I did not believe I needed to be unnecessarily humiliated about details relating to that time.

When I would share in my testimony that Mr. Warner did not allow me to go to a doctor alone or at all, etc., Mr. Lawrence would challenge me in regards to my answers. He would ask me, "Did you have your own keys? No one was threatening you, were they?" Mr. Lawrence was either very naive to the fact that I was operating in the realm of the "battered wife's syndrome" throughout my marriage, or he was very aware of the fact that I had been battered by his client. I believe Mr. Lawrence was using my previous mental history as a sideshow in Court to cover up the crimes his client had committed against me–battering, ritual abuse, and marital rape.

At my temporary custody hearings, Oregon State District 8 Senator Betsy Close, who had been a trusted friend, also harmed me through her testimony. When my attorney asked Betsy Close what she meant when she stated that she did not believe I had grounds for divorce, she answered, "the only grounds for divorce, as described in the Bible, are 'desertion or fornication'." Betsy Close didn't believe mental abuse was grounds for divorce.

When my attorney, Mr. Gearing, asked Ms. Close what she recommended I do while living in the midst of abuse, Betsy Close said that I should call 911." Chris and Betsy Close had offered their home as a safe home for my children and I during a time I was experiencing abuse and violence from Mr. Warner in 1985. In Court, and under oath, she denied ever being a safe place for me and my children. (Please see Court Transcripts and Tapes: Tape 2 of February 29, 1996, for more of Oregon State District 8 Senator Betsy Close's views on domestic violence.)

In October 2014, Barbara A. May, PhD, RN, Professor Emerita of Nursing, Linfield College, Portland, Oregon, shared her views on Betsy Close's 1996 court testimony, *"In my opinion, 'just call 911,' is a good sound bite and plays well to those looking for a simple answer to a complicated problem. In an ideal world, that might be all that is necessary. It reminds me of the Reagan's "just say no," slogan during the zero-tolerance war on drugs program in the 80's. Unfortunately, we are not living in an ideal world and those living in a situation where abuse is occurring are well aware of this. They are smart people who know they need to weigh the pros and cons of taking that step in the context of their situation. Safety for themselves and their children (if there is any), is paramount in the decision-making.*

"Depending upon their situation a "911" call may lead to what the victim perceives as an unsafe outcome if, for instance, officers decide to arrest both parties. If there are children, they may be taken by Child Protective Services and foster care. Maybe when officers respond to the call, they harbor their own biases about IPV and no one is arrested, but the victim is now punished further for making the call. Maybe the call results in one or more fatalities. There are many examples as to why calling "911" can be complicated and yield a negative outcome. Anyone looking for simple answers to a complicated problem such as IPV has no grasp of the dynamics involved in this problem.

"Resolving this problem will take a comprehensive effort at macro and micro levels from global collaboration down to individual actions. Then, if all the stars were aligned at all these levels, an individual could indeed trust that making a "911" call would have a positive outcome." (My mentor, Dr. Barbara May, as well as many physicians, counselors and advocates throughout the country describes my Oregon court case as "obscene" and the individuals who were a threat to my safety and survival "toxic.")

Betsy Close shared during her testimony that I had called her before the court hearing and told her I wanted to drive to a cabin and kill myself and my baby, Zachary. This was totally untrue! I had not spoken to her for several months per the orders of my attorneys and due to my own common sense. She was a friend to my rageaholic/abusive husband. They both shared similar extreme religious ideologies. I knew she would betray me; I just didn't know to what extent.

As I listened to her on the witness stand, I was horrified at the lies and distortions. I could not understand why she acted so viciously and invented such a twisted story. I loved my baby, Zachary, loved my life and was doing all I could to escape the hell that had been created for me in the past. I was not suicidal. I desired to protect myself and my children.

My attorney read a letter in Court that Betsy Close had written me praising me for being a loving, nurturing mother, and thanking me for the gentle mothering style I had not only with my own children, but with her children as well. I babysat her children while she attended "Right to Life" meetings and other political events.

When court recessed, she came towards me in a very aggressive and hostile manner. Friends in the courtroom and Christopher Vasquez, an Air Force cadet, (now a pilot and Major in the Air Force) moved to protect me from her. Judge Norblad ordered Ms. Close removed from the courtroom for disorderly conduct. I have not heard from Betsy Close since the trial. Someday, I would like an apology.

> A wise man told me: "Coral, we are all born with a triangle inside of us. This triangle has three razor- sharp points. If we lie and tell un-truths to injure or harm another, it turns and makes us hurt, bleed and feel pain inside. When people become habitually 'untruth tellers' the triangle spins so quickly that the pointed sharp edges are worn down to a circle that just spins and spins. They no longer feel any pain when they lie."

I believe Betsy Close, now a newly appointed Oregon Senator (District 8) is an obstacle to women and children seeking safety and wholeness. Ms. Close holds many extreme fundamentalist beliefs that are a detriment to woman and children as well as the general community. Her viewpoints promote domestic violence and loss of lives.

As long as individuals, such as Betsy Close, are in office who fail to recognize the severe and far-reaching consequences of domestic violence to our society, women in situations like mine will have to prepare for the worst. Anyone who denies a woman's (or a child's) right to be safe, especially when that denial is cloaked in a paternalistic and legalistic religious dogma, contributes to the prevalence of the abuse. Betsy Close is such a person and the wrong choice to represent the people of Oregon.

Betsy Close and other brutalist Christians is the reason I pray, *"Jesus, protect me from your followers."* Many of us wonder what makes legalistic fundamental Christians so cruel and mean.

When my attorney, Mr. David Gearing, questioned my brother, Don Hall, on the witness stand about visiting me in the spring of 1994 at the "Wings of Love" half-way house, my brother wept as he explained the dangerous and filthy living situation in which I was left while too ill to take care of myself.

It also grieved me to watch Mrs. Helen Warner, my husband's mother, on the witness stand. She lied about me and supported her son, in hopes that my babies would be removed from me. She "produced" a note that I had written, claiming to the Court that it was a suicide note. She claimed I dropped this note when picking up some items from the home in January 1996. It was the note I had written over a year earlier and wore in my shoes in the event that I died while living in Washington with my brother. I was very ill at that time from my breakdown, and also pregnant. The yellow post-it-note simply stated, "If you find this body, please call (503) 757-2069, Richard and Therese Vasquez, my friends. I am separated from my husband." I had left the note in my hiking boots. During that time, I took extended walks and was still in an unwell state of mind. I threw the note away the summer of 1995, after Zachary was born. I believe my husband must have taken it out of the garbage and saved it in his "black book" of my infractions.

Helen Warner does not believe God recognizes divorce. In her mind, I am still married to her son and he has rights over me. (Just as she considers herself still married to the man who divorced her over thirty years ago.) She does not believe a person can have spirituality apart from her narrow interpretations of Catholicism." Four of her non-Catholic daughter-in-laws left Helen Warner's sons. (Two of us suffered serious mental breakdowns.)

Mr. Warner's parents, Helen and Bernard Warner, and his brothers and sisters, Bernie, Peggy, Ray, Dennis Warner, and Donna (Warner) Bronkhorst, fully supported him, emotionally and financially, during the court trials even though they had very limited information about our life in the past years. Two of his brothers, Steve and Ed Warner, and his father, Bernard Warner, did not attend the court trials.

The Warner family proudly wears a T-shirt that simply states, "You messing with me–you're messing with the whole family." My attorneys commented to me that they had never seen a group of such hateful looking people as the Warner family. I am thankful that looks do not kill. Mrs. Warner's testimony was shocking, but consistent with who she is and her belief system. Her lies are her version of the truth.

The five individuals, Mr. Marty Warner, Mr. Bill Heard, Mr. Brian King, Mrs. Helen Warner and Ms. Betsy Close, who were so adamant about my rights of motherhood being removed from me, were also pro-life and "Right-to-Life" activists and legalistic fundamental Christians. I found this ironic and hypocritical! (Betsy Close was a founding member of Options Pregnancy Care Centers, a private non-profit group in Corvallis, Oregon. Marty Warner was a representative for Oregon Right to Life).

"Most "pro-life" positions are not really pro-life; they are no-choice. Their positions are designed to protect traditional gender roles and patriarchal institutions and, specifically, institutional religion. The Catholic Bishops and Southern Baptist Convention—both leaders in the charge against reproductive rights— represent traditions in which male "headship" and control of female fertility have long been tools of competition for money and power. They use moral language to advance goals that have little to do with the wellbeing of women or children or the sacred web of life that sustains us all.

"The arguments they make to attain these ends are powerful emotionally but not rationally. They appeal to antiquated and brittle conceptions of God. They appeal to the crumbling illusion of biblical and ecclesiastical perfection—and the crumbling authority of authority itself. They corrupt the civil rights tradition and turn religious freedom on its head. They play games with our protective instinct and cheapen what it means to be a person. They lie." - Valerie Tarico, *Nine Ways to Beat the Patriarchal Christian Right*

Judge Norblad felt comfortable with having Helen Warner, my mother-in-law; assume the role of caretaker in our home. Mrs. Warner was in her 70's. She did not have to take any mental or physical exams. To Zachary, my infant son, Helen Warner, was a stranger. Zachary had never spent time with her.

The younger children reported to me on visitation weekends their fear of their grandmother, and said during the day they often stayed and hid in the work shop while she was taking care of them because of the abuse they had experienced from her.

After a few months, Helen Warner was no longer available in this capacity, so the children were being watched by various baby-sitters, many who were strangers. My younger children commented how frightening this was for them.

My attorney, Mr. David Gearing, told me at the beginning of my divorce trial, "Kathy, people lie in court." I consoled myself throughout the years of court trials and trauma with one of my favorite quotes, "Pure truth, like pure gold, has been found unfit for circulation because men have discovered it is far more convenient to adulterate the truth, than to refine themselves." Charles Caleb Cotton, Lacon (1825)

1ˢᵗ Sgt George Kidd and Coral Theill at Montford Point Marine Association Marine Corps Birthday Ball, November 2012

Bearing Witness

As usual, those who don't have the resources to defend themselves are the ones who pay: the *children, the poor, the shunned - all the abused. We put or leave them out there as human* sacrifices, and instead sing the praises of the rich, the famous, and the well-connected. Can't we have a heart and justice for those without a means of defense? Is it a form of Stockholm Syndrome that we so often want to identify with the powerful and the abusers? - *Susan West*, Virginia

BONSHEÁ is an incredibly honest, intimate, and shocking look at one woman's arduous journey towards safety and freedom from an abusive husband and his religious-cult mentality. Coral's story is an amazing account of sacrifice, betrayal, and a woman's desperate attempt to extract justice from the American legal system for the safety of her children.

BONSHEÁ Making Light of the Dark is a wake-up call and a tribute to the "spirit of women." *–Tashi Smith*, Teacher, Oregon

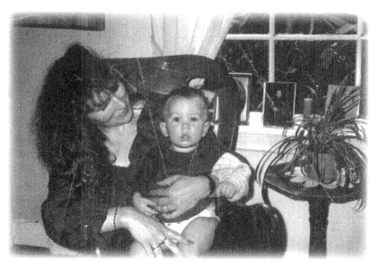

Coral Anika Theill, aka Kathryn Y. (Hall) Warner, with her son, Zachary David Warner, in Corvallis, Oregon, April 1996, on a "visitation weekend" after she lost custody of her children when she sought safety and a divorce.

"Truth crushed to the earth will rise again." - Dr. Martin Luther King, Jr.

V

Rape is Torture, Judge Albin Norblad, Impairment of Judges, How I Became a Brood Mare and Egg Donor for the Church and State, Legally Changed My Name

---

On March 1, 1996, during the temporary custody hearing, Judge Norblad asked my husband, while he was on the witness stand and under oath, why he had impregnated me during the time I was suffering a mental/nervous breakdown. [The response is given below.]

Judge Norblad's lengthy career has included a number of controversial and high-profile cases. As a juvenile court judge during the 1970's, Norblad made hundreds of unpopular decisions, reportedly sending more youths to MacLaren Youth Correctional Facility than any other judge in the state. He is known as the "hanging judge."

In 2002, the judge was disciplined by the Oregon Commission on Judicial Fitness and Disability with a thirty-day suspension following a drunk driving incident, an action which was upheld on appeal to the state Supreme Court.

Judge Albin Norblad Laughs about the Rapes I Suffered

COURT TRANSCRIPT

JUDGE NORBLAD: "Sir, I have one question. Maybe this is curiosity, more than it has to do with the case. If your wife was going through so much emotional difficulties, she realized it, and you realized it, why did you attempt to have an additional child and two pregnancies?

MR. WARNER: We didn't attempt to have an additional child.

JUDGE NORBLAD: No, you succeeded, I guess.

MR. WARNER: Yes, sir. Zachary's pregnancy was a surprise. We were trying to avoid that.

(Note: No contraceptives were used. I was living with my brother out-of-state at the time.)

JUDGE NORBLAD: Twice?

MR. WARNER: The other pregnancy was a surprise as well. Both those.

(Note: Pregnancy No. 1 during my mental/nervous breakdown. This pregnancy ended in miscarriage.)

JUDGE NORBLAD: Okay.

MR. WARNER: I was very committed to doing my part to avoid pregnancy.

JUDGE NORBLAD: All right. Thank you. You can step down.

MR. WARNER: As you can tell, Kathy and I have not had too much difficulty conceiving. (Laughs)

JUDGE NORBLAD: Yeah, I got that figured out. (Laughs)

My friends and I wonder what Mr. Warner meant by, "I was very committed to doing my part to avoid a pregnancy." These two pregnancies pushed my health farther over the edge. It was not a humorous situation. What is humorous about rape?

Throughout our marriage Mr. Warner often referred to me as a "cow or a horse in need of being bred." Mr. Warner insisted on sexual relations immediately before and after the birth of each my children. He had no regard for the risk of infection he subjected me to or the pain he caused. He used me sexually when I was physically ill and during my breakdown. He made me promise before we were married that I would never say "no" to him. I thought he would have respect and decency, but I was mistaken. Mr. Warner had bitter memories of his mother. He detested seeing his father sleeping on the couch and said he would not be treated like that.

My Body Feels like a Crime Scene: Invisible Victims

The most painful and insidious act committed against me was being raped by my ex-husband during the period of my mental nervous breakdown. One day, after I had attempted to cut my wrists by an electric grinder to escape life with Mr. Warner, he taped my wrists and drove me to a motel and raped me. The next day I was forced to meet with Mr. Tom McMahon, a Christian counselor and writer. He also told me I was selfish and needed to learn how to "obey."

> Until now, to survive the court trauma and shock, I kept my feelings regarding the rapes deep within me. I can't find that woman, –the empty shell with bandaged wrists any more. She was mentally gone, spiritually stripped and being used like a whore and a brood mare by the man who "*legally owned her.*" This fact leaves me at a loss for words and is probably one of the reasons I felt compelled to change my name. I don't know Kathy Hall, anymore. I believe the day she was raped while so physically, mentally and emotionally broken, she died.
>
> Severe trauma can so impact our ability to recognize our self, that even the face in a mirror is a stranger.
>
> On April 22, 1999, I legally changed my name to Coral Anika Theill at the Marion County Courthouse, in Salem, Oregon. Kathy Hall was laid to rest.
>
> Andrea Dworkin, in her book, *Intercourse*, analyzes the institution of sexual intercourse and how that institution,

as defined and controlled by patriarchy, has proven to be a devastating enslavement of woman.

Helen Benedict, 1992, *Virgin or Vamp* wrote, "I prefer to characterize rape simply as a form of torture. Like the torturer, the rapist is motivated by the urge to dominate, humiliate and destroy his victim. Like a torturer, he does so by using the most intimate acts available to humans - sexual ones."

I was not the only woman Mr. Warner treated badly. During the years 1993-1994, Mr. Warner was a supervisor over Debbie Custis, at Hewlett Packard. Sexual harassment allegations on a gender basis were reported against Mr. Marty Warner by fellow employees and a former supervisor who worked with Ms. Custis. He continually harangued her that she should be at home—women did not belong in the work place, and he made suggestive and disparaging comments when they disagreed, such as, "I don't know if this is a personal problem we're having or if this is something you are going through at this time of the month." (Documentation available).

Mr. Warner was never reprimanded for his behavior and suffered no consequences. Ms. Custis found Mr. Warner's derogatory attitude towards women so difficult she tried to transfer to another department. She was hired by another department within the company, but her supervisor and facilities manager would not allow her to transfer. Mrs. Custis is still healing from the abuse she suffered from Mr. Warner on the job site and worked in the same department with Mr. Warner until he transferred to Clair Company in the fall of 2001.

Two other women who he abused in the workplace and in our own home also contacted me. One of them sought the assistance of an attorney, the second women regrets that she did not have the monies to seek legal help and protection from Mr. Warner.

My physicians and counselors have accurately described my marriage as a prison, or sweat shop. I have stated to counselors that within the confines of my marriage I lived more or less like a legalized prostitute. Instead of cash, I was given shelter and food. Batterer's objectify women. They do not see them as people. Overall, they see women as property or sexual objects.

Some people have wondered what was "wrong" with me. Why did I stay so long in such an unhealthy and abusive environment? My answer is simple. Abuse and trauma leave an individual in a state of numbness - you become the walking dead. When you are numb, you are not in a state of mind to be planning an escape. You think about how to survive the next day or you think about death and suicide. It is as if you are a soul neither dead or alive wandering in a half-world seeking redemption without hope of ever finding it. While living with abusers, hope is not within reach.

Why do women stay with their batterers? This question has been fueled by those who believe that remaining with a batterer indicates stupidity, masochism, or co-dependence. Far from being accurate, such labels prove dangerous to victims because they tend to absolve batterers of responsibility for their crimes. Many women return to their abusers for the sake of their children. food, and shelter.

"Domestic violence represents serious violent crime: this is not co- dependence, for there is nothing the victim can do to stop the violence, nor is there anything she does to deserve the abuse. Domestic violence victims stay for many valid reasons that must be understood by lawyers, judges and the legal community if they are to stem the tide of homicides, assaults and other abusive behavior. That abuse victims make many courageous efforts to flee the violence is too often overlooked in the process of judging them for now being with the batterer." - *Sarah M. Buel,* Clinical Professor of the University of Texas School of Law, Former Domestic Violence, Child Abuse and Juvenile Prosecutor

Today, I am appalled when I realize the desperation I felt to appease Mr. Warner during our marriage. My physicians and counselors have since shared with me the traits of "Stockholm Syndrome." Many aspects of my life were out of my control.

"Stockholm Syndrome" was described in response to a situation in which a bank was robbed in Stockholm, and a number of people in the bank were held as hostages for several days. With time, the hostages began to identify with the robbers, and defended them against the police.

"A strategy of trying to keep your captor happy in order to stay alive becomes an obsessive identification with the likes and dislikes of the captor which has the result of warping your own psyche in such a way that you come to sympathize with your tormentor!" *"Stockholm Syndrome"* by Kathleen Trigiani

"Denial of terror and anger, and the perception of their victimizers as omnipotent people help to keep victims psychologically attached to victimizers. High anxiety functions to keep victims from seeing available options. Psychophysical stress responses develop." *The Stockholm Syndrome: Not Just for Hostages,* by Dee L.R. Graham, Edna Rawlings, and Nelly Rimini

I have twenty years of mental scars to prove what I am saying is true. I was severely abused by Mr. Warner and his religious leaders and counselors during my illness. After questioning Mr. Bill Heard, one of the religious counselors my husband had taken me to during my breakdown, my attorney, Mr. David Gearing, commented that I could have died under the "care" of these unqualified counselors. He spoke the truth.

Mr. Warner and his religious counselors told me, during my illness, that I had not learned how to submit to the spiritual authorities God had placed over me, namely my husband and his religious leaders, and that God was chastising me for not being a submissive wife. They told me I was in "sin" and was a "selfish woman." Mr. Bill Heard stated to my husband during my breakdown that "God's living example of cursed women is to be self-sufficient, that I was spiritually confused because I was in sin, that I was in rebellion and that I had a proud and critical spirit." Mr. Bill Heard testified in Court that Mr. Warner was the more qualified and competent parent.

"A woman has a right to safety—in real life, not abstractly. A lot has to change before safety is possible. All the implicit assumptions about women's inferiority have to change.

Women will not be free unless we are not any longer treated as objects, which includes sexual objects. We are human beings; we are the center of our own lives. We are not things for men to act out on. We will never be free unless we stop the notion that violence is okay." - Andrea Dworkin, *Escaped & Hunted: The Battered Woman*

Bearing Witness

"I discovered Coral's story while doing research for a graduate school paper about the injustices of the family court system. Coral's story is about decades of severe abuse that would crush just about anyone's spirit and soul. This memoir certainly contains harrowing details that are almost too difficult to read at times. However, the reader is brought into Coral's intimate world and is invited to see the world through her eyes. It is almost as if she gently guides the reader to what she somehow knows will be challenging information to absorb. What is so deeply admirable about Coral is that although she has basically been through hell and back (more than once), she is able to have a positive view on life and humanity, as she is able to view life through a compassionate lens of how she can help others.

Although part of public awareness, society has a tendency to resist knowing about abuse. The idea of this type of denial operates on a social level, not simply an individual level. A common response to learning about abuse is to banish it from consciousness, which explains why courts, evaluators, and everyday people often believe stories of abuse are fabricated. This is an important book that should be read by anyone in the legal, teaching, mental health, or healthcare professions."

- Danelle Givner, LSW/LMSW October 2020

"To do evil a human being must first of all believe that what he's doing is good ... "Ideology [or religion] - that is what gives devil-doing its long-sought justification and gives the evildoer the necessary steadfastness and determination. That is the social theory which helps to make his acts seem good instead of bad in his own and others' eyes, so that he won't hear reproaches and curses but will receive praise and honors."
- Russian dissident Alexander Solzhenitsyn

VI

Removal of my Children by an Order of the Court, Visitation, Relinquishing of Custody, Patriarchal Religion, Battered Wives & Divorce

The younger children and I traveled to Wamic, Oregon, to stay with my brother for a few days while we waited for the judge's decision. My attorney, Mr. Gearing, called my brother to inform him of the court order. We were at an outside telephone booth at Pine Hollow Resort. My brother told me that I had lost the children. I ran toward the woods wailing in pure agony. My brother's girlfriend, Theresa Cagle, a deputy sheriff, ran after me. I looked deep within myself for answers of how I was going to survive the trauma of being separated from my children. I did not find any answers, just a small voice that said, one minute, one hour, and one day at a time. Theresa Cagle drove with me to Portland the next day. I met with my attorney. Debbie Dresler was also present and showed support during this time.

After the Court Order, dated March 5, 1996, was read to me by Mr. David Gearing, I asked my attorney to contact Judge Norblad, Mr. Warner and Mr. Warner's attorney, Mr. Mark Lawrence. I begged permission to be granted a couple of weeks to wean Zachary. They all said, "No."

I stayed with friends, Rich and Therese Vasquez, in Corvallis, Oregon, until Sunday, March 10, 1996. I made numerous phone calls to Marty's family, including his uncle, Mr. Tom O'Halloran in Tigard, Oregon, and friends to ask them to speak with Mr. Warner about the Court Order–but no one seemed to care. Mr. Tom O'Halloran made this comment about his sister, Helen Warner, "She has a way of taking her religion (Catholicism) to extremes." Ms. Patricia Cox, Mr. Warner's custody evaluator even called me to check up on me and make sure I wasn't going to run. I told her that I felt like running, but I wasn't stupid. I knew I would be arrested. I told her I was obeying the Court Order.

> Many professionals who have read accounts of my story say they are shocked and appalled by one common denominator–the number of women who betrayed me during my life and at the time I finally sought safety, both on professional and private levels.

> I believe that women reacted to my situation in the only way they knew how–support the men and the religious leaders who supported my husband. Psychologist Dee Graham believes that since our culture is patriarchal, that all women suffer from "Societal Stockholm Syndrome"–to varying degrees.

Because they knew it would be impossible for me to deliver my children in compliance with the Court Order, my friends, Debbie Custis and Candy McGuire, came to the Vasquez's home on Sunday, March 10,1996, to pick up my three youngest children and deliver them to Mr. Warner's home.

"The day Coral was forced to turn her three youngest children over to Mr. Warner because she had lost custody; I was the one who took the two youngest girls (Rebecca and Hannah) to their father," says Debbie Custis. "They cried or screamed the entire trip. It was one of the most gut-wrenching things I've ever seen. Candy McGuire took six-month-old Zachary in her car."

> The last night I was with my children, I spent the night awake, trying to come to terms with the imminent separation we would be experiencing the next day. With everything in my body screaming, "This is wrong!" I had to put on a mask of normalcy in order to minimize the trauma for the children.

Prior to the children leaving with my friends, I shared with my children that they would be living with their father because this was what the Court decided was best, but I would still be able to visit them every other weekend. I will never forget the looks of horror and confusion on my children's faces, and the sound of their cries as they left.

> "A culture that requires harm to one's soul in order to follow the culture's proscriptions is a very sick culture indeed. This "culture" can be the one a woman lives in, but more damning yet, it can be the one she carries around and complies with within her own mind." –Dr. Clarissa Estés, *Woman Who Run with the Wolves*

When the children arrived at his home, Mr. Warner asked Debbie and Candy, "What do I feed him (Zachary)?" I believe he truly thought I would return with the baby. He thought keeping the children would keep me.

After the removal of my young children and nursing infant, my natural mothering and bonding chemicals that are so strong especially after the birth of a child sent me into physical and emotional shock. I did not cry, I howled from the pain of the abrupt removal of my nursing infant and baby.

The breast pump didn't work very well, and my breasts were engorged with milk. I couldn't sleep because of the emotional and physical pain. My friends, Lynn Eisler and Debbie Custis, slept near the doorway of the home I was staying at the first week because during the night I kept getting up and wanting to go get my baby, Zachary. I couldn't understand what had happened, I never will.

I gradually learned that my survival depended on me keeping the precious memories of being a mother and the bond I felt for my children in a detached place.

> I no longer feel the daily joy of being a mother, and I miss that. For my wellness to remain intact, it takes an enormous amount of emotional effort, awareness and courage to keep the precious memories I have of my children in the background. The survival of the court trauma proved more difficult in some ways than surviving eighteen years in this marriage because when I finally found strength to try to get out–the help I had depended upon from the law, the court, etc., all betrayed me. Justice did not come.

I continue to long for healthy interaction with my children and miss them more than words can describe. Spiritually, I understand what has happened. I understand money and power buy justice. I rebuild my balance each day by mediation and by accepting the fact that everything for the moment is exactly as it should be because society has willed it so. I continue to pray for the highest good for all. I continue to believe in surprises, miracles, imminent possibilities and "One Fine Day."

I met with Mr. Warner, and his pastors and elders from Bridgeport Chapel in Monmouth, Oregon, the week my nursing infant and children were removed from me with the same request. I told them the breast-pump was not working well for me and I was in a lot of pain. They said nothing and did nothing.

I believe my ex-husband and his religious supporters were calloused to my well-being because my well-being is not compatible with their idea of sex—possession, power, control, manipulation, and ego gratification. Their God condones kidnapping and rape: Numbers 31:17, 18, Deuteronomy 20:13, 14

Ellen Callen, a member of Bridgeport Community Chapel, was also present at this meeting. I will never forget Pastor Ron Sutter's stone-cold face. He reminded me of my favorite quote from Maya Angelou, "People will forget what you said, people will forget what you did, but people *will never forget how you made them feel.*"

"Despite the documentation of the breadth of this problem [domestic violence] it remains a "myth" to many pastors. Although 40 percent of battered women report that they first went to their pastors for help, most pastors deny the existence of violence among members of their congregation. **The "absence" of the problem represents the failure of the minister to acknowledge its existence and his or her willingness to address it."** - Judith Herman, M.D.

No attorney has been able to help me, and several of them have been verbally, emotionally, spiritually, and financially abusive towards me. I love and respect myself and cannot tolerate or subject myself to more abuse and also have to pay for it. My first attorney, Mr. Alway, sent me a threatening letter in October 1998 after I had left a message with his staff that I had handed my transcripts from my attempted marital rape trial to professionals and physicians. He is well aware that he did not defend or help me in the court trial. I paid him a healthy fee for his negligence and poor representation.

Mr. David Gearing told me during court recess that I reminded him of a mentally ill idiot (because I occasionally used the word "God" when I answered questions). I told him I was alive today because I believed in the divinity in myself and a higher power outside of myself. I told him that ego will always come to an end.

I do not understand why one of the attorneys did not initiate criminal rape charges against Mr. Warner. Instead, both attorneys were more interested in how much I was going to pay Mr. Warner for child support for a baby I conceived by rape during the period of my mental/nervous breakdown. By state law, Mr. Warner's actions towards me are considered Rape Count 1, a Felony.

In the summer of 1995, I had met Julie Caraway. My husband and I had invited Julie and her business partner to our home to recommend remodeling ideas and renovation plans. Several months later, I was in court and Julie Caraway attended the court hearings. During the court proceedings I could not bring myself to see the possible loss of my children—the thought that was so obvious to her.

From her inner wisdom and maturity, Julie sensed that my children would be removed from me, and she also understood the shock I would go through. After court adjourned, she came towards me and said, "Kathy, some of us are going to have to hang on to your ankles for the next couple of years, but you will be okay." She had years of experience to foresee that human nature, without spirituality, often leans toward abuse of power. I was too naive to understand the lack of sensitivity and moral principles many people operate from—and the future events that were about to unfold in my life.

Patriarchal Religion, Battered Wives & Divorce:
Legally Imprisoned in the Name of God

Divorce is not the scandal; rather it is the cover-up and condoning of abusive behavior which is the scandal of the Christian community and an embarrassment.

Escaping an abusive marriage is no easy task for many evangelical women, many of whom have pastors that say physical and mental abuse is no reason for divorce. The fear of reprisals and repercussions from husbands, pastors, the religious community and the judicial system prevents many women from seeking safety and wholeness. They are experienced with the ways abuse and trauma operates in their home. To seek safety would often mean subjecting themselves to further abuse in our judicial system as well. The choice to stay in domestic violence is not a choice at all. It is just the lesser of two evils. A battered woman weighs what kind of abuse she is most familiar with and can possibly survive. Fear of the unknown is often a crushing deterrent.

Another pastor said, "Kathy, removing an infant from a mother is sometimes necessary." Kathy Stuewe, Mr. Warner's friend and baby-sitter, said, "Look what you have done to your husband and children. Kathy, you are going to go to hell." Mrs. Kay Dixon, a pastor's wife and teacher of one of my daughters, said, "Kathy, you have torn your home down with your own hands. You need to get away from your evil, Jewish psychiatrist (Dr. Kuttner)." I did not know Mrs. Dixon, but she appeared as if she knew me, through comments by Mr. Warner. I was repulsed by her anti-Semitic comments and told her I was going to hang up.

> During the pregnancy of my eighth child, Dr. Charles South, my obstetrician of sixteen years, encouraged me to get the best attorney in the country and file for a divorce. He used very strong language that day. When Dr. South was questioned by the private investigator during my divorce hearings, Dr. South stated, "I wonder what is wrong with her that she would stay with a man like Mr. Warner." I offer him this story for an answer. He was aware in January of 1995 that I was still healing from my breakdown that was a result of my ex-husband's abuse and neglect. In the early months of my pregnancy I lived with friends and was still in a semi-vegetative state. I know he could not have foreseen the horrors I would encounter as I followed his advice. I stopped by his office after the court hearing in March 1996 with a breast pump instead of a baby. He was shocked. He immediately made some calls, but there was nothing that could be done. A Court Order is the law of the land, no matter how inhumane.

> I still wake up with night terrors. The memory of being forced to give up my children is a continual torment to my body, mind and soul. Time has helped me find peace in the pain. I have learned that "perfect peace is when pain is as welcome as lack of pain."

"When woman is brought before our man courts, and our man juries, and has no bruises, or wounds, or marks of violence upon her person to show as a ground of her complaint, it is hard for them to realize that she has a cause of appeal to them for protection: while at the same time her whole physical system may be writhing in agony from spirit wrongs, such as can only be understood by peers." - *Elizabeth Parsons Ware Packard*

Author and advocate, Elizabeth Packard, wrote the above paragraph 145 years ago in her true life story and book *The Prisoners Hidden Life or Insane Asylums Revealed* (1868). Elizabeth Packard was unjustly incarcerated in an insane asylum in the 1860s, because she didn't hold the same ideology and beliefs as her legalistic, Christian husband.

Elizabeth Packard came out on the other side better than I did, since she was set free from her oppressor by the courts, and retained the support of her children. After reviewing her story, it is my opinion that the courts and religious systems have both regressed over the past 100 plus years.

Nothing, nothing prepared me for the horrors that tens of thousands of women, including myself, experience in America's family court system.

Visitation was ordered to take place in the home every other weekend. Mr. Warner and his mother, Helen Warner, were to leave for the weekend when I arrived. Sometimes Mr. Warner continued doing his chores and made no attempt to leave on time.

I was greeted with hostility by my older children upon my first visitation to the home. My 17-year-old daughter was holding my baby, Zachary. I longed to hold him. My breasts were still engorged, painful and full with milk. My 17-year-old twins glared at me when I asked to hold Zachary. They said, "He is our baby, not yours." Mrs. Helen Warner, my mother-in-law, had the same hostility towards me. My daughters learned well from her example. Although my younger children were happy to see me, they were pressured in the following months by their older siblings and their father to reject me.

I was given permission, by the Court, to call my children during the week. Often, when I called, Mrs. Helen Warner would answer and refuse to allow the children to talk with me. She would state, "The children are where they belong." My attempts at calling were often futile. During the time I was permitted to call the home, no one would answer, and I would leave messages on the answering machine.

The power struggle that had characterized my marriage with Mr. Warner was continued by my twin daughters when I would come to the house for visitation. They controlled the schedule and activities, withheld the baby and children from me, interrupted my time with the younger children, locked the phones away and locked doors, and reported on me to Mr. Warner's attorney after I left the house on weekends.

After each visitation, Mr. Lawrence arrived at the home to interrogate the children about the visitation. He told them he was their "friend". Judge Norblad ordered Mr. Warner to encourage the young children to visit me. Judge Norblad was misinformed as to Mr. Warner's intentions and motives. There could not be a relationship with the children unless I was under Mr. Warner's total control and submitting to his abuse.

Mr. Warner eventually gave me permission to take the younger children, who wanted to see me, on visitation to my apartment during the weekdays. This relieved me of the abuse issues from my older twin daughters and I was able to keep my new job. (I worked Thursdays through Sundays). Mr. Warner agreed to this because he would not have to leave his home on the two weekends a month that I was there visiting the children.

I invited my twin daughters to have time with me at my apartment and they accepted that offer once, but I found them in my apartment going through my personal papers and other private items while I was returning from the pool with the other children. Since that event they did not return to my apartment or choose to see me again—their choice.

> Mr. Lawrence and Mr. Warner used my suggestion with Mr. Warner regarding my having the children at my apartment rather than at their home in Court stating, "that I did not participate in court ordered visitation during the past six months."

> Although I visited with my children every other week during the weekdays and baby-sat for Mr. Warner on occasion in my apartment, they insisted that this was not court appointed visitation. Theresa, age 11, and Joshua, age eight, chose to see

me only a few times during the two-year period of my visitation privileges.

In March 1996, Mr. Jack Meier, of Bend, Oregon, wrote Mr. Warner a letter regarding his feelings after hearing the Court's judgment. Mr. Warner and Mr. Meier had worked together at CH2M Hill, an engineering firm in Corvallis, Oregon. Mr. Meier had heard about court hearings through his daughter, Debbie Dresler, of Portland, Oregon. Here are a few excerpts from his letter:

> "I am appalled by your non-Christian behavior! To take a nursing baby from his mother's breast, to turn your children against their mother and put them in charge of her, and to withhold common acts of decency from a wife you have controlled for most of her married life are the acts of a hardened heart, and <u>are not Christ like</u>.

> "I don't know where you found those "Christian" lawyers, or how the judge could have ruled as he did. It is neither right nor just. Kathy deserves better. She should not be deprived of the three youngest children. They need their mother and her love." (Please see letter by Mr. Jack Meier in documentation.)

> In her book, *Necessary Losses*, Judith Viorst speaks of a young child's experience of prolonged maternal separation. Separation from the mother gives rise to profound feelings of despair and finally, detachment, as the child becomes apathetic and shuts down loving feelings. If in early childhood, especially during the first six years, we are too deprived of the mother we need and long for, we may sustain an injury equivalent to being doused in oil and set on fire. The pain of such deprivation is unimaginable. The healing is hard and slow. The damage, although not fatal, may be permanent.

My physician, Dr. Kuttner, says that removing a nursing infant from a mother is equivalent to castrating a man. To ease the shock and to help prevent me from being admitted to a mental hospital, Dr. Kuttner prescribed a low-dose tranquilizer. I took one-third of a tablet when needed for a few weeks. This was the last time I took medication. To this day, I suffer from the trauma of the abrupt removal and absence of my children.

> A friend, Sue Kettles, from Philomath, Oregon, wrote in a letter dated May 4, 2001, "I, too, was stunned that a court judge would take a nursing baby out of your arms to give to a man who would then have someone else care for your son. I think it would have killed me. Your strength in surviving that small portion is amazing. I think you've endured every mother's worst nightmare—losing your babies; having them taken from you by force. I'm so sorry that Marty would even allow such a wrong thing to happen. You've been through more than any one person should ever have to go through." Your friend always, Sue

Pediatricians, who had known me for years as a devoted and nurturing mother, were shocked over Judge Norblad's decision. Professionally, they understood the psychological harm this would cause the children, especially a nursing infant, and to me. Mothers have a chemical in their bodies called oxytocin. It is why we feel protective, nurturing and bonded to our children. The removal of a young child puts a mother not only in shock, physically, mentally and emotionally, it puts her in shock chemically. I was strengthened by my life verse from the ancient text of Isaiah 42:3 during this time.

> "A bruised reed He will not break. And smoking flax He will not quench; He will bring forth justice for truth."

My attorneys would not allow the pediatricians to call Judge Norblad because it might make the judge upset to have someone challenging his decision. They said if the judge finds out the public's dismay over his decision, he might be harsher towards me in the final divorce hearing.

> For the years involved in this litigation I witnessed attorneys relating to Oregon's judges the same as a fearful citizen relates to a tyrannical ruler. We are not the land of the free and brave. We are a people who lack courage to speak out against our oppressors.

In the spring of 1996, I also made contact with my oldest son, Aaron. We started a new relationship based on two people who had escaped a home filled with threats and abuse of power. I continued to be a champion for Aaron and was thankful he was doing as well as he was with the trauma and changes surrounding his life. He would call me often between our visits, and I shared with him wisdom that I had gained in my own survival.

In the months between the temporary custody hearing and the final divorce trial, (March through October 1996), Mr. Warner set up appointments to meet with me alone to talk about settling out of court. On one such occasion, we took a walk in the woods to discuss settlement issues. Mr. Warner shoved me against a tree and attempted to sexually assault me. I reminded him I was no longer his wife and he eventually let me go. We had been legally separated for seven months. In the months and years that followed, Mr. Warner continued to touch me or hug me, although I continued to tell him this was inappropriate. A friend of mine, Marilyn Gaines, helped me distance and protect myself from Mr. Warner by picking up and returning my three younger children to their home for me.

I also agreed to meet with our mediator, Mr. Willett, but it was no use. Mr. Warner would not agree to any compromise in settlement. Most of the appointment time with the mediator was used up by Mr. Warner's issues regarding my mental health.

During the summer of 1996, I meditated on what I should do regarding my children. They are all equally precious to me and it made no sense to seek custody of only the baby or the younger three or four children. The message to the other children would be confusing. I understood the bond my older twins had toward my baby, Zachary. I also understood their anger over my breakdown.

Mr. Warner continually threatened me, "You will get nothing." My twin daughters would make comments to the effect, "I will destroy this (name of item) before you will ever get it."

> "Fathers who battered the mother are twice as likely to seek sole
> custody of their children as are non-violent fathers." -*American*
> *Psychological Association*

Dr. Jean Furchner's custody evaluation report was finished in June 1996. Her report was positive. I had met with her a couple of times and she had met with my children in the home. Most of her comments were correct. Although, when she interviewed and reported statements made by Mr. Warner's supporters, they,

116

of course, were hostile and damaging in their comments of me. She also made an erroneous report regarding my son, Aaron. She states he had a close bond to his father. Aaron never spoke with Dr. Furschner and did <u>not</u> have any relationship with his father.

> Her report states, "Myrna Phillips, M.Ed. has seen Kathy with her youngest child and comments on her gentleness and kindness. Debbie Dresler says, by letter and in telephone consult, that she feels Kathy Warner has spent years being an outstanding mother, and she speaks of the sadness of the current situation. She has known the family for about twenty years. She sees Marty Warner as having translated his intense religious zeal to mean that anyone in disagreement with him or his wishes is in ungodly rebellion. Mrs. Dresler said that Marty presents himself well, but she feels he will not tolerate anyone who thinks differently than him, and is very invested in male dominance. She sees him as constantly correcting and punishing his wife, and even setting up the oldest twins to do the same, and feels he is now punishing her by alienating the children from her. She said he encourages the children to believe that Kathy is just choosing employment over motherhood for trivial reasons, or because she is mentally ill. Mrs. Dresler came by the home on 3/24/96, when Kathy was there for the first visit, to find that many rooms were locked, all the phones had been locked away, the older girls critical of their mother."

Dr. Jean Furchner further states, "Lynn Eisler has also known the Warners for about twenty years, neighbors at first and later always keeping in touch. She describes Kathy (Coral) as a wonderful mother and parent, creative and bright in her activities with the children. She recalled Kathy coming to stay at the Eislers' during her depression, Marty dropping by regularly, emphasizing about how she needed to submit. She said Kathy would ruminate about her guilt, how she should try harder, and Marty would play on that, with talk about "If only you had done this or that..." Mrs. Eisler feels that Kathy has made a great comeback, pulled herself together and made great strides.

"Shirley Walsh knew this family in their early years but has seen less of them recently. She remembers Kathy (Coral) as a great mother, "the epitome of a lovely housewife, loving her kids,...devoting her life to them." She adds that Kathy has "spirit and character," and also expresses amazement at Kathy's comeback in recent months. She recalls Marty as very intense, sometimes rather strange in his social interactions."

Furchner continues, "Tashi Smith knew this family in the fall of 1995 when she was tutoring with the children. She said Kathy (Coral) was doing the home schooling, a highly intelligent woman, creative, not content to just assign busywork but always looking for genuine learning and creative methods. Ms. Smith uses the expressions "a sweet disposition...a real strength about her." She said Mr. Warner made a very good impression at first, but she said he would often come home late in the evening, go straight into his study, walking right past the children and Kathy without a hello to anyone. She said he would sometimes express irritation that supper was not ready, but he would not offer to help. Tashi recalls seeing the children very subdued when their father might be angry, recalls Mr. Warner coming out of the study to spank the five-year-old for a small spill, an ordinary five-year-old mistake.

"Ursula Hay was in the home briefly as a housekeeper, invited by Kathy (Coral), and she comments that Mrs. Warner is loving, caring of the kids, doing baking, doing things with the kids...always with something out for the kids to do...not messy but active.

"Karen (Heinz) Lague was a neighbor for about eight years, and has known them longer than that. She expresses her admiration for Kathy (Coral), her organizational ability, her responsibility with the children. She says Kathy is calm, loving. She said Marty was unusual, often would not allow his wife to go to the doctor, always controlling. She worries that he can justify any behavior he has decided to adopt, with no self-doubt, confident in his rightness.

"I also spoke to Ms. Debbie Custis, the employee who worked with Mr. Warner and who found herself harassed, lectured to, etc. and generally treated with condescension by him. She also uses the word "controlling" with Mr. Warner, said he was derogatory to women and she finally found his attitude so difficult that she transferred to another department."

The following two sections from Dr. Furchner's report are from Mr. Warner's supporters. These people had only known our family for a short period of time—while we were in crisis.

"I also spoke with Bill Heard, who describes himself as a biblical counselor, working out of Riverside Counseling in Roseburg. Mr. Heard reports that he came to think of Marty as always seeking for answers but felt Kathy was looking for a way to end the marriage. He thought Kathy (Coral) had been a very good mother in earlier years, as adamant in her religious beliefs as Marty, re: homeschooling or women remaining in the home. In the long run, he said, he had to think of Marty as the more reasonable of the two."

"Mrs. Marijo Sutter, (wife of Pastor Ron Sutter - Marty's pastor) has known the family since last fall, and they allowed Marty to stay with them for the weeks while he was out of the house [restraining order against him]. She comments that Mr. Warner is a great father, said both parents had some problems."

Dr. Furchner further adds in her report comments from the children, "Sarah and Rachel have happy memories of the family's early years. They describe their mother happy, active, going to the library, teaching, shopping, doing laundry and cooking; the younger ones would nap for a while in the p.m. while the older ones did school work. They said the homeschooling had gone pretty well until three years ago, when their mother began to become depressed." They described Kathy as affectionate. Their comment was that they had been "deeply loved by both parents." Their relationship with their mother seems to have deteriorated during the last two or three years, they said, partly because of the demand on mother's time by all the younger ones and partly because of her depression. They began doing more and more with Dad, in turn, and say he loves all of them."

"Theresa has vivid memories of the family together, happy, and felt that the family members were kind and loved each other. She says Mom did not let them watch too much TV and would instead provide better things to do. Theresa was frightened by her mother's depression, said she had been accustomed to her mother running the household and found her mother's inability to function quite frightening. I thought I heard a child's anger at a parent's inability to be there for them, and she in turn says she has learned to rely on her father.

"The other saddening feature of Theresa's long talk was her bitterness to her mother about the divorce: she says that "Mom started it" and says that she has been shown the property list of things the mother wants (!) and thinks that Dad "will be on the street" if Mom takes everything, thinks Mom should not be allowed to take anything at all, that this whole divorce is all mother's fault, etc. "She's just causing a whole lot of problems." she says, and talks further about the property list and the financial strain on her father. I asked her if Dad had talked with her about how most couples share belongings, but she said no, that mother should not have anything, etc."

One custody evaluator recommended I be given custody of my infant, Zachary, and the three-, five- and eight-year-old. Another custody evaluator recommended I only be given custody of Zachary. I also understood the emotional repercussions this would cause my younger children; had I only been given custody of Zachary.

> Through all the trauma I had found a spiritual reservoir within me that knew no depth. I relied on this strength in the decision I would soon have to make and knew my children needed each other and did not need the further trauma of being separated from one another.

A friend recommended I read Khalil Gibran's *Prophet* about this time. His verses gave me wisdom that would comfort and strengthen me in the months and years ahead.

THE PROPHET

> "And a woman who held a babe against her bosom said, Speak to us of Children. And he said: Your children are not your children, They are the sons and daughters of Life's longing for itself. They come through you but not from you. And though they are with you yet they belong not to you.

> You may give them your love but not your thoughts, For they have their own thoughts. You may house their bodies but not their souls, For their souls dwell in the house of tomorrow, which you cannot visit, not even in your dreams. You may strive to be like them, but seek not to make them like you. For life goes not backward nor tarries with yesterday. You are the bows from which your children as living arrows are sent forth. The archer sees the mark upon the path of the infinite, and He bends you with His might that His arrows may go swift and far, Let your bending in the archer's hand be for gladness; For

even as He loves the arrow that flies, so He loves also the bow that is stable."

No matter what the court had decided, I put the beautiful memories I had of my children in a sacred place. Each one of my children had shown me a new and beautiful universe through his/her eyes. As a mother, each day was a journey of new experiences and new joys. I am still in awe in the gift of motherhood and am grateful for the days, months, and years I shared with each one of my children.

Ugly Shoes

No woman deserves to wear these shoes.

I am wearing a pair of shoes.

They are ugly shoes.

Uncomfortable shoes.

I hate my shoes.

Each day I wear them, and each day I wish I had another pair.

Some days my shoes hurt so bad that I do not think I can take another step.

Yet, I continue to wear them. I get funny looks wearing these shoes.

They are looks of sympathy.

I can tell in other's eyes that they are glad they are my shoes and not theirs.

They never talk about my shoes.

To learn how awful my shoes are might make them uncomfortable.

To truly understand these shoes, you must walk in them.

But, once you put them on, you can never take them off.

I now realize that I am not the only one who wears these shoes.

There are many pairs in this world.

Some women are like me and ache daily as they try to walk in them.

Some have learned how to walk in them so that they don't hurt quite so much.

Some have worn the shoes so long that days will go by
before they think about how much they hurt.

No woman deserves to wear these shoes.

Yet, because of these shoes I am a stronger woman.

These shoes have given me the strength to face anything.

They have made me who I am.

I will forever walk in the shoes of a woman who has lost a child. ~ Unknown

Although I had fired my attorneys in the spring of 1996 for financial reasons, they continued to work for me until the divorce trial. Before my divorce trial, in October 1996, I relinquished custody of all eight of my children to my ex-husband by a video-taped deposition. I was fully aware of the mental and emotional abuse that awaited me in court if I had continued to fight for custody. My attorney bills, by this time, had become insurmountable–$90,000 and I was physically, mentally and emotionally frail from court trauma. When I called my attorneys to dismiss them from working on my case, I was working one full-time labor job and two part-time night jobs to support myself, and I knew that my attorney fees were going to exceed any settlement that I might receive.

I choose to relinquish custody of my children in the fall of 1996 because I knew my older children were brainwashed and despised me. I also had no monies for ongoing court costs. My decision to not seek custody of my baby and younger children was a message to all eight of my children that they were loved equally.

The deposition was taken at the office of Mr. Mark Lawrence, my ex-husband's attorney. As I was climbing the stairs to where the deposition would be held that day, I collapsed. I remember going numb. My basic maternal instincts were being forcibly cut away. I did not believe that relinquishing custody was the right thing to do. There was nothing in my emotional make-up to prepare me for the irrational decision I was forced to make. However, I consoled myself with the thought– "He is no fool who gives up what he cannot keep to gain what he cannot lose." I had no other choice but to give up that which was most precious to me, my children. In the next few months and years, I learned the raw truth of the saying, "You do not know love until you know love's anguish."

My attorney, Mr. Gearing, was very disturbed with me during these depositions. He told me, "Kathy, if you would have fought for your children, I would have represented you pro bono." He did not understand. This was a spiritual decision I had made for myself and my children, not a legal maneuver. My counselors and I both understood that Mr. Warner would have destroyed me if I had received custody of any of my children. There was no choice.

The courts gave me NO CHOICE, as you cannot choose one child over another. Experts also acknowledged the fact that if I had custody of any of my children, I would most likely be stalked and/or end up dead, due to my ex-husband's belief that his patriarchal empire remains intact.

Mr. Warner and his attorney, Mr. Lawrence suggested that I might consider working as "Mr. Warner's baby-sitter" during the day and then keeping my full-time job at night. Although I would have loved the opportunity to be with my children, I did not want to have any contact with Mr. Warner or be his employee. Also, this arrangement did not allow me any rest or sleep. I said, "no" to their offer. I was grieved to learn that my youngest child, Zachary, was being cared for by day-care providers.

Mr. Warner and his attorney, Mr. Lawrence, were pleased during the deposition. They had won. They had taken away my children. They did not know, though, that they would never be able to take away my soul, my dignity, my inner joy or my freedom–those things that are a part of our sacred ground. No one outside ourselves can rule us inwardly. When we know this, we are truly free.

> William Styron, in his book, *Sophie's Choice*, expresses some of my spiritual and emotional feelings concerning the loss of my children. He writes, "What Sophie is forced to do is not a choice at all, but is instead a torture without rational foundation, and her experience permanently and irrevocably erodes her sanity and her ability to continue living."

Bearing Witness

We have known Coral for 33 years and realize after reading *BONSHEÁ Making Light of the Dark,* that we were unaware of so much about her life for most of those years. We only saw her as a peaceful, generous, and dedicated wife and mother.

We sadly realize that because we ourselves were so caught in the web of the authoritarian, religious influence, that even if she had tried to share her true life with us, we probably would not have been able to "hear" her and would have repeated spiritual platitudes to her and not been able to believe the true extent of her situation.

We are filled with admiration for her and are amazed at her courage, strength of character, and integrity. Her story truly inspires us to examine our beliefs more carefully, to be more true to ourselves and become more aware and sensitive to those around us. *—Bob and Shirley Walsh*, Washington

Coral Anika Theill at the Beach, 2018

"For to be free is not merely to cast off one's chains, but to live in a way that respects and enhances the freedom of others."
-Nelson Mandela

VII

Divorce Hearing, Children are Sacred Beings—Not Pawns to be Abused

Before my divorce hearing, Mr. Warner arrived at my apartment late one night and left a single red rose and this note: "Dear Kathy, I don't know how to say it. I only hope and pray the Lord will intervene to allow you to feel what I am trying to share. I want you to know that I love you and the children God has gifted us with. I remain committed through His Grace and mercy to be all that He would have me be for you and our children. I call upon the Lord and ask that you might prayerfully consider the magnitude and lifelong significance to the children, to you, and to me of what you are about to do. I love you and am committed to grow and build. I know and truly believe that all things are possible with God. I remain faithfully yours. I love you, Marty"

The first day I realized I had no more fear of those who wished to harm me was in October 1996, during my final divorce hearing in Salem, Oregon. Judge Albin Norblad, Circuit Court Judge of Oregon, arrogantly asked me what I had done with myself since he had taken my baby and children from me six months earlier. I said, "Well, your honor, I worked two jobs (80-hour work weeks), stayed in touch with counselors and good friends, and enrolled in exercise classes. But, your honor, I just want to say one thing, "If you take a baby from a mother who does not have a good support group, you will be dredging her out of the Willamette River." He was shocked I would be so bold, but I was putting out a warning that what he did to me on March 10, 1996, was beyond cruel. His actions were inhumane.

At my divorce hearing, in October 1996, Judge Norblad was shocked I was not fighting for custody of my younger children. He didn't understand. Although my custody evaluator's recommendation to the Court was that I be awarded custody of my four younger children, I wanted a divorce, not a custodial war. My children are precious gifts, not pawns or possessions to be fought over.

Mrs. Helen Warner was present in the courtroom praying with her rosary beads. Mr. Brian King, an elder, and Pastor Ray Birch, with bibles in hand, were also in attendance in support of Mr. Warner. Ellen Callen also attended one of the hearings, as well as my brother, Don Hall.

I was asked in Court to share with Judge Norblad my life and survival since the removal of my young children and baby. I told the judge that I had rented an apartment and obtained employment, and continued counseling with Dr. Kuttner. I also told the Judge Norblad that I had survived the abrupt removal of my nursing infant. With the help of my physician and the support of a few friends, I had avoided being admitted to a mental hospital from the shock.

Mr. Lawrence called to the stand an expert, Dr. Robert Male, on vocational and economic analysis. He had put the information in a computer program and calculated my "worth" in the job market. From his calculations I should have been making $11.00 per hour and $27,965.00 per year with benefits. I was, at the time, earning $6.00 at a night job and $8.50 an hour at a day time warehouse job. I never will understand where that $11.00 per hour position was for a woman who had been out of the job market for eighteen years and had suffered a mental breakdown.

I think it is humorous that Mr. Lawrence and Mr. Warner spent much effort to prove to the court that I was mentally ill, emotionally unfit, and "crazy", then in a swooping gesture put an expert on the stand stating to the court that "I was an intelligent, charismatic, and successful woman." My attorney asked the expert if he had ever talked with me or met me. He said, "No." His calculations for my earning ability came from my having been a pilot when I was seventeen years old, and my two years working as a court reporter twenty years ago.

Dr. Jean Furchner's custody evaluation to the Court reported that:

"Martin presents himself as a loyal supportive husband who has tried to hold the family together, tried to make sense of his wife's mental illness. He professes his love for her, denies trying to control her or demand that she be submissive; Mr. Warner's portrayal is that Kathy often behaved in certain ways that she later came to dislike and would then project onto him as his demands." I asked Mr.

Warner to examine his possible contribution to the difficulties in the marriage, encouraging him to regard the ultimate depression as the culmination of many years of difficulty. He said he was a hard worker, and at first said he was away a lot. Asked again to consider the question of his own contribution to the marital unhappiness, he says that perhaps he has an "inability to perceive and minister to Kathy's need...don't know how I can help or contribute," a perception of the problem which still defines it as Kathy's mental health. Mr. Warner denies that he is dominant in the relationship, certainly does not see himself as controlling or intimidating...denies being sexually demanding, feels offended by her portrayal of him as someone who wanted her home and pregnant."

Dr. Furchner stated that I exhibited traits of those who experience Post-Traumatic Stress Disorder.

Dr. Jean Furchner interviewed Dr. Charles D. South, my obstetrician. Her report states:

> "I spoke with Charles D. South, M.D., who is OB/Gyn who delivered the twins and has seen Kathy through several of her deliveries. He said she had a very difficult time at the last delivery, with Zachary, hemorrhaging and in distress; the doctor wanted to start the IV and other therapy and was opposed by Mr. Warner; he said he finally had to intervene and begin the treatment because the patient was in real trouble. Dr. South states that he has been disillusioned by Mr. Warner, who presented himself early as a doting father but who has allowed his beliefs in male dominance and his control needs to interfere. He comments that Kathy was probably passive and notes her recent depression; he comments that he has come to see this patient as mentally abused in the marriage."

Judge Norblad stated, in Court, that he was giving me half of the estate, which was Oregon law. Later, he signed a court order giving me visitation rights and a portion of the estate that was heavily taxed upon withdrawal. My taxes, attorney, medical and court related fees exceeded my settlement. Mr. Warner's attorney bills were only about one-third the amount of mine. He was awarded the home which was debt-free. He also has numerous accounts and assets which were not touched.

In his written opinion and in court, Judge Norblad described my ex-husband as a "control-freak," and a "stable man." I have since learned that stable in court, means non-emotional, non-feeling. In that sense, the judges' words are true. Judge Norblad counseled Mr. Warner that if he did not change some of his control issues with his children, that as they got older, he would lose them.

Custody evaluators, Ms. Patricia Cox and Dr. Jean Furchner reported that Mr. Warner cannot accept any responsibility for the failure of the marriage. Ms. Cox said of Zachary "the abruptness with which he was weaned certainly must have been traumatic for him."

Dr. Kuttner testified that my marriage had been detrimental to my physical and mental health and that I might suffer another nervous breakdown in the near future if I was not protected from further trauma. Judge Norblad acknowledged that my health was frail, but ordered me to pay my ex-husband child support for the next eighteen years in the amount of $500.00 per month knowing that on my income, I would not be left with enough to cover my own living expenses. Evidently, he didn't consider financial trauma to be a problem. (Mr. Warner was ordered to pay a $500.00 spousal/medical support for eight years in case I had another breakdown).

On the last day of my divorce hearing in October 1996, my attorney, Mr. David Gearing, began his closing statements with, "Your honor, first of all I want to make some general statements. This has been...I don't know if I can talk..." Mr. Gearing broke down and wept. Judge Norblad called for a recess until Mr. Gearing could regain his composure.

> Mr. Gearing continued, "What I was going to say is this case has been one of the most difficult cases that I have handled since I have been a member of the bar. A case in which the Court has earned its pay (laughs) in making a very, very difficult call in a very difficult situation. Mrs. Warner's response to the pedente lite decision has been extremely courageous. She did not allow herself to fall apart. She recognized that she had a responsibility to her family, to get on her feet, move on, take care of herself, get a job, and start earning money. With attorneys and judges that see a lot of divorces it is not secret—it is pretty rare for a spouse to—not rare, it happens, sometimes. It is not uncommon for spouses to make no effort, whatsoever, to improve themselves vocationally during the pendency of a

case and sit and do nothing and be a burden on the estate and on their spouse.

"Mrs. Warner needs help from Mr. Warner in the future, but did everything she could as quickly as she could to obviate that burden and to move forward with her life after what was a crushing decision [from the Court] to a person who was undeniably fragile. We know her condition. The Court has seen her testify. Doctors have testified. She is a fragile person and that is all the more remarkable that she did what she did, and I have the utmost respect for her and I hope everyone in this courtroom does. It would be naive to ignore Mrs. Warner's past health. She gave and she gave and she gave until she fell flat on her face. And she needs to walk away from this with half the assets. And there is no reason why she can't.

"The Court has ruled on visitation and Mr. Warner runs his household with–he is a very strict, loving father. He believes that love, at least from what I've heard, is shown by giving guidance and requiring his children to do and behave in an appropriate way as he sees it. There is no denying that he loves his children tremendously and that he runs his home in a way that is strict and orderly. He had the strength to take custody in this case, which the Court determined Mrs. Warner did not.

"Mrs. Warner has made the ultimate sacrifice that she will probably ever make in her life by conceding the issue of custody of those children who she loves dearly and who she gave her heart and soul and seventeen to twenty hours a day of her time to for seventeen years." Mr. Gearing, in his closing argument, asked the Court to instruct Mr. Warner to teach the children to respect their mother.

Judge Norblad was very impressed that Mr. Warner had a large debt free estate and numerous savings, stock and IRA accounts. He complimented us in court for our frugal lifestyle and financial abilities. He stated that Mr. Warner was "unbending and controlling" and questioned how Mr. Warner was going to deal with teenagers. Judge Norblad stated in Court that he "was impressed, very impressed with how I was getting along." He also stated that the older children's anger towards me was misplaced, and the circumstances of my breakdown were not in my control.

During the divorce hearing it was revealed that Mr. Warner had disobeyed the Restraining Order that his own attorney, Mr. Lawrence, had filed on January 4, 1996, that froze our accounts during the year and a half of litigation. Mr. Warner made large withdrawals ($12,000.00) from these accounts during this time. Mr. Warner suffered no consequences, although this action was a direct violation of Court Orders.

> Domestic violence counselors have introduced me to a term that describes Mr. Warner's favorable treatment in Court– "privileged entitlement". Our courts have not shed the fundamental belief that a man is master of his household–and as long as he provides financially, he is a "good" father and husband.

In court, Mr. Warner was given permission by Judge Norblad to read a "love letter" he had composed for me. After he finished, Mr. Warner reached out to hug me, I told him, "No, it would be inappropriate."

> I left the courtroom believing it was finally over, but I was naive. My court and legal trauma had only begun. Mr. Warner does not believe in losing, and even though he had custody of the children, my divorcing him was a great loss of face (and free labor.) He and his attorney would attempt to teach me who was in control.

> I learned that anyone can endure tyranny, but it takes true courage to embrace freedom.

I was working a full-time job and two part-time jobs at minimum wage at the time of my divorce hearing including a daytime warehouse job and night time hostess job. I sold my beeswax art part-time to supplement my income. (I had not worked outside the home for twenty years and I did not have a college education.) While working eighty-hour work weeks, I was barely able to support myself. I do not believe the judge took into account the disparity between Mr. Warner's assets, health, and income and my own.

My attorneys recommended I appeal the decision, but I could not. I did not have the $40,000 to $60,000 to appeal the case or the emotional and physical stamina to survive more court hearings.

Financial advisors and accountants went over the judge's decision with me and estimated that between my income, the attorney fees, tax penalties, child support, loans and bills relating to my divorce, my monthly deficit would be **minus** $2,000 per month. My take home pay was $950.00 per month. My paycheck barely covered rent, food, utilities, gas, car insurance, medical bills, clothing and misc. I had no monies extra for child care in the event that I was working overtime on my scheduled visitation weekends.

> I was recently told by attorneys that it would cost another $20,000 for me to take my ex- husband to court over contempt of court issues.
>
> Judge Norblad did award me my personal journals at my divorce hearing. My ex-husband stated to me that he has my journals, but they are "his", not mine and has refused to relinquish them. He and his religious counselor, had taken them from me before my divorce. I wrote in my journals during my illness. I have never had the opportunity to re-read them and would like to do so someday. I believe it would aid my healing process for me to revisit those times in my journals, as they are part of my truth.

In 1997, several months after the divorce I received a card and letter from Mr. Warner stating: Not having you here...sure puts a damper on things. Miss You!

> "Dear Kathy (Coral),
>
> "I would very much look forward to getting together with you. It has been over four months since you and I have had a chance to truly talk and share with each other. Please let me know if you would ever be open to getting together as friends for dinner or an evening of dancing. I am fully committed to you and the children and will do all that I can to build our relationship and family. I look forward to hearing from you and would be blessed to look forward to a date with you. Your friend and husband, Marty"

The church aided my ex-husband throughout the divorce because of their opposition to divorce, their hatred toward women, and their beliefs regarding patriarchal authority and the obedience of woman. I believe that clergy are often trained to see only the goal of saving the marriage at all cost, rather than the goal of stopping the violence. Their beliefs are based on domination, not respect.

Fundamental churches in America emphasize the importance of the submission of women "in all things." I wrote Mr. Warner's pastor a brief note once and suggested he preach a sermon from a verse in the book of Malachi, "Woe, to you who deal treacherously with the wife of your youth." My belief regarding divorce is simply this: Cruelty and abuse within the marriage nullifies any marriage covenant.

> The indifference and apathy I have experienced from the so-called "spiritually-minded" Christian people grieves me to this day. Their response to my trauma and abuse is far removed from the meaning of "Christ-consciousness" that their institutions claim to represent. Instead of vessels of love, compassion and understanding, they became my judges, my jury and my executioner.

> I have discovered through the years that our society is quick to judge and condemn. Could it be because the greater portion of our society is only operating from fear and religious indoctrination and not from true spirituality and the teachings of the great masters who taught and patterned their lives in love, compassion, understanding, non-judgment and forgiveness?

> It saddens me to see so many individuals wearing jewelry and T-shirts with the motto, "What Would Jesus Do?" I don't believe these people, who are so quick to model these fashions, even have a clue.

> The hostile Christian individuals involved in my divorce case reminds me of the adage, "Some people are so heavenly conscious, they are no earthly good."

During my early court hearings and proceedings, several Christian friends drew me into their life and read copies of my mental files, court orders, personal papers and private notes and letters. After my initial court proceedings and loss of my children, they withdrew their friendship. I learned throughout the years of court trauma who I could trust and who was most likely to betray me. The treachery and betrayal of "friends" came as great shock.

Often the concern some well-meaning people have shown me is not from empathy or compassion but from a more voyeuristic motive. They want to be privy to the secrets and informed about the drama of my life. Even when it has not been malicious, it certainly has a toxic effect - especially when people start fueling slander and gossip.

A true friend is someone who desires and gives mutual respect, empathy and support. Relationships and friendships are two-way streets. Some friends require a one-way street – especially in regards to religion and politics. One-way friendships are those where someone tells you they respect your views, but do not wish to hear them and proceed to share their views. A one-way relationship isn't a friendship.

Just because someone gives you aid; doesn't mean they are your friend. Many times when people help others, it has to do with fulfilling their needs. A friend does more than just support you in one specific area. Friends respect, empathize, and support each other.

Some individuals, who have assisted me, believe it gives them license to speak or treat me disrespectfully. I am grateful for their aid. Are they my friends? Absolutely not. Many people throw words around like 'love' and 'friendship,' but actions speak louder than words.

> To protect me from further harm, I mentally erected a 10,000-foot brick wall in my mind. Once in a while, I removed a brick to peer out to see if it was safe, then I would quickly put it back in place.

> As I healed and acknowledged my own medicine, I was able to take down the wall. It was no longer needed.

Bearing Witness

I first met Coral in 1996. We quickly became good friends. She is an outgoing and generous person and was so even during the time she was going through incredibly difficult divorce proceedings. We lived in the same apartment complex for a while and I got to meet several of her younger children. When they would come to visit, they often played with my children. I was able to witness firsthand the bond of love between Coral and her children. I was confident that Justice (or at least common sense) would prevail in the courts and these bonds would be respected. Sadly, this was not the outcome.

BONSHEÁ is the result of a lot of hard work and I am very proud of Coral. She has told her story. If we ignore it, shame on us. Coral's manuscript is complete but the story is not finished. There will come a day when the legal proceedings will begin again. I hope by that time her story will have touched enough people that there will be public outcry for true justice. Until that day, I hope *BONSHEÁ* provides hope and strength to others who find themselves in similar situations. – *Mike Gordon,* Arizona

Coral Theill visiting her relatives in Denmark for the first time in 1997

"Our lives at times seem a study in contrast... love and hate, birth and death, right and wrong... everything seen in absolutes of black and white. Too often we are not aware that it is the shades of grey that add depth and meaning to the starkness of those extremes." - *Ansel Adams*

VIII

Counselors, Trip to Denmark, Healing, Stigma Associated with being a Non-Custodial Mother

I am thankful for my mentors and friends who helped and encouraged me to explore spirituality and to discover who I truly was, apart from the pseudo-Christian community of my past.

I shared with my mentors years ago that I was going to spiritually jump out of a plane (explore my spirituality apart from my past) without my parachute. I was confident the universe would catch me, and it did. I found myself and my soul.

> I believe when individuals become more aware of themselves, they discover their true self, the spark of divinity, that is within each of us. Healing comes when you realize that your trauma is not who you are. Trauma is what has happened to you or what has been done to you by people who have not become aware of their own divinity <u>and the divine</u>. Until you become acquainted with yourself, you are in spiritual poverty.

After over six months of working eighty-hour work weeks, Dr. Kuttner, wrote a disability waiver and recommended a six month leave of absence. My divorce became final in March 1997 and I used $550.00 of the settlement monies to buy a round-trip plane ticket to Denmark.

In May 1997, I visited my relatives and friends in Denmark. It was a very healing experience. They are a sensible, humorous, civil and humane people. During my visit, I observed equality between men and women and personal boundaries honored and respected.

I visited a church while I was in Denmark. My relatives (humorously) told me that churches are visited by tourists, the mentally ill and the senile. I believe their healthy attitudes are a result of not being subjected to the fundamental and patriarchal doctrines and attitudes that are so prevalent in America's churches and society today.

My relatives and the friends I made in Denmark were very disturbed by my story and the injustices I had experienced in America's courts. Their society would not punish a woman for escaping marital abuse or for defying a man's power over her. Their judicial system would not remove a nursing infant from a mother. The thought of a woman/and or wife being raped and beaten while suffering a mental/nervous breakdown was incomprehensible to them.

> They perceive America as a primitive country that is caught up in power, control and violence. They consider our society overly fanatic and religious. They often shared with me, "When America stops treating people like animals, then your citizens will stop acting like animals." My experiences validates their concerns about the inhumane treatment of innocent people in America. In their society, money and influence do not buy justice.

After visiting my relatives in Denmark in May 1997, I received this letter from them.

> "Dear Kathy, (Coral)
>
> "Until now I was only worried about the burger culture of fat Americans. After your visit I learned that I should probably be more worried about lots of weird Americans. I feel very bad about your law system where money and influence seem to be able to buy justice, and also about the huge difference between rich and poor.
>
> "You have told the horror story of your life and by your presence here, we have met a survivor, a very strong character, an open, humorous, intelligent and knowledgeable woman

with good argumentations for her opinions. Your very positive and humorous style has thrilled us all.

"We have talked about life-quality, sex, humor, religion, man-woman relationships and "Nordbagges" (Viking horses) in a very open way and it has been a pleasure to have you here - you are welcome back." With much love and affection,

Mogens, Anne-Marie, Jacob and Christian Theill, Hornslet, Denmark

Coral Anika Theill modeling authentic Danish dress in 1998

In all, between 1996 and 1999 there were eight court hearings relating to my divorce and fifteen hearings relating to our children and child support issues. I participated in approximately thirty-five hours of depositions that were oppressive, mentally abusive, and cruel. I have spent tens of thousands of dollars for legal representation, and presently owe over $150,000 for attorney fees and court related costs. I underwent five psychiatric exams to prove my mental well-being to the court. Since December 1995, I have spent a total of approximately forty-two days in court, twelve hours of psychological exams and thirty-five hours of depositions. Physicians have stated that it would be difficult for anyone with this schedule and trauma to keep a job, let alone their health!

I continued counseling with Dr. Kuttner in 1996 and 1997. He confessed that when he first met me in 1993, he did not believe me, but believed my abusive husband. In describing my husband after my divorce, he said, "Marty Warner is a cross between Saddam Hussein, David Koresh and Ike Turner." During one therapy session he loaned me a book that would be very instrumental in my healing—*Man's Search for Meaning in Life*, by Dr. Viktor Frankl.

In the spring of 1997, Dr. Kuttner introduced me to Dr. Barbara May. Dr. May taught me how to *empower* myself and thrive in my survival. Her expertise in the field of domestic violence, and her support while I suffered through more court trauma, encouraged me. She taught me about resilience and the importance of trusting and listening to my inner voice, my truth. Most importantly, Dr. May believed me. She also helped me understand the illness of those who have mastered abuse. She said my ex-husband had not only mastered abuse, he appeared, from his actions, to have the "Ph.D. in power, control and abuse issues."

On one occasion, Dr. May gave me a hand-out entitled "Criminal Thinking and Behavioral Errors." She had made check marks next to statements she felt represented my ex-husband's behavior. ("Criminal Thinking Behavior Errors" hand-out is included in the documentation.)

Dr. May continues to encourage me and my journey in this life. She recently wrote me, "Calvin Coolidge once said, 'Nothing in the world can take the place of persistence. Talent will not; nothing is more common than unsuccessful men with great talent. Genius will not; unrewarded genius is almost a proverb. Education will not; the world is full of educated derelicts.' Coral, you are nothing, if not persistent." I took her statement as a compliment.

From 1995 to 1998, my eldest son, Aaron, lived in foster homes that were arranged by Mr. Warner. In the spring of 1998, Aaron requested that he be allowed to live with me. Since March of 1996, I had arranged visits through his foster parents. The last foster parents Aaron lived with were Phil and Carol Jones. Mr. Warner had set up this arrangement with the Jones'. Mr. Jones was an elder at Mr. Warner's church, Bridgeport Community Church.

The Jones did not honor my visitation rights with Aaron and actually created obstacles to my spending time with my son. I made two separate arrangements to come and pick him up for his birthday. Both times, at the last minute, they said I could not see him. I once said to Mrs. Jones, "I hope your God does not punish you to the extent that you are punishing Aaron and I."

The next time I tried to pick Aaron up for a visit, Mr. Jones demanded that I apologize to him and his wife. He was incensed I would share my feelings with them and my disappointment in how they used our visitation as a weapon and tool for punishment. I refused to apologize to them and left. They continued to badger my son with their religious dogma. Aaron was subjected to ritual abuse from this couple and often felt suicidal while in their care. He did not appreciate or agree with their alternative view of reality.

In June of 1998, Mr. Warner offered to give me custody of Aaron, who was then seventeen. I was open to this arrangement, but told the judge that I would want my child support payments to Mr. Warner adjusted, and I wanted protection from any further harassment by Mr. Warner. I did not want the issue of having my son live with me be a legal open door for Mr. Warner. The judge set a hearing date for July 1998.

The judge told me before the next hearing that my visitation rights would be in full effect. I told the judge that I didn't have any visitation rights. The Jones were in control of my rights and sometimes that could be defined as no visitation. I shared with the judge, specifically speaking about Mr. and Mrs. Jones, that I believed these individuals lacked the ethics necessary to act, in good faith, as foster parents and that they used their religious beliefs to harm others.

A foreign exchange student from Argentina lived in the Jones' home with Aaron. He stayed at my apartment several times when Aaron visited me. He told me that the Jones' were the most rude and abusive people he had ever known. He said, "Their religion does not impress me."

> Like the story of the emperor with no clothes, religious-minded people are most often the last to realize their hypocrisy and how spiritually impoverished they truly are.

That same week I called Aaron at the Jones' home and I was told he no longer lived there. They would not tell me where he had been taken. I later found out, after making numerous calls that Aaron had been taken out of the foster home he was living in and placed in a run-away home for youths, even though Aaron was not a run-away. (Aaron was distressed by this sudden placement and was not allowed to call me before or after he was moved.)

Aaron was put in prison clothing and was not allowed to leave the premises. He was to fill out workbook materials daily about his shortcomings. I was not allowed to see him or talk with him without special permission. I was told as soon as I signed Mr. Warner's custody papers that his attorney, Mr. Daniel Van Eaton, had drawn, Aaron would be released. In other words, this was just another one of Mr. Warner's tactics to add further trauma to my life. He didn't seem to mind that he was sacrificing his own child.

In the meantime, I was allowed a visitation with Aaron and he was encouraged by the fact that I was doing everything I could to rectify the situation. Aaron was quite depressed, and it traumatized me to see the condition of the building that he was living in. It reminded me of my stay, during my breakdown, at the half-way house on Killingsworth in Portland. During this time, my Danish relatives arrived to visit me. I shared with them the situation and they nodded their heads in disbelief and said, "America is very sick." I arranged for a hearing with a judge in Polk County. I typed a letter to the judge during the night and left the next morning for the hearing.

The Honorable Judge Wallburg was alarmed that Aaron had been taken to a home for run-aways when he had a mother who was emotionally involved in his life and willing to have him live with her. Judge Wallburg told me to "go get your son, now, Ms. Hall." I asked the judge if I needed any papers, and he said, "No, go get your son out of there." As I was leaving, I heard Judge Wallburg reprimanding one of the individuals responsible for this fiasco. Aaron was thrilled to see me and we went home to my apartment. He met his relatives and started planning a trip someday in the future to Denmark.

Despite the fact that I was now fully responsible for Aaron's medical bills, support and food, my child support payments were never reduced. I was expected to continue paying the full amount of $500.00 per month (despite the fact that the twins had turned nineteen and legally I should have been released from supporting them). However, I was grateful for the fact that I no longer had to go through the Jones' to see my son.

While my son, Aaron, lived with me in 1997, I shared *"The Credo"* from Leader Effectiveness Training, with him. It states simply,

"You and I are in a relationship that is important to me, yet we are also separate persons with our own individual values and needs. So that we will better know and understand what each of us values and needs, let us always be open and honest in our communication. Whenever I'm prevented from meeting my needs by some action of yours, I will tell you honestly and without blame how I am affected, thus giving you the chance to modify your behavior out of respect for my needs. And I want you to be as open with me when my behavior is unacceptable to you. And when we experience conflict in our relationship let us agree to resolve each conflict without using power to win at the expense of the other losing. We will always search for a solution that meets both of our needs–neither will lose, both will win. Whenever you are experiencing a problem in your life, I will try to listen with acceptance and understanding in order to help you find your own solutions rather than imposing mine. And I want you to be a listener for me when I need to find solutions to my problems. Because ours will be a relationship that allows both of us to become what we are capable of being, we will want to continue relating to each other–with mutual concern, caring and respect."

As I healed and reached higher levels of consciousness, it became more and more difficult to go back in the darkness—America's courtrooms. To give you an illustration of the Polk County judicial system, this is what my son, Aaron and I observed in July 1998. We were in the Polk County courtroom of Judge Charles E. Luukinen in Dallas, Oregon, for a final custody hearing involving Aaron. Judge Luukinen sentenced another juvenile to one week detention. Why? The young boy was Hispanic, clean shaven, clean cut, nicely dressed in clean olive-colored pants and shirt with a black belt. Judge Luukinen seemed overly displeased with the youth's clothing. He stated that he was sentencing the youth to one week of detention for daring to come into his courtroom dressed like a gang banger. The people in the courtroom were aghast. I often wonder what the youth learned from this harsh sentence.

Aaron has recently been able to reestablish a relationship – although a strained one - with his brothers, sisters and father. We are estranged at this time.

Aaron harbors a tremendous amount of anger towards me. He blames me for his crimes and their consequences.

Many people are concerned about the impairment of judges in America's judicial system. It appears, from their records, that many judges have no regard for the safety and well-being of women and children. They execute judgments that, in many cases, are viewed as bizarre and inhumane with no repercussions to their careers.

In July 1997, Dr. Kuttner wrote a letter to the Commission on Judicial Fitness and Disability. Dr. Kuttner stated in his letter, "I have spoken with other therapists and attorneys in this area, and understand that Judge Norblad has a reputation for making capricious and bizarre decisions, but that no attorney feels safe to question them."

The Judicial Fitness Commission responded to Dr. Kuttner's complaint by saying they saw this as only his (Dr. Kuttner's) complaining because he disagreed with the judge's decision. They didn't think there was anything wrong.

The fear of reprisals and repercussions from husbands, the religious community, and the judicial system prevents many women from seeking safety and wholeness. They are experienced with the ways abuse and trauma operates in their home. To seek safety would often mean subjecting themselves to further abuse in our judicial system as well. The choice to stay in domestic violence is often not a choice at all. It is just the lesser of two evils. The woman weighs what kind of abuse she is most familiar with and can possibly survive. Fear of the unknown is often a crushing deterrent.

On May 28, 2001, a friend wrote these comments to me, "I hope you have felt that I wanted to be there for you and yet I was unsure at times if I was really able to do anything to help you.

> "I am sorry that I was not able to help you more, Coral. I tried, in any way I thought appropriate. There were times I felt great concern over the possible retaliation of Mr. Warner should he find out who we were and that we were involved with you in any way. I am sorry for that. I/we have never been in a situation like this where we want to help someone so greatly, but unsure of how much is safe. I know you understand this and I know

we are not alone in these feelings and how unfair they are to you in such great need. No one should ever be at loss for where to go for help and to feel safe." Much love, (name withheld)

LIFE Magazine, USA Today and many other magazines have featured articles on women in prison in America. They report that women prisoners are allowed to keep their babies with them for eighteen months while serving their sentences, (Florida Statute 944.24). I am haunted by this single question. Why was I treated lower than a criminal by Oregon's judicial law system? I was a faithful wife and mother for almost twenty years. Presently, I have fewer rights than a criminal in America and I have no criminal record and have no history of alcohol, drug or child abuse.

> Loving non-custodial mothers face a stigma in society that is reprehensible and unjust. People assume these mothers do not have custody because they are drug addicts, alcoholics, child abusers, or they just didn't want their children. While there certainly are cases of abusive mothers who give up their children and walked away, in more and more cases today, fit and loving mothers are losing custody of their children against their will.

Sable House, a safe home in Dallas, Oregon, was called numerous times by my friends and myself about my court hearings. They did not respond to any calls or attend of any of my court hearings. I sought help from Sable House in 2004 while I was homeless, disabled and destitute due to ongoing court trauma. My ex-husband took our court case to the Oregon State of Appeals. I had no legal representation due to poverty and was expected to write a legal brief. Deborah Thompson, Director of Sable House, responded, "We cannot help you. Go sell more candles and books."

A safe home employee in The Dalles, Oregon, didn't have time to help and told me to call the District Attorney in The Dalles myself. I shared with her that I have called and written him several times, but he has never responded. I went to a couple safe home support group meetings in Salem, Oregon, and was alarmed at the victim mentality that was being taught by the facilitators. Also, I noticed that many of the safe home facilitators I contacted had the same fundamentalist thinking processes as my ex-husband. Many of the facilitators were very unhealthy-minded women.

I survived childhood abuse and many acts of violence from my former husband. I have been exploited and abused by attorneys. I have survived the silent violence of the court system.

So far, I have sought help from seven judges, seven attorneys, seven doctors, several counselors, two custody evaluators, a private investigator and bodyguard, two sheriffs, a policeman, three district attorneys, a mediator, Pastor Ron Sutter, Bridgeport Community Church, four safe homes, including Sable House in Dallas, Oregon (none became actively involved), C.A.S.A., (Court Appointed Specialty Advocates) for Children, Inc., former Washington State Senator Harriet Spanel, Father Pat McNamee, Father Mihlton Scarpetta, former Governor Ted Kulongoksi, Governor John A. Kitzhaber, Governor Kitzhaber's Council on Domestic Violence, Oregon Statewide Law Advisory Committee, Oregon Attorney General Hardy Myers, Oregon Attorney John Kroger and Oregon Attorney General Ellen Rosenblum, the Oregon Attorney General's Sexual Assault Task Force, Governor Kate Brown, men and women's activist groups, La Leche League, American Civil Liberties Union (A.C.L.U.), the Crime Victims' Compensation Program, the Disciplinary Counsel of the Oregon State Bar Association, the Veterans Administration, the Oregon Medical Board, the National Coalition Against Domestic Violence, Naomi Sterns, Staff Attorney for Domestic Violence and Homelessness, the National Organization for Women (NOW), U.S. Senator Ron Wyden, U.S. Senator Jeff Merkley, President Barack Obama and local and national media. (None of these individuals or groups could help me and some of them became a part of the problem.) I believe I have fallen through the cracks of America's judicial system.

In my experiences in religion, in court, in 'therapy', and *even among the people at shelters and advocacy groups*, when there is a power differential between people there will be abuse (of power) and exploitation. Power does not like to be challenged- and in order for their systems to run smoothly, they insisted on my playing the role of subject, patient, victim or whatever fits within their hierarchy.

Trauma expert Dr. Sandra Bloom, describes social systems as organisms with an internal logic of self-preservation and self-replication. In our society as a whole and within each of the groups that function as systems within the whole, the top power strata is like the brain and heart, the mid-level people are the other vital organs. These require the most in resources to function. The lowest on the power ladder are the extremities - and resources will be shunted away from them to preserve the vital organs if there is ever a perceived threat to the system.

Bloom speaks of homelessness and poverty as "violent aspects of our society." They are the result of a social system pulling resources away from the lower level of society to feed the head and torso of the organism. The problem is that as cells are destroyed in the extremities, that destruction further stresses the organism and if not addressed will eventually cause the death of the entire organism.

"Justice is itself the great standing policy of civil society and any departure from it under any circumstances lies under the suspicion of being no policy at all." –quote found in the Justice Building in Salem, Oregon.

Coral Anika Theill wearing vintage black dress in Washington D.C., 2018

Bearing Witness

I must say, Coral that if Stevie Wonder read your story, he could clearly see that there is gross injustice in your case. In other words, a blind person can see that you have been, and continue to be wronged. For you to not have a criminal record (of any kind), and to be kept from your children, forced into poverty and in essence forced into hiding (state address protection program) it is plain to see that our system is severely flawed. I have heard stories similar to this in Utah. Their laws are totally different than the laws of other states. For the authorities to basically turn a blind eye is sickening to say the least.

How can clergy persons, law enforcement, judges and other women for that matter put another person (man or woman) through something like this? There is neither rhyme nor reason for this to have happened and for it to continue to happen. You gave birth to your children. They are more yours than they are your husbands if you ask me. Men play their one part in causing pregnancy, but the woman does the rest. Again, absolutely nothing criminally causing them to have made such a drastic move in removing your children from you and preventing you from all contact with them, but they have found a way to separate you physically from them.

Bringing your personal story, your life to the forefront will hopefully put fire under someone's butt to look at this from a different perspective than those who in the past have, reopen the cases and bring justice and closure to this matter. Although you don't know the magnitude of those you have touched, know that your story has been an inspiration to many. – *Sergeant Major Brian Jackson*, USMC (Ret)

"Power without love is reckless and abusive, and love without power is sentimental and anemic. Power at its best is love implementing the demands of justice, and justice at its best is power correcting everything that stands against love." - *Dr. Martin Luther King, Jr.*

IX

Going into Hiding, Child Support Hearings, District Attorney, Court Orders, Judgments, Post Traumatic Stress

Before I moved and went into hiding, one of my older daughters was still very angry towards me. She would take out her rage on the younger children by hitting, kicking, biting and smothering them. This frightened my younger children. They continued to share their fear of returning to the home when their older sister was in charge. I spoke with Mr. Warner about this and he said, "Theresa is getting help from Mr. Bill Heard in Roseburg. When my friend, Debbie Dresler heard this, she stated to me, "Kathy you must try to help Theresa protect herself around these sick men." Theresa did not welcome me in her life. I am helpless in protecting her or any of the children anymore.

> In several states, when a custodial parent allows an older child to abuse a younger child, the parent will be charged with child abuse.

When my younger daughters would visit me they would boldly tell me, "Mommy, we have been told not to listen to you and when we are older, we will understand more." However, when I would put them to bed in the evening, they would talk for hours telling me of abuse issues in the home and how they felt safe in talking with me. They shared with me that their father was often on the phone in his office and wasn't available to talk with.

On one occasion, one of the children's neighbors and friends, Mrs. Marilyn Gaines, heard my younger daughters express some of the abuse issues in the home regarding their father and some of the people responsible for their care. Mrs. Gaines was so disturbed by their statements she wrote her phone number inside their shoes instructing them to call her if they ever needed help.

In October of 1998, I signed an "At Risk" form with the district attorney's office in Polk County, went into hiding and moved out-of-state. This ended my attempts at visitation. I was concerned that trying to see my children was hurting them because Mr. Warner used my visitations to manipulate and degrade me. Psychologically, the children would be spared being used as pawns by Mr. Warner to harm me. On visitations my children would ask if we could all run away together. I said that was impossible. I did tell them several months before I left the state that because of the present circumstances I would have to leave and may not see them for a long time.

I shared an analogy with a judge during a hearing with my eldest son regarding issues with visitation. I told the Court that during World War II, Nazi soldiers would strap American P.O.W.'s to the front of their tanks. As their tanks approached American soldiers, the American soldiers had two choices: either shoot at their own men to protect themselves or be taken over by the enemy. None of us are prepared, psychologically, to make either of these two choices.

My physicians were supportive of my decision to seek safety. They also understood the possible repercussions that would arise as I sought freedom and safety from my ex-husband's power and control. I continue to believe that an abused individual should not have to <u>ask permission</u> from our judicial system to seek safety and wholeness, and should not have to fear repercussions for doing so.

I moved out-of-state and experienced some success in my beeswax art business. The pain I felt from the loss of my children by my being several states away and unable to see them was even more severe than the abrupt removal of my children in March 1996. This time I knew I may not see them until they were adults–if and when they decided to find me.

My 17 1/2-year-old-son, Aaron, had a job in Salem, and chose to stay in Oregon and move in with friends. I continued to help support him financially and emotionally through the years. Even though I was living in hiding, I gave my minor children my P.O. Box address and my voice mail. After my move, one of my twin daughters left a disturbing message on my voice mail stating, "*We will find you, Mother!*"

> I share with my counselors that I have compassion for my ex-husband and abusers because I respect their soul journey and understand that for what they know, they are doing the best that they can. I basically perceive them as disabled. I learned I could remove myself from their path and their toxicity so I didn't get destroyed by their fears and lack of understanding of who they truly are.

I tried, by phone, to reconnect with my mother after my move. She told me, "It is your fault you lost your children." She also said, "Kathy, you should be taking care of me." I realized that this relationship was also too toxic for me. I choose to have no further contact with my mother, but I did send her letters and gifts, though, and wished her wholeness and peace. She passed away in 2010. I have found I function best in mutually accepting relationships. These past years I have learned the value of letting go and walking away from anything or anyone that keeps me from healing.

At the same time, I went into hiding, I investigated getting child support adjusted because the twins, now nineteen years old, were living out of the home and I had been awarded custody of my 17-year-old son, Aaron. Deputy District Attorney Martha Hill, in Dallas, initiated efforts to get my child support payments lowered. Judge Brockley, fully aware of my circumstances, gave me permission to testify by a phone hearing for my safety and mental well-being.

In November, I participated, by phone, in a hearing regarding the child support issues. Several weeks later, I received a court order, signed by Judge Brockley, nullifying my privileges to testify by phone, although my circumstances had not changed. This was confusing to me and my physicians. Mr. Daniel Van Eaton, my ex-husband's attorney, and Mr. Warner, moved the Court for an Order for disqualification of Judge Sid Brockley from further proceedings. For reasons unknown to me, Mr. Warner and his attorney, Mr. Van Eaton, had Judge Sid Brockley disqualified from further involvement in the proceedings.

My ex-husband and his attorney obtained numerous court orders against me. One Court Order demanded my address while I was living in hiding! (I could be reached through my voice mail and P.O. Box.) Another Court Order was for me to submit to a psychological exam. I wondered why. I had no contact with the children or my former husband and I lived out-of-state. I started losing hope and felt *this would never end.*

One motion for contempt against me stated that I had disobeyed the provisions of the Judgment of Dissolution of Marriage by not providing my physical address. They also alleged that I had made derogatory comments about Mr. Warner and asked the Court to impose upon me the maximum financial sanction sought–$3,000.00. (I had not been living in the State of Oregon for several months!) After my last Court hearing regarding these orders January 25, 1999, I began to write my story and document my experiences in my marriage and the Oregon judicial system.

My ex-husband and his attorney were contesting my child support payments being lowered by the State of Oregon. My support payments were automatically being paid through a bank. Deputy D. A. Hill advised me to drop the case for support modification. She reminded me that the Court would traumatize me again, and Mr. Warner's attorney would hurt me. She asked me if this was worth another breakdown. In other words, since the Courts, my ex-husband and his attorneys have a history of being harsh with me, I should seek no justice.

Dr. May has stated that my situation is one of the most extreme and violent cases of abuse she has encountered in her twenty years of psychiatric practice. She was present at one of my court hearings in January 1999 and observed the oppressive nature of my court hearing. Judge Luukinen was presiding. Mr. Warner was represented at that hearing by Mr. Daniel Van Eaton.

I was representing myself and had no legal counsel. Judge Luukinen told me to get an attorney. I told him that was impossible and that no attorney will represent me because of the bizarre nature of the case, their fear of possible reprisals from Mr. Warner and my former unpaid attorney bills. The judge repeated himself and told me to get an attorney. I felt so overwhelmed and exhausted, I broke down and wept. Dr. May calls this case "obscene" and the individuals in the court system in Polk County "toxic."

Dr. May, an expert and scholar in the field of domestic violence and abuse, explained to me why people project blame on the victim in regards to domestic violence and abuse. She shared that people are ignorant about the complex dynamics of domestic violence and/or they just don't want to know about something that is uncomfortable to look at. People are often threatened by something they do not understand and project their discomfort on the victim. She added, "Coral, pity them for their insensitivity and their blind spots."

Dr. May met with me and my friends, during this time, to talk about what I should do in the midst of my present court trauma. I took Dr. May's advice one day and just walked away from the court trauma, leaving Mr. Warner and his attorney to find someone else to play court with. I was tired. I could not continue to play the role in the script Mr. Warner and Mr. Van Eaton had written for me. I thought I could walk away and start a new life. I was wrong. My ex-husband and his attorney were just beginning to legally stalk me. If I did not show up in court, there would be bench warrants for my arrest. Since 1995, I have had to participate in forty-two court related hearings due to my divorce. In 1999 my physicians suggested I leave the country to save my health and life.

> I came to understand the Scriptural proverb, "In the multitude of counselors there is safety." There was wisdom imparted by all my mentors and counselors. The Circle of Life became more apparent to me as I saw the synchronicity in my call for help to the Universe, and how various individuals were placed in my path to assist me.

Mr. Van Eaton sent me a deposition notice that arrived *after* the scheduled hearing. District Attorney Hill dropped the case. I was unable to afford an attorney. I was not represented in Court and lost by default several months later. As a result, I was counter sued by my husband for *his* legal fees of $3,311.27, my visitation rights were officially removed and my child support payments were doubled to $1,074.00. Judge Luukinen increased my support payments based on the facts presented by Mr. Warner and his attorney. Their facts were lies. This all happened as a result of the State of Oregon initiating efforts to lower my child support payments. A Court Order now reads that visitation rights were removed from me (their mother) for the *best interest of the children*.

In January 1996, Mr. Warner and his attorney, Mr. Lawrence, stated to the Court that Mr. Warner was able to care and support all eight children, including a nursing infant. They said they would prove I was emotionally unfit to be a mother because I was mentally ill. To this day, I wish my attorney, Mr. Gearing, would have asked Mr. Warner, while on the witness stand, his personal definition of mental wellness for me. Mr. Warner's task was to prove to the Court, in whatever way he could, that I was "crazy." What other reason would I have for leaving him? Mr. Warner also continued to state, in court, that he wanted me back. I humorously shared with friends and attorneys, "Why would a good father want a crazy woman to raise his children?"

Now, the great contradiction is child support. I do not understand how Mr. Warner and his attorneys expect someone they claim to be "mentally and emotionally unfit" to be self-sufficient and pay over $1,000 a month in support. There are numerous affidavits and sworn statements by Mr. Warner to the Court, in his own words, regarding my fragile mental health and my previous mental/breakdown. Then in December 1998, Mr. Warner and his new attorney, Mr. Daniel Van Eaton, sent me a Court Order for a psychological exam!

After receiving an onslaught of judgments and court orders from Mr. Warner's attorney, an advisor gave me this excerpt from *The Merchant of Venice* by William Shakespeare for encouragement and humor. "This is the kindness I'll show. Come with me to a solicitor. Sign your irrevocable bond, and–for fun–if you don't repay me on such a day, at such a place, such sum or sums as are in the contract, let the forfeit be agreed for a full pound of your fair flesh, to be cut off and taken from whatever part of your body I choose."

I moved back to Oregon in February 1999 to take care of my legal difficulties. In the summer of 1999, I again moved out-of-state.

> Trauma has left me with limited physical, emotional, and financial reserves. It has been difficult to heal while I have had to represent myself and participate in Court the past few years. Even though Mr. Warner and his attorney play "Christianese" and continue their legal maneuvers through the court system, I continue to believe that someday this will end.

> A court order could prohibit this man from coming near me, but by manipulating the legal system, my former husband is harassing me as truly as if he was stalking me in person. Since their religious belief system condones their actions towards me, I do not believe Mr. Warner and Mr. Van Eaton will be satisfied until they "break me." They believe their vindictive god needs to punish me and they are the vessels here on earth to do God's will.

In June 1999, I contested the judgments on child support and judgments for attorney fees recently filed against me. My physicians sent affidavits to the judge in regards to my health and recommended I not appear in Court. However, the fact that Mr. Warner can continue to threaten me through the judicial system and that he has the power to harm my children is doing more to keeping me on the slippery slope than anything else. (Please see attached document listing the court orders, affidavits, hearings, motions, etc., related to my divorce case from 1995 to 1999. It is eight pages, single spaced.)

During this time, I wrote letters regarding my case and sent documentation to Governor Kitzhaber, Margie Boulee of *The Oregonian*, Gloria Allred, Attorney at Law in California and to local and national media. Tashi Smith, a school teacher in Oregon involved in my case, wrote Pastor Ron Sutter, Mr. Warner's pastor. I wrote to Pastor Sutter, Mr. Brian King, an elder at my ex-husband's church, Pastor Sutter's wife, Mrs. Marijo Sutter, and George and Ellen Callen, a couple from my ex-husband's church who initially became very involved in my case, but never heard back from any of them. (Ms. Smith's letter to Pastor Ron Sutter is included in documentation.)

My doctors diagnosed me with Complex Post Traumatic Stress Disorder due to decades of abuse, torture, sexual assaults/molestation, rape, ritual abuse, cult "brainwashing, and finally court abuse and trauma. Complex Post Traumatic Stress Disorder (C-PTSD) is a combination of PTSD and Stockholm Syndrome. In 1998, my physician signed a certificate of disability for me because of my fragile mental condition. Fragile is not mentally ill. Fragile means: easily broken, easily destroyed.

Post-Traumatic Stress (PTS) is a psychological and emotional response to the traumatic events of a person's life. It affects hundreds of thousands of people who have survived natural and man-made disasters, war, inner-city violence, domestic violence, rape, child molestation and abuse. In the past PTS was referred to as shell-shock and combat fatigue.

Trauma survivors find themselves re-experiencing the trauma in their mind. There are many symptoms including an agitation and a constant state of being on the lookout for danger, night terrors, flashbacks, avoidance of places or people which remind them of the traumatic event, irritability, feeling trapped, emotional shutdown or numbness, a feeling of being disconnected from the world around them and the things happening to them. Survivors can't control these feelings or stop them from occurring. The brain and body respond to traumatic events in a very intense physiological way. Traumatic events overwhelm the usual methods of coping that give people a sense of control, connection and meaning. Trauma survivors and combat veterans can feel an overwhelming sense of powerlessness, the belief that nothing can be done to stop the flood of violence, terror, war and explosions that they experienced and witnessed.

There are coping skills, however, to help one empower oneself and own and embrace one's own trauma.

I have learned there is a mystery in healing from trauma. There is something there–the past trauma–that needs to be processed, healed and resolved.

> There is a positive that lays in the negative of the traumatic experience. When we are triggered and re- experience the trauma, we are given the chance to let light into that room and see the experience emotionally and spiritually. As we embrace our trauma, it becomes our *medicine*–a positive force. "**Making light of the dark**" is the binding force that can help empower you. When we understand that, the violence no longer owns us. The traumatic experience is revealed and knowing this you are at peace–the trauma is no longer a threat to your present consciousness.

> PTS helps us make resolution with the past. We must ride with it, not run from it. PTS is not only a mental experience, but is a spiritual and karmic experience, as well. Once you address the trauma clearly, own it and recognize it, you can release the impact of what occurred and what is not serving you. The past has no business in the present. The memories are painful, but they can't hurt you.

> Until healing and forgiveness takes place, we hold our own soul hostage. To heal, we must dance the opposites, forgive and be forgiven. To heal, we must relive the experiences in our emotions and transform the trauma–" **make light of the dark.**" We then heal ourselves by embracing the pain body within us.

> "To know ourselves in our greatest darkness is our opportunity to heal that part of ourselves that we least choose to experience.

To find our balance we must know our extremes. We must know how we respond in the darkest of the dark as well as the lightest of the light, and embrace both, to heal the judgment of our experience and find the power of our truest nature."
–Greg Braden, *Walking Between the Worlds: The Science of Compassion*

"That which does not kill you will make you stronger." –Friedrich Nietzsche

At a 2006 court hearing in Polk County, with Judge Paula Brownhill presiding, Mr. Warner was awarded the 12% interest on the $4,900 child support debt, so another $1,200 was awarded to him. My passport is now permanently revoked because of past due child support. Mr. Warner has attempted to get my driver's license suspended in the past due to child support owed.

I find it incomprehensible to pay my abuser huge fees in child support. It would take away from my integrity and would definitely thin my soul. I believe that there is nothing that can happen to me behind bars that hasn't been done to me already. I am encouraged by the promise in Isaiah 54:17 "No weapon formed against you shall prosper."

> My script for my life involves wholeness, dignity, honor and self-respect. I avoid participating or involving myself in anything that would thin my soul. My vow to myself was first stated by Booker T. Washington, "I will never allow any man to drag me so low that it would cause me to hate (or despise) him."
>
> The shame of my abuse lies upon the community who refuses to help or stop it. Domestic violence and abuse begins in the minds of a community that allows and accepts it.

As I began to seek the Truth that would create wholeness for me, my mentors assisted me in remembering who I truly was apart from my trauma. They taught me how to respect and honor the sacredness of my being.

Together, my counselors, physicians, mentors and friends have all brought me from a devastating past to wholeness. Through their assistance, I am in touch with the wildish part of my soul, again. Most of all they helped me understand Dr. Viktor Frankl's wise words, "To live is to suffer, to survive is to find meaning in the suffering." I am thankful for my past because it has pushed me to reach a higher level of consciousness and a deeper awareness of who I am.

> "When we heal the imbalances created from our past wounds and embrace life from our present viewpoint, we see our experiences from a new perspective. Eventually, if we can let go of the past, we are able to be authentically grateful for our wounds, our harrowing experiences, and the brutality that we may have endured. Through healing those wounds, we become *healed healers* who have embraced our own suffering and transformed our lives. Healed human beings stand tall as examples for others. Nobody can belittle the life of a healed healer. The human being who has authentically healed his or her past has an unshakable, intimate knowing of the value contained in the journey of healing the self and in the bravery required of all spiritual warriors." *Dancing the Dream: The Seven Sacred Paths of Human Transformation*

Since escaping my husband and the religious circles that surrounded our family life, I no longer experience panic attacks, insomnia, migraine headaches or mental breakdown.

"The mind is never right but when it is at peace within itself."–Lucius Annaeus Seneca (4 B.C.-65 A.D.)

In these past years I have learned that I have a right to live without fear, to be treated with respect, to have and express my own feelings and opinions, to be listened to and taken seriously, to set my own priorities, to say "no" without feeling guilty, to ask for what I want without reprisal, to ask for information from others, to have my own needs met, to have privacy and support and friendship.

Bearing Witness

This truly happened to this beautiful, wonderful woman and mother. I can never fully explain to all of you how horrendous this was. Not only did I try to help Coral, her husband was my supervisor at the time and I was battling my own personal hell with Warner in the work place.

He was a disgusting, sexist man, who had no business supervising women in any capacity. He tried/did talk to me "privately" about Coral (captive audience) and my heart ached for her. I didn't even know her at the time and I was sickened for her. I only had to deal with him at work, she had to live with him in her own personal prison!!

It's hard for me to revisit in my mind and memories working for him [Marty Warner]. I was stressed, anxious, and depressed all the time. I don't know how Coral has survived his lies, abuse, sick ideologies, losing her children (yes, I delivered the girls into his hands when she lost her court case, and still remember the screaming and crying coming from my back seat when they were pulled away from their mother).

I've seen Coral Theill go through pain and suffering at the hands of Marty Warner, and the court system that would drive most people insane. I've seen her lose everything in this world that could possibly matter to her except her hope that justice would eventually come to her aid. I've seen Ms. Theill pick herself up time and time again in her attempt to right an extreme wrong. I've read Coral's book she's written in an attempt to help other victims of domestic violence and hopefully explain to her children why she is no longer in their lives.

I've sat back and watched and listened as time after time she's been denied justice and human compassion from the very people who say they are advocates for domestic violence.

I submitted to the courts an affidavit that documents the abuse I suffered at Hewlett Packard from Coral Theill's ex-husband, Marty Warner, in the hopes that the legal system will understand what happened to Coral Theill is real, is cruel and continues. (*Affidavit is included in Coral's memoir).

I know it's real because I lived through eighteen months of emotional and mental turmoil, fear and doubt in my professional abilities at the hands of the same man that brought his wife to a state of emotional and mental breakdown.

I salute you Coral, want nothing but happiness for you, and grew to love you very much. - *Debbie Custis*, April 15, 2015, Fr. Hewlett Packard Employee, Oregon

"Neutrality helps the oppressor, never the victim. Silence encourages the tormentor, never the tormented. Sometimes we must interfere." – *Holocaust survivor, Elie Wiesel*

X

Filed Marital Rape Charges Against Mr. Warner, Marital Rape Laws, Domestic Violence is Encouraged and Condoned by Christian Leaders, Dominionist Christians

In March 1999 and May 1999, I filed criminal rape charges against my former husband in Dallas, Oregon, (Polk County) with Deputy Sheriff Terra Wilson, and The Dalles, Oregon, (Wasco County) with Police Officer Jeff Miller. At the time of the rape and assault, I was living apart from my former husband with my brother and healing from a mental/nervous breakdown I had suffered after my seventh child was born. In October of 1994, Mr. Warner picked me up from my brother's house, took me to a motel and forced me to have sex while I was in a nearly catatonic state. I became pregnant.

While I was being interviewed and taped by a Polk County Deputy Sheriff about the marital rapes I had suffered, Polk County Deputy Sheriff Bernie F. Krauger walked by and made an inappropriate comment to me. *"What took you so long to report the rapes?"* he said. I will never forget his ignorant and rude comment. I hope Polk County Sheriff Mark Garton will use my own story to train his deputy sheriffs and staff so no rape victim is ever shamed and treated like this again. I highly recommend the documentaries, *"Unbelievable"* and *"The Keepers"* as well as my published memoir, *BONSHEA Making Light of the Dark* - a local Polk County story - as educational tools for all law enforcement and court officials.

Sergeant Steve Baska, from The Dalles Police Department, investigated and documented the evidence and facts of the rape I reported to them. In June 1999, Sergeant Baska called me and told me that the documentation of the rape was on the desk of District Attorney Donna Kelly. The district attorney told him that they would not prosecute because "a jury would never convict a husband of rape." I believe District Attorney Donna Kelly is not in touch with the views of the community. I know the community feels differently. Many people are appalled, outraged and disgusted about this case, but are afraid to confront my abusers because of fear of reprisals.

Law makers, attorneys, district attorneys, police and society suffers from "rape illiteracy." There is manipulative rape committed by dates and husbands and intimate partners, not to mention fathers and uncles, babysitters and teachers. There is rape that is quietly coerced under threat, there is rape that is cooperated with in order to survive, there is culturally proscribed rape, and there is rape without physical force. It is all still rape.

Many people believe rape is justifiable, if the husband commits rape. Even though our laws say differently, many prosecutors refuse to "enforce" them.

Police informed me that a crime had been committed against me and that the laws are written to protect people from criminal acts being committed against them. If the District Attorney will not prosecute documented cases of rape, then the law should be removed from their books. It confuses the general public when they are informed about written laws, but then see the criminals who committed the crimes suffer no consequences.

Rape Count I as described in Chapter 743, Oregon Laws 1971, 163.375:

Rape in the first degree. (1) A person who has sexual intercourse with another person commits the crime of rape in the first degree if: .... (d) The victim is incapable of consent by reason of mental defect, mental incapacitation or physical helplessness. (2) Rape in the first degree is a Class A felony. (1971 c.743 s.111; 1989 c.359 s.2; 1991 c.628 s.3)

(3) "Mentally defective" means that a person suffers from a mental disease or defect that renders the person incapable of appraising the nature of the conduct of the person.

(4) "Mentally incapacitated" means that a person is rendered incapable of appraising or controlling the conduct of the person at the time of the alleged offense because of the influence of a controlled or other intoxicating substance administered to the person without the consent of the person or because of any

other act committed upon the person without the consent of the person. (5) "Physically helpless" means that a person is unconscious or for any other reason is physically unable to communicate unwillingness to an act.

While the legal definition varies within the United States, marital rape can be defined as any unwanted intercourse or penetration (vaginal, anal or oral) obtained by force, threat of force, or **when the wife is unable to consent** (Bergen, 1996; Pagelow, 1984; Russell, 1990). On July 5, 1993, marital rape became a crime in all 50 states, under at least one section of the sexual offense codes. In 17 states and the District of Columbia, there are **no exemptions from rape prosecution granted to husbands.** Oregon is one of the 17 states.

Dr. Raquel Bergen, in her document, "Marital Rape," writes, "Despite the fact that marital rape has not been criminalized for long in the United States, it is clearly a serious form of violence against women and worthy of public attention. The research to date indicates that women who are raped by their husbands are likely to experience multiple assaults and often suffer long-term physical and emotional consequences. Marital rape may be even more traumatic than rape by a stranger because a wife lives with her assailant and she may live in constant terror of another assault whether she is awake or asleep. Given the serious effects, there is clearly a need for those who come into contact with marital rape survivors to provide assistance and challenge the prevailing myth that rape by one's spouse is inconsequential."

Dr. Bergen also writes, "In a study of battered women, Bowker (1983) found that they ranked clergy members as the *least helpful* of those to whom they had turned for assistance. The emphasis of some religious institutions on wives' responsibility "to obey their husbands" and the sinfulness of women's refusal to have sexual intercourse with their husbands, perpetuate the problem of marital rape. Most researchers of marital rape agree that rape in marriage is an act of violence - an abuse of power by which a husband attempts to establish dominance and control over this wife. While the research thus far reveals no composite picture of a husband-rapist, these men are often portrayed as jealous, domineering individuals who feel a sense of entitlement to have sex with their "property."

> I do not understand why the criminal actions of my ex-husband were not brought up by attorneys during my civil divorce trial. Both Mr. David Gearing and Mr. Mark Lawrence were aware of my previous breakdown and my pregnancy at the time of

my breakdown. I believe injustice and negligence has been committed by these attorneys.

"A Florida legislator who opposed criminalizing rape in marriage stated, "The state has absolutely no business intervening into the sexual relationship between a husband and a wife." In other words, the state has legally created that relationship and has protected the husband's forced access to the wife. It is this conception of privacy–keeping the wife sexually subjugated to the husband as a matter of law–that cloaks the abuse of wives in legitimacy and a secrecy that stops interference. The right of a man to use his wife the way he wants has been the essential meaning of sexual privacy in law." Andrea Dworkin, *Intercourse*

This is where domestic violence originates. Conforming to this ideology contributed to my mental/nervous breakdown in 1993. Dworkin also writes, "Anyone whose legal status is that she exists to be touched, intimately, inside the boundaries of her own body, is controlled, made use of: a captive inside a legally constructed cage." In 1979, Bob Wilson, a state senator from California, while talking to women lobbyists eloquently stated, "But if you can't rape your wife," the lawmaker asked, "who can you rape?" The answer, of course, is "no one."

In these cases, intercourse remains the fundamental expression of male rule over women, a legal right protected by the state especially in marriage. My case speaks loudly of the insidious crimes that are legally permitted and condoned under the guise of state-sanctioned domination of males in marriage. Laws must be changed to protect vulnerable people who cannot protect themselves. Presently, women prisoners around the country are winning lawsuits against guards who have raped and impregnated them. One woman prisoner was awarded $100,000.

Until our country becomes more healthy-minded in matters of sexuality, rape cases will continue to be a horror for women in America. In our country, sexuality is often synonymous with power, control, possession and ownership.

In 1893, Matilda Joslyn Gage, author of *Woman, Church and State*, wrote, "An investigation of the laws concerning woman–their origin, growth, and by whom chiefly sustained–will enable us to judge how far they are founded upon the eternal principles of justice and how far emanating from ignorance, superstition and love of power, which is the basis of all despotism." Matilda Joslyn Gage was a committed abolitionist and leader in the National Woman's Suffrage Association. She was adopted into the wolf clan of the Mohawk nation in 1880. Her courage in almost single- handedly standing up to the oppressive forces of right-wing Christianity led to Gage being written out of official suffrage history. Gage gave up her place in history in the fight for religious liberty.

District Attorney, Mark Hesslinga in Polk County told Deputy Sheriff Terra Wilson, from the Polk County Sheriff's Office, that he did not want my case investigated. The district attorneys in Polk and Wasco counties have ignored my case and not responded to my letters and phone calls. Consequently, they are sending a very strong message to children, young adults and the

community that sexual crimes and violence committed against women will be ignored and tolerated.

"Today, the men as a body politic have power over women. They decide how women will suffer: which sadistic acts against the bodies of women will be construed to be 'normal.'"

–Andrea Dworkin, Intercourse

As the years passed by, I gave up hope for a healthy relationship with my children because of their father's religious view of women and his disrespect towards me. My children were told by their father and his religious supporters that I am "sick, wicked, evil and immoral." They were told that I abandoned them. They attended Santiam Christian School near Corvallis, Oregon, and were taught the same Christian principles that have oppressed woman and children for centuries.

I asked Mr. Warner why he would not allow me to participate in the children's school activities Mr. Warner replied, "You are an enemy of the cross of Christ."

Mr. Warner's Christian supporters taught my own children to shun me. According to their interpretations of their rule book - the Bible, these misled Christians decided what rights I have. They treated me with the same disdain they believed their god has for me.

I moved out-of-state after two years of trying to see my children under Mr. Warner's restrictions and the court order. It became increasingly difficult and too painful for me to hear my young children's cries for help. My ex-husband used visitation as a means to control me further. He could use the children to punish me. Since my divorce, no one outside Mr. Warner's family and limited church community has been allowed to help my children sort through the past, their parents' divorce and their mother's former psychiatric episode.

During the earlier years, I strongly believed my children needed professional help. Two of my daughters had suicidal thoughts, another daughter spoke of running away, an older daughter hit, kicked and smothered the younger children and spoke of wanting to kill me (according to the other children). My youngest son, Zachary, screamed at the end of my visitation weekends and often had to be physically removed from me. This broke my heart and even though he was less than two years old, I'm sure he bears scars, too. The only "help" my children received was purification sessions with religious counselors. My eldest twin daughters have not spoken to me since before my divorce in 1997, their choice.

Dr. Gabor Mate teaches that we have two basic survival needs: attachment (since we cannot take care of ourselves at birth so must have a caregiver) and authenticity (the ability to be in touch with and trust our own innate gut knowing- so we can perceive and deal with or leave dangerous situations.) Often children discover that following their authentic gut knowing and instincts threatens attachment with their caregiver (who may be embarrassed or angry and insist the child do what they are told.) Children often learn to sacrifice their authentic connection to their own inner knowing to preserve the attachment upon which their life depends. Gabor Mate, M.D., is author of, "*In the Realm of Hungry Ghosts: Close Encounters with Addiction*"

I was distraught over the fact that I was forced to give up my children so they could remain in a dysfunctional household fraught with abuse. Since there was no intervention, my children will learn the art of manipulation and lies to survive. They will be conditioned and learn to keep family and church secrets. They will be unable to hear the voice inside that we are all born with that tells us when we are *not safe* and that tells us we have value.

I have not seen or had personal contact with my five minor children since 1998 The pain I continue to feel is far beyond tears. I am comforted by the words in Psalm 50:15, "Call upon me in the day of trouble; I will deliver you, and you shall glorify Me." Each day I hope that my grief will subside, but it continues to feel raw. I believe in the words of Isaiah 61:3, "He will give them beauty for ashes, the oil of joy for mourning, the garment of praise for the spirit of heaviness."

Sarah and Rachel both married in the summer of 2001, each marrying young men they met at their father's church. They informed me, by letter, of their wedding plans and that I was not invited. My mother, grandmother, brother and aunts, uncles, and cousins were invited to attend their weddings. I am not welcome in my daughter's lives.

I hope they receive professional and spiritual help someday. They were with my abusive mother when she died in 2010, but failed to acknowledge that my mother had and been a predator/pimp to me as a child. My twin daughters and son-in-laws consistently support predators and dismiss victims.

On February 18, 2000, I spoke with an assistant in Governor Kitzhaber's office briefly about my case and the past four years of trauma in Oregon's judicial system. She suggested I get an attorney. I shared with her that I cannot find anyone to represent me because of the complicated and bizarre nature of this case; my unpaid former attorney bills and court related fees amounting to over $150,000.

She also suggested I contact a State Representative. I shared with her that one state representative, Betsy Close, had been involved in my divorce case and is a close friend of my ex-husband. My ex-husband and Betsy Close hold many extreme religious beliefs in common. They, most importantly, believe divorce is a sin. Her testimony in court reflected this religious viewpoint and hostility.

I wrote the Governor's Council on Domestic Violence about my concerns regarding domestic violence and the marital rape charges I had filed with the Polk and Wasco County Sheriff and Police Departments. Several months later I received a letter from Renee Kim, Grants Coordinator for the Oregon Department of State Police.

Ms. Kim wrote that the Council did not have an answer for my very difficult situation. She also stated in her letter that the Council "has learned that the Polk County criminal case was not filed because the district attorney believed there was insufficient evidence to prove the charges beyond a reasonable doubt. The criminal justice system must approach the suspect as presumed innocent and can only proceed with charges when there is substantial independent evidence, which can prove the case. The civil divorce case, which had a much lower burden of proof, allowed a lot of negative attacks against you and most of that evidence would be used against you in testimony in any criminal case."

Domestic violence is a complex problem with roots in an oppressively hierarchical, patriarchal violence-accepting society. I believe that domestic violence is a crime. Yet, fundamental evangelical Christian movements (cults) that thrive today refuse to speak out against domestic violence, rape, incest and abuse because their doctrines are the foundation for conditioning women and children to accept abuse.

In America domestic violence is still acceptable. People are living in ignorance about this subject...even in the churches.

I agree with Matilda Joslyn Gage, a progressive visionary of women's rights and human liberation in the late 1800's, that the Euro-American patriarchal Christian/Catholic religions are the root cause of violence in our society today. The greatest obstacle to woman's freedom and equality lies in the teachings of the church: that woman was created inferior to man, brought sin into the world and is therefore under an especial "curse." I know these teachings to be false and support my statement with my life testimony and documentation.

One cannot read the Bible story of Hagar and not think of those who live among us who are oppressed and voiceless. Hagar fled her abusers, but God sent her back to a brutal and oppressive environment. From the perspective of Hagar, God is not a liberator of the oppressed. If we do not speak on behalf of the oppressed and abused or give a voice to the voiceless, we are not neutral.

I have asked numerous people throughout the years if they ever heard an in-depth sermon from the pulpit -Christian/Catholic/Jewish - **on Domestic violence, rape and childhood abuse and molestation.** So far, 100% respond "no." I never heard any sermons or teachings on these topics in all my forty years of "church going" - but these events were occurring in my life. When I sought help from abuse, pastors and priests told me, *"You need to learn how to submit and obey your husband."* As a child I was taught to *"obey my parents, teachers and elders."*

Some Christian theologians, such as the Rev. Marie Fortune and Mary Pellauer, have raised the question of the close connection between patriarchal Christianity and domestic violence and abuse. Steven Tracy, author of *Patriarchy and Domestic Violence* writes: "While patriarchy may not be the overarching cause of all abuse, it is an enormously significant factor, because in traditional patriarchy males have a disproportionate share of power. So while patriarchy is not the sole explanation for violence against women, we would expect that male headship would be distorted by insecure, unhealthy men to justify their domination and abuse of women."

Teachings of Jesus: Compassion and Unconditional Love

Progressive Christians believe in the teachings of Jesus – a message that speaks about love, compassion, empathy, forgiveness, acceptance, helping the unfortunate and living nonviolently. They believe Jesus' teachings contain nothing misogynistic, homophobic, nor do they condemn divorce, contraception and abortion. Progressive Christians are "pro-life," in contrast; **legalistic fundamental Christians are merely "pro-birth" - hypocritical fraudsters.**

Progressive Christians understand that love and fanaticism are incompatible.

Fundamentalist Christians have a very literal and legalistic interpretation of the Bible. They believe that the Bible was written by God, and that all of the genocide, war, slavery, misogyny, homophobia and other loathsome things were authorized by the Almighty and that defines their political beliefs. They use prayer for selfish and narcissistic purposes and profess a sanctimonious piety and a total sense of superior existence. From football to indicting weather events as the will of God, these people are devoutly delusional.

Progressive Christians, on the other hand, have a different perspective regarding the beliefs about the Bible. They see the Bible as a set of documents written, edited, translated and selected by humans. Prayer is more about a spirit of gratitude and often inspires acts of generosity toward others.

Legalistic fundamental Christians many times are prejudiced and excessively insular. They often pass their prejudices onto their children. Some, who are in

167

positions of power, impose narrow views on us all, causing wars and political strife. The worst part is these people have fierce motivation and they are not going away. Dominionist, (a movement of politically active conservative Christians in the United States working toward either a nation governed by Christians or one governed by a conservative Christian understanding of biblical law), and fundamental Christians have a deep, dark, abiding sense of purpose.

The late Francis Schaeffer, Sr., Jerry Falwell, and Rousas John Rushdoony are a few of the Christian leaders who promoted the Christian Dominionist and Theonomy movement. Christian Dominionist such as Sarah Palin, Michelle Bachman, Rick Santorum, and Pat Robertson believe that the United States is "one nation under God," with the Bible **and their beliefs** trumping existing law and the Constitution - *America's version of the Taliban.*

Pat Robertson has even suggested beating a wife as punishment for her disobeying her husband.

Dominionist and legalistic Christians, "The Tea Party," John Birch society and others manipulate their members to stop worrying about poverty, compassion, helping the downtrodden and injustices and rather focus on politically marginal issues like homosexuality, contraceptives and abortion. They would like the public to be sex-obsessed against women rather than discussing real political issues. Fighting to take away women's rights is more important to fundamental Christians and the Pope than stopping pedophilia and greed. The ideology and rhetoric of anti-abortionists reflects their contempt of women and their need to punish "female fornicators." but not men.

> "I distrust those people who know so well what God wants them to do because I notice it always coincides with their own desires." - *Susan B. Anthony*

Thirty years ago, Rushdoony shared his views with Frank Schaeffer, Jr., "We must establish God's kingdom by degrees. We can't start by saying that God demands that we put homosexuals to death! We need to begin with things like helping form home schools and electing our people. Someday we'll be in a position to establish *biblical law in America.*"

Dr. James Dobson, *Focus on the Family,* is perhaps one of the most powerful figures in the Dominionist movement. Former Alaska Governor and vice-presidential candidate Sarah Palin is living proof that a female misogynist can exist - someone that doesn't want other women to think for themselves, *but wants them to think as she does.*

America was founded on principles of greed, religious intolerance and slavery. Christians like to rethink the reality to make it sound better but the Pilgrims came here because they were "better" than the fallen masses of Britain and Europe. Instead, they created a land where women and children had no rights, where people could be bought and sold and where blacks were only partially human. Four hundred years later things are still pretty backward. As a society, we are slow to look at our own mirrors and shadows.

The fundamental Christian conservatives want to "take us back to the good ole days." The so-called "religious right" believes that Christian values will save society from its sins. Each person should seriously study and learn how the Christian Church has attempted "to save" societies in the past.

For the past 1,000 years white Europeans and Euro-American "Christians," have been on a planet wide rampage of conquering, plundering, looting, exploiting and polluting the Earth as well as raping and killing the indigenous communities that stood in the way.

Americans eliminated tens of millions of Native Americans so effectively that Adolf Hitler considered it a model for purging Germany of Jews and other undesirables.

In the late 1690's the Christian Church revived witch trials in Salem, Massachusetts, instigating a reign of terror on women. Many believe this widespread church and state-sanctioned torture and killing of "witches" set the stage for modern society's acceptance of violence against women. (See *Burning Times* Film Documentary)

America fostered the Ku Klux Klan and African-Americans were subjected to decades of lynching, racist violence and Jim Crow Laws in their communities without the protection of the government. We, a Christian nation, seized the property and imprisoned Japanese American citizens during WWII.

Jeff Sharlet exposes the far-right conservatives and the "elite" fundamental Christian establishment in society in his book, *The Family: The Secret Fundamentalism at the Heart of American Power.* In public, they host Prayer Breakfasts; in private, they preach a gospel of "biblical capitalism," military might, and American empire. Citing Hitler, Lenin, and Mao as leadership models, the Family's current leader, Doug Coe, declares, *"We work with power where we can, build new power where we can't."*

Sharlet's discoveries dramatically challenge conventional wisdom about American fundamentalism, revealing its crucial role in the unraveling of the New Deal, the waging of the cold war, and the no-holds-barred economics of globalization. The question Sharlet believes we must ask is not "What do fundamentalists want?" but "What have they already done?"

Part history, part investigative journalism, *The Family* is a compelling account of how fundamentalism came to be interwoven with American power, a story that stretches from the religious revivals that have shaken this nation from its beginning to fundamentalism's new frontiers. No other book about the right has exposed *The Family* or revealed its far-reaching impact on democracy, and no future reckoning of American fundamentalism will be able to ignore it.

Domestic Violence is Encouraged & Condoned by Christian Leaders

The work of James Dobson and John MacArthur perpetuate the problem of domestic violence among evangelical Christian families. They are dispensing life-threatening advice to abused Christian women. "Both Dobson and MacArthur are high-profile evangelical leaders with enough influence and ability to make a positive contribution to the plight of battered women which would result in lives being saved." Instead, "their words are often used to send Christian women back into the danger zone with counsel that encourages them to try and change violent husbands or return to violent homes as soon as the 'heat is off.' The last time I looked, assault was a crime, **but Christian women are generally not encouraged to report that crime."** – Jocelyn Anderson, *Woman Submit! Christians and Domestic Violence*

In her book, *Trauma & Recovery*, Judith Herman, M.D. explores the cultural dynamics of collective repression and denial and why people tend to shun and try to silence trauma survivors.

How our culture regards trauma and traumatized people is very important to those trying to become reintegrated into society after massive psychic shock.

Judith Herman maintains that the function of domestic violence is to preserve male supremacy. **"Perpetrators understand intuitively that the purpose of** their behavior is to put women in their place and that their behavior will be condoned by other men [women] as long as the victim is a legitimate target. Thus, women live with a fear of men which pervades all of life and which convinces women that their weakness is innate and unchangeable.

*"The legal system is designed to protect men from the superior power of the state but not to protect women or children from the superior power of men. It therefore provides strong guarantees for the rights of the accused but essentially no guarantees for the rights of the victim. **If one set out by design to devise a system for provoking intrusive post-traumatic symptoms, one could not do better than a court of law.**"*

I will always treasure the memories and joys of motherhood. Being abused by my husband, his cults and their leaders, and enduring violence, is not a part of God's marriage covenant. I believe when there is violence and cruelty; the marriage covenant is permanently severed. Mr. Warner, at the time of our divorce and to date, found his support from family members, the community, the judicial system, and pastors, elders and church members at Bridgeport Community Church,

Their church doctrine did not believe I had a right to divorce. Crimes of violence are supposed to be endured. **It disturbs me that many Christians cannot find compassion in their hearts for victims of violence (women and children), due to their strict *adherence to church theology.***

I have concluded that many individuals who embrace anti-abortion ideology and legislation regarding "legitimate rape" truly do not love babies or mothers – their rhetoric and laws are about contempt of women and their need to punish "fornicators."

Throughout Euro-American history, women and children were considered legal property, the chattel, of the father or husband. By taking his name, the wife "belonged" to her husband. Today, women and children are not legal property, but attitudes have been slow to keep up with the law and many men still believe it is their right or privilege to control women. I experienced, first hand, the truth of this statement when I sought safety from my husband and left with my youngest children and baby in January 1996.

A few months before I finally left my husband, I had gone on an extended trip (without Mr. Warner) with my younger children, and nursing infant to attend the funeral of Betsy Close's father. I was sane and strong enough to make this trip, and encouraged by Mr. Warner to take the children and my nursing infant. When I left the home seeking safety from my ex-husband a few months later, I was labeled mentally ill, psychotic, suicidal and emotionally unfit to be a mother and became a "criminal" to be hunted by the Sheriffs.

At my temporary custody hearing, my attorney, Mr. David Gearing, in his opening statements to the Court, February 28, 1996, said, "Her, (Mrs. Kathy Warner), custody is being challenged now, willfully, intentionally, with full knowledge and with acknowledgment of her husband as to her qualities for 20 years. She has been fit, proper and capable of doing that for twenty years. And, now, we are calling into question her emotional stability and mental health and ability to raise these children. She has been given that role. It is a distraction. We have three doctors who are ready, willing and able to testify, on rebuttal, if necessary. They give her a clean bill of health."

Some attorneys and advisors believe that the Circuit Court Judges of Oregon used me as "an example" to show what they do to women who defy their power.

> "Liberty is the only thing you cannot have unless
> you are willing to give it to others."
> –William Allen White

Bearing Witness

I am often angered by the so-called religious who are very quick to minister to offenders but pay no attention to the victims the perpetrators leave in their wake. Anyone who does not get involved with helping victims and stopping offenders from committing acts of violence or manipulation perpetuate the problem. Unfortunately, government and the legal system in this country have bent over backward to protect offenders for fear of punishing someone who is innocent rather than focusing on the innocent who have been injured by offenders. An awakening of mega proportion is needed for everyone to stand up and demand that violence be stopped. - *Ray Ramirez*, Crime Victim Advocate, Texas

BONSHEÁ engaged my attention immediately, and then enraged me. The author has endured huge suffering at the hands of brutalists hiding behind the masks of pseudo-Christianity and "justice for all." The author continues to stride toward the light in her own life-at huge personal cost-and to bring her story forward for all to consider and act upon. – *Karen Goldammer,* South Dakota

"Learning how to be kind to ourselves, learning how to respect ourselves, is important. The reason it's important is that, fundamentally, when we look into our own hearts and begin to discover what is confused and what is brilliant, what is bitter and what is sweet, it isn't just ourselves that we're discovering. We're discovering the universe." - Pema Chodron, *When Things Fall Apart*

XI

Stigma Associated with Mental Illness, Invisible Victims

Mr. David Gearing stated that he believed my case would have been handled differently if I had been healing from cancer instead of a nervous breakdown. Dr. Jean Furchner, my custody evaluator stated in her report to the Court, *"There is little in the current situation that will foster any respect for the mother...the emotional message of derogation is the issue."*

> Our country needs understanding and compassion to lessen the stigma of mental illness. People recover and heal from mental/nervous breakdowns just as they do cancer or a broken leg. I have met many individuals who have recovered from breakdowns who are productive members of our society. I have observed one admirable trait in all of them, compassion.

"It is not the mentally ill we should be concerned about, as it is the carriers." – Dr. Charles Kuttner

After my divorce, I experienced emotional healing from alternative forms of medicine including cranial sacral and reiki treatments from massage therapists, Myra Cook and Vicki Allsop. Reiki is a system of healing in which the healer acts as a conduit for divine light. I believe these treatments are successful because they provide safe and healing touch. During these treatments I felt emotionally safe with my therapists and was able to experience and release grief. (More information can be found in the book, *Hands of Light: A Guide to Healing through the Human Energy Field* by Barbara Ann Brennan.) In my life, the only safe and unconditional love and human warmth had been from my children. Their absence left me shattered. Together with their skills and compassion, these two women helped put me back together.

Vicki Allsop shared these words of wisdom with me, "You can live without food for forty days, you can live without water for eight days, you can live without air for twenty minutes, but you cannot live thirty seconds without hope."

Trauma and abuse contribute to mental/nervous breakdowns. Over ninety percent of women in mental hospitals are believed to be the victims of childhood sexual abuse.

> "Women who were physically or sexually abused in childhood may suffer for a lifetime from a distorted response to stress," reports *The Dallas Morning News*. Researchers at Emory University in Atlanta compared stress hormone levels and heart rates of women who had previously been abused with those of non-abused women while the women were performing a stressful task. Those who had suffered child abuse showed markedly elevated levels of stress hormones and increased heart rates in response to stress. The researchers conclude that, "there may be a permanent biochemical disruption in the way their bodies respond to and regulate stress," states the newspaper.

Christine Pahl, MS, LPC describes the complexity of trauma with this analogy, "Trauma is like an open wound on the arm that is cut deep and infected. Too frequently "treatment" only covers the injury making it appear to heal from the outside leaving the infection still festering underneath the scar. When someone inadvertently touches the "scar" the person reacts. The severity of the reaction depends on the amount of infection. If someone is living in a toxic environment the infection of the wound is compounded and the assault on the wound continuous."

People fear and are threatened by that which they don't understand. During the two years of my mental illness, my ex-husband, Christian and Catholic friends, family and counselors treated me as a cursed and "demon-possessed" woman, instead of a woman suffering from years of childhood and marital abuse and physical exhaustion.

Dr. Sandra L. Bloom, author of *Creating Sanctuary* argues that psychic health is virtually impossible in our society because we have become desensitized to violence, we have normalized repression, and we have created institutions that repeatedly traumatize the most vulnerable among us. She dares to define violence as more than sexual, emotional, or physical abuse. Allowing our citizens to go hungry or homeless, denying them a quality education or medical care, and tolerating laws and policies that perpetuate these conditions are all forms of violence. Bloom suggests that these hostile acts – unaddressed, regulated, permitted, accepted - are perpetually shaping our culture and threatening the very possibility of our healthy existence. She writes, "For the most part, we have lost our awareness of the true social nature of human existence, of tragic consciousness.... Within our segregated, individualized, demystified, and fragmented lives we avoid resonating with the suffering of others. We are not our brother's keepers."

When my mother learned of my breakdown, she told me God was punishing me because I had not obeyed her and served her "enough". The word enough became the buzz word for my breakdown. I wanted to die because I could not work faster or give more. "Enough" was beyond my reach.

> While living with an abusive partner or parent, you carry an enormous amount of guilt because you can never get it right or perfect for them. You run faster, but it is never fast enough. Counselors and professionals have shared with me that my mother and ex-husband are the ones that belong in a mental hospital or prison.

A close friend of twenty years, Cindy Haugland, shunned me and treated me as if I were refuse during this time. I wasn't a part of her religion. In her opinion, that was why I was suffering a mental breakdown. I have since come to realize that people often accuse and project on to others the shadows within themselves.

A few years later, after my divorce, Cindy's young son, Eric Haugland, and her parents, Mr. and Mrs. Gene Fowler, watched her bully and humiliate me because I did not adhere to her legalistic Christian ideology. I left their home and never returned.

The reason people awaken is because they have finally stopped agreeing to things that insult their soul.

Betsy Close, phoned me, during the time of my illness, and told me that God had cursed me. She sent me numerous letters exhorting me to repent. (I have copies of her letters to this day.) She disapproved of my taking medication (low-dose tranquilizers) during my illness. In her words, "Kathy, taking tranquilizers will open you up to demonic strongholds." She and her husband, Chris, participated in a Pentecostal cult in Corvallis, Oregon. I tried to caution her of the dangers of this cult, but she dismissed my warnings. Her views extend to prejudice against anyone who does not conform to her fundamentalist doctrines.

Some people cannot give up their hatred because it would force them to look at their own pain.

"We don't see things as they are; we see things as we are." Talmud

<hr />

Presently, no one seems to have the ability or the authority to help me become truly emancipated from my former husband, Mr. V. Martin Warner. There are still outstanding judgments, court orders and contempt orders hanging over my head that could eventually land me in prison. Also, no one has had the ability to get help to the children. Some people's choices give others no freedom. This country will never experience liberty until all citizens are free and safe.

I want to be emancipated from my ex-husband and the Oregon courts.

In August 1999, Mr. Warner's attorney, Mr. Daniel Van Eaton left a message on my voice mail stating that Mr. Warner may agree to settle out-of-court regarding some of the court orders, contempt orders, etc., if I would sign a document stating I would stop my book writing and contacts with the media. (I have a copy of their voice mail message). He said that if I did not agree to their request, they would continue their court actions against me. I never returned the call.

In the years that followed, while I lived under an address protection program, my ex-husband "hunted me." My neighbors in Montana were contacted by Mr. Warner's investigators inquiring about my whereabouts and activities. I left Montana so he could not find me.

Since my divorce hearings, I have suffered four physical (not mental) breakdowns from exhaustion. I have left the country twice (Denmark) and seriously contemplated not returning because of legal and emotional trauma. I returned to America to write this story with the hopes that eventually the community would respond to the injustices I and others have encountered within the judicial system. It is time for a champion who will advocate for women and help right some of these wrongs before others must endure this kind of destruction.

New legislation is needed that would promote the safety, wellness, and wholeness for women, children and families involved in domestic violence and abuse incidents in Oregon and throughout America.

> Legislation is needed that would allow mediators, physicians, mental health providers and guardian ad litems whose expertise involves domestic violence, rape, child abuse and molestation issues to preside over court hearings. This bill would change the present laws regarding Circuit Court Judges presiding over court hearings (in Oregon State) and put decisions in the hands of those trained to understand these issues.

> The rights of young children and infants in domestic violence situations and divorce cases need protection. A Guardian ad litem and/or a child advocate should be appointed to represent the best interest of the children.

An "Address Confidentiality Program" under the Governor or Attorney General's office, to protect victims of sexual assault, domestic violence and other crimes of violence, needs to be put in effect in all states.

Legislation is needed that would encourage extensive education programs relating to abuse issues and violent crimes against women and children in schools, colleges and police academies. Although a majority of calls that police respond to are related to domestic violence, it is reported that police academies offer only sixteen hours of domestic violence training.

"The sad fact of twentieth-century history is," as Albert Einstein remarked, "that the development of our technology has out-stripped the development of our humanity to the extent that an unparalleled destruction of human life was made possible in the form of the Holocaust." This has been my personal holocaust.

Holocausts and suffering are caused by society's indifference. Elie Wiesel says, "indifference to suffering makes the human inhumane." Evil is the absence of empathy.

The once carefully guarded problem of domestic violence and the judicial/law system can be compared to the Jewish Holocaust. The holocaust in Germany was not caused by Hitler. James Redfield writes, "Hitler could do nothing without the cooperation and support and willing submission of millions of people. At some degree, the larger group of the German society allowed itself to remain indifferent and apathetic to the suffering of the Jews. It was the "collective consciousness" which provided the fertile soil for the growth of the Nazi movement. Hitler seized the moment, but he did not create it." *The Tenth Insight*

Bearing Witness

Coral Theill's **BONSHEÁ Making Light of the Dark** is a "must read" for all interested in women, women's health, children, and our court systems. I find myself going back, again and again, to re-read parts that strike so close to my heart. Coral is such an utterly honest voice telling of a deeply caring person that has traveled an unforgettable journey in life. This story reaches out to anyone that reads it. It touches lives in a remarkable way that is most profound. It deeply saddened me to realize that in this day and age, violence in the shelter of one's home, under the guise of religion is condoned and sanctioned. It is unbelievable that our local court would sanction the removal of a nursing infant from the mother. Domestic violence is tolerated by our society and in the courtrooms. It continues as a "silent violence." Coral has told a sad, truthful story to her children and the world to enable them to make this a better place for everyone to live. – *Jean Weisensee,* R.N., Oregon

Coral's book, **BONSHEÁ** is the most unbelievable document I've ever read. It's mind blowing to realize that women are still being treated as chattels in the 21st century in today's modern America. As long as we buy into religions, government, and judicial systems that are patriarchal, and treat men as demigods, this will continue. I felt like my heart was being ripped out of my chest when I read about Coral's children being taken away, especially her breast-fed baby. This is a mother's worst nightmare. I don't know how Coral managed to live through this and have the wherewithal \to write this manuscript. She is an amazing lady that has earned my respect and admiration. – *Marti Barnard,* R.N., Alaska

Is it being overly simplistic to find it incomprehensible that with such extensive public knowledge regarding the horrendous crimes committed against Coral, not one attorney has been willing to stand up and help this woman fight to see that justice is served? - - *Rieve Rockwell,* Pediatric LVN, *California*

"The outstanding achievement of twentieth century physics is not the theory of relativity with its welding together of space and time, or the theory of quanta with its present apparent negation of the laws of causation, or the dissection of the atom with the resultant discovery that things are not what they seem; it is the general recognition that we are not yet in contact with the ultimate reality. We are still imprisoned in our cave, with our backs to the light, and can only watch the shadows on the wall." - *Sir James Hopwood Jeans* (1877 – 1946) English physicist, astronomer and mathematician

XII

Closing, Matilda Joslyn Gage, Women, Church and State, 1893

In November 2000 I had a brief conversation by phone with Mr. Warner. My eight-year- old daughter had sent me several letters asking me to please call her. She stated that she missed me and needed to hear my voice. I asked Mr. Warner if he could change the court order that prohibited my contact with the children, so I would be able to call Hannah. (In the spring of 1999, Mr. Warner and his attorney presented a court order to Judge Luukinen to remove all my visitation rights. I was not represented and was unaware of the hearing. Judge Luukinen signed the Court Order.) Marty's reply was, "Kathy, I told you what I would have to do to you if you did what you said you were going to do"– (leave him, divorce him, seek safety, equality and write this book.)

From education of Afghan schoolgirls to veiling in France, female sexuality and freedom has come to symbolize a global conflict "over the nature of the self," argues David Jacobson, a University of South Florida sociologist, in *"Of Virgins and Martyrs: Women and Sexuality in Global Conflict,"*. He writes, "In an honor society, patriarchal and tribal traditions dictate that a woman's body belongs to and serves the community. An interest-based society privileges self-determination, the sovereignty of the individual over her body, and ownership of one's own capital, be it economic, cultural, or social."

> Mr. Warner believes an individual needs to have "permission" from him and "authorities" to leave and seek safety. He does not believe in individual harmony and peace. He believes in seeking obedience and worship from those around him. His mother expected this behavior from him, he expects it in turn from his family.

> When people have been abused or used up by others, it is difficult to find your balance and center. Our energy has been exploited and we continue to give ourselves away. Our abusers convince us through manipulation and lies that we are under an obligation to be abused and used. When an individual escapes abuse, they find wholeness and they find their center and balance, their home. Their center becomes their Universe, not the abuser.

In the phone conversation Mr. Warner said he wanted to meet with me alone at a restaurant. I told him that would not be possible. He said we had made a commitment together and to the children and that he wanted to work on figuring out a way we could "co-parent" the children. I said that I did not agree with his parenting methods or religious beliefs. He said we would have to work out a detailed plan of my intentions with the children for future phone contact. I said my intentions were love. He said we would have to meet with his attorney. End of conversation. Last contact. I wrote my daughter, Hannah, that I was sorry I could not call her that I would try to send her a tape recording of my voice.

Shortly after our phone conversation, I received a letter from Mr. Warner dated December 5, 2000.

He merely states that, "You have shared with me, both in our conversations and in your letters, and have demonstrated, that you currently do not share the same values or spiritual perspective as those of our family. That certainly is your prerogative. However, due to our present significant differences in values and faith, it is understandably difficult for you to be supportive of our family's goals, values, and vision. Consequently, your interaction with the children tends to bring about considerable confusion, disharmony and, though you certainly do not intend it, is quite disruptive and counter-productive. Please forgive me if this offends in any way, for I certainly do not intend it so. Rather, I am trying to answer your question and practice discernment and judgment concerning the effectiveness and fruitfulness of your calling or visiting with the children at this time. *(Brainwashing is only effective as long as there is no outside interference.)* I want the children to always have the fondest memories of you as their mother and to honor and respect you."

> The fact that I do not agree with Mr. Warner's patriarchal and cult mentality does not make me unspiritual or a bad role model for my children. I believe that teaching my children healthy thinking patterns regarding abuse issues is disruptive and inconvenient for Mr. Warner, not the children. In America, a parent can be banned from seeing his or her own children because they do not attend a cult or condone cult behavior.

Mr. Warner and his supporters and family members told my children that I was crazy, mentally ill, wicked, evil and immoral, not under the "blood of Jesus," and that I had abandoned them and joined a motorcycle gang.

We are often asked to "respect people's religions." In the first place, many religious ideas are very disrespectful to human beings and are not worthy of respect. Secondly, what about people respecting our religion in return? How can one respect a religion with ideas that harm other human beings?

> In his December 5, 2001 letter Mr. Warner further added, "I have gained considerable insight in all that I have been through and from other couples who have gone through marriage and relational difficulties as they go through their 40's and 50's. I thought I would share them with you for your consideration and reflection. This is a time (the 40's and 50's), especially for a woman, when her body is going through significant changes and hormonal adjustments, often with devastating impacts on her perspective of life and the world about her. This is definitely is not unusual or abnormal. Certainly, a woman should not feel guilty or that there is something wrong with her when this occurs.

> "Several women and couples have been helped greatly by working with their doctor, taking appropriate hormonal supplements to naturally regulate and balance their hormones

during this frightening and challenging time. They have found that they did not need psychiatric or mood modifying drugs, but rather natural and healthy hormonal supplements to assist their bodies in self-regulating during these few transitional years, thus allowing them to have a restored and focused perspective on life and the world about them. I thought this was quite insightful and thought you might find it encouraging, also. I wish you well and keep you in my prayers. I would be happy to talk with you if you ever have a desire." Sincerely, Marty Warner

After six years of separation and divorce, Mr. Warner still felt a need to "instruct" me in women's issues. His statements reflect his deficiencies of truly understanding the real issues. I was not menopausal yet—just somewhere in between estrogen and death!

In 2002, I wrote to Dr. Kuttner in reference to my seeking visitation and asked,

> *"If my children are living in this "world" where they have learned "to protect their captor," what would me coming into the picture do to this set-up—for them psychologically?*
>
> *"These are heavy questions and I don't know the answers. I feel led to attempt to bring light back into their lives. I know their captor will do all he can to extinguish any light in their camp. Is this all too dangerous and foolish?" – Coral Anika Theill*

Dear Coral,

"I know how much you long to give those children a life-line from their P.O.W. camp. But, as you know, you're not in a position to rescue them. So, I think that not only you, but those children, are at risk of a great deal of pain. Marty will find ways to punish them, confuse them, confound them for every bit of positive emotion they may have toward you.

"I think the metaphor you have to use is that they are chained in prison, that you can't unlock the chains, and that it's not a matter of your visiting; you're having to tear them partially from the chains. They will be left, still in chains, but broken and bleeding by the time Marty is done with them.

"I really am aware of how much you want to do the right thing for them. I think it's better for them to have a concept of you as a distant, possibly despised woman who shows little signs of reaching out to them, e.g., by any letters you get through, etc., than someone they have real contact with. Again, I will stress: it's not as though their jailer-father was a reasonable person.

"It's a tragic situation that is not fair to either you or the children. Alas, that's the way it's been for these many years and will so remain. Treasure Aaron. He understands." - Charles H. Kuttner, M.D.

I wrote my children letters and sent them gifts each month, until Judge Paula Brownhill signed a court order in December 2003 revoking my right to send them letters, cards or gifts. I do not know if they received the items I sent them. I have shared by letter to my children that I will be here for them when they reach the legal age of eighteen, and as each child reaches eighteen, I have offered to support them in getting professional help in dealing with the events of their childhood. They have not responded.

> I am grieved that my children had to witness their mother's breakdown. Although, psychologically scarring for them, I did not plan my breakdown or wish that they would have to suffer.

> I realize some of my children view me as someone who ruined their life and family. I honestly believe that the life they had before my breakdown was more psychologically damaging, i.e., witnessing a man's (their father) absolute control over his wife and children.

> The Universe could not support that—something had to shift. My breakdown was a catalyst to a balancing of power.

In May and June of 2001, I received letters from a friend, Debbie Dresler. Here are some excerpts from her letters.

Dear Coral,

"It is totally unimaginable how that man (Mr. Warner) can destroy his children's hope and security to try to punish you and maintain the image he holds of himself in their eyes. I hope some day they can get to a place of help and healing. I do believe what you said about your inability to stop him from hurting them. Revenge is such a controlling force in his life. I doubt that he can see the world from anyone's point of view than his own and would never even wonder if his behavior hurts them. Any outsider can look at that situation and bleed emotionally if not physically. I don't believe it is in him to even consider that a perspective outside his own driven nature has any validity. There isn't much hope in that outside of prayer.

"I believe that you were an excellent mother and loved your children very much. You always had a special way with children–you were fun, patient, gentle and interested in them as individuals. What a tragedy that they are robbed of that relationship.

"If you are in touch with a relative who has any contact with the children, perhaps that person can convey that your door is always open to them when they are of an age to exercise their own options. Aaron did. Perhaps the others will find that path when it is available to them.

"I don't wish many people "peace" because it sounds so trite and "60's" but I genuinely wish that for you." - Debbie

My sixteen year-old daughter wrote me a letter in July 2001. I had not heard from her for almost three years. She shared that her father "didn't do anything wrong."

She further writes, "He (God) has a plan for you too, mom. If you would just listen to him and surrender your life to him. Oh mom, please, God has so much in store for you, he wants to be a part of your life. You just have to surrender your own will and give it all to Him. There is hope for all of us, mom. You can never go too far. God wants all of us to draw close to him. He will take away our old sinful hearts and will replace them with new shining clean ones. We can all have a fresh start. Oh thank you Jesus, for dying for me and for taking away all my shame. Satan wants me to have a crummy life and he'll do anything to make me suffer but I won't let him have a stronghold in my life because he has no place in me, no power over me, and no unsettled claims against me. Because all has been settled by the blood of Jesus. Praise the Lord!!" Theresa writes, "I forgive you for all you've done to us (the family). You make me cry. I love you and will be praying for you. Your daughter, Theresa

I sent a reply to Theresa the following week. I thanked her for her letter and told her I was sorry that she felt I had failed her. I told her that I valued her opinions, feelings and thoughts. I wrote her, "There is not one moment I do not think of you with your well-being in mind."

Not Allowed to Attend my Brother's Funeral

The court order sought by my ex-husband and abuser, denying me visitation privileges in 1999 also created complications in July 2009. I was not permitted to attend my own brother's funeral. My brother's pastor reported that my ex-husband was attending the funeral, as well as my younger children. According to the Oregon Court Order, I could be arrested for attending the funeral due to being in the same vicinity of my younger children - a violation of Judge Paula Brownhill's court orders. I emailed the pastor my eulogy for my brother's service.

I believe the courts and churches that are so adamant in punishing women who seek safety have not yet realized the long-term ramifications for the victim. As a child, I could not have imagined that Court Orders, due to my ex-husband's wrath, would prevent me from adequately grieving for the loss of my only brother and sibling. Only in America.

Morality is not determined by the church you attend nor the faith you embrace. It is determined by the quality of your character and the positive impact you have on those you meet along your journey.

Coral Theill at Modern Day Marine Expo 2012

We are as Sick as Our Secrets

In 2003, my ex and his attorney filed a Motion of Contempt against me due to attending my sixteen-year-old son's football game at Santiam Christian School, at my son's request. At the game, my ex-husband violently abused my 11-year-old daughter, Hannah. There were many witnesses, including me; charges against my ex were filed with the Corvallis Police Department, children and parents shared their testimony. The abuse charge against Mr. Warner was dismissed due to Mr. Warner's and Hannah's testimony that "nothing happened." Children living with abusers learn that accepting abuse and keeping quiet is "safety." Secrecy and denial become a way of life. A few years ago, my ex-husband served as a foster parent for a troubled 15-year-old boy from Bridgeport Community Chapel.

In the years that followed, due to severe brainwashing, my children shun me and some of my children have written me "religious hate letters." My adult children have invited batterers, rapists and child abusers/molesters to their weddings and events, but I, their mother who protected them, am not welcome.

My eldest daughter, Rachel, was married in 2001. Her husband, Jesse White, posted a comment, July 16, 2007, on one of Tim King's published articles about my life story expressing his complete disbelief of the facts - asserting that my life story was a lie. He defended my ex-husband, Mr. Warner saying, "*I do not believe I have met a man that has influenced more people in a positive manner.*"

Jesse White wrote, "The enormous pain that has been caused by those of you who think you know the truth by reading a one-sided story is a serious injustice. The hurt and pain that my wife has to live with, brought on by her mother, and now recurring with comments posted by those who do not seek the entire truth saddens me to no end."

In response, many people posted comments addressed to him. In the correspondence which followed, my son-in-law, Jesse White, continued to believe I had caused more pain to my children by publishing my story and that I should have left out their true identities. To this, I respond, "*Abuse deserves no privacy.*"

I agree with the words of Judith Herman, M.D., "Without some form of public acknowledgement, all social relationships remain contaminated by the corrupt dynamics of denial and secrecy."

Half-truths are not enough, and my hope is that someday my children will find the truth in this book and they will understand why their mother, *who loves them deeply,* is not in their lives. It causes me pain every time I think about the new families that are being told so many lies about the missing mother in the family.

Response to Jesse White's Letter by Debbie Custis, July 16, 2007

Coral's son-in-law, Jesse White wasn't in the Warner's life nor was he in court for the proceedings during the time Kathy (Coral) was being abused by Marty and the court system in Oregon. I was. I also worked with and for Mr. Warner. Trust me, he can "just flip on an internal switch" when he feels it's necessary to appear to be a well-adjusted, upstanding member of the community. Feel fortunate that you're not a "woman" and that Mr. Warner feels no need to "control" you!

You didn't see Coral with her three youngest children, her patience, the love and the bond that was so clearly there for all to see while she was in hiding from her husband, living from hotel to hotel, with no money, and no food, entirely dependent on friends and yes, even some strangers that wanted to help her. It's easy to be kind, loving, and nurturing during the good times; Coral was all those things during the hard times as well.

You weren't there during the court proceedings. You didn't listen to the absolute absence of feeling for his wife and her trauma in his answer when the judge asked "why would you continue to have marital relations with your wife in her current physical and mental condition." I was there. I was also outside the courtroom walking the baby when I couldn't stand to hear any more of what he said in court.

You weren't there when the court decided to take Coral's children away. You didn't see a woman sobbing, rocking back and forth consumed with the kind of grief that only another parent could understand and yet, not wholly fathom.

You weren't there when we picked up the three youngest children and delivered them to Mr. Warner. You didn't hear the screams and sobbing of the two little girls in the back seat of my car on the trip to Mr. Warner's. You never had to watch a grief-stricken mother trying to pump painfully engorged breasts because her six-month-old nursing baby had just been wrenched from her.

Tell me something, what had Coral ever done to deserve this? Coral Theill was a warm and loving mother. She was also a good wife. To this day she loves her eight children deeply, even the ones who no longer call her mother. Coral was the sole nurturer, caregiver, and teacher in that family for many, many years. At least half of those wonderful, talented, children you speak of received their foundation from their mom.

It saddens and sickens me that all of the wonderful things the children learned from their mother; all of the warm and happy memories that should be Coral's legacy to these children have been tossed away like yesterday's garbage.

That, sir, is the real tragedy. – *Debbie Custis*

(NOTE: Letters to my son-in-law. Jesse White, from Judy Bennett, Coral Theill, Debbie Custis, Bruce McLelland and advocates are included in the "Letters" section, as well as Jesse White's letter to Tim King/Editor of Salem-News.com.)

In 2003, my daughter and son-in-law, Sarah and Ben Bobeda, InFaith Ministries, were present in court supporting Marty Warner, my ex-husband. At the time, I was homeless, destitute and disabled. They appeared to be pleased to hear I was sued for several thousand dollars and that I would not be allowed any further contact with my younger children. They did not speak with me and looked at me with contempt. By supporting Mr. Warner, they **condone rape, domestic violence, child abuse, molestation and court abuse.**

My children's pastors and school teachers have, unfortunately, encouraged their hatred and intolerance of me. (My mantra is Holly Near's song, *I'm Not Afraid*)

Although my children have erased me from their lives, I am not dead, I am very much alive, and I have a face, and a name.

I have been and will always be very involved in their life, even if it is only through prayer. I am praying that someday my children will choose to become "aware, awake and conscious" concerning details of their past and present and recognize that I have always loved them and tried to protect them. Their lack of awareness regarding their own life will greatly affect those around them. I pray my children will find good role models and mentors. I also pray that someday my children will find the courage to walk through the unpleasant details of their past.

I wish that divorce was only between adults, but the reality is divorce transcends the couple who took wedding vows, touching, and too frequently, hurting all those within the couple's family and community circle.

I wrote this letter in 2011 to my youngest daughters, Hannah and Rebekah,

> *"There has never been a day that I do not think about you and send you good thoughts and prayers. I am always praying for your highest good. Since 1999, I have lived under a "state address protection program" so your father cannot contact me. For years, I sent all of you gifts, cards and letters frequently, but from the questions in the letters I received from you, I do not believe you ever got them. In 2003, your father went to Court to revoke my right to send you letters and gifts. I continued to purchase birthday and holiday cards, but never sent them. I heard from others how very angry and disappointed you were with me. I do not blame you if you despise me, but I believe your anger is based on misinformation from your father, family, relatives, church members and school teachers."*

I also gave my daughters information on how to contact my friends so that they could learn, when they were ready, the "other side" of their own family history.

Many of the pastors and Christians my children have chosen to socialize and worship with, embrace and support their father, Mr. Marty Warner, a man who has committed criminal acts against his former wife and children. This does not support my children's well-being, only their delusion of themselves and their family.

M. Scott Peck, author, *People of the Lie*, explains, "It is not the sins of these people that lead to the label of evil (despite our feelings to the contrary at times) – because we have all sinned and fallen short of the glory of God (Romans 3:23) – but rather it is the 'subtlety and persistence and consistency of their sins. This is because the central defect of the evil is not the sin but the refusal to acknowledge it."

Throughout the past years of journey work, I learned that, 'Forgiveness is not the misguided act of condoning irresponsible, hurtful behavior. Nor is it a superficial turning of the other cheek that leaves us feeling victimized and martyred. Rather, it is the finishing of old business that allows us to experience the present, free of contamination from the past.' - *Joan Borysenko, Ph.D.*

You will never know where you are going unless you truly understand where you came from. It is important to take care of the "contamination of the past."

Benton County District Attorney Haroldson shared this profound insight: that while I escaped long term violence in my home, I was shot with a poison arrow in my back – the abrupt and permanent removal of my children as well as ongoing court trauma. He said, "Coral, you have left a legacy. Your published book, *BONSHEÁ*, is available to anyone you wishes to know the truth. Choose life!"

> Many children who have no contact with their protective parent have clear functional amnesia. They have no memories other than those created and re-created by the controlling parent. These children successfully re-program who and what they are outside as well as within.
>
> "What good is a conscience if it is not awakened?" – Harry Belafonte, *"Sing Your Song"*

I was not invited to my daughter, Theresa's, graduation in 2003. I bought her a beautiful Danish crystal candle holder and Hawaiian lei (garland). I asked one of Theresa's fellow students at Santiam Christian School to delivery my gifts to my daughter. As I left the parking lot, I saw my ex-husband and his relatives walking to the gymnasium to attend the graduation ceremony. They continue to support his abuse of me and my children.

On July 29, 2003, I received this letter from my daughter, Theresa, when she was eighteen.

> Mom,
>
> I am sorry but I don't think I am able or willing to write or contact you anymore. When I first started writing you I was excited and hoped things had changed, but as I've heard more from you I realize that you are still the same. I wish things were different but they aren't.
>
> By writing you I feel as though I have opened Pandora's Box and so many evil awful things are flowing out of it and I need it to stop. You are like that box holding terrible things within.

We are two very different people and hold dissimilar morals, qualities, values and attitudes about life.

You say to believe in the truth and the truth will set you free. I am free Mom, I believe in the one truth. Jesus also said, "I am THE way, THE truth and THE life, no one comes to the Father except through me." There is no other god, no other way to be saved. Until you believe in the one true God, you will be in misery, confused and deceived. Your past will continue to chase you nipping at your heels. **Satan desires to destroy you Mom and he loves what you are doing for him. He'll continue using you as a vessel and when he's through with you he'll tear you down and throw you away.** I grieve that things are this way but you are a discouragement to me and I don't want to hear from you until you have changed.

Sincerely,
Theresa

P.S. As for college issues, I have found a wonderful university that I can afford and Dad is bending over backward to help me out and provide for me. We are both working together to pay for it. Don't ever think badly of him, or think he is holding me back from doing what I need. You don't know what the situation is here.

(NOTE: At the time of Theresa's graduation, I was homeless, had a full disability, and destitute.)

My son, Aaron, lived with me when he was seventeen and nineteen and I paid for his medical, college, food and housing expenses, while I paid Mr. Warner child support for Aaron and children who were 25 years old. All in all, I spent over $25,000 from 1998-2002 in assisting Aaron, personally and in legal matters, until I could barely care for myself financially.

My daughter, Theresa Warner married Jason Arnold, son of Jay and Betsy Arnold, from Dallas, Oregon, in March 2008. They were married by Pastor Gregory V. Trull, a professor at Corban University and senior pastor of Valley Baptist Church.

I phoned Pastor Trull and asked why he did not contact me, her mother, in regards to my daughter's wedding. He was cold and aloof and said that my daughter wanted nothing to do with me. My youngest daughter, Hannah, is now engaged and it hurts to have no contact with her. It is difficult to be shunned by your children and to know that the family and church secrets are being perpetuated.

Rigid fundamentalists have no understanding of what trauma does to a person. They limit all issues to a spiritual realm to the exclusion of the fact that we are physical, emotional, psychological and spiritual beings. Fundamentalist still visit doctors for their physical ailments but psychological "wounds" are deemed "spiritual" issues in their camp.

When I am no longer here, who are my children going to hate and blame?

> "I imagine one of the reasons people cling to their **hates** so
> stubbornly is because they sense, once **hate** is gone, they
> will be forced to deal with pain." — **James Baldwin**

In my search for wholeness these past years, I embraced spiritual truths that bring peace to my life. I believe these truths to be universal – compassion, peace, non-judgment, and unconditional love.

As I live out my life today, I am still disturbed by the actions of many abusive people from my past, especially those involved in my court trials. My counselors became aware I was reaching wellness when I could acknowledge that the way I had been treated was not correct. It would not be correct for anyone.

I value my life, respect myself, and I believe I am equal to others. I am most disturbed by the fact that I had to seek, beg and ask for permission from the judicial and religious society, to get safe. No individual should have to seek permission to get safe!

The physical, mental, and emotional toll of surviving the negligence, abuse and trauma from the individuals who are part of my story will last forever. Although I risked everything to escape from my ex-husband, and in some ways I lost everything, I have never been more sane or more sure that the choices I made were the only choices I could make and survive.

I questioned a judge's decision and power over me and saved my own life. In Oregon, a judge's "black robe" legalizes his right to commit cruel and unjust acts. Oregon gives judges the same absolute authority over me that a marriage license gave my ex-husband. So far, neither the judges, attorneys, hostile witnesses, nor my ex-husband have been held accountable for the cruel acts committed against me. Oregon's law system has given them all a legal right to commit acts that would otherwise be viewed as criminal, depraved and inhumane.

I believe Mr. Warner and his attorney received a twisted sense of satisfaction from the pain they caused in the many hours of depositions, hostility in Court and the sudden stripping away of my children. Neither they, nor the judges, and witnesses who twisted the truth in Court, have been held accountable for the damage they have done. The law protects them and gives them the right to legally abuse me.

In June 2001, I filed a formal complaint against Mr. J. Mark Lawrence, my former husband's attorney, with the Disciplinary Counsel's Office of the Oregon State Bar Association. In my letter I simply state that "Mr. J. Mark Lawrence failed to comply to the Oregon State Bar's "Code of Professional Responsibility – January 20, 2000" in regards to egregious actions towards me in Polk County Civil Case No. 95P-20689 and Case No. 95P-20693 in Polk and Marion County Courts between January 4, 1996 through October 15, 1996. I understood that this may be a futile attempt for justice, but I believe we must voice issues of abuse, even when they are legally accepted by our judicial system and the society. (Letter and complaint to the Oregon State Bar Association Disciplinary Counsel's Office and the Oregon State Bar's letter of response is listed in available documentation.)

I was informed by Kateri Walsh of the media relations department for the Oregon State Bar Association that Mr. J. Mark Lawrence had been admonished by the Disciplinary Counsel in 1994 and that there are several other complaints pending against him.

On August 2, 2001, I received a reply from the Oregon State Bar Disciplinary Counsel. The letter, written July 30, 2001, by Mary A. Cooper, Assistant Disciplinary Counsel, stated, "While you allege that your husband pressed his case solely to harass and maliciously injure you, that clearly was not the case. You and your former husband had significant issues between you relating to the custody of your children. These clearly needed to be addressed. Mr. Lawrence, as he was required to do under the disciplinary rules, vigorously advocated for his client's position. DR 2-109 (A) (1), is not violated under such circumstances."

"I reviewed the transcript of proceedings you submitted from a hearing on January 4, 1996, with a view to whether Mr. Lawrence's questioning was unethical (1). (1) I did not, however, review the many hours of videotaped and audiotaped material you provided the Bar inasmuch as you did not identify any specific part of those extensive materials that you believe support your claims. *(Note: I identified in my complaint that the evidence of my allegations would be found in these video and audio tapes.)*

"During that hearing, which addressed whether the court should leave in effect a restraining order you had obtained against Mr. Warner, Mr. Lawrence cross-examined you. The issue at the hearing was whether Mr. Warner had placed you in fear of imminent, continuing, serious bodily injury. You alleged that Mr. Warner had attempted to rape you at a time when you were suffering adverse health consequences from the delivery of your eighth child. Mr. Lawrence questioned you about your sexual relationship with your husband, in an attempt to demonstrate that you were mis-characterizing the nature of your husband's actions. He also questioned you with regard to a mental breakdown you apparently had in 1994, which led you to consult with various doctors and led to your eventual hospitalization. *(This is an inaccurate presentation of the facts by Mary A. Cooper.)* This line of questioning was apparently aimed at your credibility as a witness."

"Though obviously unpleasant for you, nothing about such questioning was irrelevant to the issues being addressed. Although I did not read or hear Mr. Lawrence's questioning of you regarding your molestation as a child, that issue too – in the discretion of the court – would be relevant to the issue of your mental health, which was a primary issue in the custody dispute." *(I am thankful, in my spirit that I do not agree with her opinions.)*

"It was an unfortunate fact that because your mental health was at issue, Mr. Lawrence was, with the court's permission, permitted to inquire as to matters which were intensely private and embarrassing to you. He did not act unethically by doing so."

"In light of the above, the Bar will take no further action on this matter at this time. Thank you for expressing your concern about one of our members. *(Copy was sent by the Bar to Mr. J. Mark Lawrence.)*

"There may be times when we are powerless to prevent injustice, but there must never be a time when we fail to protest." — *Elie Wiesel,* Nobel Laureate, and Holocaust survivor

After the traumas of childhood, twenty years of subjugation to Mr. Warner and his extreme religious views, a breakdown and rapes by my husband, the treatment by the courts was a **final outrage.**

I believe my human rights were violated by specific people, my husband and his attorneys, my attorneys who did nothing to halt the humiliation I experienced in Court, the judges who allowed the process to continue and supported the frivolous and unwarranted claims Mr. Warner made–his onslaught of court orders to try to force me to return–to maintain his control on my life, and the religious community that was so blinded by an abhorrence of divorce that they closed their eyes and their hearts to the truth.

I would like the satisfaction of an apology from all of these people. Restitution is not likely, but resolution is necessary. I did not believe I would survive the court trauma, but that does not mean I have given up on getting justice. I believe that if you do not seek or ask for justice, you are victimized twice. My children, who I loved, nourished and cared for and will always love, are still caught in a home that is not good for their hearts and souls.

> I do not and will never understand the society I live in today. During my breakdown I endured and survived much pain and crawled my way back to health. I was greeted by a society that literally slammed the door in my face.

There are individuals mentioned in my story who refused to acknowledge the horrors of my survival of marital abuse and my cry for help. They became an obstacle to my basic human rights – freedom and safety. I am holding them responsible and accountable for the continued trauma I have experienced throughout the past several years. I am requesting that the acts of disrespect, dishonesty and violence against me be acknowledged and resolved.

In my research and studies, I found a profound quote on responsibility and accountability in Lucy Dawidowicz's book, *War Against the Jews.* Her words accurately portray how I feel. I believe that many of the injustices of innocent people in this country are a result of specific individuals, especially those in power, ignoring their own responsibility in given situations. Dawidowicz writes:

"Responsibility means accountability or answerability for one's actions and their consequences. Historical responsibility is defined as an individual's answerability for committing or failing to commit acts that would have affected the outcome of any given situation."

When my children are adults and ask me what I did to help them, I will tell them, "I spoke the truth." When they ask me why my case remained unchallenged, I hope I don't have to tell them, "Nobody cared."

I will continue to share my truths in a legal and non-violent manner. Non-violence does not threaten. Non-violence leans until something, some day, moves. "Non-violence is a way of life for courageous people. Non-violence seeks to defeat injustices, not people. Non-violence always chooses love instead of hate. Non-violence holds that the universe is on the side of justice and that right will prevail. The goal of non-violence is reconciliation and the beginning of healing."–Mary Manin Morrissey

I have concluded, by my present circumstances, that the judicial and religious organizations and people who have aided my former husband all embrace the same views regarding women and children. They believe male power is absolute over women and great harm will come to those who question and/or defy that power. I believe this is the mentality that causes and perpetuates abuse.

In his book, *Man's Search for Meaning*, Dr. Viktor E. Frankl writes, "When we understand the *why* we can do any *how*." Understanding that our religious and judicial systems are based on patriarchal power and control has been the secret of my survival through these past years of horror.

Liberating myself through the power of forgiveness has been a continual strength.

People ask me what I have learned from the local religious and judicial systems these past 17 years. I candidly share with them that I have learned that in America's dominator society "my body is not mine, but belongs to the community that upholds male dominance and female possession and ownership. By being possessed (occupied) the female becomes weak, depleted, and usurped, in all her physical and mental energies and capacities by the one who has physically taken her, by the one who occupies her. Her body is used up, and the will is raped. In our society, *"masculinity is still measured by how well a man controls his wife in the house and his horse in the field."* – Andrea Dworkin

As a body of people, "a collective consciousness," we should be aware and conscious of where and to whom we gift our energy. If we continue to condone those in power who harm and victimize innocent people, then we will continue to witness injustices against those who are vulnerable and unable to protect and defend themselves. I believe my life and my experiences these past few years reveal a moral dilemma for the religious organizations and judicial systems that exists today.

I firmly believe that the Euro-American patriarchal Christian/Catholic religions are the root cause of violence in our society today.

Domestic violence is supported by the judges, district attorneys and law enforcement agencies and religious organizations who treat the victim (women and children) like a criminal and ignore reported crimes of violence. As long as our religious and legal systems remain complacent and unsympathetic towards women and children, domestic violence and child abuse will remain at epidemic proportions in Oregon and throughout America.

If we teach violence in our homes–these places that are supposed to be safe–these situations will lead to a violent society. The violence and pain in individuals, in families and communities, often reflects the violence and oppression we have experienced. People begin to act the same way they have been treated.

"An eye for an eye makes the whole world blind." –Gandhi

Historically, violence against women has not been treated as a "real" crime. This is evident in the lack of severe consequences, such as incarceration or economic penalties, for men guilty of battering their partners. Rarely are batterers ostracized in their communities, even if they are known to have physically assaulted their partners. It appears that "having a relationship with the victim" is an excuse for their crime.

> "Addiction to the drug of superiority and dominance is the deepest and most ignored underlying cause of male violence."
> Author unknown

Our judicial system is a product of the community we live in. The courts represent the prevalent views regarding women and children in our communities. Their judgments are a reflection of the patriarchal religious structure of this country today. The judges are the instruments of the local community "seizing the moment of power" that has been given to them. Although many people were appalled and shocked by the removal of my nursing baby per Court Order, the community stood by, watched and did nothing. I believe a majority of the religious community believed it was God's way of punishing me for divorcing my husband.

Christianity continues to encourage a fear-based authoritarian structure that has segregated people into positions of superiority or inferiority. This type of tyranny prohibits personal empowerment and demands unquestioning obedience and submission. Many people believe the judicial system in America is structured in the same manner as the patriarchal church system.

Albert Einstein spoke profoundly when he said, "The significant problems we face cannot be solved at the level of thinking that created them."

Unless we speak out against the injustices in our society, we become accomplices to the individuals and institutions that are an obstacle to women and children's wholeness, safety and wellness.

I choose not to participate in the silence that protects perpetrators and isolates survivors.

A judge's signature on a white sheet of paper can be a shattering experience for an individual. I believe judges in America will continue to use their absolute power until people wake up from their "huddled fear". When society responds from a higher state of consciousness spiritually and emotionally, they will desire a justice system that uses emotional and intuitive energy. Until then, our judicial system is best described by the slogan, "America–Where the criminal is protected and the victim harassed."

May these words of hope encourage you in your pursuit of truth, "A brighter day is to come for the world, a day when the intuitions of woman's soul shall be accepted as part of humanity's spiritual wealth; when force shall step backward, and love, in reality, rules the teachings of religion; and may woman be strong in the ability and courage necessary to bring about this millennial time." – Matilda Joslyn Gage, *Women, Church and State, 1893*

A mother does not forget her children.

"Our lives begin to end the day we become silent about things that matter."
- Dr. Martin Luther King, Jr.

Coral Theill at Silent Vigil at White House – Mother's Day, May 2010

"Patriarchy needs god to justify injustice." – *Nawai El Saadawi*

Epilogue

Invisible Shackles
by Coral Anika Theill

Most individuals prefer not to hear the story of how a cultured people turned a blind eye to consenting to the "legal kidnapping of children through America's family courts" and how the majority of our society, consisting of cultured people, remained silent.

Many women grow up in homes in which they were conditioned and groomed to be victims. They marry sociopathic abusers, have children with them, and lose custody and contact of their children when they become stronger and choose safety.

Nurturing and loving mothers losing permanent custody of their children is such depressing subject matter. But we cannot indefinitely avoid depressing subject matter, particularly if it is true.

Every day, all women in our society deal with male domination. Women are verbally intimidated, bullied, battered and killed by men, but our society is in a state of denial about the truth and severity of the abuse. Raising the consciousness of this violence against women is the beginning of what it will take to bring it to an end.

To heal and recover from violent crimes, survivors need the community to create the conditions for an experience of justice. Some experience of justice is the prerequisite for forgiveness and eventually for healing.

Susan Brown-Miller has said *"rapists are the shock troops of patriarchy."* It follows that the men who batter and psychologically abuse women are the army of occupation - forcing subjugation and servitude.

Gloria Steinem spoke about domestic violence at the 40th Anniversary of *Ms. Magazine* on October 11, 2012. *"The home and our country is the single most dangerous place for woman - it is not the street*," she said. "Since 9/11 there have been more women killed by their husbands and boyfriends than all the Americans killed in Iraq and Afghanistan and the 9/11 attack combined."

It is not hard to take sides against Al Quaeda; it is more difficult to take sides when the violence involves someone you know. A great deal of the trauma resulting from abuse remains private. Society accepts domestic violence as "just the way things are." Society does not experience the kind of urgency and outrage that followed the 9/11 tragedy.

Oprah Winfrey has shared on her program, *"America is the safest place in the world for women."* Tens of thousands of Americas "mothers of lost children" would be quick to disagree with Oprah's words. We bear invisible, but permanent battle wounds from years of abuse in America's family court system. Our mental scars and years of court documentation prove that seeking safety in America often costs more than money. The price of safety in America has been too high for all of us - it cost our children and our right to be a mother.

"Coral's story is extremely common in the U.S. today," said Patricia Evans, nationally known author of the books, *The Verbally Abusive Relationship, Verbal Abuse Survivors Speak Out, Controlling People, and The Verbally Abusive Man-Can He Change*, "Hundreds of thousands of fine, intelligent, loving, giving mothers have lost their children via the family court system.

"How can this enslavement be happening in the United States? Because power over the innocent is condoned. Power over those who have what one wants is condoned. Power over the poor is condoned. Furthermore, there is no oversight of the family court system, nor is there any standard for determining justice in custody cases."

The controversial PBS Documentary *"Breaking the Silence: Children's Stories,"* illustrates some of the ways a wealthy abuser can use the justice system as a tool of abuse. A non-custodial mother remarks: "to lose one's children in such a way would unmake any woman." And it is true. Taking a woman's children is the last great punishment an abuser can scar them with. **To be publicly and permanently branded 'unfit' is a new scarlet letter. It can and will scar an entire family for life.**

Many women who seek safety from long term abuse in America will lose custody and permanent contact with their children, especially if they have reported

206

criminal acts of abuse in their homes or have suffered from a serious depression due to the abuse. I believe individuals who support the removal of babies and children from good, nurturing mothers should be held accountable, legally and spiritually.

Experts at the Leadership Council on Child Abuse and Interpersonal Violence estimate that more than **58,000 children** each year are either placed into dangerous homes or forced to go on unsupervised visits with their alleged abusers by divorce courts that simultaneously deny the children's safe, protective parents' access to their sexually and physically abused children.

Many battered mothers who have lost custody of their children will end up homeless due to the ongoing court abuse they are subjected to in America. I know this to be true, as I was homeless, too, due to my ex-husband, Mr. Marty Warner, legally stalking me in Oregon's courtrooms for the past decade, i.e., forty-two court related hearings related to my divorce since 1996.

Unfortunately, even though being aware of this epidemic, talk show hosts and the general news media refuse to address this topic. Court trauma and abuse continues in my life as well as for thousands of mothers in the United States. I often wonder *"Does America hate mothers?"*

Charles Pragnel, Child/Family advocate writes, "The law in the U.S.A. and its implementation by the Courts represents the will and the wishes of the people of America. It is important therefore that every American is aware of what is happening in their name.

"Yet, while politicians are rightly condemning human rights abuses in foreign countries, they are blind to or are ignoring the human rights abuses of America's children which are occurring daily in the Family Courts of America."

There are not always two sides to every story

Our determination to pursue truth by setting up a fight between two sides leads us to assume that every issue has two sides—no more, no less. But if you always assume there must be an 'other side,' you may end up scouring the margins of science or the fringes of lunacy to find it.

This explains, in part, the bizarre phenomenon of Holocaust denial, among other denials, *and that river flows through lots of courtrooms.*

The child rape and molestation scandal at Penn State is an example of what is epidemic throughout America. Many of us who have been victims of sex abuse crimes are ridiculed, threatened and dismissed. Those in positions of power know what has occurred, but often dismiss the victim and protect the criminal. The victim becomes invisible.

Former Oregon House Representative, and newly appointed Oregon District 8 Senator Betsy Close, just like Joe Paterno, is guilty of protecting an abuser and criminal. She fully supported my ex-husband personally and in Court in 1996. Protecting one of your own, when they have committed horrific inhumane acts against another is one of the worse offenses you can commit in life.

Marty Warner is just one man, but it took a proverbial village and the Oregon judicial system to hide decades of overt abuse.

While many people focus their outrage on the judicial system alone, it's easy to lose sight of broader problems that assist in the culture of abuse — like churches, family members and the local community. These elements, too, played a role in the corruption and silence that has allowed a man like Marty Warner, and others like him, to operate untouched for so long.

As a human rights advocate, and advocate for the safety of women and children, I hand delivered a MEMO to all Oregon State Senators and Oregon State Representatives at the Capitol in Salem, Oregon on March 20, 2003 to inform them that Oregon House Representative Betsy Close had personally aided an abuser and did not believe a Christian woman had the right to divorce her husband in cases of severe abuse.

**Family Courts and Fundamental Legalistic Christians
are the Real Weapons of Mass Destruction.**

"Remembering and telling the truth about terrible events are prerequisites both for the restoration of the social order and for the healing of individual victims.

"The conflict between the will to deny horrible events and the will to proclaim them aloud is the central dialectic of psychological trauma. When the truth is finally recognized, survivors can begin their recovery. But far too often secrecy prevails, and the story of the traumatic event surfaces not as a verbal narrative but as a symptom. The psychological distress symptoms of traumatized people simultaneously call attention to the existence of an unspeakable secret and deflect attention from it.

"Without some form of public acknowledgement, all social relationships remain contaminated by the corrupt dynamics of denial and secrecy." – Judith Herman, "*Trauma and Recovery*"

We do the perpetrators a favor when we do not speak about the abuse.

Mothers of Missing Children

A few summers ago, I watched the news of two missing boys who were found and returned to their families. My heart was filled with gladness for the parents. I wept while watching their reunion as I know and understand the anguish of losing a child. I thought about the "missing children in my life." I have not had visitation privileges in fifteen years or the right to send my children gifts or correspond with them since 2003. I know where they are and who they live with, but there are no search and rescue teams, police, sheriffs, FBI or other state, government agencies, church groups who care to assist the parent and child in reuniting.

Society accepted the circumstances that I and thousands of mothers have been forced to survive as **normal.** Some individuals who have **deep legalistic religious persuasion** believe that the cruelty and injustices I have experienced are God's way of punishing me for seeking safety and divorcing my abusive ex-husband.

One attorney informed me I would need one million dollars for attorney fees in order to ever have contact with my children again. For the right to love and see my children, monies would be needed for legal fees due to my ex-husband's legal stalking and a decade of battles in court. I realize I live in a very sick and twisted society and it hurts.

I find it ironic that America, while involved in two wars in the Middle East, insists that they were improving the women's lives in Iraq and Afghanistan, while the hearts of tens of thousands of America's mothers were lying on the ground.

Marital Rape and Abuse Victim Seeks Justice

The advocacy system, as is, can offer no help or assistance in cases like mine. I have not received any help with my case from local, state, or from anyone or group on a national level, even though my case history in Oregon courts has been documented by many advocates as one of Oregon's most violent and obscene cases.

Even though I have written hundreds of letters throughout the years to Oregon state legislators, to the media, lawyers and legal advocates, to the Governor of Oregon's Council on Domestic Violence and the former Attorney General's Sexual Assault Task Force in an effort to seek help and promote awareness for the need for better laws for women and children escaping domestic violence and abusive situations, there is often no response. Domestic violence organizations and programs are failing victims.

The letters received from the Oregon State Bar, and the Governor's Council on Domestic Violence were shocking. Legal aid cannot and will not help and U.S. Staff Attorney for Domestic Violence, Poverty and Homelessness, Naomi Sterns, in Washington DC, was of no help either.

I was physically and mentally incapacitated during the time of my breakdown and unable to consent, and suffered repeated sexual assaults by my husband, Mr. Warner. My children were allowed to remain with the man accused of these crimes. My contact with them was completely, suddenly and arbitrarily removed.

No woman who has been raped and suffered the abuse I have endured should be forced to pay her wealthy abuser and rapist monies.

Dr. Barbara May has been involved in my case since 1997. Throughout these past years she shared extraordinary wisdom and insights with me that helped transform my life from victim to survivor.

She writes, "Coral A. Theill is an abuse survivor who has been resourceful on her own behalf against all odds. She lives below poverty level income and has had to live out of her car at times in the past. Unfortunately, she has continued to be systematically beaten down and broken down in a variety of ways by other individuals, by her family, by her community, and by society despite her efforts to try and eke out a so called, 'normal life.' Anyone, even the strongest person, reaches a breaking point, especially when all avenues turn into dead ends and you are let down, rejected, and turned away by everyone again and again. An excerpt of a letter I sent to District Attorney John W. Fisher, JD of Polk County Oregon on August 2, 2006 typifies just one example of many I have on how the system failed Ms. Theill.

"Having just heard the news from Coral that she will have to appear at a court hearing next month, I am appalled by what is happening to her in the name of the law. I am extremely concerned about her mental health which is what prompted my letter. I appeal to your sense of humanity to please see what you can do to seek true justice in this matter." (I received no response to this plea from D.A. Fisher and Ms. Theill was required to appear in court). — Barbara A. May, PhD, APRN, BC, Adult Psychiatric-Mental Health Nurse Practitioner, Professor of Nursing, Linfield College (November 2003)

Many mothers who seek safety from abuse are routinely prohibited from having even the most basic contact with their own children, not because they were unfit parents, but because they were outspent, out represented, and out-maneuvered in a court atmosphere not prepared to understand the needs of families dealing with domestic violence. To unnecessarily and violently separate a woman and her young children can represent the gravest form of abuse, with major social ramifications in generations to come.

To harass and exhaust a victim through repeated, frivolous court actions aimed at punishing and controlling her, beyond the point where a victim is physically, mentally, or financially able to defend herself, is a form of legal stalking. The family court system, as it is, does not yet recognize this, and the advocacy system is literally not financially able to help these survivors spend thousands and thousands of dollars defending themselves year after year in court.

Many individuals have developed a form of post-traumatic stress disorder (PTSD) that Dr. Karin Huffer describes as Legal Abuse Syndrome (LAS). It is a psychic injury, not a mental illness. Abuse of power and authority and a profound lack of accountability in our courts have become rampant.

I will continue to seek justice from a corrupted system that protects those in power and rejects those without the resources to seek redress from the corrupters.

Awareness that such things can even happen is the first step toward change.

Justice, Vindication, Restitution

A few years ago, I received a letter from Governor John Kitzhaber's office telling me to go get an attorney and go through THE APPROPRIATE channels. There are no appropriate channels for help in Oregon and of course, being destitute, there is no legal help.

"One of the overwhelming issues for Coral became the sheer expense of paying for lawyers.

It is part of the reason that she did not appeal the custody decision or the settlement—and it is the reason that so many judgments and court orders hang over her head. It seems that in our society justice is as much in the hands of the lawyers as our health is in the hands of doctors. Since most of us have a very true sense of what is right and wrong, it is hard to accept that our legal system puts justice out of our grasp." – Judy Bennett, Oregon, Editor

I Want to be Emancipated from Mr. Marty Warner and Oregon Courts

Presently, I have not had contact with my children for 15 years, was sued for twice that I earn as a fully disabled woman, was homeless for three years, living in my car off and on, due my ex-husband legally stalking me, i.e., forty-two court related hearings from 1996-2006 and the financial exploitation of George Amiotte.

I attended community college classes for two semesters, and received straight A's, but the stress of ongoing court trauma, the Oregon State of Appeals case, disability, poverty and homelessness was too great, so I did not take any additional classes. Since 1995, attorney and court related fees and expenses have amounted to over $200,000.

My passport was revoked years ago due to a $5,815.74 Child Support Summary Judgment my wealthy ex-husband has against me through the Polk County District Attorney's Office. In 2003, Judge Paula Brownhill ordered that I could not visit, write, phone or send my children gifts.

Due to the Child Support Summary Judgment hanging over my head, I have been threatened with jail time as a "punishment" and my driver's license could be revoked. Well-meaning individuals have confronted my ex-husband this past year in regards to the judgment requesting that he dismiss it by signing a "Child Support Summary Judgment Dismissal "In Kind" Form. *Mr. Warner informed them he will never dismiss the judgment.*

In November 2011, my trusted friend and editor, Judy Bennett, from Monmouth, Oregon contacted me. She had received a surprising call from a woman who had attended a Christian rally nearby. The woman had met my ex-husband, Marty Warner, at the rally. He told her and other individuals that I had committed suicide and was dead. Even though he claims I am dead, I continue to receive notices from Polk County trying to collect the judgment he has against me for child support each month.

Justice needs our voice.

When I was homeless and living in my car in 2003, I asked my wealthy Christian brother, mother and grandmother for assistance in monies for food. They each had considerable wealth and claim to be Christians. My relatives would not help me.

Sadly, my brother, Don Hall, and his girlfriend died in a tragic plane accident July 8, 2009.

I had no contact with my brother for six years prior to his death; this was his choice. His fundamental legalistic Christian ideology caused him to shun me. It made me sad, but there was nothing I could do but respect it. I missed him greatly and always loved him and always will.

My grandmother passed away in 2009. She was 98 years old. My mother passed away in 2010 at 76 years old. My adopted mother, friend and mentor, Addie Archer also passed away in 2010. I learned that grief for our abusers has a sharper edge than the grief for those who loved us.

After I became homeless, I contacted my close relative, **Harriet A. Spanel**, former Washington State Senator (D), Bellingham, WA, and asked for help, per the recommendation of my physicians and mentor, Dr. Barbara May. Fr. Senator Spanel, a devout Catholic, was close to my abusive mother who committed crimes against me. I spent many holidays with her and her family as a child.

I received no response from former Washington State Senator Harriet Spanel throughout the years of my survival.

On November 4, 2003, I hand delivered a copy of my published book and a letter about my case to United States Attorney Karin Immergut, U.S. Attorney's Office and Judge Michael Mossman, Portland, Oregon and sent a copy to Washington State Senator Harriet Spanel (my relative). I did receive a kind letter from U.S. Attorney Karin Immergut.

"There comes a time when silence is as powerful as betrayal." - *Dr. Martin Luther King, Jr.*

In 2012, I wrote my ex-husband's close relative, **Father Pat McNamee**, Portland, Oregon, and asked him if he could advocate for me and my children. Father McNamee counseled us before we were married and officiated at our wedding ceremony. In my letter, I shared details about the abuse I suffered, news articles, documentation and information about my published book. He wrote me a short note saying, *"Sorry to hear about your poor marriage."* I reached out for help, and he slammed the door - literally, and figuratively!

In her book, *Trauma and Recovery,* Judith Herman writes, "It is very tempting to take the side of the perpetrator. All the perpetrator asks is that the bystander do nothing. He appeals to the universal desire to see, hear, and speak no evil. The victim, on the contrary, asks the bystander to share the burden of the pain. The victim demands action, engagement, and remembering. . . .

"In order to escape accountability for his crimes, the perpetrator does everything in his power to promote forgetting. Secrecy and silence are the perpetrator's first line of defense. If secrecy fails, the perpetrator attacks the credibility of his victim. **If he cannot silence her absolutely, he tries to make sure that no one listens.** To this end, he marshals an impressive array of arguments, from the most blatant denial to the most sophisticated and elegant rationalization. After every atrocity one can expect to hear the same predictable apologies: it never happened; the victim lies; the victim exaggerates; the victim brought it on herself; and in any case it is time to forget the past and move on. The more powerful the perpetrator, the greater is his prerogative to name and define reality, and the more completely his arguments prevail.

"The perpetrator's arguments prove irresistible when the bystander faces them in isolation. Without a supportive social environment, the bystander usually succumbs to the temptation to look the other way. This is true even when the victim is an idealized and valued member of society. Soldiers in every war, even those who have been regarded as heroes, complain bitterly that no one wants to know the real truth about war. When the victim is already devalued (a woman, a child), she may find that the most traumatic events in her life take place outside the realm of socially validated reality. Her experience becomes unspeakable. . ..

"To hold traumatic reality in consciousness requires a social context that affirms and protects the victim and that joins the victim and witness in a common alliance. For the individual victim, this social context is created by relationships with friends, lovers, and family. For the larger society, the social context is created by political movements that give voice to the disempowered..."

My Children

As long as society, victim advocate groups and the judicial system, chooses to turn a blind eye whenever control and manipulation tactics are practiced by a custodial parent through courtroom litigation in order to separate child from mother (or father); and refuses to act against this lowest and most hateful form of spousal revenge, justice cannot be served. As long as those who hold the power fail to acknowledge and support the rights of non-custodial parents, justice cannot be achieved.

I have not seen my children since 1998 due to Court Orders, poverty and the fact that I live under a state address protection program. My children's spiritual advisors are from Bridgeport Community Church, Monmouth, Oregon, and unfortunately, Santiam Christian School. A kindergarten teacher at Santiam Christian School announced, in front of the class and parents, that my youngest son, Zachary, had been abandoned by his mother (me) and that was why he was not participating in making a "Mother's Day gift." This was a lie and a horrific statement to say to a child! Parents who witnessed this incident phoned me to share their disapproval of the teacher's comments.

Benton County District Attorney John Haroldson and Dr. Barbara May offered to professionally speak to the teachers and administration of Santiam Christian School in 2003, but the administration wanted nothing to do with hearing from these two experts and learning any truth about my case. I sought an attorney to assist me with my legal rights to my children's school records. To date, Santiam Christian School did not adhere to Oregon law in this matter.

My son, Joshua Warner, has erased me from his life. He was also the student body president while attending Corban University, Salem, Oregon. *On his website he indicates he was born in Albany, Oregon, to Marty Warner and that growing up in a family of eight was "easy."* (No mother mentioned – he must have been hatched?) I remember being blind while pregnant with him, due to his father's brutality - easy for Joshua, not easy for the mother.

In Joshua's early years, I often protected him from his father's rage. Mr. Warner's weapons of brutality consisted of his fists, his fraternity board, belts or logs. Once, when I was pregnant with my seventh child, I put my body in between my son and my ex-husband while he attempted to beat Joshua. After this incident I wanted to report my husband to the police, but instinctively knew my husband and his religious supporters would be protected by the system. Joshua and his wife, Annie, have shunned me also, and remain friends with my abusive ex-husband and his supporters. They condone batterers and child abusers.

In 2011, I called my oldest son and asked him if he would tell my son, Zachary, who is still a minor, that I remembered his 16th birthday. I said, "Don't tell Zachary Happy Birthday for me, or else I will get contempt orders from the Court, but tell him I reminded you about his birthday." I broke down and wept as I relayed this message because it was just too crazy and insane!

Reporting Unethical Judges and Attorneys

Dr. Barbara May, Professor of Nursing at Linfield College wrote a two-page MEMO to Kingsley Click, Oregon Court Administrator, reporting Judge Paula Brownhill's abuse in my case. I also wrote a letter reporting the abuse I had suffered from Judge Brownhill. We wrote our letters of complaint because Judge Brownhill serves as "chair" of the Oregon Statewide Family Law Advisory Board Committee.

Judge Brownhill continued to rule against me while she has presided over my case, assisting my abuser, Mr. Warner, over and over. We had hopes that our complaints would remove her from the "chair" position, but we were dismissed.

The staff attorney who gave me the address to the Oregon Court Administrator informed Judge Brownhill that I had reported her. She gave Judge Brownhill my private email.

I was shocked to receive an email and letter from my presiding judge. Judge Brownhill complained that my physician and counselor, Dr. Barbara May, and I reported her abuse to the Oregon Court Administrator in Salem, Oregon, and asked me via an email what my problem was. I did not respond to her and find it inappropriate for her to have written me.

The kind of violence, abuse and suppression perpetrated by so many of our organized religions and government agencies is truly shocking and can only continue by our refusal to look AT IT rather than the OTHER WAY.

Every Victim Longs for Justice, Vindication and Restitution

After my divorce in 1996, I sought help by writing hundreds of letters to the media and to local, state and national advocate groups, to no avail. I met with journalists and editors of The Statesman Journal, Albany Democrat Herald and The Gazette Times. They refused to expose my story. Personnel at the Albany Democrat Herald were especially rude and would not publish my editorial.

I also have twenty years of documentation and mental scars to prove that there is no "help" within America's church and religious system. I am thankful for the heartfelt support and compassion from doctors and friends, but no one seems to have the ability or authority to help me become free and emancipated from my former husband. He plans to destroy me and ruin my life. I still believe I have the right to "*life, liberty and the pursuit of happiness.*"

On December 19, 2003, I was sued for an additional $4,900.00 in child support to be paid to my ex-husband, Mr. Martin Warner. I am now under the Polk County District Attorney's Support Enforcement Division. At this time, I was virtually homeless, unemployed and was disabled.

My ex-husband and his attorney offered me "state supervised visitation" with my children. I refused their offer. I did not want my children to view me as "unfit, mentally ill, or criminal" due to this arrangement. I am not a criminal. I am not "mentally ill." I am a nurturing, loving mother and I do not need "supervision."

I was also ordered to have no further contact with my children. All contact by mail is prohibited. I am not allowed to send my children gifts or attend any school activity or games. I was given the right to write my children one last letter. Judge Paula Brownhill recommended that Mr. Warner provide psychological counseling for the children so they can better understand why their mother is not in their life.

Mr. Warner was suing me also for writing my book, *BONSHEA*, writing my children, for e-mailing my children and for attending my high school son's football games. The judge did not respond to Mr. Warner's complaints.

My ex-husband was disturbed that Shirley Peterson, a friend, was a supporting me in the court hearings. One morning, Mr. Warner called Shirley at her home at 6:00 a.m. He said, "You need to get under the blood of Jesus." She was alarmed and told me "no one has ever spoken to me like that.

While I was homeless in 2004, I enrolled in college to improve my life, but was forced to leave college after a couple terms due to my ex-husband and his attorney, Mr. J. Michael Alexander, Salem, Oregon, appealing our case to the Oregon State of Appeals in 2004, CA No. 124851. My ex-husband was not pleased that my child support had been terminated in December 2003.

Even though I was homeless, destitute and disabled, he requested another $50,000 from me in child support. (Mr. Warner owns a large debt free home and acreage, has stock, savings and retirement accounts and income from working as a professional engineer for thirty-five years.) I was again forced to defend myself and write my own sixty-five-page legal brief without a law degree, while homeless, with no resources and no legal assistance, further adding to my trauma.

After this case, Mr. Warner initiated another case against me with the Polk County courts for further child support. None of these suits were successful but neither did they dismiss previous judgments or put an end to the harassment.

The Oregon State of Appeals denied Mr. Warner and his attorneys appeal to sue me for his alleged day care fees, etc. throughout the years. Mr. Warner was also contesting the fact that I did not want to see the children once a month for supervised visitation. I refuse to be treated as though I am mentally ill or a criminal after being a good nurturing mother to my children for twenty years. A breakdown is not a crime and people do recover, especially if they get safe from their abuser and rapist.

In October 2006, there was another hearing in Polk County, Judge Paula Brownhill presiding. I requested a phone hearing due to poverty and disabilities. I had no attorney and was unable to afford travel. Judge Brownhill denied me a phone hearing indicating that she did not want someone with PTSD on the phone in her courtroom. I was not represented in person or by an attorney. Mr. Warner was awarded the 12% interest on the $4,900 child support debt, so another $1,200 was awarded to him, with 12% interest each month.

My passport is now permanently revoked because of past due child support. Mr. Warner has attempted to get my driver's license suspended in the past due to child support owed. I have heard of other mothers in similar situations who could not afford child support due to disability and poverty and ended up in jail until someone "found them" and helped provide legal help. Their only crime: poverty. I hope and pray that is not my demise.

I am praying to be emancipated from Mr. Warner and the Oregon courts.

Coral Anika Theill and Vic Browne, Montford Point Marine, Congressional Gold Medal Recipient, 8th and I Marine Barracks, Washington D.C., Montford Point Marines Congressional Gold Medal Commemorative Ceremony July 28, 2012)

Closing

In 1998, my physician and mentor, Dr. Charles Kuttner, asked me a profound question during our last therapy session. He asked me to share with him why I had spent twenty years of my life with my abusive ex-husband. He asked me why

I had not sought help sooner and why I had protected my abusers throughout my childhood and my adult life. I could not articulate the words he was asking me to express in his office. I can now. I found my voice.

In short, abuse dulls our senses and instills fear. We lose our voice and identity long before it has had a chance to form. My "protectors" never showed up as a child. As an adult, those who I went to for help, did not show up either, including Dr. Charles H. Kuttner.

Dr. Kuttner only needed to look in the mirror for the answer to his question. Within one year I would report the abuse and threats I suffered from his friend, George Amiotte. Dr. Kuttner would dismiss my cries for help and embrace my abuser.

The balancing act of trusting your own boundaries and recognizing where people are in *their* development is a continual lesson in life. I always see the *potential* in people rather than seeing who they are being in the present moment. As we journey with people, they will show us who they are.

Today, when people show me who they are, I BELIEVE THEM.

As I look back at all the negative experiences, as well as the cruel and abusive people that showed up in my life, I am reminded of the severity of my past. I believe the amount of abuse a person is subjected to will be similar to the number of predators, perpetrators and energetic vampires who will show up as "teachers." Each person was a mirror to the past torture I had experienced. They were each a unique gift - allowing me to see the depth of abuse of my past and help me realize that I NO LONGER ACCEPT ANY ABUSE OR DISRESPECT FROM ANYONE - NO MATTER WHAT. I found my voice in the courtroom, I found my voice by standing up to abusive therapists and advocates, and I found my voice by standing up to those who thought they could strip me further. *Finding our voice is a gift.*

The journey of healing is a personal one for each man and woman and not to be judged. It took me a long time to "find my voice." I am thankful for my journey as my past assists me in my writing, advocacy, and gives me a unique overview of the dynamics of the world around me. My collapse in 1993 was from decades of abuse and cruelty, but mostly because my voice and identity had been stripped away at a young age. My voice was removed before it could ever "form." *"If our lips don't speak it; our bodies will scream it." - Clarissa Estes, Ph.D.*

To this day, I remember the terrifying fear I felt for years as a child and also during my marriage that had me lying awake shaking some nights. Every form of abuse has a long-lasting effect on each one of us.

I have learned to value the horrifying scars of my childhood and past as valuable raw material for soul work.

Although I am only one small voice, I believe "a single pebble affects an entire ocean."

I need someone to tell this story to the world so that other women who are trapped and oppressed can hear that there is a way out. This story must be told so that the society that aids and abets the men and the religions that seek to treat women as slaves might change and my suffering will not have been totally in vain.

Dallas, Oregon, Polk County Court Update

From November 17, 2017 through April 11, 2018, I attended five court hearings regarding my child support judgment in Polk County, Dallas, Oregon. Mr. Joel Corcoran, U.S. Senator Jeff Merkley's assistant, recommended I file a Motion in Polk County courts regarding this unjust judgment. In 1999, I was sued for twice I earned for child support at a hearing I was not informed about and was not present.

Before the Polk County April 11, 2018 court hearing, my editor Judy Bennett, wrote all my eight children a personal letter informing them about the details of my health and the court hearing. *See Letter from Judy Bennett in Letters & Documentation*

Numerous affidavits were filed by mentors, long term friends, and neighbors for my court hearings in 1996 documenting the abuse I had suffered. Glen Schmauder, fraternity brother and my ex-husband's former friend, filed an affidavit for the April 11, 2018 court hearing, on my behalf. Glen was one of the groomsmen at our wedding in 1976. Mr. Warner lied to Glen during their conversations for 15 years following our divorce in 1996. He told Glen that I was committed to a mental hospital and that he was raising our eight children by himself. Glen and his wife, Carol Schmauder, have since read my published memoir and have reached out to me with compassion and support.

Prior to my 50th court hearing, Barbara A. May, Ph.D. RN, PMHP, Professor Emerita of Nursing, Linfield College, Portland, Oregon wrote an affidavit and "letter of support." She sent a copy of this letter to Judge Monte Campbell, Presiding Judge, Oregon Governor Kate Brown, the Polk County District Attorney and Oregon Attorney General Rosenblum. Dr. May did not receive a response. Numerous national advocates also contacted Governor Kate Brown and Oregon Attorney General Ellen F. Rosenblum on my behalf - to no avail.

While attending my 50th court related hearing on April 11, 2018, Polk County District Attorney John Adams insinuated I was a liar. My ex-husband, Marty Warner, referred to me in court as mentally ill, crazy and dangerous. My adult children and in-laws were present in the courtroom to support Marty Warner.

Judge Campbell read a vile and obscene hate letter that was addressed to me, out loud in court. The letter was composed by my son, Aaron Warner. My son, Aaron, was angry with me, as I questioned him on the witness stand about my monetary support to him which included college tuition, medical, food, housing, transportation and court fees in the amount of $25,000. He said, while on the witness stand, "You had me arrested." I replied, "Yes, Aaron, parents, teachers, police, pastors and priests are required by law to report the sexual assault of children."

As a disabled and destitute woman, I was ordered on April 11, 2018 by Judge Monte Campbell to pay my wealthy abusive ex-husband $3,815.74.

On April 11, 2018, Judge Monte Campbell said he felt I had a need to "fight with my ex-husband in court" all these past years." I believe he forgot that it is my ex-husband that has been legally stalked me for over 20 years – 50 court related hearings to date - and that I live under a state address protection program from him.

My friends set up a GoFundMe fundraiser and raised the $3,815.74 and made full payment to the Polk County District Attorney's office who had supported and represented my rapist/abuser, Marty Warner since 1999. I was finally a FREE WOMAN on July 4, 2018, thanks to friends and supporters from all over the world. The Polk County District Attorney's office had revoked my passport in 2004 due to this judgment. The D.A.'s office forgot to file the proper paperwork after my judgment was paid in full, so my passport was denied in the summer of 2018. U.S. Senator Ron Wyden's office assisted me in getting my passport expedited.

An assistant at the Polk County District Attorney's office told me that my ex-husband had asked them to keep the "CASE OPEN," even though he had been paid in full. The assistant said that he reminded my ex-husband that he had been paid in full and that the case was CLOSED.

At this time, my ex-husband was working as an engineer for Public Works, Monmouth, Oregon and all our eight children were adults and no longer living with him. His estate was worth over ½ million dollars. Court abuse and legal stalking was my ex-husband's way to continue his abuse, terror and control of me.

After escaping the most torturous, malicious and damaging abuse, all you want to do is recover, pick up the pieces of your shattered life and move forward. This is when the most intensive campaign is launched by the abuser. *You find yourself being re victimized by the system* and by the abuser's enablers and "*flying monkeys.*" Instead of getting understanding and sympathy, you get further beaten down. No victim is fully prepared for this onslaught.

The movie ***Spotlight***, stirred deep emotions in me as I reflected on the abuse I suffered silently as a child, in my marriage, churches and now in Oregon's family court system. The message of "Spotlight" is simple—survivors will see their perpetrators and enabling institutions (whether family, school, sport, court or religious) unmasked for what they are. **The truth has that effect**.

I feel encouraged by the #Metoo movement. I believe, in time, the movement will create change by exposing America's rape culture, toxic masculinity and how patriarchy perpetuates the abuse many of us have suffered. People are saying NO MORE. I hope the #Metoo movement will empower those who have been threatened, blamed and shamed for the abuse and/or crimes committed against them. The work of movements like #MeToo is crucial, and it must continue. Ending violence, rape, sexual assault, and sexual harassment, and combating the stigma and victim-blaming that survivor of these crimes face, are vital tasks that are far from complete.

I have the greatest respect for women who stand up to tyranny and oppression and fight for freedom and justice. Often, they battle alone, with children in tow, and with the enemy entrenched in their home, in their minds, and sleeping in their beds. These are the extreme and painful conditions under which I, and women all over the world, set out to make their escapes from domestic violence and terror. And even so, right up until today, the bravery of women's struggles for freedom is still too often met with the cruelty of questions like *"Why don't you just get up and leave?"* instead of being given the admiration their struggles deserve.

> *"The accounts of rape, wife beating, forced childbearing, medical butchering, sex-motivated murder, forced prostitution, physical mutilation, sadistic psychological abuse, and other commonplaces of female experience that are excavated from the past or given by contemporary survivors should leave the heart seared, the mind in anguish, the conscience in upheaval. But they do not.*
>
> *"No matter how often these stories are told, with whatever clarity or eloquence, bitterness or sorrow, they might as well have been whispered in wind or written in sand: they disappear, as if they were nothing. "The tellers and the stories are ignored or ridiculed, threatened back into silence or destroyed, and the experience of female suffering is buried in cultural invisibility and contempt... the very reality of abuse sustained by women, despite its overwhelming pervasiveness and constancy, is negated. **It is negated in the transactions of everyday life, and it is negated in the history books, left out, and it is negated by those who claim to care about suffering but are blind to this suffering.**"* —Andrea Dworkin, *Right Wing Woman*

I have learned that confronting abuse and violence is ugly and requires difficult self-examination. **Accepting collective responsibility costs more.**

"We know through painful experience that freedom is never voluntarily given by the oppressor; it must be demanded by the oppressed." – *Dr. Martin Luther King, Jr.*

Therapist Exploitation and Abuse

How our Society Enables Batterers, Abusers and Predators
Re: Dr. Charles H. Kuttner and Mr. George D. Amiotte
1997-2005

These past several years, I have had the privilege and honor of meeting hundreds of fine Marines and service members as well as many wonderful people who assist veterans and our wounded warriors.

The individuals mentioned in my story below reflect a dark side of human nature and does not represent the majority of individuals who work with trauma victims and veterans.

While in the midst of surviving the horrors of my divorce case and Oregon court trauma, my psychiatrist and counselor, Dr. Charles H. Kuttner, committed a breach of confidentiality in 1998-1999, giving my personal client information and phone number to a friend of his, George D. Amiotte, a Native American and former Marine who was involved in PTSD and trauma counseling.

Dr. Kuttner invited my son and me to attend a PTSD workshop at his office. He introduced George Amiotte, the facilitator, as a former U.S. Marine Corps Veteran, Oglala Lakota wisdom keeper, western medical practitioner (P.A.), filmmaker and artist.

Mr. Amiotte learned traditional tribal medicine from Frank Fool's crow and Pete Catches. As one of the founders of the Native American-based therapy for PTSD, he conducts PTSD workshops and healing circles for the Veterans Administration and serves as staff and faculty for numerous veteran's associations and educational institutions. During his five years with the Marine Corps in Viet Nam, he was awarded the Purple Heart, the Bronze Star and Vietnam's Cross of Gallantry with Silver Star. His film company, Heaven Fire Productions, is located in Los Angeles.

Dr. Kuttner repeatedly told me how brilliant and insightful this man was, but if he was introducing George Amiotte honestly, he would have said this: "Coral, within a year you will be the victim of financial and therapist exploitation by Mr. Amiotte. He will threaten you, stalk you, and strip you of your life savings. You will end up bankrupt. When you seek safety from him, he will take out his rage on you. He will beat and strangle you to an inch of your life. When you seek help within the judicial system, he will not comply with the court orders or restraining orders.

"He will sign promissory notes and promise to restore a portion of what he robbed from you, but that is a lie, too. You will be destitute and be living out of your car while your past court trauma in Oregon escalates. You will go without food, adequate shelter, and medical care and will have no vehicle or means of transportation for years due to poverty and disabilities. As your trusted physician, I will violate the code of client confidentiality and betray you by giving your client information to George Amiotte, who is not a licensed therapist.

"When he requests your whereabouts and phone number, I will violate your trust and give him your private information, without your permission. When you contact me and report you are being threatened and abused by Mr. Amiotte, I will dismiss your pleas for help. When you report me to the Oregon Medical board and submit the numerous letters I wrote to you admitting that I violated your client confidentiality, I will rely on the "good Ole' boys club" and they will dismiss the case. In reality, George Amiotte is a narcissist, sociopath, pathological liar, batterer and thief. By his words and behavior, he is a misogynist and racist."

Mr. Amiotte's tactic is to win the trust of V.A. therapists and psychiatrists, and then prey on their patients. (I was not the first woman he pursued and exploited, or the last.) I was later stalked, threatened, robbed of tens of thousands of dollars by Dr. Kuttner's associate, Mr. Amiotte.

Dr. Kuttner attended several of Mr. Amiotte's Native American PTSD workshops for Veterans Administration and Veterans Affairs employees and veterans and said he accomplished amazing psychological and spiritual growth during his first workshop with Mr. Amiotte. While I counseled with Dr. Kuttner, he appeared obsessed with Amiotte and would talk about him at length during my therapy sessions with him.

226

Dr. Kuttner believed George D. Amiotte had the capacity for strong ties to the spiritual and that the group facilitation he has done had demonstrated that.

While counseling with Dr. Kuttner, he would mention how he wished Mr. Amiotte and I could meet and date. I became uncomfortable with Dr. Kuttner, but he was the only counselor I was seeing at the time. Dr. Kuttner felt Mr. Amiotte would be helpful in assisting me in trauma recovery and PTSD issues. After losing my eight children, including my nursing infant in 1996, per court order, Dr. Kuttner would find it humorous to tell me lewd jokes and say, "Coral, what you need is a good screw." I did not share his sense of humor.

At this time, Dr. Barbara May was working on her degree and studying under Dr. Charles Kuttner. She would joke about Dr. Kuttner trying to be a Jewish matchmaker for me. In hindsight, being Dr. Kuttner's client became an awful nightmare and very inappropriate. I wanted to stop counseling with Dr. Kuttner as I became uncomfortable with his obsession of Amiotte and his inappropriate methods of counseling.

At one of my last therapy sessions in 1998 at Dr. Charles Kuttner's office in Albany, Oregon, he instructed me to hold a basket his wife had made. Dr. Kuttner proceeded to hold a feather over my head while he "checked out" my auras, he said. Afterwards he told me, "Coral, just as I thought, your auras inform me you have not had sex yet since your divorce." Dr. Kuttner is one of the reasons I caution trauma victims and survivors about therapist abuse and exploitation.

Dr. Kuttner once asked me why I had not sought help when I was a child and why I had protected my abusers throughout my childhood and adult life. He would continue to show me his ignorance regarding child abuse, Stockholm Syndrome and domestic violence in the coming months. He was also overbearing when it came to pushing me to speak more about my painful childhood. He recommended hypnotism in therapy and I refused. I discontinued my counseling with him in 1998. I began counseling with Dr. Barbara May in the summer of 1997. Her expertise is trauma recovery for abused women.

Even though I was no longer a client to Dr. Kuttner, he had called me and requested that my son and I attend a one-day PTSD workshop that he was sponsoring at his office in Albany, Oregon. Dr. Kuttner exposed his clients to Mr. George D. Amiotte, the facilitator of the PTSD workshop in 1998.

Mr. Amiotte was an unqualified and unlicensed therapist/PTSD workshop facilitator for the Veterans Administration. After the one-day workshop, Dr. Kuttner called my home and said that Mr. Amiotte wanted me to attend his next workshop at the Veterans Affairs Camp Chaparral in Yakima, Washington. I declined. In 1998, Mr. Amiotte was banned from the Veteran's Affairs Camp Chaparral, at the Yakama Nation due therapist abuse of clients and victims.

Mr. Amiotte asked Dr. Kuttner for my phone number. At this time, I lived under the District Attorney's "At Risk" program (address protection) so my ex-husband could not harass and abuse me. Dr. Kuttner complied with Mr. Amiotte's requests. The code of client confidentiality was disregarded by both of them. At this time, Mr. Amiotte was in a mentoring relationship with Dr. Kuttner. Dr. Kuttner revealed personal client information with Mr. Amiotte without the permission of his clients, including me. Mr. Amiotte took good notes and would use that information to exploit and abuse me.

Because of the events of my traumatic past, I was "easy prey" for Mr. Amiotte. Initially, I thought Mr. Amiotte was an advocate for veterans and trauma victims. Within a two-month friendship/relationship with Mr. Amiotte, he had robbed and depleted all my accounts, used my credit cards, damaged my car, and threatened and stalked me. Within one year, after seeking safety from him, he broke into my apartment, violently beat and strangled me and attempted to murder me.

While threatened by Mr. Amiotte, a very unhealthy triangle developed in my life, due to the fact that Mr. Amiotte and my physician, Dr. Kuttner, were close friends. Privately, I felt Mr. Amiotte would report any effort I made to defy his authority or domination over me to Dr. Kuttner and others in his inner circle as *"mental episodes."*

Mr. Amiotte often called Dr. Kuttner at his home. He had a privileged relationship with my physician. I also understood that if I attempted to share with Dr. Kuttner what was truly going on in my relationship with George Amiotte, he would believe his mentor, trusted friend and therapist, George Amiotte, and not me, his client. Visitation with my children was dependent on Dr. Kuttner's testimony in future court hearings.

One of my physicians, Dr. Roger Jacobson, recommended I hire a P.I. to thoroughly scrutinize any person I would become involved with due to my abusive past. Since Dr. Kuttner knew and respected Mr. Amiotte, I did not feel led to follow Dr. Jacobson's advice. Although, when I first met with Mr. Amiotte in April 1999, I introduced him to many of my close friends, including Addie Archer, Ron and Judy Bennett, Bob and Shirley Walsh and my older son. They enjoyed meeting and visiting with him. My friends encouraged me to learn to trust others and that all men were not like my ex-husband and his religious supporters.

Mr. Amiotte shook my son's hand and promised him that he would take good care of his mother and protect her. Mr. Amiotte said, "Aaron, trust me, you will never have to worry about your mother's safety again." Due to the abuse and violence I have suffered from Mr. Amiotte, my son has no respect for Mr. Amiotte nor the people and organization that continues to enable and coddle him – the Veteran's Administration.

Mr. Amiotte presented himself to me and my friends as an advocate, and he sent letters to individuals involved in my court proceedings in Oregon for interviews for a documentary. We were all outraged later when we learned, by my experiences, that Amiotte was a batterer, predator and a con artist. Predators are often so believable at first, but they cannot maintain their masks for long. My friends contacted both Dr. Charles Kuttner and Mr. George Amiotte about their abuse. Dr. Kuttner did not respond and Mr. Amiotte would curse at my friends on the phone and hang up.

Even though I sensed "red flags" in my initial interactions with Mr. Amiotte, I had been desensitized from decades of abuse. In the past, I was often harmed when I dared to speak up or seek safety. I was in shock from the loss of my baby and children in my recent divorce. There were few friends and I had no family support in my life. I was able to recognize the fact that I was being treated abusively by Mr. Amiotte, but my reaction time was slow due to the horrific consequences I have suffered in the past years from abusers.

George Amiotte knew about my previous breakdown, loss of children, the past cults I was forced to attend and the court trauma through his association with my physician, Dr. Kuttner. Once, Mr. Amiotte asked me if I was the woman Dr. Kuttner discussed with him that was raped by cult leaders. I said "no" that must have been another one of Dr. Kuttner's clients.

Mr. Amiotte began to request monies from me then would degrade me and tell me he was going to tell Dr. Kuttner that I was mentally ill. I realized I had found myself in a "boxed canyon" – and could not find my way out due to my love of my children and my fear of Dr. Kuttner and Mr. Amiotte – both powerful and well-respected therapists. I told Mr. Amiotte that I was disabled and needed my savings account for my ongoing court hearings in Oregon, my children and for my medical and health needs. I learned he did not care about me as a human being - he hated me.

He often became hostile over the fact that I remained in contact with my mentors, including Dr. Barbara May. On one occasion, I left my own home and stayed in a hotel (when he would not leave) because he would not stop speaking about my mentors in a profane and derogatory manner. Any questions I had about my own recovery or safety were, in his eyes, psychological problems.

A favorite technique for narcissists is to debilitate your identity by leveling false accusations and/or questioning your honesty, fidelity, your "true" motivations, your character, your sanity and judgment.

Sadly, predators, such as George D. Amiotte, are skilled at cruelly manipulating tender consciences, causing their victims to have a mistaken view of themselves. The truth is that abuse survivors tend to attract repeat offenses simply because they are wounded and hurting; and predators, like beasts of prey, perceive the wounded as an easier target.

In June 1999, I agreed to meet Mr. Amiotte's friends and family in South Dakota. He threatened and forced me to type a letter to my financial institution in the office of Dr. Robert Phares' secretary, Rosemary Slater, at the Black Hills V.A. Hospital in Hot Springs, South Dakota. He used the monies to purchase twenty-six acres of property as he was preparing for Y2K in 2000. He believed what was mine was his.

I was in debt for taxes due from the early withdrawal of my IRA account. Mr. Amiotte had no job, no savings, and had a bad credit record and had no intention of ever restoring my accounts or paying me back for all the debt I incurred from his financial exploitation of me. Sadly, I had no monies for an attorney to assist me in legal action against Mr. Amiotte. Although I did manage to get a Summary Judgment against him eventually, he refuses to pay.

To date, I have survived all types of abuse, including childhood sexual molestation, physical abuse, rape and ritual abuse. Financial abuse has been the most difficult of the forms of violence I have experienced to date. The lack of financial security dictates whether we can obtain shelter, food, health care or legal assistance in America.

When I would question him about the financial bankruptcy, I faced due to him fleecing and emptying my accounts, he would threaten me and would tell me to "act right." He would say, "When are you going to stop "putting my head in sh-t? Coral, I really get tired of you and the way you are. You are having menopausal symptoms." He then would become enraged, throw things at me and terrorize me. My health deteriorated rapidly.

George Amiotte knew my triggers well and accused me of having psychological problems. My vulnerability was mental abuse. Sometimes I submitted to his threats to avoid further cruelty and mental anguish. Mr. Amiotte failed to recognize me as a human being. He did not respect any of my own boundaries.

Before I began to live in my car in 2002, I asked Mr. Amiotte what I should do. He suggested I live in a tepee or a recently flooded Native American Christian campground. I lived out of my car and with friends temporarily for the next three years. The Veterans Administration, Dr. Kuttner and Mr. Amiotte's friends were aware of my plight, but did not care and continued to support my abuser.

In the summer of 1999, I left a message with my physician Dr. Kuttner requesting that he meet with me in person some day in the near future regarding my concerns about his mentor and fellow colleague, Mr. Amiotte. Dr. Kuttner did not respond to me, but met with George Amiotte instead. **Dr. Kuttner dismissed me, the victim, and supported Mr. Amiotte's abusive treatment of me.** Mr. Amiotte called my mentor and counselor, Dr. Barbara May, in the summer of 1999. She suggested he get help from a licensed qualified male counselor. He did not heed her advice.

I also reported the abuse to Mr. Steve Becker, a V.A. employee at the Black Hills V.A. hospital and a friend of George Amiotte. He truly didn't want to hear what I had to say. Mr. Becker was too preoccupied in promoting George Amiotte's PTSD workshops.

During this difficult time, I stayed in touch with Dr. Barbara May, Professor Emerita of Nursing, Linfield College, Portland, Oregon. She said, "George worked fast." In a matter of a few months, I had been ruined financially. I did not perceive his hidden agenda or covert intentions.

After my life savings were depleted by Mr. Amiotte, my accountant went over the damage with me and shared the bad news. The debt I incurred from Mr. Amiotte was well over $150,000, which included the taxes I owed for early withdrawal of accounts, credit card debt and loss of interest on the account. Mr. Amiotte had also damaged my leased car.

Although I was still in contact with Mr. Amiotte and trying to get him to repay money he had taken, I avoided many of Mr. Amiotte's questions for fear that my answers would make him angry. I became weary of appeasing his temper. When I could no longer sustain this way of life, I sought help and this caused Mr. Amiotte to take his rage out on me. Seeking outside help and intervention also elevated the level of danger I lived under.

> Years later, I understand this truth: if someone or something
> does not make you feel more alive, it is too small for you.

I wrote and called Dr. Kuttner once again about the abuse and threats I suffered from his friend. Instead of responding to me, Dr. Kuttner wrote a letter to George Amiotte. Dr. Kuttner's letter to Mr. Amiotte increased the level of abuse.

Dr. Kuttner also sent a memo to my mentor, Dr. Barbara May, about the reports of abuse I had sent him reporting that *my calls were an annoyance to him.* I received a copy of this memo.

I was shocked that this person who claimed to be concerned for my welfare had so trivialized my life. *Dr. Kuttner's cold response and words pushed me into a very dark place.* I decided, at that time, that I would not open myself to further humiliation by calling for help. I began a long process of "taking care of myself" in a very unsafe situation that almost ended in my death AT THE HAND OF Mr. Amiotte.

Since 2004, I have had no contact with Dr. Kuttner. My calls for help to Dr. Kuttner were dismissed as "harassment." In all my years of recovery, the pain I suffered from Dr. Kuttner's breach of my client confidentiality and his siding with my abusers has been traumatizing for me.

One year later, after I reported the crimes of violence and threats to Dr. Kuttner, George Amiotte, Dr. Kuttner's friend and mentor, beat me severely and attempted to murder me.

Therapist exploitation and abuse violates and destroys the fragile element of trust victims struggle to build again. After my experiences with Dr. Kuttner and Mr. Amiotte, my trust was shattered.

I spoke with my friend and adopted mother, Addie Archer, at the onset of being threatened and robbed by Mr. Amiotte. She also understood that I might face jail time as a penalty for the huge taxes I owed and would most likely end up homeless and living out of my car due to all the debt I incurred from Mr. Amiotte. She recommended I do all I could to hold him accountable for his actions. I observed through the years that Mr. Amiotte could "yes me to death, but he never meant what he promised.

"Memory says, 'I did that,' Pride says, 'I couldn't have done that.' Memory yields." – *Friedrich Wilhelm Nietzsche*

What I have learned by George's behavior is that he wasn't interested in other people or their basic needs. It was all about George, his Vietnam pain, his Native American issues, his trauma, his tragedies and sadly, domination games. Instead of equality, domination games consist of how much the one in power can control, punish, threaten, humiliate and destroy another person.

George Amiotte would often threaten me by saying, "I am a trained Marine. I can take you out anytime I want, bury you, and no one will find you and no one will know who did it."

He demanded that I open another credit card line as I was destitute and I did. His relationship with me was based on "robbery and exploitation." I lived separately from him, I was not his girlfriend and was not involved with him, but he still maintained control over my life. **I lived in fear of his rage.**

Finally, when seeking safety, and unable to appease my abuser with the monies he demanded, I was beaten and strangled in an attempted murder incident by Mr. George D. Amiotte, in Olympia, Washington, August 6, 2000. He beat me in the face and head, ears and arms and breasts, pulled my hair and pinned me down on the floor and beat and strangled me. I begged him for my life, but he kept on beating and choking me. When he would stop for a moment, I would gasp for air. I finally cried out to him, "George do you need to rape me?" The fact that I was forced to make this statement was a very low moment in my life. It brought back many past memories of my childhood sexual abuse. I would try to flee from my apartment, but he would drag me from the door, throw me on the floor and begin to choke me again.

I escaped from my apartment screaming, *"He is trying to kill me. Help me!"* The incident had lasted over 20 minutes. I did not believe I would escape with my life. This was a night I almost became a statistic. Several neighbors and police came to my aid. Mr. Amiotte was arrested by Tumwater Police Officer Ross Rollman and Lt. John Stines and was transported to the O.P.D. jail where he was booked for Assault D.V. He spent the night in the Tumwater, Washington jail.

Mr. Amiotte explained to neighbors and the Tumwater Police that *nothing happened* and it was "only a verbal argument and that we did not get physically violent with each other." His statement does not explain the red marks that were noted on my neck, ears, shoulders and arms. Neighbors also testified that my skin was very red and scratched.

Police reports note that there were **red marks and swelling just below the collar of the shirt I was wearing, that my right ear was red and that I had visible red marks on my left bicep and shoulder and several red marks up and down my arms and shoulders.**

Mr. Amiotte called my phone number over a dozen times that night. I did not answer.

I realized again, the huge consequences in attempting to get safe from an abuser.

Shelton Police Officer Troy Wiktorek, my neighbor, wrote in his affidavit to the Thurston County Superior Court, "On August 6, 2000, at about 2300 hours, I was in my apartment located at 1221 Mottman Dr. SW, #J-104, when I was awoken by a woman screaming. The screams appeared to be coming from an apartment above mine or nearby. The screams appeared to be in the nature of someone fighting for their life. As I exited my front door, I saw the joining neighbors standing there with a phone in hand and was told they were on the phone with the 911 dispatch reporting the screams. The neighbors appeared very concerned for the safety of the woman in apartment #J-203. I ran out to the parking lot area and turned back towards the apartments just in time to see an Indian male exiting apartment #J-203. The male appeared to be in his 50's, his hair was long and appeared to be uncombed.

"He was wearing a white colored Gi with dark color pants. The male appeared to be intoxicated, as he staggered down a flight of steps. I approached the male and could see that his eyes were bloodshot and that he smelled of intoxicants. He would not make eye contact with me. He had what appeared to be car keys in his right hand. I requested the keys, he handed them to me without incident. The male would not converse with me at any time during our contact. I asked the male to sit down and wait for the police to arrive. Moments later the Tumwater Police arrived and took control of the situation. I am a Shelton Police Officer and from my experience as a Police Officer, the nature of the screams I heard on that night would have been of someone who was being hurt, not just two persons arguing."

I obtained a protective order against Mr. Amiotte the next day. George violated the protective order. He would call and talk as if he was the "victim" in this violent incident. Later, Mr. Amiotte threatened my life telling me that "he was a trained Marine and he could take me out any time he wanted, bury me and no one would know who did it, or know where I was." I calmly replied that if anything happened to me, he would be the first-person police would investigate.

At the restraining order hearing August 30, 2000, Mr. Amiotte arrived in court dressed in green surgery scrubs and a stethoscope hanging around his neck. His attire was bizarre! The judge ordered him to fully comply with the Washington state licensed batterers treatment program and also counsel monthly with Rev. Joanna Trainor. I went over my financial documents and records with Mr. Amiotte dozens and dozens of times. Mr. Amiotte acknowledged the monies he had taken from me and signed a promissory note, in front of witnesses, for $31,500 promising to make monthly payments. He failed to do so.

At the time I obtained a restraining order against Mr. Amiotte, he was ordered to surrender his weapons. He joked later saying that his gun collection was with family and friends.

Dr. Barbara May has been my mentor and counselor for the past fifteen years, and she believes I was suffering from Stockholm Syndrome from Mr. Amiotte. Her words are true. When you become numb from abuse; you are not in a state of mind to plan an escape. You are thankful your captor has not killed you. It is reported in studies on Stockholm Syndrome that high anxiety functions often keep victims from seeing available options.

It took me an hour or so to scrub the black marks on my floor in the entryway of my apartment due to being dragged away from the door as I sought to escape

Mr. Amiotte. During this time I began to pour over the scar map of my psyche attempting to learn what led to what, and where to go next. I began all over again picking up the pieces of my shattered self.

I looked deep down inside for the "tough girl" to help me survive another episode and chapter of violence and abuse-but sadly, I could not find her. She was all used up. She was gone.

After the attempted murder incident, Mr. Amiotte was invited to speak at a local Native American Domestic violence convention in Washington State. Mr. Amiotte moved forward as though nothing had happened. He literally became an expert on domestic violence overnight. My recovery and injuries were of no concern to him. At the time he attempted to murder me I was recovering from a 102-degree fever and was very weak. Mr. Amiotte was aware of my illness at the time he assaulted me. That same night he had officiated as "chief" at a local Sundance, a Native American spiritual ceremony. Many veterans and Native Americans admire George as a "wisdom keeper."

Due to preparing for upcoming court hearings regarding the financial exploitation I suffered from Mr. Amiotte, I was given wrong information about the protective order. They recommended I have the P.O. order modified so I could have contact with Mr. Amiotte in court.

On April 18, 2001, Mr. George D. Amiotte was permanently terminated from Hoy & Nickle Associates Domestic Violence treatment program. His counselor, Ann Phillips, reported that he failed to comply with court orders and the requirements of the domestic violence treatment program. They admitted that there was a breakdown in communication between his counselors and the courts.

His state licensed counselors gave me information from the Trimodal Typology of Batterers stating that George Amiotte represented a **Type II – Sociopathic Batterer.**

"This is an individual socialized into a belief and value system which endorses or at least condones violence as a pragmatic or excusable method for dealing with problems. He may have a diagnosable personality disorder and is likely to have some level of substance abuse problem. While he uses violence in a variety of settings to meet his needs he is unlikely to have a criminal record. His violence is more severe, likely including use of weapons or injuring the victim, is not apologetic, threatens to kill the victim or do more violence, and is likely to make sexual demands after violence."

If it wasn't for the court errors and the unwritten law of familiarity within our society, Mr. Amiotte would be in jail.

Until 2000, Mr. Amiotte was a licensed P.A. (Physician's Assistant) in Washington State. After he assaulted me in August 2000, he was disqualified from obtaining his Washington State P.A. license.

When I reported the crimes that Mr. Amiotte had committed against me to V.A. directors and employees, many of them sided with my abuser and some of them called me a liar. Their dismissal of me was as traumatic as the violence and abuse I had suffered.

Mr. Amiotte was angry that I reported the abuse to friends and V.A. employees. He expected me to hide, like an abused child, and not talk about it. My fault lies in not having any other reference for relationships besides my abusive ex-husband of twenty years and an abusive childhood – terror and horror were the norm. In the coming months and years, I also understood the serious repercussions I would suffer if I choose to seek help to survive the ongoing violence and abuse from George Amiotte. The unspoken message I got from George was that the matter of the attempted murder incident and financial abuse would be kept private.

Keeping secrets binds up our energy and impacts our health and well-being.

The freedom that I gained when I broke my silence about the abuse I suffered from Mr. George Amiotte and Dr. Charles Kuttner I wouldn't trade for anything. **My voice is more important to me than my safety. Once secrets are exposed to the light, they lose their power over you.**

Mr. Amiotte enjoyed humiliating me, calling me names, i.e., "whore, slut," intimidating me and threatening me. I stayed in contact for a short time to seek restitution, but he never had any plans of paying me back for the monies he robbed from me. Due to the combination of court litigation in Oregon by my ex-husband and the financial exploitation by George Amiotte, I ended up living out of my car for a few years and was essentially bankrupt. Mr. Amiotte keeps his property in another person's name to avoid a lien due to the Summary Judgment I have against him.

I believe "Evil (ignorance) is like a shadow. It has no real substance of its own; it is simply a lack of light. You cannot cause a shadow to disappear by trying to fight it, stamp on it, by railing against it, or any other form of emotional or physical resistance. In order to cause a shadow to disappear, you must shine light on it." - *Shakti Gawai*

In 2002, George Amiotte was hired as a consultant by the Black Hills V.A. in South Dakota per Mr. Steve Becker and Dr. Robert Phares recommendation. He was paid $65.00 per hour. At Mr. Amiotte's 2002 workshop for the Black Hills V.A. employees and staff in Hot Springs, South Dakota, Amiotte said, "*There's one lesson that everyone needs to learn in dealing with returning veterans regardless of their race. **Respect them...that's basically it**. Respect them, be there for them, love them. I know how they feel.*"

Mr. Amiotte could learn some lessons about "respecting others - their boundaries, their resources and money, their bodies, their life and their very soul. Mr. Amiotte characterizes the quote, "If you can't be a good example, you'll just have to be a horrible warning."

Since he was terminated from the Hoy & Nickles court ordered batterer's treatment program in Washington State in 2001, Mr. Amiotte promised me he would counsel with Mr. George Twiss, Director of Cangleska, a domestic violence shelter at the Pine Ridge Reservation in 2002, but failed to keep his promise.

In 2003, Mr. Amiotte was aware I was homeless, living out of my car and was without adequate shelter and food. He was also aware I was involved in ongoing court litigation in Oregon due to my ex-husband legally stalking me. I called him in regards to the promissory note and monies he owed me. In February 2003 he stated, "Coral, I won't be like other jerks and leave you living on the street. I will pay you back what I have promised to you." George did not make any payments, but continued to call and leave messages on my voice mail wanting to get together for lunch. Later he told me he owed me nothing.

I reported the acts of violence against me to Mr. Amiotte's psychiatrist, Dr. Ralph Hummel, and individuals who Mr. Amiotte claimed were his friends and mentors, i.e., Bob Coalson, Steve Becker, Mr. Bill Wheeler, Faith Spotted Eagle, Doris Peters, Tribal Judge Lorintha Warwick and Dr. Alfonso R. Batres, Director of Veteran Affairs Chief Officer, Readjustment Counseling Service. Several of these individuals have participated with George in victim advocate work.

When Mr. Amiotte wrote me a hostile and threatening letter in March 2003, I was staying with friends. I began to block my door with furniture and boxes. This was an automatic response to the former incident of violence with Mr. Amiotte. I thought about his friends at the V.A. and Dr. Charles Kuttner and understood that they suffered no consequences in their relationship with. Amiotte and could go to bed at night knowing that they were safe. I did not have that same freedom and right.

I understand that Mr. Amiotte hates me because the acts of violence he committed against me **exposed his 'dark side.'**

Tashi (Smith) Gremar commented on Mr. Amiotte's 2003 threatening letter, "His repulsive, irate and immature attitude is intended to scare you away from pursuing him to give you back your money and to try to misplace blame on you for his poor choices. I do not respect his decisions or his "scare tactics." The only truth in that letter is that he is indeed in dire need of "getting it together," yet amazingly he continues to fail to get professional help. For him to punish you for his crime is not okay. And it is a crime. I feel angry that he is portraying himself as the "victim," (poor me, look at all have been through and all I have to deal with). The only person he has to be angry with is himself and I find it repugnant that a grown man will not take responsibility for his actions but instead tries to lay his blame on others. For such a big, tough vet, he sure does act like a little helpless baby. Coral, you are a good person and you're much too refined for all this garbage."

I was invited to be a guest speaker at the Thurston County Domestic Violence and Sexual Assault Task Force meeting by Thurston County Sheriff Dan Kimball. In March 2004, I gave a report of the details surrounding the domestic violence incident involving Mr. George Amiotte and offered insights of the breakdown in communication and services. The Task Force, i.e., deputy sheriffs, judges, police officers, probation officers, and domestic violence advocates wish to know where the services are failing in domestic violence situations and how they can avoid failures such as this one in the future. There was a failure in the system. Mr. Amiotte was not held accountable for his lack of compliance with the domestic violence treatment program.

Another difficult component in surviving domestic violence is the "real fear" of future incidents if your abuser should become angry toward you again. Restraining orders are just a piece of paper. I discovered that my post-traumatic stress symptoms were not as severe when I would be in contact with Mr. Amiotte by phone because I would know where he was and "where and at whom" his rage was directed. I understood the phrase – *keep your friends close, your enemies closer.*

At the Task Force meeting, I learned that the VA Puget Sound Health Care System, Seattle Division had banned Mr. Amiotte from working or contracting with them. They were protecting themselves from future lawsuits. Seattle V.A. police attended my speaking engagement in March 2004. The VA Puget Sound Health Care System American Lake Division in Tacoma, Washington also banned the Native American Veteran's healing circle from meeting at their hospital due to Mr. Amiotte's involvement with that group.

I attempted to stay in touch with Mr. Amiotte for a while due to the financial exploitation issues. I soon realized that this was a waste of time. Safe Place, the local domestic violence shelter, helped me obtain an attorney to seek a Summary Judgment against him.

I never recovered financially and Mr. Amiotte did not make payments on the promissory notes or the Summary Judgments I had against him. He did acknowledge receiving the Washington State Mason County Summary Judgment of $31,000 and sent an attorney who was working on the case a check for $500.00 in 2004. That same month he closed his bank accounts and left the area. No payments have been made since. I have had no monies or attorney to help me garnish or collect and being an American Indian, it is difficult to enforce the Summary Judgment and find and attach his assets.

Washington State Crime Compensation Program awarded me monies for counseling fees and I met with my mentor and counselor, Dr. Barbara May. Dr. May commented, as she assisted me in healing from the attempted murder incident by George D. Amiotte, "Coral, from the long-term sexual abuse you suffered as a child and the long-term survival of domestic violence, during the twenty years of your previous marriage, you wear what we therapists call a 'Red X' on your forehead. Predators, like George, can spot you a mile away. Her statement made me sad. I asked, "Dr. May, what can I do to wipe the 'Red X' off?" She looked at me and said, "I don't know, Coral."

Dr. May assisted me in collecting the shattered pieces of my "self" after these incidents with George. In one of my counseling sessions, I listed the abusive characteristics of Mr. Amiotte: thinking there are no consequences for his behavior, depriving me of money, taking my money and making me beg for money, restricting my access to food, clothing, work, and health care etc. He destroyed property belonging to me, believed in male supremacy, was pathologically jealous, cruel, self-righteous, and self-centered. He denied or minimized his abusive behavior, needed to be in control of every situation, yelled, and used angry expressions or gestures, shunning, humiliation, and manipulation tactics.

He isolated me from family, friends and counselors, accused me of infidelity, accused me of insanity, and ignored or minimized my feelings. Physical abuse included: slapping, beating, throwing items at me, pushing, choking, throwing me around the room, and restraining me. Verbal abuse included name-calling, i.e., referring to me as a whore and a slut. The sole purpose of his behavior was to dominate, manipulate and control me.

I shared with Dr. May my experiences with the Veterans Administration employees and their response to the attempted murder incident and financial exploitation I suffered from George Amiotte, i.e, they condoned his behavior, endorsed him and hired him as a consultant and PTSD workshop facilitator. After sending police reports and documentation to the Veterans Administration, I was told I had harassed them and not to contact them again.

Dr. Barbara May commented about my attempts to expose George Amiotte to the V.A., "Coral, the only one who truly 'gets it' is you—you are the expert of domestic violence knowingness. I continue to be in awe of your strengths. George knew that he could beat you up to an inch of your life because there would be little or no consequences. If he had harmed anyone else, he would be held accountable by our society. Domestic violence and spousal/partner abuse is *acceptable* in our society. I wonder if Mr. Amiotte has found his next victim."

Dr. May commented, "Mr. Amiotte is a predator and a sycophant. **His behavior toward you is unconscionable given the fact that he has worked for years in a caregiver role as a P.A.**" She recommended I read, *Anatomy of a Spirit: The Seven Stages of Power and Healing,* by Caroline Myss, Ph.D., to assist me in my healing.

I shared with Dr. May the fact that Mr. Amiotte would often "leave" his gun license at my residence. She told me this was an intimidation tactic and no accident, but a way to psychologically create an "element of fear." Mr. Amiotte carried guns in his vehicles and had numerous guns, swords and weapons in his home.

Dr. May commented, "Coral, the *most dangerous abusers* are those who appear with both components: the good and the bad. When you are experiencing the healthy moments, it is difficult for you to remember the moments of terror. It becomes more confusing and you begin to forget the moments of terror because the present moments of calm are so welcome and refreshing. You also wish to dismiss the violence because of the shame and fear involved in the abuse. What makes Mr. Amiotte dangerous as a therapist is that he uses 'victim advocate and trauma specialist lingo and terminology,' but has not integrated it into his behavior. He therefore, lures and seduces unsuspecting individuals and victims into believing he espouses empathy and sensitivity. Dr. May added, because she understood Mr. Amiotte's true nature, "Coral, you will never see a dime of your monies returned from him."

There are other abuse issues that I suffered from Mr. George Amiotte that are documented with my mentors, physicians and counselors that will remain confidential because they are too shameful to mention. Domestic violence evolved into other forms of abuse. Terror and threats became the norm.

After the attempted murder incident, my abuser, Mr. Amiotte spoke to my son and told him that his mother (me) was suffering from delusions, created by her counselors, Dr. Barbara May and Rev. Joanna Trainor. My son was shocked by the derogatory manner in which he spoke about women and individuals of other ethnicities.

Mr. Amiotte had no therapist license or a P.A. license since his attempt on my life in 2000, but even though the V.A. informed me that they hired only licensed PTSD workshop facilitators, he continued to conduct workshops for veterans.

In February 2005, Oregon Circuit Court Judge Tom Hart read the documentation I submitted, including court records and a dozen letters written by my physician, Dr. Kuttner, admitting his breech of my client confidentiality and phone number. Judge Tom Hart was alarmed and recommended I report this physician immediately to the Oregon Medical Board.

Numerous physicians, nurses, advocates and professionals who were familiar with this case of "therapist exploitation" also recommended I report Dr. Kuttner and Mr. Amiotte to protect their future victims.

I reported my physician, Dr. Charles Kuttner, of Portland, Oregon, to the Oregon State Medical Board in 2004, and gave them pages of documentation of my physician's letters admitting what he had done.

The Oregon Medical Board's ruling was in favor of my physician, Dr. Charles Kuttner. The physician's breech of my client confidentiality and unethical behavior, and abuse did not qualify as "misconduct or unethical." The case was closed – business as usual.

An Oregon Circuit Court Judge, did, though and Judge Tom Hart wanted to give me a jury trial as he was appalled and shocked by what this doctor had done to me, but an attorney who handled the filing of this case, filed one day too late, missing the deadline with the statute of limitations. My friend and editor, Judy Bennett, supported me by attending the court hearing. I still hope for apologies and restitution from both of these therapists, and I pray for their future victims. Both of them continue to counsel trauma victims and veterans.

Letter from Judy Bennett (my friend and editor) to Dr. Charles Kuttner in February 2005.

> Dr. Kuttner,
>
> I am a friend of Coral Theill and I am writing because I want you to understand the full impact of your actions on her life. I can believe that you were seduced by George Amiotte on some level – he is charismatic and professes a knowledge and spiritual enlightenment that is very attractive. But the fact is, George Amiotte is as damaged as any of the trauma victims he claims to help. There is a side to him that is very violent, masochistic and egomaniacal. That is the person to whom you gave Coral's personal information and phone number.
>
> In giving personal information, you may not have named Coral, but in discussing your "patient" George easily figured out Coral's case history and used that information to manipulate and ultimately abuse her. You set her up, and the outcome was wrong.

George systematically cut Coral off from her friends, exhausted her financially, made many promises to deceive and bind her emotionally - and ultimately beat her and misused her sexually.

During the period of time she was with George, Coral tried to contact you - and you were in contact with George, but you would not talk to her and indeed complained that she was harassing you. Can't you understand that she needed help?!

I was present in court on Monday when the suit against you for negligence and malpractice was dismissed because too much time had elapsed since the initial offense. I can tell you honestly that if the judge had been able to find any way to rule in Coral's favor he would have done so. You got off on a technicality and the ineptness of the attorney that originally filed in Coral's behalf.

Coral once shared a parable that you had sent to her regarding the difference between heaven and hell. In hell, all the people are starving and miserable because they are all seated around a table laden with food but the utensils have handles that are so long there is no way they can get the food to their mouths. In heaven, the same scenario, but everyone is happy and full and having a good time - because they are all feeding each other. You have failed that basic test of human compassion. You failed Coral as a therapist and counselor. And you failed as a friend. She asked you for help in getting free of George, she asked you for help in getting George to pay money that he admits he owes to her. She finally asked for you to be held accountable for the consequences of your actions.

At present, Coral is destitute. Because she had a promissory note and a subsequent summary judgment against George Amiotte for money he owes to her, she was denied help from Social Services - that case is being reviewed but a hearing is probably still six months away. Housing assistance has a 2-3 year waiting list. She is taking courses at community college and working part time, BUT SHE HAS NO PLACE TO LIVE and minimal income. She is staying in her car and a few nights here and there with friends. She has less than $400 a month income to live on. She is exhausted and frail. The situation is a direct result of the relationship with George Amiotte which you encouraged and orchestrated.

You have admitted you "made a mistake" in giving George Coral's phone number - "against your better judgment." But you did it, and you have done nothing to rectify the situation. I suspect that you feel this is not your fault - perhaps you even feel you were used by George too, at the least you see this as a problem between George and Coral. But you are responsible for their being together in the first place. As a therapist you should know better than to play matchmaker!

Coral would never have filed suit against you if you had made the slightest move to help her either emotionally or financially. I wish this had gone on to trial because I think you behaved unethically and should be held accountable. But I also am glad Coral is spared the horror of depositions and prolonged anxiety. I'm glad she had the guts and the brains to stand up for herself, whatever the outcome.

It would be nice to think that you would apologize and even make some effort at restitution. That seems unlikely though, in view of the way you have treated Coral in the past. She was your patient. She is still vulnerable and "disabled" by a lifetime of trauma. You put yourself in the position of being part of the problem. Shame on you.

Sincerely,
Judy Bennett

Judy Bennett received no response from Dr. Charles Kuttner.

For many people power and control over others IS their existence. Domestic violence is not about anger but about trying to instill fear and wanting to have power and control in the relationship. Batterers and abusers treat others inhumanely because they lack three necessary components for spiritual health: being self-critical, showing empathy and walking in humility.

The Oregon Medical Board's ruling was in favor of my physician, Dr. Charles Kuttner. The physician's breech of my client confidentiality did not qualify as "misconduct or unethical."

Even though I contacted the V.A. and sent them my restraining orders, police reports (that indicated strangulation marks on my neck), affidavits of witnesses and statements from the counselors who terminated Mr. Amiotte's court ordered treatment program due to non-compliance, the V.A. believes Mr. Amiotte is more valuable as a speaker than the horror I experienced from the crimes he committed against me. (Mr. Amiotte was a guest speaker at the Veterans Affairs "Serving Returning Veteran's" Conference in Seattle, Washington in 2011.)

I learned that many Native Americans take care of their own often at the expense of others. I was never allowed into Mr. Amiotte's "sacred circle," but my money was good enough for him and his friends. Through the years I knew Mr. Amiotte, he displayed and voiced his prejudice and hate toward women, white people and minorities. He called my money "his grub money" and white people "squatters" – as he did not believe we belonged in America.

Psychologist Carl Jung wrote, "The best political, social and spiritual work we can do is to withdraw the projection of our shadow onto others." Many people are slow to acknowledge their own shadows.

After the attempted murder incident Mr. Amiotte said, "Coral, I wanted to teach you a lesson, scare you." For my safety, I added George Amiotte's name to my state address protection program, due to his threats on my life.

On January 28, 2004, Ms. Diane Callison, a probation officer and Thurston County Domestic Violence Task Force member in Olympia, Washington called me. She checked on Mr. Amiotte's records in municipal court. She said that the municipal court had received the letter of April 2001 from Mr. Nickle's office regarding his non-compliance and termination. Ms. Callison shared with me what should have happened is a continuance in this matter, but clerks recorded the letter in their system as a letter of compliance, instead of non-compliance and termination. Mr. Amiotte should have had to appear in court again.

Ms. Callison also expressed her concerns regarding the police department, municipal court judge and prosecutor commenting that this case should have been handled as a felony instead of a misdemeanor because of the severity of the violence, noted red marks on my neck and arm, battering, choking.

In short, Mr. Amiotte suffered little or no consequences for his violent behavior. Mr. Amiotte believes he lives above the law.

Dr. Kuttner wrote me nearly a dozen letters admitting that he had violated client confidentiality by giving my case history and personal information to Mr. Amiotte. Dr. Kuttner wrote me a letter indicating that he "hoped that Mr. Amiotte would not murder me." Dr. Kuttner also wrote me a letter apologizing for introducing me to his colleague calling him a "snake." He wrote me a letter saying, "Coral, Mr. Amiotte steals your money and your soul."

For many people power and control over others IS their existence. Domestic violence is not about anger but about trying to instill fear and wanting to have power and control in the relationship. Batterers and abusers treat others inhumanely because they lack three necessary components for spiritual health: being self-critical, showing empathy and walking in humility.

While I was in shock from the loss of my children and the ongoing court trauma in Oregon, I was "prey" for these two "pseudo therapists." The abuse and exploitation by my doctor and his unlicensed associate traumatized me.

In 2003, Dr. Kuttner backpedaled after I was almost murdered by his friend. He protected himself by writing me a letter dated Jan. 22, 2003, "Coral, if asked for my input on Mr. Amiotte having a license for counseling, I would say he is absolutely unqualified due to ethics violations. I've told him that, both in a letter and in person." Dr. Kuttner shared that he felt Mr. Amiotte is both a predator and con artist. He said, "But as I look into the situation in retrospect, I see a wolf, hovering around an injured, but beautiful deer and going in for the kill." He added, "George is so ill he is beyond recognizing his need for help."

On January 31, 2004, I wrote a letter to Mr. Anthony Principi, United States Department of Veteran Affairs and Dr. Alfonso R. Batres, Director of Veteran Affairs Chief Officer, Readjustment Counseling Service, to advocate for myself and others who will be victimized by Mr. Amiotte, and to prompt the V.A. to improve their practices for hiring workshop presenters and contract employees. I included a manuscript dealing the abuse I have suffered and included police reports, court documents, regarding the man who had attempted to murder me in August 2000, Mr. George Amiotte. My abuser, Mr. Amiotte considered Dr. Alfonso R. Batres as a friend and associate and talked with him on the phone. I hoped Dr. Batres would take this matter seriously. Sadly, I did not hear back from them and Mr. Amiotte continued to work for the Veteran's Administration. Silence is the same as approval.

Unfortunately, Amiotte has many supporters, enablers and a "cult following" within the V.A.

My goal is to help expose how our society "enables" batterers, abusers and predators.

Dr. Barbara May, asked me to request that Dr. Charles Kuttner contact V.A. employees about this matter.

Later, Dr. Kuttner attempted to report his concerns regarding Mr. Amiotte's abuse issues to Mr. Steve Becker, V.A. employee in Hot Springs, South Dakota, but was met with resistance, also. Mr. Steve Becker did not seem to take the court documentation, police reports, restraining orders, affidavits, legal promissory notes and documented reports of violence against me seriously. He is Mr. Amiotte's friend and has supported Mr. Amiotte and his seminars for years.

Amiotte's followers defended him because they are spellbound. His cult-like following within the Veterans' Administration demanded no accountability. He could continue his abusive and violent behavior. I did not fit in his *pretend* world with his *pretend* people where the ego is encouraged and integrity dismissed.

There are V.A. employees who believe it is insignificant that I have been battered. They are simply saying: *"We are of value in our society, you, Coral, are not."*

Not all veterans and V.A. therapists who attended Mr. Amiotte's V.A. PTSD workshops were enamored with him or a part of the "George Amiotte cult phenomena."

I am not the only person alarmed at the workshops Mr. Amiotte conducts for the V.A. Several people contacted me after attending his workshops to share their reactions:

"I witnessed George Amiotte humiliate V.A. psychiatrists and civilians during his workshops. This behavior is acceptable to George's V.A. 'cult followers.' I believe our American veterans/soldiers and taxpayers deserve better."

"George wants us to leave his workshops believing that **no one** has experienced the depth of pain and trauma that he survived in his three tours in Nam."

248

"George is a womanizer. I don't appreciate his 'in your face' methods." (The last comment is a component that most cult leaders use as a method of psychological control over an audience, i.e., making them ill at ease.)

In 2004 Mr. Amiotte purchased a $4,000 vehicle from Mr. Steve Becker, a V.A. employee at Hot Springs, South Dakota, even though Mr. Amiotte knew I was living out of my car due to the debt I had incurred from him. Mr. Becker called Mr. Amiotte to make sure the $4,000 check was in the mail for the vehicle. Mr. Amiotte did not play power and control games with his friend, Steve Becker as he put the monies in the mail immediately. Mr. Amiotte said he bought the vehicle in the event his daughter, Lalena, needed it. I know Mr. Becker would not be pleased to wait for years for payment on this debt. Mr. Becker was of value to Mr. Amiotte. I was not. At this time, I had a $31,500 Summary Judgment against Mr. Amiotte.

I am requesting that Mr. Amiotte sell his properties and pay me in full for the Summary Judgment I have against him so I can pay my creditors and taxes due. Individuals in the Hot Springs area have contacted me and shared that they approached Mr. Amiotte about purchasing his land. Mr. Amiotte told them that he will not sell his land.

Sadly, throughout the past several years, Mr. Amiotte has continued to lead a life of violence and abuse. A few years ago, he threatened his neighbors' lives. I have also received letters from women he has counseled who were abused by him, too.

Rev. Marie Fortune writes, "There is little empathy or sympathy, a deflection of attention away from the agent of the trauma and a tendency to silence or ostracize the victim altogether. The moral substance of this trauma is murky. And since the perpetrator most likely is someone known to both the victim and her community, bystanders prefer not to get involved."

Confronting abuse and violence is ugly and requires difficult self-examination. Accepting collective responsibility costs more.

I have learned that victims suffer not only from the abuse they experienced but also from the threat of meaninglessness and powerlessness that comes with it. People who experience the trauma of violence at the hand of someone they know, (i.e., a partner, parent, relative, therapist, teacher, pastor, or priest) - struggle to make meaning, usually in a context of isolation, if not moral condemnation and victim blaming.

The sad fact is this: you will not know you have been victim of a "con" until afterwards. Con artists have perfected their work, their art, so well, that you will not recognize them until it is too late.

Several months after Mr. Amiotte attempted to murder me, he asked me if I would be a phone contact for him while he attended a two-week PTSD workshop for his combat trauma at the Seattle, Washington, V.A. hospital. I agreed to do so. He later asked me if I would assist him with his "Coyote Crossing PTSD Workshops" and I declined. He does not respect me, he does not respect people, and he does not respect himself.

On July 12, 2012, George Amiotte was arrested for eluding police, drunk driving (.216 blood alcohol level) and possession of marijuana in Mason County Washington, Cause No. 12-1-00282-7. Prosecutor Erik Sigmar is handling the case. Mr. Amiotte's trial date is March 4, 2013.

Since the Veterans Administration and Veterans Affairs has incorporated Native American teachers, such as Mr. Amiotte, as a part of their curriculum, I will share a few insights and wisdom from Jamie Sams, author of *"Dancing the Dream: The Seven Paths to Human Transformation.* She says she has seen many succumb to this form of "distraction," ignoring their own ego issues and spiritual bankruptcy at the expense of others.

Jamie Sams describes Native American teachers such as George Amiotte as *"Twilight Masters"* – individuals who have mastered the use of the light and dark sides of human nature in order to control or manipulate others. Twilight Masters also use the lure of claiming to be spiritually enlightened in order to draw others of goodwill in their way of thinking. By masquerading as spiritual, caring individuals, the Twilight Master influences or bends the resolves of other spiritually committed individuals in order to serve his or her hidden agendas and selfish aims.

"Enlisting the assistance of dark elemental entities and by demonstrating dark behavior, people can become Twilight Masters. Bending the will of another to your own is what the Southern Seers call BAD Medicine. Individuals use energy and focused personal intent to exact the desired outcome from others. Using this form of invasive psychic energy is a *breach of trust and a rape of the Sacred Spaces of others."*

After years of abuse and court trauma, and now more violence, betrayal and therapist exploitation, I identify with the character of the Vietnamese woman portrayed in the movie, '*Casualties of War*' starring Michael Fox and Sean Penn. A group of American soldiers invades a Vietnamese village and capture a young woman. They gang rape her and force her to march with them on their patrol. When they were "finished with her," they shot her and threw her over an embankment.

Dr. Kuttner's betrayal of me, dismissing my pleas for help regarding his associate Mr. Amiotte, then becoming annoyed with me when I reported I was being threatened, financially exploited and abused, has caused me much reflection.

There would not have been any professional consequences to Dr. Kuttner had I been murdered. I would have only been a "statistic."

I would never allow these two cowards, or their friends and colleagues, in my life today.

Mr. George Twiss, former director of Cangleska, Pine Ridge, South Dakota, shared that many Lakota men now have joined Warrior Societies to be held in accountability with one another so abuse incidents such as the one I experienced will not occur. Mr. Amiotte is accountable to **no one.**

One of Mr. Amiotte's mentors in the past was medicine man Frank Fool's Crow who taught that humility was the component of a great leader. He is humble and honest and sincere. He is not profane. He is not violent. Fool's Crow said that a spiritual man must be measured by their manner of life. When someone has offended or harmed another individual, he must do everything he can to restore that individual so he does not lose his power.

Unfortunately, numerous Native Americans from the Pine Ridge Reservation (SD) and the Skokomish Reservation (WA) where Mr. Amiotte lives support and enable him—even after hearing about the violence I suffered from him.

To heal and recover from abuse and violent crimes, survivors need the community to create the conditions for an experience of justice. For the perpetrator, the goal is the possibility of a change or "repentance."

I have asked myself, "What does the human spirit need in order to heal and move on?" (This can be applied to veterans as well). Victims need a safe place to share their pain and be acknowledged, they need compassion, they need to know that they (and others) will be protected from their perpetrator, they need accountability—someone to hold their perpetrator accountable, they need restitution or material compensation for the losses incurred by the perpetrator and they need vindication (not revenge) —to be set free. Scars remain, but healing is sufficient so as not to continue to be held in bondage to the trauma.

Resolution, restitution and apologies from Mr. George Amiotte are needed in this case.

When there is no justice, there is truly no healing.

I continue to believe in surprises, miracles and "one fine day."

Left to Right: *George Amiotte, Peter Fonda and Coral Anika Theill, August 1999 at Sturgis Motorcycle Rally*

Peter is wearing my Viking Helmet and is riding the "Captain America" chopper from the film 'Easy Rider.'

Peter Fonda's "Captain America" chopper from Easy Rider — easily one of the most iconic motor vehicles in movie history. The [Easy Rider] bike evokes powerful emotions even in non-bikers. It personifies the '60s, all of the good and the bad that decade brought.

Toxic Leadership in the U.S. Marine Corps

After over twenty years of advocate work in a volunteer capacity, interviewing hundreds of Marines and author of numerous articles about Marines and wounded warriors, I joined the National Naval Officers Association at Camp Pendleton and Quantico Marine Corps base per the invite of Gerald Hampton, Oceanside, California.

During these years, a decorated Marine attempted to murder me, robbed, threatened and stalked me, while his Marine colleagues and employees of the Veteran's Administration condoned his behavior. I have been slandered, betrayed, deceived, bullied and sexually assaulted – all by Marines.

Secretary of Defense Lloyd James Austin, III, asked advocates to communicate with him so he could address the epidemic of sexual assault in the military. He is welcome to read this story regarding my experiences as an advocate for military members and Marines. A majority of them condoned the deplorable behavior of their fellow Marines.

I joined the NNOA because I am a civil & human rights activist as well as a reporter for the U.S. Marine Corps, Wounded Warriors and military. I believe racism and misogyny are so deeply intertwined, that they cannot be disentangled. We really cannot talk or advocate about one without talking and advocating about the other. It has been my experience that patriarchy has promoted misogyny as well as racism. Sadly, my experiences as a member/volunteer for the NNOA mirrored the abuse of my past traumas – betrayal, obscene disrespect and shaming by Lt. Colonel NaTasha Everly, USMC, and Colonel Christopher Shaw, USMC

It is my hope that the officers, leaders and members of the NNOA will become more informed and educated about toxic patriarchy, domestic violence, rape and the #MeToo movement in the future. Local, state and national advocates were shocked and alarmed when they learned of how Colonel Shaw and Lt. Colonel NaTasha Everly treated me, a domestic violence and rape advocate. Sadly, their actions may have been *business as usual.*

Unchecked power is a very sick drug. It is the same component that causes the epidemic of abuse and rape in our society, homes, workplaces, places of worship, schools as well as the government and the military. From my experiences in the NNOA, many of their members are pseudo-Christians and pseudo leaders. Their treatment of me resembles how cult leaders act and respond to their members.

I believe good leadership empowers people. Good leaders DO NOT WIELD AUTHORITY OR POWER or act like bullies and cowards.

In 2014 Major Zerbin Singleton, USMC, President of the Camp Pendleton National Naval Officers Association (NNOA) asked me to write an article about "Leadership." In a twist of events, *I wrote an article about how not to lead*, **"Exposing Abusers & Enablers in the National Naval Officers Association."**

It is my hope that the acts of obscene disrespect, dishonesty and abuse against me be acknowledged. I hope the NNOA will find evolved mentors and create positive changes.

I've been thinking about what it would be like in today's environment to be a "good" cop, Marine or soldier who believes in true justice, equality and the ideals of the Constitution. Peer pressure applied within a uniformed organization is intense and can be quite heavy handed. Go along to get along. Don't be a rat. Stand with your brothers and sisters. It requires immense courage to stand up for what's right against the tide of peer pressure.

Because of my life's history, I think of the 1968 My Lai Massacre.

Lieutenant William Calley led his unit in a slaughter of old men, women and children of a Vietnamese village. There were soldiers in that unit who simply went along to get along; did horrendous things they didn't know they were capable of doing; and later regretted it. It was only because another soldier and his helicopter crew, flying overhead, saw what was happening and took steps to stop it, that it ended. For doing the "right thing," Warrant Officer Hugh Thompson was not rewarded; just the opposite. The military culture and its supporters made his life miserable for many years.

In the months and years to come, I suspect many "good" cops, Marines and soldiers will be faced with a tough decision, just as Hugh Thompson Jr.

The National Naval Officers Association already showed me who they are regarding addressing abuse and disrespect - shun, shame and discard the victim.

After six decades of severe abuse and traumas as well as twenty years of surviving abusive Christian/Catholic clergy, leaders, members and cults, my experiences in the NNOA *has left ash on my tongue.*

Coral Theill pictured with Jeff Galloway, Olympian,
marathon runner and author, February 2012

I have honored my survival of the abrupt removal of my young children and baby, on March 10, 1996, by purchasing a hat on the anniversary of the day I no longer was allowed to be a mother.

About the Author

"It has been said, time heals all wounds. I do not agree. The wound remains. In time the mind, protecting its sanity, covers them with scar tissue and the pain lessens. But it is never gone."

-Rose Kennedy

I have come to appreciate the mystery of human suffering. When we can truly embrace our pain and suffering and are able to be authentically grateful for our wounds and the brutality that we may have endured, we become 'healed healers.'

Alice Walker's wise words have become my personal mantra, "Resistance is the secret of joy, we should challenge whatever oppresses us, anything we love can be saved, the way forward is with a broken heart, we should lead and not project on others what they should do for us, and we are the ones we have been waiting for."

Difficult experiences in life have softened rather than hardened me.

I have a positive, inspiring deep warrior soul, a brave gypsy heart, a renaissance woman, survivor/overcomer extraordinaire and an angel with a sword standing tall for the Good when it has to be!

My passions include support of our troops and wounded warriors and assisting those who have experienced trauma and crisis in their journey back to wholeness and 'self.' I remind those around me, 'your trauma is not who you are, it is just what happened to you.' I believe we are all bonded together by the fact that each and every one of us faces personal trials, trauma and crisis. Our challenge is to reframe and use the tragic moments in life for personal empowerment and for encouraging others.

I understand quantum physics and destiny plays a role in our lives. I believe there are no accidents in life and in synchronicity. Beauty is how we treat people around us. Love wants the highest good for the other. Respect is not casting your shadows on others.

I believe there is beauty in the ashes, sanity is madness put to good use, normal is only a setting your dryer, too much of a good thing is wonderful, and sexuality is a 'state of mind.' I don't have any baggage, but do have a classy luggage rack. Through the years I have learned that 'gray is a beautiful color.'

My past training and professional work experiences include: pilot training and ground school, court reporter, legal secretary, sales, home renovation, logging, fork lift driver and warehouse worker, professional modeling, freelance reporter, artist, advocate, writer and author.

My own favorite quote: *'No one outside ourselves can rule us inwardly, when we know and understand this, we are truly free.'*

In 1997, 1999 and 2018 I visited my relatives in Denmark and traveled to Sweden. I was refreshed by their love, humor and hospitality and their civil and humane society. Since 1997, I have lived in many different states and have also had the opportunity to experience living on several Indian Reservations within the United States. My homes have been my car, small motel rooms, cabins, and numerous small apartments. I take my contentment with me, live in my 'now moment,' and "blow with the wind."

My self-care activities range from reading a diverse body of spiritual, alternative health and self-improvement books, as well as literature, history, and poetry. I also enjoy dancing, singing and physical fitness programs. These activities have combined to enrich and strengthen me physically, mentally and spiritually. In my spare time, I enjoy volunteer work, research and writing, decorating, bargain hunting at second hand shops and creating new designs for my pure beeswax candle and keepsakes business.

I continue to pray for the highest good for all and envision a healed, whole and conscious society. I encourage those around me to "go to the edge of the light, to listen deeply and feel their inner guidance." I am thankful for my past because it has pushed me to reach a higher level of consciousness and a deeper awareness of who I am.

I am at peace with my life and my past and have learned the importance of honoring myself. I no longer embrace the ideological rigidity and doctrines of patriarchal religions and "Christianity," but wish to help those who are being abused "in the name of God."

As a youth I did not believe in the "us" and "them" mentality that is prevalent in American churches. I felt equal to my fellow man. The doctrines and beliefs of Christianity seemed too limiting to me. I felt interconnected to all mankind and nature. Compassion, unconditional love, peace and non-judgment **were** an automatic response to my personal belief system and moral code. I did not see the fruit in myself or others as we embraced the dogmas within Christianity. It was difficult for me to participate in the arrogance of the church and their teachings regarding the "lost, damned and unsaved."

When I finally left organized religion at the age of forty, I was reborn. The world suddenly became a much larger place and the people in it more interesting and beautiful. I could breathe and smell, see in color and dream. I became less fearful and judgmental. I appreciated my body, my life and my friends more. I had no absolute answers, which opened me up to new and interesting ideas. The entire universe became my church and everything and everyone in it my friend. I can worship 24/7 — anywhere at any time because all places are holy, sacred and special for me as are all people. I belong to the biggest church of all - the infinite universe and everyone is in it.

I believe our goal should not be eliminating religion, but illuminating the tactics by which it commands obedience and discourages doubt so that people can recognize these and reject them. It is more important that we all make up our own minds, use reason to guide us, and do not passively rely on faith or authority of religious leaders. Rather than keep our thoughts in captivity, we should set them free to explore wherever they wish - to seek out different viewpoints, to question fearlessly, and most importantly, to expose *all* ideas to the fire of testing. The ones worth being kept will survive. Humanity has a vast potential to accomplish things as yet undreamed-of, but blind faith will never take us there. If we are to become aware of the dangers that beset us and enter into a future where we can realize this potential, this is the way we must learn to live.

I truly believe the Universe sets in motion experiences in life for our soul's longings and desires to be met.

Even though I have left and walked away from organized religion, I believe in walking my talk. My personal moral code goes beyond the doctrines, dogmas and commandments of the religious-minded. I make my decisions from a place of unconditional love for myself, my Creator, and for my fellowman. I believe in personal accountability and responsibility for my thoughts and actions and believe that I create my own reality. "First do no harm" and "how can I help" are basic mottoes from which I base my discernment.

Being true to myself and resonating that truth to the Universe and to those around me is a highest priority. Einstein said that our actions are a reflection of our belief system. I continue to envision a whole and healed world. I believe our survival as a human race is dependent upon emotional and spiritual enlightenment apart from religion.

For my personal spiritual, emotional and physical health, I understand the truth of 'living your way into the answer.' Rainer Maria Rilke writes, "I beg you to have patience with everything unresolved in your heart to try to love the questions themselves as if they were locked rooms or books written in a very foreign language. Don't search for the answers which could not be given you now, because you would not be able to live them. And the point is, to live everything, live the questions now, perhaps, then, someday far in the future, you will gradually, without even noticing it, live your way into the answer."

My understanding and personal belief about love is best expressed by Anne Morrow Lindburgh. She wrote, "People talk about love as though it were something you could give, like an armful of flowers. And a lot of people give love like that - just dump it on top of you, a useless strong-scented burden. I don't think it is anything that you can give… Love is a force in you that enables you to give other things. It is the motivating power. It enables you to give strength and power and freedom and peace to another person. It is not a result; it is a cause. It is not a product; it produces. It is a power…It has taken me a long time to learn. I hope it will stay learned and that I can practice it."

I believe in the basic values of this country, life, liberty, pursuit of happiness - the necessity of basic human rights for all people, the golden rule and the social contract that says that those who have been given much should help those who are without.

I remind those around me to not forget the millions of women and children who are veterans of intimate wars and private anguish and for whom terror at home is *business as usual*. One in four women will experience violence at the hands of their partner at some time in their lives and one in three women will be the victim of sexual assault.

I hope by sharing my story, that other women (and men) who are trapped in similar situations—(and there are thousands of them), will be able to travel the path I have been forced to take a little more successfully.

In 2002, while writing and publishing *BONSHEA,* I was living out of my car, destitute and disabled. I was the victim of theft and an attempted murder incident by George Amiotte, an unlicensed therapist who worked for the Veterans Administration. I have shelter now and time has healed some of the pain. I continue to live in awe and radical amazement of life and will never stop hoping for justice, restitution and vindication.

I believe in seeking to defeat injustice, not people. I believe that the Universe is on the side of "justice" and that right will prevail.

Coral Anika Theill is available for speaking engagements and interviews. You may contact her at: coraltheill@hotmail.com or visit her website: www. coralanikatheill.com

Coral Anika Theill Professional Modeling Headshot
Photo Credit: Wen McNally Photography

Awards and Honors: In 1998, I received a professional model of the year award, in 2001 I was a guest speaker at Linfield College, and 2002 recipient of a Writer's Award from iUniverse Publishing Company. In 2004 **BONSHEÁ Making Light of the Dark** was used as a college text for nursing students at Linfield College, Portland, Oregon. *BONSHEÁ* is available in numerous libraries throughout Oregon as well as the Matilda Joslyn Gage Foundation Religious Freedom Room.

In 2008, Gene Deutscher, a U.S. Marine Combat Veteran, nominated me for the '*Woman of Courage Award.*" I was selected for the award by impressionist artist, Andrea Harris. In 2011, I was the recipient of the Lester Granger Award from the National Montford Point Marines Association for my advocacy and articles on the Montford Point Marines.

To help raise the consciousness about the mistreatment of mothers in America's courtrooms, I participated in a Silent Vigil for Mother's Day at the White House in 2010.

My article, *Montford Point Marines: Honoring and Preserving Their Legacy,* was published in the February 2011 issue of Leatherneck Magazine, my *Exclusive Interview with Commandant of the Marine Corps General James F. Amos on PTS and TBI* and *Invisible Battle Scars: Confronting the Stigma Associated with PTS and TBI* was published in the October 2011 issue of Leatherneck Magazine. *Invisible Battle Scars* is cited in the U.S. Army War College Psychological Notes, has been used as a college text for Marines studying at the Marine Corps University, Quantico, Virginia and was published in *Short Rations for Marines (And FMF Corpsmen),* an anthology of Marine Corps stories.

In honor of Mother's Day 2014, the Pixel Project Survivor Stories Interviews featured my story to help raise monies for the National Coalition Against Domestic Violence. In 2014 I submitted a request for a hearing with the Inter-American Commission on Human Rights and on August 1, 2015, and August 1, 2016, my Oregon case history was filed with the Claim Submitted to the United Nations on Modern Day Human Rights Crisis. I was assigned a USA case number in October 2016, On January 5, 2016, my Polk County Oregon case history was submitted to the United States District Court as a 'Declaration of Support' in Adkins v Adkins #15-754 addressing the due process violations in family courts across the United States. In 2016, I was a guest speaker for the Rotary Club in Fredericksburg, Virginia, in honor of Domestic Violence Awareness Month.

The *NEW YORK CITY ALLIANCE Against Sexual Assault* published my Oregon story of surviving marital rape in their book, *RECLAMATION: A Survivor's Analogy* by Survivors of Sexual Assault on March 1, 2018 in honor of the #MeToo movement. *RECLAMATION* is available at Amazon.com. Proceeds from the book are donated to assist rape victims.

Presently, I serve on the Board of Directors of the Montford Point Marines of America, Inc.

Live Your Best Life

by Dawna Markova

I will not die an unlived life.
I will not live in fear of falling or catching fire.
I choose to inhabit my days,
to allow my living to open me,
to make me less afraid,
more accessible,
to loosen my heart until it becomes a wing,
a torch, a promise.
I choose to risk my significance,
to live so that which came to me as a seed goes to the next as blossom,
and that which came to me as blossom,
goes on to fruit.

Coral's Professional Modeling Headshot After Divorce

I Believe

by Coral Anika Theill

I BELIEVE each soul has a responsibility for the entire world and that our personal losses can be a vehicle to experiencing a greater good. Surrendering lost dreams helped me prepare for new dreams.

I BELIEVE we all embrace the hope and dream that humanity can be free to act humanely and that someday all people will resonate Christ-consciousness, compassion, non-judgment and peace toward one another.

I BELIEVE in the inherent worth of every person. People are worthy of respect, support, and caring simply because they are human.

I BELIEVE in seeking to defeat injustice, not people.

I BELIEVE that the Universe is on the side of "justice" and that right will prevail.

I BELIEVE in working towards a culture that is relatively free of discrimination on the basis of gender, race, sexual orientation, national origin, degree of ability, age, etc.

I BELIEVE in the sanctity of the human person. I oppose the use of torture and cruel or unusual punishment including the death penalty. (http://www.innocenceproject.org)

I BELIEVE in the importance of democracy within religious, political and other structures.

I BELIEVE In the separation of church and state; and the freedoms of speech, association, and expression.

I BELIEVE in the importance of individual believers determining evil influences and policies within their chosen faith group, and advocate for their correction. If the beliefs people have adopted prevent them from feeling love, equality and inner connectedness with all mankind, then I believe that they must challenge their beliefs and integrity.

I BELIEVE in the importance of education - that people are not truly educated unless they have studied at least the world's major religions and ethical systems. They need to learn of the good and bad impacts they have had on society.

People need to understand the religious sources that inspired Gandhi and Albert Schweitzer, and to commit their life to the alleviation of human suffering. But they also need to learn the shadow side of religion: how religious beliefs have contributed to hatred, intolerance, oppression, discrimination, as well as mass murders and genocides in such places as Nazi Germany, Bosnia, East Timor, Kosovo, Northern Ireland, the Middle East, Sudan and countless other countries.

I BELIEVE in respecting another's religion, but if their religious beliefs cause harm or are being used to abuse another, then I must speak out against the abuse.

I BELIEVE that domestic violence is a crime and that the symbol of "patriarchal ownership" is shameful and should elicit public condemnation. The chattel laws of the past have roots in an oppressively hierarchical, patriarchal violence-accepting society. There is a point at which behavior becomes predatory and malicious—a point at which one is morally obligated to separate themselves from that person.

I BELIEVE in protecting children and object to the government's lackadaisical approach to fighting human trafficking.

I BELIEVE in the United Nations Declaration of Human Rights and the integrity and value of international law.

I abhor Genocide, corruption, colonialism, needless war and greed.

I applaud Civil Rights, Humanitarian Activism, strength, courage and resistance to state terrorism.

I protest the contamination of the earth, particularly water supplies, military base toxicity, Monsanto, Agent Orange and GMO food.

As a non-military writer researching the subject of Marines and Post Traumatic Stress, Traumatic Brain Injury and Suicide Prevention, I feel a deep gratitude to our servicemen and women and believe our society needs to do more to respect, understand and support those returning from deployment in conflict zones.

Afterword

by Judy Bennett

"It takes two to speak the truth. One to speak, and another to hear."
–Henry David Thoreau

"When I came upon this quote, used as a chapter intro in a murder mystery, it struck home. I have known Coral for several years and helped her with some of her writing, but, even though she had asked, I had stopped short of making a commitment to helping her finish a manuscript recounting her story.

I have the tendency, as do most people to shy away from the overly dramatic–to resist that which seems a bit unbelievable or "crazy." This quote from Thoreau brought me face to face with the question, "Did I believe Coral was telling the truth?" The answer was yes, and the question for my conscience became, "What is my responsibility to that truth?"

Truth does not exist in a vacuum. Any event is subject to the changing perceptions of the participants and the interpretations of society–and the language used to communicate. But Coral's story had remained remarkably consistent, and the documentation was very complete. What had changed over the years I had been friends with Coral was her capacity for examining the details of the events that wove together to create such trauma in her life.

My own life has been very untraumatic. I'm very happily married, my parents have always been loving and supportive, and no one has ever abused me. I have been lucky–or blessed. And what "bad times" I've had have been tremendously important lessons in life.

Even the experiences I have had with church and my own spiritual life are different from Coral's. I was raised in the Presbyterian Church. Although I made a conscious decision to leave the church at about the age of 17 and have not been back, I have an appreciation for the fact that within the church, people are striving for a world where good prevails.

My own spirituality has no definable dogma attached. I believe strongly that there is a spirit of godliness in all people and that for good to overcome the ills of the world everyone needs compassion. I tend to be an optimist, to believe that truth and justice will win. But I am also a bit cynical and feel that a lot of people deserve what they get. Sort of like the Karmic principles of Buddhism, with a twisted sense of humor.

Getting to know Coral and her story challenged some of my basic beliefs—as does any situation where we ask, "Why do bad things happen to good people?" But working on this project has also reawakened some trust in my own intuitive knowledge—which I had neglected in favor of the practical and the day-to-day survival skills in a busy and increasingly technological world. It is impossible to know Coral as she is today without recognizing the strength she has found in putting her trust in the Universe.

I met Marty Warner and some of the children before I met Coral—she was Kathy then. I was always impressed with the kids—they were intelligent and confident and talked easily with adults. Marty seemed to be a nice guy, and the only clue to the family's religious leanings was that all the kids had Biblical names—and maybe that there were so many of them.

Over the next few years, I encountered the Warner family occasionally in the small town we all lived in, and somewhere along the way I met Kathy. She was always with several of the children and I was impressed with the ease and grace she showed in managing all the tugs for attention from the kids. She was full of patience and creativity, and the kids were beautiful, happy, intelligent, polite and outgoing. (It was hard, as I began to know what was happening to Kathy—and later, working on this manuscript—to reconcile this image of a beautiful family, with the darkness that engulfed her.) It wasn't until she separated from Marty that I began to get to know Kathy.

I was not directly involved with the years of court cases—and that is the portion of this history that has been the hardest for me to understand. I have always believed that right must triumph and that our system of justice is basically sound. I cannot believe that most of the people involved meant to cause Coral pain. But they did—and it is a measure of all of us that many people hurt her by just not wanting to get involved. Others held so desperately to a concept of Christian righteousness that they would not accept truths that they had seen with their own eyes.

Because of Coral's fragility (fragile does not mean mentally ill), the court put the children in the custody of their father. The issues that Coral desperately wanted addressed in court—the mental abuse of cults, abuse in a marriage, marital rape, authoritarian and brutal practices in child rearing—were not subjects that the court would consider within the context of a divorce trial. By the final custody hearing, Coral felt that the only chance for survival was to let Marty have the children–fighting over them would hurt them too much.

One of the overwhelming issues for Coral became the sheer expense of paying for lawyers. It is part of the reason that she did not appeal the custody decision or the settlement–and it is the reason that so many judgments and court orders hang over her head. It seems that in our society justice is as much in the hands of the lawyers as our health is in the hands of doctors. Since most of us have a very true sense of what is right and wrong, it is hard to accept our legal system puts justice out of our grasp.

Working on this story originally was difficult because much of it has been a process of helping Coral fit together the pieces of her life. Some parts have been so painful and raw for her that for years she could not examine them and find words to express them. Other parts had been examined so much–kind of like picking at a scab–that it was a matter of peeling away scar tissue to find the underlying truths. I have been the dispassionate voice asking why, what and how. Sometimes I forced Coral to go deeper and look at details of events that made her uneasy. I hope that by doing this without judging her or being emotional I helped lessen the pain of reliving these events.

The first edition of this book represented an incredible personal journey for Coral. Just writing one's life story is more than most people can accomplish. To write a story that examines so much personal trauma is even more difficult. It evolved from a pile of journal pages and a trail of post-it-notes and reminders stuck on the bathroom mirror, through early versions cut into paragraphs and strewn on the bed, and hundreds of edits–filling in details, clarifying and digging deeper. In the end, the words–Coral's own words–flowed like a river that has broken through a dam.

When she decided on rewriting and updating the book, my job was more that of a true editor – reading the copy and making suggestions and corrections, but Coral had found her voice and her confidence. She had healed in many ways, and with that increased strength has come a healthy measure of anger. In the intervening years there has been some more trauma, but also growth, joy and discovery.

The saddest part of Coral's story will always be that her children were robbed of her love, grace, strength, creativity and joy. They have been taught a lop-sided perspective on events, distorted by a religion that is based neither on love nor compassion. I hope that someday this story will help all of Coral's children understand that their mother loves them very much.

I know that Coral struggled with what to tell and what to hold back in telling her story. I pressed her to tell as complete a story as possible – it was past the point where half-truths would do. What Coral's children do not understand is that what set in motion the events that led her to stand up to her husband and escape from her marriage – was an effort to PROTECT her children from harm.

The reason this book exists at all is because she was driven to document her life– for the sake of her children and adults they are becoming. I know that finishing this will help Coral put to rest some of her demons and move further into the light. I also hope this tale of survival helps others who read it to find strength and compassion.

People who think Coral's story cannot be true are living in a world of make believe. It is time we open our eyes to what is going on behind closed doors and hidden behind "righteousness".

I have tremendous respect for Coral's grace and intelligence – and for her unwillingness to give up. She will never be free of the pain, but some justice – and apologies from those that failed her – would do wonders.

Shalom, Coral. Thank you for including me in the journey. I am proud to have you as a friend.

- *Notes* -

SPIRITUAL JOURNEY

OBSERVATIONS & CONCLUSION

Learning how to be kind to ourselves, learning how to respect ourselves,
is important. The reason it's important is that, fundamentally, when
we look into our own hearts and begin to discover what is confused
and what is brilliant, what is bitter and what is sweet, it isn't just
ourselves that we're discovering. We're discovering the universe.
- Pema Chodron, *When Things Fall Apart*

Dear Reader,

The following words are who I am, what I believe and spiritual truths and universal laws that have sustained me in this life. Many of the feelings and insights of truth have always been with me and are part of why I could survive *in the world I found myself*—and why, even in that world, I could experience such joy with my children. Much of the vocabulary

and the articulation of spiritual truths have come from a great deal of time spent seeking knowledge through reading, meditating, and listening to the wisdom my counselors and mentors have imparted. These activities have aided me in my search for wholeness since losing my children.

Spiritual Journey and History

I am a deeply spiritual woman. I respect the sacredness of my being. I believe in walking in the path of the Bodhisattva—one who embodies compassion and lives solely for the purpose of allowing others the gift of their own growth and enlightenment. I honor the female component of the divinity. I believe we can achieve Christ-consciousness—Christ centered thinking and actions apart from religiosity. The wisdom and writings from, Buddhism and Eastern thought, Jewish mystics, Native American spirituality and ancient texts and traditions encourage and inspire me. The use of ancient tools and meditation bring peace to my life.

I appreciate the profound insights from great thinkers and writers such as Albert Einstein, James Allen, Helen Ellerbe, Andrea Dworkin, Matilda Joslyn Gage, Carl Jung, Greg Braden, Thomas Moore, Elie Wiesel, Joan Borysenko, Judith Herman, M.D., Gabor Mate, M.D., Jonathan Shay, M.D., Clarissa Pinkola Estes, Ph.D., Alice Miller, James Baldwin, Bertrand Russell, Maya Angelou, Wayne Dyer, Christine Northrup the Dalai Lama and Viktor Frankl. Their writings, along with encouragement and insights from my counselors and mentors, helped me to graciously reframe my past and learn to respect the sacredness of my inner being and soul.

Today, I relate to the definition of a mystic: A mystic sees God everywhere, looks for God in all people, develops humility about self, hungers after God, is always growing, knows there is more, looks for ways to give themselves away, gives up the need to be right, is tolerant of other's viewpoints, resists the temptation to take life for granted, is spiritually connected, but at odds with the community, feels rich that God will provide, sees things from a higher perspective, and is sometimes branded a heretic. Mystics are ordinary people who live in radical amazement.

A meditation and prayer I say for myself and all those around me, *'There is nothing in me that believes in lack, negation of any kind, confusion, or discord. There is no belief in chaos, disease, weakness or limitation. I recognize the abundance in the Universe. I see myself surrounded by plenty. The universe is orderly and harmonious. I draw on its inexhaustible energy'*

I also identify with the definition of a witch—one who bends; one who is flexible—in other words, one who can enjoy the scenery while taking a detour. Witches were wise women (witch means wise woman) who were skilled in the use of herbal remedies. I relate to the term "heathen." Heathens were those "who worshipped in the heathers."

Thomas Moore, in his book, *Care of the Soul*, taught me a beautiful analogy of suffering. I cling to the wisdom of his words. Moore writes,

"Care of the soul sees another reality altogether. It appreciates the mystery of human suffering and does not offer the illusion of a problem-free life. It sees every fall into ignorance and confusion as an opportunity to discover that the beast residing at the center of the labyrinth is also an angel. The uniqueness of a person is made up of the insane and the twisted as much as it is of the rational and normal."

"The Greeks told the story of the minotaur, the bull-headed flesh-eating man who lived in the center of the labyrinth. He was a threatening beast, and yet his name was Asterion–Star. We have to care for this *(our)* suffering with extreme reverence so that, in our fear and anger at the beast, we do not overlook the star."

The "star" is the psychic energy and medicine I have discovered within me and the ability to travel to the "ethers or my own Avalon."

Trauma has helped me tap into my own intuition and energy. I feel and sense people and places strongly. One such example was an incident in South Dakota in 1999. I was staying in an old hotel in Hot Springs. I could not lay down on the bed and became increasingly uncomfortable in the room. I finally left in the middle of the night and slept in my car. The next day I was shopping in the local health food store and shared my experience with the owner, who had previously befriended me. She was amazed at my sensitivities and told me that recently a Native American woman had been raped by a white man in that same room. The woman sought help, but the police "lost" evidence and her abuser was never prosecuted. The local safe house employees assisted the woman during her trauma.

We all possess psychic energy, and intuition, but so many people have been taught to dismiss or ignore it. The biggest obstacle to hearing and listening to our "inner voice" is man-made religion and dogma. We are taught and programmed by religious institutions not to question authority. When we believe this lie, we deny the life force that we were born with–we might as well not be here.

All of life's answers are truly inside each one of us. All we need to do is take off our masks, be quiet and listen. I have learned to trust and respond to my inner voice. When I listen inside, I discover who I truly am apart from the conditioning and brainwashing so prevalent in our society, culture, politics and religion. Intuition is like hearing a song played only once—you must respond to it when it offers itself, for it seldom plays the same song twice.

Life is a curriculum for learning unconditional love for ourselves, our Universal God and for our fellow man. We seek and draw to ourselves that which we need to learn. We teach that which we need to learn. Life is also an experience of becoming humane. Humane means "one who embodies mercy." Mercy is kindness in excess of what is expected.

In the past few years, Greg Braden's book, *Walking Between the Worlds—The Science of Compassion,* has been a handbook for me. Evolved people in the Scandinavian countries and also here in the Americas encouraged me to study Greg Braden's book and the truths of mirroring, quantum physics and magnetics. Greg Braden teaches the importance of resonating unconditional love, peace, non-judgment and compassion. This is the energy that will change the world. His book is a universal handbook for "collective healing," global peace and graceful transition.

Braden writes, "Total forgiveness of myself and others generates liberation in my life and produces that inner joy that no one can rob. Forgiveness transcends us to a higher state of consciousness. The act of genuine forgiveness, I believe, contains the energy that generates miracles. Forgiveness liberates the psyche and soul from the need for personal vengeance and the perception of oneself as a victim. More than releasing from blame the people who caused our wounds, forgiveness means releasing the control that the perception of victimhood has over our psyches."

Rev. Joanna Trainor, teaches that forgiveness is not the act of holding in silence a past hurt out of some act of "polite silence." We release ourselves and the other person, and we stop the emotional holding pattern. We do NOT ignore the issue, avoid the issue, or downplay the truth of the issue, to "make believe." Resolution and apologies are acts of healing...both sides are able to STOP BEING VICTIMS OF EVENTS, IGNORANCE AND HIDDEN ACTS. She states that speaking out and requesting that the violence committed against us be acknowledged and resolved is an act of self-respect, love and healing. Seeking resolution is NOT seeking revenge.

In my quiet times, I still feel moments of raw pain from my past. I look at it for what it is, a catalyst for me to find the sacredness of my inner being–to realize more of myself and who I truly am. I believe how we think and act and how beautifully our spirit responds to our challenges is all that matters. Dr. Viktor Frankl says, "Each man is questioned by life; and he can only answer to life by answering for his own life; to life he can only respond by being responsible." He also states that "the only thing man cannot take from you is your attitude in any given set of circumstances."

When reflecting on the impact of trauma and tragedy in the world around me, I am encouraged by the words of Sharon Salzberg's, author of *Faith: Trusting Your Own Deepest Experience,* "What others have done before is impacting reality as we experience it right now. What any of us do right now has an effect over the reaches of time and space. Even when we feel helpless, we can find support in this truth. We can, with love and compassion, continue to offer our hearts beyond the hurdle of pain, stirred by faith to act the best we can in the life we all share together.

"We may not comprehend why there is so much suffering in this world, why some people behave so badly toward others, but we can count on hatred never ceasing by more hatred, but only by love. We can't predict how our actions will turn out, but whatever we do will have impact and consequences.

"There is no knowing what the future holds, or what lies on the horizon, but no matter what happens, the lives we live each day are part of a greater whole. We can place our faith on these certainties."

> "When you come to the edge of all the light you know and are about to step off into the darkness of the unknown, faith is knowing one of two things will happen. There will be something solid to stand on or you will be taught how to fly." –Barbara J. Winter

In these past few years, I was "taught how to fly."

Don Miguel Ruiz teaches in his book, *The Four Agreements* that there are four agreements that offer a powerful code of conduct that can rapidly transform our lives to a new experience of freedom, true happiness and love. I agree with the Toltec wisdom he shares: "Be impeccable with your word, don't take anything personally, don't make assumptions, and always do your best." He also shares that once we have mastered the awareness of who we are (love) and become spiritual warriors by stalking our own emotions and reactions so we can break free of the knowledge that enslaves us, we are ready to master love which is Life itself. Love in action can only produce happiness, which is heaven on earth. He teaches that the problems in our society begin with the domestication of a child, the same technique that is used with animals–punishment and reward. He says, "What we call education is nothing but domestication of the human being." His books are a must read for each person seeking inner peace and happiness.

I hope by sharing my story, the consciousness and awareness of society will be raised and the quality of life will improve in America. As a mother, I long for a safe and healthy society for my children to grow up in.

I have been counseled to count the cost of sharing honestly my experiences with a society that doesn't want to hear what they need to hear. The cost of staying silent is greater. I have discovered there is only danger in keeping secrets. If violence cannot be talked about, **it cannot be stopped.** I believe I have a responsibility to speak for women who are too traumatized to voice or write their pain and for those who are no longer living.

In the preface of Elie Wiesel's twenty-fifth anniversary edition of *Night*, Robert McAfee Brown wrote, "When Elie Wiesel was liberated from Buchenwald in 1945, having also been in Birkennau, Auschwitz, and Buna, he imposed a ten-year vow of silence upon himself before trying to describe what had happened to him and over six million other Jews. When he finally broke that silence, he had trouble finding a publisher. Such depressing subject matter. When "Night" was finally published, over twenty-five years ago, few people wanted to read about the Holocaust. Such depressing subject matter. But we cannot indefinitely avoid depressing subject matter, particularly if it is true, and in the subsequent quarter century the world has had to hear a story it would have preferred not to hear–the story of how a cultured people turned to genocide, and how the rest of the world, also composed of cultured people, remained silent in the face of genocide."

Brown continues, "Having confronted the story, we would much prefer to disbelieve, treating it as the product of a diseased mind, perhaps. And there are those today who–feeding on that wish, and on the anti-Semitism that lurks near the surface of the lives of even cultured people–are trying to persuade the world that the story is not true, urging us to treat it as the product of diseased minds, indeed. They are committing the greatest indignity human beings can inflict on another: telling people who have suffered excruciating pain and loss that their pain and loss were illusions. Perhaps there is a greater indignity; it is committed by those who believe them. *Night*, with its understated eloquence, stands as the permanent refutation of both kinds of baseness."

In his acceptance speech for the Nobel Peace Prize, Elie Wiesel said, "That I have tried to keep the memory alive, that I have tried to fight those who would forget. Because if we forget, we are guilty, we are accomplices. And then I explained to him *(Elie Wiesel as a young boy)* how naive we were, that the world did know and remained silent. And that is why I swore never to be silent whenever and wherever human beings endure suffering and humiliation. We must always take sides. Neutrality helps the oppressor, never the victim. Silence encourages the tormentor, never the tormented. Sometimes we must interfere. When human lives are endangered, when human dignity is in jeopardy, national borders and sensitivities become irrelevant. Wherever men or women are persecuted because of their race, religion, or political views, that place must–at that moment–become the center of the universe."

In her book, *Working with Your Chakras*, Ruth White writes about the spirit within us, "Beyond our behavior patterns and reactions to life, untouched by flaws of personality, character or morality, even within the most apparently vicious criminal, this spark burns on. When we know it in ourselves and honor it in others, it is nearly impossible to be inhumane."

One of the most profound Scriptures in the New Testament is also the shortest, "He (Jesus) wept." Humanity cries out for a non-judgmental, compassionate people, a people who resonate unconditional love and peace toward one another.

The following quotes have helped sustain me in the midst of trauma and crisis:

> "I promise that in no matter what disturbing circumstance I find myself or another, I will remember it is temporary, not eternal. As I apply unconditional love to myself and the circumstance, I have the strength to master the task. My spirit, my soul, and my identity is enhanced by my resolve. I am thankful for the opportunity to prove to myself that I have the power of resolve. I find pleasure in the mastery of the event." (Author unknown)

> "Knowing others is wisdom; Knowing the self is enlightenment, Mastering others requires force; Mastering the self needs strength. Wander where there is no path." –Lao Tsu

"A soul is forged out of fire and rock crystal. Something rigorous, hard in an Old Testament sense, but also as gentle as the gesture with which his tender fingertips sometimes stroked my eyelashes."
–The words of Etty Hillesum written in a concentration camp

All knowledge of the earth's past exists all around us as electromagnetic fields of information. Rupert Sheldrake, a British biologist, calls this "morphogenic fields". What has been suppressed for centuries is now surfacing in our consciousness. People are becoming aware of their pain and speaking their truth–the beginning of their walk in healing and wholeness.

> In her book, *I Know Why the Caged Bird Sings*, Maya Angelou writes, "The free bird leaps on the back of the wind and floats downstream till the current ends, and dips his wings in the orange sun rays and dares to claim the sky. But a bird that stalks down his narrow cage can seldom see through his bars of rage, his wings are clipped and his feet are tied so he opens his throat to sing. The caged bird sings with fearful trill of the things unknown, but longed for still and his tune is heard on the distant hill for the caged bird sings of freedom. The free bird thinks of another breeze on the trade winds soft through the sighing trees and the fat worms waiting on a dawn-bright lawn and he names the sky his own. But a caged bird stands on the grave of dreams his shadow shouts on a nightmare scream his wings are clipped and his feet are tied so he opens his throat to sing. The caged bird sings with a fearful trill of things unknown but longed for still and his tune is heard on the distant hill for the caged bird sings of freedom."

"Women and men all over the planet are finding the courage to break through the collective morphogenic fields of shame, fear, and pain. People are breaking the silence–releasing secrets that keep all of us trapped. People are saying, "No, more." By doing this people are changing the morphogenic field of fear and silence." –*Women's Bodies, Women's Wisdom*, by Dr. Christiane Northrup

> Singer, Tina Turner, is a beautiful example of someone who stepped "outside of the given" into a new morphogenic field. Her deep spirituality has inspired me and her example has encouraged me on in times of crisis. In energetic terms, she has become the light she radiates.

Another example of an individual creating a "morphogenic field" for her people, specifically women and the poor, is the late Phoolan Devi, hero and legend, once outlaw-turned legislator. Phoolan Devi was assassinated July 26, 2001, in India before the completion of my story. Her life is portrayed in the film, "*Bandit Queen*." She was a daughter of a low-caste family and was sold into marriage at age 11. She later fled her brutal husband and fell in love with a highway robber. Her lover was killed by upper-caste men from the village of Behmai who took her prisoner and raped her repeatedly. She escaped and formed her own gang. Gang members mowed down 22 upper-caste men with machine-gun fire.

She was jailed for 11 years. Her story is one of survival, courage and anger. Her anger from the acts of violence committed against her propelled her to acts of rage. I believe she did the best she could in an extreme situation. She chose violence and revenge–a place some people go when their anger fails to empower them. Some individuals choose to be their own justice system where there is no policing and justice in the society. This was her choice–not the best choice, but a choice. Although I do not agree with the act of violence, I honor her survival and the champion she became for women and the poor.

She stayed true to her path as a woman and refused to live out the role that she was born into–a sex slave and servant for the man who "owned her."

Breaking the silence and "telling secrets" takes courage. A few years ago, I believed by sharing my truth and breaking my silence, my very life would be threatened. "For many of us, telling the truth and coming off fear is like an addict coming off drugs. I believe the only way people can get through this fear is with the help of others who've also experienced it and come out on the other side. Imbalance of head and heart turns people into addicts. In energy terms, any behavior motivated by the fear of internal growth qualifies as an addiction." –Dr. Christine Northrup, *Women's Bodies, Women's Wisdom*

Dr. Northrup writes, "In the past, millions of women healers and wise women, and the men who have supported them, have been killed for telling the truth. It is little wonder, given the collective history, especially of women, that we are afraid. I believe when we deny this fear or discount its presence in others, we only give it more power. We need not judge it in others or in ourselves, but acknowledge it and move toward healing."

"Great spirits have always encountered violent opposition from mediocre minds."–Albert Einstein

Northrup further states, "When a person enters into the work of healing their body and speaking their truth, they must break through the collective field of fear and pain that is all around us and has been for the past five thousand years of dominator society. Rupert Sheldrake states that once a person steps outside of the given, breaks through a morphogenic field, it makes it easier for others to do the same by tapping into the new morphogenic field. This has been proven in setting world records. Once a world record has been broken, suddenly athletes all over the world begin breaking it."

In his book, *Walking Between the Worlds: The Science of Compassion*, Greg Braden writes, "You must become that which you choose to have in your life. Someone must live a new truth first. Someone must have the wisdom to recognize the possibility, the courage to become the possibility and the strength to live that possibility as a reality. The reality must be lived among us, in a world that may not always support that truth. That someone becomes the living bridge. By anchoring the possibility of a greater expression of life into our grids, that possibility becomes available for the next one with a similar desire to rise above the conditions of that which life has offered them, then for the next and the next and so on." I choose to become *a living bridge*.

The study of mirroring and quantum physics has given me guidance and peace. Greg Braden teaches, "When we start looking at ourselves, we should start looking for reflections–because the opposite is the important thing: looking for opposites. Opposites exist in the same place. If you look in a mirror, you see everything backwards from the way that it is. But it is a perfect backwards, because you are seeing the left on the right and the right on the left–it's a perfect reversal. Sometimes what you are looking for is what you are, and sometimes what you are is what you are looking for! Always look at the reflection. I have learned that each person is a mirror to you, showing you who you are in that moment. By careful observation you can see your opponent's reaction to what you are offering."

"Some mirrors (*people*) show us not what we are but, rather which we judge. If you don't like what someone is showing you, look to yourself. These are the patterns that you have become within yourself. These are the patterns that you identify with so strongly that you often do not see them. The source of your irritation with another's action may be the mirror of those qualities of character that you judge in life. There is a good chance that others may be reflecting back to you the very patterns that you have become within yourself. Life offers a series of mirrors that each man and woman will encounter on the path to know themselves. Relationships are your opportunity to see yourself in all ways. Each relationship mirrors a reflection of your beliefs, judgments, bias or lack thereof, as you interact with others. It is through the temples of our relationships that we remember our truest nature. In that memory, once again we return to a sacred place." –*Walking Between the Worlds–The Science of Compassion* by Greg Braden

> *"Perhaps love is me gently bringing you back to who you really are and not who I want you to be."* –Antoine de Saint-Exupery, *The Little Prince*

My belief about the sacredness of each individual's soul journey in this life can be best described in the following story. "Once a group of Siamese monks covered their precious golden Buddha with an outer covering of clay to keep their treasure from being looted. The golden figure lay hidden for centuries. We are all like the clay Buddha covered with a shell of hardness created out of fear, and yet underneath is a golden essence, our real self. Sometime along the way we began to cover up our natural self. Our task now is to discover our true essence once again." –*Jack Canfield* (adapted)

The Christ and the spirit of Christedness I have come to understand is described in Gary Zukav's book, *The Seat of the Soul*. He shares that Christ and Gandhi knew non-judgmental justice. "What is non-judgmental justice? Non-judgmental justice is a perception that allows you to see everything in life, but does not engage your negative emotions. Non-judgmental justice relieves you of the self-appointed job of judge and jury because you know that everything is being seen–nothing escapes the law of karma–and this brings forth understanding and compassion. Non-judgmental justice is the freedom of seeing what you see and experiencing what you experience without responding negatively. It allows you to experience directly the unobstructed flow of the intelligence, radiance and love of the Universe of which our physical reality is a part. Non-judgmental justice flows naturally from understanding the soul and how it evolves."

Gary Zukav teaches that evil is the absence of Light. He writes, "Understanding that evil is the absence of Light does not mean that it is inappropriate to respond to evil. What is the appropriate response to evil? The remedy for an absence is a presence. Evil is an absence and, therefore, it cannot be healed with an absence. By hating evil, or one who is engaged in evil, you contribute to the absence of Light and not to its presence. Hatred of evil does not diminish evil, it increases it. Understanding evil as the absence of Light does not require you to become passive, or to disregard evil actions or evil behavior. If you see a child being abused, or a people being oppressed, for example it is appropriate that you do what you can to protect the child, or to aid the people, but if there is not compassion in your heart also for those who abuse and oppress—for those who have no compassion—do you not become like them? Compassion is being moved to and by acts of the heart, to and by the energy of love. If you strike without compassion against the darkness, you yourself enter the darkness.

"A compassionate heart is more effective against evil than an army. A compassionate heart can engage evil directly—it can bring Light where there was no Light. Understanding evil as the absence of Light requires you to examine the choices that you make each moment in terms of whether they move you toward Light or away from it. It allows you to look with compassion upon those who engage in evil activities, even as you challenge their activities, and thus protects you from the creation of negative karma. This is the appropriate response to evil."

Observations

My story reflects the prevalence of "pseudo-Christianity" in America today. Spirituality for many has become a self-righteous hobby. Many of the religious people I mention in my story used their spirituality as a license to judge, condemn, control and harm me. This is a perversion of how humans should conduct themselves with one another. True spirituality bears the fruit of unconditional love, peace, non-judgment and compassion. I believe that Christianity has helped to create a society in which people are alienated not only from each other but also from the divine.

During the 70's, America experienced a wave of people involved in the "Jesus Movement." This movement was fanatical about Jesus, repentance, salvation, being "born again" and "spirit-filled." At the age of fifteen several friends, teachers and pastors introduced me to a form of mental "slavery" in America. It has many names: Fundamental Christianity, Catholicism, the Evangelical and Pentecostal/Catholic Charismatic movement, Fundamentalism and "Bill Gothardism."

The teachings of these organizations were like a slow drip of dark fluid covering the light of my soul. We were not to question the teachings. We were to blindly accept them. Confusion was prevalent among those of us who continued to reason and think. Every Christian/Catholic sect had their own interpretations of the Scriptures—different truths. Every religious leader representing these groups had his right interpretation of the truth.

Because of the controlling and manipulating manner in which most children are raised in America, young people are prime targets and are easily swayed by or enticed into the cult phenomenon. In the tenets of Roman Catholicism, the largest cult in the world, you are mandated to "give over your will and your mind." The history of "missionaries" for Catholicism and Christianity was to send people to "occupy and take over"—somewhat like war, but with teachers and churches, not tanks.

Since the beginning of European colonization throughout the world, the first contact between indigenous peoples and the explorers and missionaries was the beginning of the spiritual and physical decay of the indigenous societies. In 1493 Pope Alexander VI, issued the Inter Caetera bull, the papal bull which declared that "...barbarous nations be overthrown and be brought to the faith itself."

It is estimated that more than 90% of the indigenous people and their nations in the western hemisphere were eventually exterminated by European weapons and diseases. The slaughter began in 1492 in the Caribbean and ended around 1910 on Canada's west coast.

The papal bull of 1493 was the first law used to commit genocide of native peoples of the Americas, and it provided the Catholic nations with a means of legal conquest. It marked the attitude of Christianity toward peoples not previously thought to exist and the concept of "just war." Their refusal to accept "papal or Christian doctrine" resulted in torture, rape, murder and annihilation.

These two societies could never live together. The Euro-American culture believed and lived out oppression of women and children and believed in the conquering of nations and tribes..." all in the name of God." (Please see article written by Jewell Praying Wolf James, referred to in documentation, *"Did God Only Endow the White Man with Sovereignty?"*)

It is reported that many Euro-American women who were captured by Native Americans and lived within their tribes did not want to return to white-man's world, even when rescued or offered release. They found the Native American culture more civilized and peaceful. They stated they were treated as equals by the men, not like a second-class citizen.

Women were valued, respected and viewed as equals in the Native American Indian culture. In their culture violence within their society was viewed as a threat to the harmony needed to survive. Many of the Indians learned violence in the Catholic boarding schools. The Indians traditional parenting was nonviolent and nurtured the spirit of the child. Christian church teaching or corporal punishment replaced this knowledge and truth.

After Catholicism and Christianity replaced the Native American's nature-based spirituality, the dominant society's negative attitudes, beliefs and behaviors toward women were adopted. "Women soon adopted female societal beliefs about the "place of women." This "place" is generally one of inferiority and subservience to men. The Euro-American image of a "good woman" is one who is rarely without a man, weaker, less intelligent and dependent." –*Domestic Violence is Not Lakota/ Dakota Tradition* by Marlin Mousseau and Karen Artichoker.

Jewell Praying Wolf James writes, "It was during the U.S. Grant Administration (1870's) that the Christian churches were in complete control over Indian Affairs and governed Indian Reservations and education. Like their predecessors before them, they believed the Indians to be savage and needing forced conversion. The religions were organized enough on the "Indian problem" to secure the drafting and implementation of the Religious Crimes Code (Department of Interior Circular #1665). Any Indian caught practicing non-Christian spiritual or religious rituals, rites, and ceremonials were automatically arrested and imprisoned, without a right to trial and jury. Ceremonial regalia and symbols were seized and burned or sold or donated to universities and museums, or private collections." (Taken from Article, "Did God Only Endow the White Man with Sovereignty?")

The Catholic Boarding Schools on Indian reservations in America were designed specially to break down the richness of the Native American's nature-based spirituality and philosophy which was the cohesion of the family, band, clan and tribe. The school's curriculum was designed to brainwash the children. There has been severe abuse, torture and sexual molestation reported and documented by Indian students in Catholic boarding schools throughout the years. Indian children were beaten for speaking their own language. President Richard Nixon, signed the Native American Religious Freedom Act in 1977, which gave the Indians permission to practice their own religious beliefs. It had been almost 100 years since the American government had stripped them of their right to practice their ceremonies.

Marlin Mousseau knows first-hand about the spiritual vacuum that creates violence in this generation of indigenous people. He is a part of Cangleska, Inc., on the Pine Ridge Reservation and works with groups of men to end the cycle of violence. In the "Afterward" of Gage's book, *Woman, Church and State*, Mousseau states, "When Christians came, they told us not to believe what we believed for thousands and thousands of years and if we did, we were punished. The government's policy was termination and then they turned us over to the missionaries and anything the missionaries told us is what we were to believe. We lost our beliefs and all these false beliefs, these man-made beliefs, were substituted and they really created the violence and the suffering."

Mousseau continues, "These cultures went without spirituality. They destroyed their spirituality. They came up with a man-made spirituality that really has no substance to it that was made up of lies. It seems that's why the killing happened, without any remorse or any apologies by the church for what they'd done. They went for a long time, probably still do, without any real spirituality."

The movie *The Education of Little Tree* accurately exposes the crimes of violence and hate by Christians and Catholics and beautifully portrays the gentleness and love known as "The Way" as taught by the Native Americans. The movie contrasts the difference between the teachings of the male-dominant Father-Son-God Religions and that of the Mother Earth Religions of Native societies. The Christian/Catholic religions promoted domination while the traditional native societies taught respect.

I continue to look for the "fruits" that Jesus spoke about in the Scriptures that would be evident of "His followers." I am repulsed by how innocent people have been tortured, raped and murdered by those who "conquer" in His name.

> Some people believe the ideology behind the Inquisition and the conquering of the Native Americans is something of the past. I was shocked to see the following statement by Father Coyne, Vatican Observatory director in a **May 25, 1992,** Vatican document regarding the Apache Indians on the San Carlos Reservation. Coyne wrote that Apache beliefs were "a religiosity to which I cannot subscribe and which must **be suppressed with all the force that we can muster."**

Thousands of children throughout America and around the world have been subject to cruelty, molestation and torture by priests, nuns, and Christian missionaries. For the past several years, many cases are getting widespread attention and some are coming before the courts. The Catholic Church is spending millions of dollars to defend priests and to settle cases out of court and out of the public eye. A black robe and collar, and the power of the church, has saved many priests (and clergy in other churches as well) from being treated as pedophiles (sex offenders) by our judicial system. The church continues to think everything can be fixed with prayer, obedience to God and purification sessions.

The Catholic Church has vast holdings of real estate throughout the world including the United States. Church property has traditionally not been under the jurisdiction of the criminal justice system. This has made it possible for priests to escape criminal prosecution for the rape, torture and sexual molestation of children as well as other crimes. If crimes committed by priests are reported to the Church, church authorities send the offenders on "retreat" to a monastery for several weeks and then reassign them to a new parish. This has allowed them to repeat crimes and a new set of children are molested all in the "name of God."

We have bishops labeling President **Barack** Obama as Hitler and Stalin and fighting affordable health care for children and parents because of contraception and supporting politicians who classify rape as "forced" or "legitimate". They want to be moral spokesmen in this society and yet they do nothing about the scandals of child rape by priests except shuffle them around and sweep them under the rectory carpet.

The Roman Catholic hierarchy is morally bankrupt and the conservative faithful are more concerned about outward forms of the religion while they rot away on the inside. They are whitewashed sepulchers and noisy gongs. (Please see 2012 HBO Documentary *Mea Maxima Culpa: Silence in the House of God.)*

> I believe the sickness of sexual predators was portrayed correctly in the controversial film *"Natural Born Killers,"* but most people missed the message the director, Oliver Stone, was giving us... that, as a society, we are slow to look at our own mirrors and shadows.

American citizens and religious leaders are often quoted as saying, "we must repent and return to the morals and principals that our founding fathers established when they first arrived to this country." Since the landing of Columbus, tens of millions of Native Americans were murdered by the hands of those who served the Catholic Church; millions of African-American people were enslaved by Christians whose lives revolved around power and greed.

It has been reported that even Hitler during the Nazi regime stated that he did not invent the idea of concentration camps for the Jews. He learned from the American government how to exterminate a people quickly by the example we established on the Indian Reservations.

Our country is guilty of the genocide of millions of Native Americans.

I often wonder what "morals and principles" these people are referring to or speaking about. I am grieved and sickened by America's church and government history.

Religious cults use covert induction, a type of hypnosis induced without the individual's awareness or consent. Cults are a product of fear. Neale Donald Walsch writes these beautiful words, "Fear is the energy which contracts, closes down, draws in, runs, hides, hoards, harms. Love is the energy which expands, opens up, sends out, stays, reveals, shares, heals. Fear wraps our bodies in clothing; love allows us to stand naked. Fear clings to and clutches all that we have, love gives all that we have away. Fear holds close, love holds dear. Fear grasps, love lets go. Fear rankles, love soothes. Fear attacks, love amends. Love never says no." The ancient text of the Scriptures state that "perfect love casts out all fear."

Studies have determined that cults are detrimental to an individual's mental and physical health. Emotional effects include overwhelming feelings of fear, guilt, anger, humiliation, hostility, anxiety, sleeplessness, depression, violent outbursts and suicidal tendencies. Mental disturbances include disorientation, confusion, nightmares, amnesia, hallucinations, delusions, depression and the inability to break mental rhythms and patterns associated with group practices. Many of the women I knew in cult and fundamentalist circles suffered from depression or mental breakdowns. Although, I have many painful memories and experiences from my exposure to cults and Christianity, I am comforted knowing that my soul was on a journey of remembering who I truly was.

Throughout the years, I have observed Christian groups training people to erect prison walls around their minds. Through twisted doctrines, you are brainwashed to allow harm and threats to be a part of your everyday life. You can no longer think or reason on your own without consulting "an authority." What a distortion of spiritual laws and universal truths! I agree with comedian George Carlin that America could get well if we could just give up organized religion. George Carlin adds, "but that would be too easy."

It grieves me to talk with individuals who are thoroughly brainwashed by their so-called Christian religious leaders. I have a brother and numerous friends who live in obedience to a religious leader or authority. At this time, they cannot be reached spiritually or emotionally. They believe they are God's remnant (set-apart, chosen). They know the truth and the rest of us are lost. I have noticed two things they have in common–they believe in sharing their religious views with you, but almost never want you to share yours with them and they exhibit in their daily lives no compassion for others.

I have come to believe that church is a place where the unconscious hide with their masks intact. They gather to support one another in their delusional and depraved viewpoints. It is as if they are drugged or asleep. I respect their soul journey, but it is sad to watch the harm that is done not only to themselves, but to others as well, all in God's name.

As I listen to adults speak about the abuse issues within their marriages, I am convinced that we live in a society where the covenant of marriage is glorified and idolized. Christian parents honor their marriage covenants to their death and sacrifice their own children. As they keep the marriage and family together, they seem oblivious to the consequences the children will suffer from witnessing the violence and abuse within their homes and parents' relationship.

Our society appears to be shocked by the violence exhibited by our youth. It is difficult for society to understand that the children learned violence at home as a way of resolving conflict. Terrorism is often taught without ammunition and bombs by those who abuse power and get what they want—no matter what the cost.

Many children in households throughout America learn "male-supremacy" and "strong over weak" messages from their parents. Children are watching, listening and learning by our interactions in the private and professional sectors. Sadly, children are learning the "domination game."

In his book, *How Holocausts Happen: The United States in Central America*, Douglas V. Porpora writes, "Mainstream Christianity consists mostly of family holidays, Sunday services, and perhaps saying one's prayers before going to bed. Its morality is largely a list of don'ts: Don't lie, don't cheat, don't steal, and don't commit adultery. The idea is to have as good a time as possible within the confines of these don'ts. Beyond the don'ts and the family holidays, religion plays little role in the lives of mainstream Christians.

Beyond lip service, there is very little of the positive and truly radical morality that Jesus preached: Serve God by serving your neighbor."

Porpora continues, "There is little in a negative morality of don'ts or in a religion of family holidays and church services to push religious concern beyond the private sphere into the political domain. It takes a positive morality of radical commitment to one's neighbor to extend the concept of neighbor to those one does not see face to face, to extend the responsibilities of neighborliness to suffering peasants in a remote country. It takes such a radical commitment to neighborliness to care about the effects of political decisions on our neighbors everywhere. That, however, is a commitment that is largely unknown in mainstream American Christendom."

I relate more to what historically is known as Gnostic Christianity. Gnostic Christianity invites people to seek a deeper sense of self that leads ultimately to the revelation that within each of us is a "True Self" that is a spark of divinity. Within this "True Self" God is known. In the Gnostic approach, the world is not viewed as a good place that was driven into sin by the acts of human beings, but rather as a place that lacks the fullness of love and moral sense that is at the heart of the divine. It is not so much that human beings are sinners, but that the world itself is deficient, only when one touches their innermost "True Self" does serenity and love truly become known to each person.

> "If you bring forth what is within you, What you bring forth will save you. If you do not bring forth what is within you, What you do not bring forth will destroy you." –Jesus, In the Gospel According to Thomas

For Gnostic Christians, Jesus Christ is a revealer of this "True Self" that is divine, and leads people into an awakening of their true nature–love. When we have developed our capacity to feel love within, love is a spontaneous, pure outpouring of feeling. The emphasis is not on doctrine or dogma, but rather on self-exploration and awakening oneself to a deeper spiritual reality. Gnostic Christians recognize that the form of Christianity and Catholicism that is practiced today is more about control and power than about truth.

Whenever a people sense the need to control and struggle for power, they are opposing the universal force that keeps things in balance. The need for control comes from a lack of trust in themselves and trust in the Universal God. This need for control creates violence, prejudice, hate and fear. Fear is the opposite of who we truly are. One way to heal from fear is to revisit it with the help of others who have also experienced it.

In her book *Cunt-A Declaration of Independence*, author Inga Muscio writes, "Since the beginning of time, most cultures honored forces which were tangible, such as the moon, earth, sun, water, birth, death and life. A spirituality which was undetectable to any of the human senses was considered incomprehensible."

The earliest religions worshipped a mother Goddess. All early religions had a female component of the divine. The loss of the female component of divinity enabled the church to lose the divine component of the female, thus women's position in the Church became so degraded that no act of torture or mutilation was deemed excessive when applied to wise women.

Matilda Gage wrote, "One of the most revered ancient Scriptures, "The Gospel according to the Hebrews," which was in use as late as the second century of the Christian era, taught the quality of the feminine in the Godhead; also that daughters should inherit with sons...The fact remains undeniable that at the advent of Christ, a recognition of the feminine element in the divinity had not entirely died out from general belief...It was however but a short period before the church through Cannons and Decrees, as well as apostolic and private teachings, denied the femininity of the Divine equally with the divinity of the feminine."

I had the opportunity and privilege to attend Carol Lynn Pearson's play, "Mother Wove the Morning." It was directed, performed and produced by Maradene and Premdaya Craig. They were drawn together through their mutual love of this play and their longing to be a part of sharing the vision of the masculine and the feminine in divine balance.

The play compels us to consider the tradition of god as male and the subjugation of women that has come as a consequence. The dramatic stories of sixteen women illustrate how the human family has longed for its Heavenly Mother, has often been denied Her, and now awakening to the femaleness of God. The play is a tool to be used in the work of "*inviting the Mother back into the human family so that our world will no longer be a Motherless house.*"–Carol Lynn Pearson

Carl Jung said that the most important psychological task humankind faces in our century is the reintegration of the feminine divine into our religious experience.

To heal and become whole as a people and a nation, we need to honor Mother Earth and her vibrations and embrace and honor the feminine goddess–the female component of the divine.

In our society, domestic violence is encouraged and condoned by patriarchal based religious organizations. The fundamental, evangelical Christian movements (cults) that thrive today refuse to speak out against domestic violence, rape, incest and abuse because their doctrines are the foundation for conditioning women and children to accept abuse. Women and children are taught shame, fear and guilt and that patriarchal hierarchy must be lived out in the homes. Patriarchal religions have proven to be devastating for women around the world. External oppression of a people leads to internal oppression.

Domestic violence has primarily arisen as a problem in the Native American population in the 20th century. In the days before, if domestic violence did occur, it wasn't tolerated. Women and men were thought of as equals. The roles shifted greatly when native people were conquered and "white man's religion" (Christianity and Catholicism) replaced their matriarchal society and nature-based spirituality and philosophy. Indian men have taken on the traits of the dominant culture and religion, and because of that, they are destroying their own now. Thankfully, many Native American children are becoming acquainted with their roots, rich spirituality and culture that "white man" tried to destroy over 100 years ago.

In her book, *Grandmother's Secrets*, Rosina-Fawzia Al-Rawi writes, "The written history is masculine and it tells us about the conquests, wars, achievements, victories, and defeats—in other words, it tells us about power. Time and space are shaped and marked through external events. Human development and evolution are measured by the yardstick of these events. So far history has been presented to us as a linear development, from prehistorical to modern times, through antiquity and the Middle Ages, with European-Christian history considered to be the highest human development. This naïve and archaic historical representation can lead to a discriminatory attitude, insofar as it considers all previous or parallel developments to be inferior. This is a superficial view which overlooks one major aspect of human life."

Al-Rawi continues, "Outer development can only be measured against inner development. This inner development relates to consciousness. The degree of development of human consciousness is a decisive phenomenon in the history of humanity. If we look at history through the lens of human development—that is, through the lens of the development of consciousness, it no longer appears to be a straight line or chain in which the individual parts are assessed according to their place. Instead of the line, there appears a unity that treasures individual cultures and sees them as enriching. In this way, the many different cultures, religions, and attitudes to life exist next to each other and inspire one other; a family of human beings, in which individuals are sources of mutual inspiration, who may further the development of consciousness among all human beings."

The superiority and spiritual pride that most Christians and Catholics resonate from their being keeps them from knowing the sacred and the divine. It keeps them from knowing the truth that we are all interconnected. If the beliefs people have adopted prevent them from feeling full of love, equality and inner connectedness with all mankind and nature, then I believe he/she must challenge his/her beliefs and integrity. Anything that creates a "them" and "us" mentality is not love. Love always unites and creates or honors oneness.

Our judicial and patriarchal religious systems are both oppressive and non-feeling. By not feeling, people can live under the false assumption that we are separate from each other. When we open ourselves to feelings, we can feel not only our own, but others' feelings as well. The nature of feelings and the power of empathy demonstrates that we are all connected, or at least potentially so, through an experience of another's pain, happiness, grief, satisfaction, pride, or shame.

> "Liberty is the only thing you cannot have unless you are willing to give it to others."
>
> –William Allen White

Our society has been taught to suppress their feelings and emotions. I believe that this is the reason for the senseless acts of cruelty I have suffered from the judicial and religious institutions. I believe many people fear emotions. Joseph Collins writes, "By starving emotions we become humor-less, rigid and stereotype; by repressing them, we become literal, reformatory and holier-than-thou; encouraged, they perfume life, discouraged, they poison it."

Conclusion

Matilda Joslyn Gage wrote in 1893, "Woman is told that her present position in society is entirely due to Christianity, that it is superior to that of her sex at any prior age of the world, church and state both maintaining that she has ever been inferior and dependent, man superior and ruler. These assertions are made the basis of opposition to her demands for exact equality with man in all the relations of life although they are not true either of the family, the church or the state. Such assertions are due to non-acquaintance with the existing phase of historical knowledge; whose records the majority of mankind (has) neither time nor opportunity of investigating.

"The wife under Canon Law (in the Catholic Church) belonged to her husband, and as a sequence to not owning herself she could not own property, and in her condition of servitude could possess no control over either her present or her future actions." Regarding her life under the Protestant Reformation, "The home under the reformation was governed by the laws in force before that period. She (the woman) was to be under obedience to the masculine head of the household. She was to be constantly employed for his benefit. Her society was strictly chosen for her by her master and responsible head. This masculine family head was regarded as a general father–confessor to whom she was held as responsible in word and deed. Neither genius nor talent could free woman from such control without his consent."

Gage writes, "The denial to women of the right of private judgment, the control of her own actions (and) the constant teaching of her greater sinfulness and natural impurity had a very depressing effect upon the majority of women, whose lowly station in life was such as to deprive them of the independence of thought and action possible to women of rank and wealth. Then, as now, the church catered to the possessors of money and power; then as now, seeking to unite their great forces with its own purpose of aggrandizement. And thus, the church has ever obstructed the progress of humanity, delaying civilization and condemning the world to a moral barbarism from which there is no escape except through repudiation of its teaching."

I believe that people do not intend to hurt another. Those who do it – including our own government – do it out of a misplaced idea that it is the only way to get something they want. People hurt others when they forget to acknowledge the divinity in themselves and in others. Evolved human beings understand spiritual laws. They will want nothing. They will have preferences, but no needs. Evolved beings lead with their soul, not their ego.

As we become *healed healers* and shamans to one another, we are given opportunities to bring pieces of our true self back as we participate in relationships, mirroring and shamanistic gifting. We must be willing to stand with another individual in the fire and not walk away. We must validate one another and be willing to sit with each other's raw pain.

> "If you don't see the face of God in the person in front of you,
> you can stop looking."
>
> –Gandhi

I believe relationships based on respect and love creates a sacred place for the unhealed places of our hearts and souls to heal. We understand and trust that this place will be protected, not violated.

Some people, and family members, are destructive and violent. They exhibit behavior that is toxic. I have learned to love and care about their soul and spirit, and separate their behavior from their spirit. I have learned to separate myself from these people, have compassion on them and choose peace. I can feel harmony with God and my fellow man as I create safe boundaries for myself.

I agree with Matilda Joslyn Gage's conclusions in her book, *Woman, Church and State*.

I believe that woman's degradation is attributed to the Christian/patriarchal position that God is strictly male. The earliest religions worshipped a mother Goddess. All early religions had a female component of the divine. The loss of the female component of divinity enabled the church to lose the divine component of the female. Death by torture was the method of the Church for the repression of woman's intellect, knowledge being held as evil and dangerous in her hands.

Gage writes, "As long as the Church maintains the doctrine that woman was created inferior to man and brought sin into the world, rendering the sacrifice of the Son of God necessary, just so long will the foundation of vice and crime of every character remain. Not until the exact and permanent equality of woman with man is recognized by the church–aye, even more, together with the accountability of man to woman in everything relating to the birth of a new being, is fully accepted as a law of nature–will vice and crime disappear form the world. Until that time has fully come, prostitution, in its varied forms will continue to exist, together with alms-houses, reformatories, jails, prisons, hospitals and asylums for the punishment, reformation or care of the wretched beings who have come into existence with an inheritance of disease and crime **because of church theory and church teaching.** (Emphasis mine)

"The most stupendous system of organized robbery known has been that of the church towards woman, a robbery that has not only taken her self-respect but all rights of person; the fruits of her own industry; her opportunities of education; the exercise of her own judgment, her own conscience, her own will.

"Under the Christian system, woman as the most rebellious against God in having eaten a forbidden fruit has found herself condemned through the centuries to untold oppression in order that the rights of God might be maintained. Yet, while constantly teaching that woman brought sin into the world, the church forgets its own corollary; that if she brought sin she also brought a God into the world, thus throwing ineffable splendor over mankind. The whole theory regarding woman, under Christianity, has been based upon the conception that she had no right to live for herself alone. Her duty to others has continuously been placed before her and her training has ever been that of self-sacrifice. Taught from the pulpit and legislative halls that she was created for another, that her position must always be secondary even to her children, her right to life has been admitted only in so far as its reacting effect upon another could be predicated. That she was first created for herself, as an independent being to whom all the opportunities of the world should be open because of herself, has not entered the thought of the church; has not yet become one of the conceptions of law, is not yet the foundation of the family.

"Looking forward, I see evidence of a conflict more severe than any yet fought by reformation or science; a conflict that will shake the foundations of religious belief, tear into fragments and scatter to the winds the old dogmas upon which all forms of Christianity are based. It will not be the conflict of man with man upon rites and systems; it will not be the conflict of science upon church theories regarding creation and eternity; it will not be the light of biology illuminating the hypothesis of the resurrection of the body; but it will be the rebellion of one half of the church against those theological dogmas upon which the very existence of the church is based. In no other country has the conflict between natural and revealed rights been as pronounced as in the United States; and in this country where the conflict first began, we shall see its full and final development. During the ages, no rebellion has been of like importance with that of Woman against the tyranny of Church and State; none has had its far-reaching effects. We note its beginning, its progress will overthrow every existing form of these institutions; its end will be a regenerated world. The End."

"If you wish the world to become loving and compassionate, become loving and compassionate yourself. If you wish to diminish fear in the world, diminish your own. These are the gifts that you can give. The fear that exists between nations is a macrocosm of the fear that exists between individuals. The perception of power as external that separates nations is the same that exists between individuals; and the love, clarity and compassion that emerge within the individual that chooses consciously to align itself with its soul is the same that will bring sexes, races, nations and neighbors into harmony with each other," writes author Gary Zukav in his book, *Seat of the Soul*.

"The greatest gift we can offer to those around us is you in *wholeness*. We must approach each situation and relationship with the knowingness of who we truly are. My commitment to myself is to come to terms with whatever it is that life shows to me. The alternative is to lose myself in the hurt from loss in my own life, giving away to numbness, anger, retribution and bitterness. None of these is my truest nature. My choice is to address these events from a place of personal peace, becoming change, moving forward with concise and definitive action rather than the crippling patterns of anger and hate. Anger transformed is power. The lack of polarities, such as anger or hate, coupled with the absence of numbness signaled an opening to compassion. I believe I have a force in me that nothing can destroy. I believe that force to be compassion. As our relationships demonstrate to us our true nature, the fallacy of darkness, fear and hate are exposed. Once healed, all that is left is compassion. – Greg Braden, *Walking Between the Worlds–The Science of Compassion*

The Prayer of the Bodhisattva

Alone, in the presence of others, I walk through the waking dream of Life,
Others see me. At the first sight of recognition, they turn away;
      for they have forgotten.
Together, through the walking dream of Life, we journey.
May the clarity of my vision guide your life in grace,
      for I am a part of you.
May my action remind you of your God within,
      my action is your action.
May my breath become the breath that fills your body with life.

May my soul become the food with which to nourish and
            quicken you.
May the words from my mouth find a place
            of truth within your heart.
Let my tears become water to your lips.
Allow my love to heal your body of the pain of life.
In your most healed state, may you remember your most
            precious gift; your divine nature.
Through our time together, may you know yourself.
In that knowing, may you find your true home,
            your God within.

The wisdom for a healthy society and relationships is perhaps best described in this story from Midrash: "A sage asked the Creator to show him Hell. In it were people on both sides of a long table, seated in front of a big pot of stew. Each person had a spoon with a very long handle, such that they could not get any food for themselves. They were perpetually starving. Then he saw Heaven. Same set-up, but the people were feeding each other."

I continue to hope that people will soon become sickened and grieved by the hate, prejudice and abuse that is prevalent among us. I envision a society that is motivated by love and compassion instead of fear. We must begin by rejecting the lies and belief system the puritan fathers brought to America. There is no "us" and "them." We are all interconnected and equal. Until we awaken to this truth, we will continue to see mankind destroy himself and those around him. I believe the condition of a society can often be measured by its prisoners.

Rosina-Fawzia Al-Rawi writes, "When we find unity within ourselves, everything around us answers us, not least nature. If our world were peopled by such beings of unity, it would be our paradise."

In his book, *The World as I See It*, Albert Einstein wrote about this paradise, "It is very difficult to explain this feeling to anyone who is entirely without it, especially as there is no anthropomorphic conception of God corresponding to it. The individual feels the nothingness of human desires and aims and the sublimity and marvelous order which reveal themselves both in nature and in the world of thought. He looks upon individual existence as a sort of prison and wants to experience the universe as a single significant whole."

When our society accepts the truth that we are all equal and interconnected, we will begin to see changes. Nothing exists in the universe that is separate from anything else. Everything and everyone is intrinsically connected and interwoven in the fabric of all life. When you are in resonance with the universe, manifestation of your true self is a natural by-product. All laws must be rooted in these beliefs. I believe this truth is the future hope of our nation and world.

Bonsheá,

Coral Anika Theill

The Eighth Amendment to the United States Constitution – Cruel and Unusual Punishments shall not be inflicted

The Eighth Amendment to the United States Constitution states that "cruel and unusual punishments [shall not be] inflicted". The general principles the United States Supreme Court relied on to decide whether or not a particular punishment was cruel and unusual were determined by Justice William Brennan. In *Furman v. Georgia,* 408 U.S. 288 (1972), Justice Brennan wrote, "There are, then, four principles by which we may determine whether a particular punishment is 'cruel and unusual'."

- The "essential predicate" is "that a punishment must not by its severity be degrading to human dignity," especially torture.
- "A severe punishment that is obviously inflicted in wholly arbitrary fashion."
- "A severe punishment that is clearly and totally rejected throughout society."
- "A severe punishment that is patently unnecessary."

And he added: "The function of these principles, after all, is simply to provide means by which a court can determine whether a challenged punishment comports with human dignity. They are, therefore, interrelated, and, in most cases, it will be their convergence that will justify the conclusion that a punishment is "cruel and unusual." The test, then, will ordinarily be a cumulative one: if a punishment is unusually severe, if there is a strong probability that it is inflicted arbitrarily, if it is substantially rejected by contemporary society, and if there is no reason to believe that it serves any penal purpose more effectively than some less severe punishment, then the continued infliction of that punishment violates the command of the Clause that the State may not inflict inhuman and uncivilized punishments upon those convicted of crimes."

Continuing, he wrote that he expected that no state would pass a law obviously violating any one of these principles, so court decisions regarding the Eighth Amendment would involve a "cumulative" analysis of the implication of each of the four principles. In this way the United States Supreme Court "set the standard that a punishment would be cruel and unusual [,if] it was too severe for the crime, [if] it was arbitrary, if it offended society's sense of justice, or if it was not more effective than a less severe penalty."

Silent Violence

September 2000
by Rev. Joanna Trainor

I met Coral, over two years ago, and thus began an amazing lesson for me. I say this because she has shown me what transpires when an individual chooses to regain the fractured pieces of the *self*. This is a story of a journey. It chronicles the events that led to Coral's shattering. These events are raw and jarring. They reveal a personal account of one woman being fed an "illusion" that ultimately stripped her of her individuality and freedom.

When any rational, sentient being attempts to conform to a dogma that conflicts with personal liberties and spiritual wholeness; then something must break. In this case, the inability to sustain an illusion created by *others* temporarily broke Coral's mind. She went through various procedures believing that her restoration would be justly determined. Her attempts to seek assistance in restoring herself were viewed as invalid, because she was deemed mentally ill and fragile. Her trust in the system–legally and socially–turned out to be another fallacy. It merely added one more level to the maze she was attempting to escape.

Her story is not comfortable to read. Its events overwhelm the heart and mind. Yet, this story was lived. It leaves one dissatisfied and uncomfortable. Why? Perhaps each of us lives with the perception that this could *not* happen. It did happen.

Part of Coral's journey home to wholeness, includes speaking *her* truth. That is why she wrote this document. She was advised to stop dwelling on the past. By addressing the past–her past–she <u>owns</u> it. She has chosen to bring it to light. It is part of her healing in the present. She will leave this manuscript available for her children to read, when they are adults. She will offer this journal to others who, like herself, awake from a harmful "delusion," and dare to journey back to wholeness.

I applaud her honesty and I respect her courage.

When I began reading Coral's manuscript, I carried an assumption that justice could, in the end, prevail. When I finished, I realized, sadly, that I had assumed <u>too much</u>. I simply felt numb with disgust. I kept asking myself...why?

Why was...a woman recovering from a mental breakdown...

1. Subjected to verbal public harassment and humiliation during these court proceedings.
2. Not appointed an advocate or guardian to support her needs, (physically, emotionally and mentally).
3. Mandated to pay monthly child support.
4. Not treated with deference.

And, finally, I asked myself...

1. Why was a nursing infant removed from his mother?
2. Why was there no child guardian/advocate appointed for this infant?
3. Why was there no review and resolution in this matter?

Imagine these events occurring when you/I are physically, emotionally and mentally whole. Now, imagine these events occurring when you/I are NOT! I feel disgusted.

I believe that justice does not reach for a "higher law," it merely reflects the current one. The current law is our legal standard. That standard is allowed (approved) by a given community (i.e. city, county, state, and nation). Our legal system is our active/passive consent to implement a set of standards...laws.

Did this community, Coral's community, agree with this example of justice? Would any community agree with this example? Did this community assume (as I did) that justice, in the end, would prevail? And, after reading Coral's story, did we all assume too much? Is Coral's story an isolated example of injustice or, simply, tragically, a current example of justice?

Perhaps, her voice, her words, serves as a "caution" for us all. Why? Maybe, we have all assumed too much. Maybe, we are all disgusted by this story. Maybe, we have learned that justice needs our voice and to that end we should speak, and assume nothing.

Some will avoid reading this document and brush it off as mere fantasy. Perhaps some will decide that ignoring a misdeed will keep them safe in the game of life. But, others will take up this account, read it, and feel that something went terribly wrong. They are the ones who know the truth about the "game" and they are choosing not to play. The "game" offers a delusion of safety. This delusion of safety failed Coral. Delusions always fail. Coral chooses to speak freely and to live fearlessly!

"Neutrality helps the oppressor, never the victim. Silence encourages the tormentor, never the tormented. Sometimes we must interfere. When human lives are endangered, when human dignity is in jeopardy, national borders and sensitivities become irrelevant. Wherever men or women are persecuted because of their race, religion, or political views, that place must–at that moment–become the center of the universe." - Holocaust survivor, *Elie Wiesel*

Coral pictured on a friend's bike

Contacts

If you believe justice has prevailed in my court case, then I encourage you to do nothing.

If you are shocked and alarmed by the injustices regarding my case, then I ask you to speak out against the injustice and intervene. Silence gives the message to the judges and district attorneys that they have done what is right, according to you, the community.

If you are uncomfortable with the circumstances I have survived, then I encourage you to let the appropriate individuals know how you feel by letter or phone. I believe we have a moral and historical responsibility to one another. What has been allowed in my court case could easily happen to you or someone close to you.

Polk County Civil Case No. 95P-20689 and No. 95P20693
Polk County Criminal Case No. 99-1141

Governor Kate Brown
900 Court St. NE
Salem Capitol
Salem, OR 97301
(503) 378-3111

Oregon Attorney General Ellen Rosenblum
Oregon Department of Justice
1162 Court St. NE
Salem, OR 97301
(503) 378-4400

District Attorney Eric J. Nisley
Wasco County Courthouse
511 Washington Street
The Dalles, OR 97058
(541) 506-2680

District Attorney Aaron Felton
Polk County Courthouse
850 Main Street
Dallas, OR 97338
(503) 623-9268

Pastor Ron Sutter
(Mr. V. Martin Warner's Pastor)
14603 Forest Hill Dr.
Monmouth, OR 97361
(503) 623-5499 (Home)
(503) 623-4082 (Work)

Pastor Bill Heard
Roseburg, Oregon

Coral Anika Theill's Oregon Circuit Court case began December 1995 to present (2013)

Judge Albin Norblad was involved in Ms. Theill's case from 1996-1997, Judge Luukinen from 1998-1999, Judge Paula Brownhill from 2003 - Present

Judge Albin Norblad, Salem, Oregon, has been removing babies and children per court order from good/nurturing mothers for almost thirty years.

Due to poverty and disabilities, I have had no attorney since 1997. No advocate or domestic violence group, on a local, state or national level, has assisted her personally or legally with my case.

Contacts

Attorneys

Attorneys Representing Coral Anika Theill
aka: Kathryn Y. Warner

January 1996 - March 1997

Mr. David Gearing

Gearing, Rackner, Engel & McGrath

121 SW Morrison Ave., Suite #750

Portland, OR 97204

Phone: (503) 222-9116

Mr. Jonathan Benson

6825 SW Sandburg Street

Tigard, OR 97281

(503) 620-1710

December 1995 - January 1996
Mr. Richard F. Alway
2581 12th Street SE
Salem, OR 97302-2153
Phone: (503) 363-9231

Attorneys Representing Mr. V. Martin Warner

December 1995 - October 1996
Mr. Mark Lawrence
235 NE 3rd, Suite 1
McMinville, OR 97128
Phone: (503) 434-9066

January 1996 – 2003
Mr. Daniel Van Eaton
350 Mission Street SE, Suite 101
Salem, OR 97302
Phone: (503) 399-8800

2004-2005
Mr. J. Michael Alexander
Salem, Oregon

A bibliography is not meant to be a tiresome list. It is not intended to teach a person what to think, but strives to give a body rich things to think about, to expose a person to as many ideas, therefore choices and chances, as possible. – *Clarissa Pinkola Estes, Ph.D.,*

Resources

Albom, Mitch. *The Five People You Meet in Heaven*. New York: Hyperion Books. 2003.

Allen, James. *As a Man Thinketh*. Barnes and Noble Books. 1992. (Reprint)

Al-Rawi, Rosina-Fawzia. *Grandmother's Secrets: The Ancient Rituals and Healing Power of Belly Dancing*. (Translated by Monique Arav) New York: Interlink Books. 1999.

Angelou, Maya. *I Know Why the Caged Bird Sings*. New York: Random House. 1977.

Arsenault, Raymond. *Freedom Riders: 1961 and the Struggle for Racial Justice*. New York: Oxford University Press. 2006.

Balch, James F., M.D., and Balch, Phyllis A., C.N.C. *Prescription for Nutritional Healing: A Practical A-Z Reference to Drug-Free Remedies Using Vitamins, Minerals, Herbs & Food Supplements*. New York: Avery Publishing Group Inc. 1990.

Bass, Ellen, and Davis, Laura. *The Courage to Heal: A Guide for Women Survivors of Child Sexual Abuse*. New York: Harper & Row, Publishers. 1988.

Bates, Major Ralph Stoney, Sr., USMC (Ret). *Short Rations for Marines (And FMF Corpsmen)*. Ordering information: *www.shortrations.com. 2013*

Bennedict, Helen. *Virgin or Vamp: How the Press Covers Sex Crimes*. New York: Oxford University Press. 1992.

Bloom, Sandra L., M.D., and Reichert, Michael. *Bearing Witness: Violence and Collective Responsibility*. Binghamton, NY. The Hawthorn Press, Inc. 1998

_____. *Creating Sanctuary: Toward the Evolution of Sane Societies*. New York: Routledge. 1997.

Borysenko, Joan, Ph.D. *Fire in the Soul: A New Psychology of Spiritual Optimism*. New York: Warner Books. 1993.

Boulet, Susan Seddon. Text by Michael Babcock. *Goddesses Knowledge Cards.* Rohnert Park, California: Pomegranate.

Braden, Gregg. *Walking Between the Worlds: The Science of Compassion.* Bellevue, Washington: Radio Bookstore Press. 1977. (A must-read book)

Branch, Taylor. *Parting the Waters; America in the King Years 1954-1963.* New York: Simon & Schuster. 1988.

Brennan, Barbara Ann, and Smith, Joseph (Illustrator). *Hands of Light: A Guide to Healing Through the Human Energy Field.* New York: Bantam Double Day Dell Publishing Group. 1988.

_____. *Light Emerging: The Journey of Personal Healing.* New York: Bantam Books. 1993. (I have found this book personally enlightening and healing.)

Brown, Dee. *Bury My Heart at Wounded Knee: An Indian History of the American West.* New York: Henry Holt and Company, LLC. *1970.*

Burton Goldberg Group (Firm). *Alternative Medicine: The Definitive Guide.* Fife, Washington: Future Medicine Publishing, Inc. 1995.

Byock, Ira, M.D. *The Four Things That Matter Most: A Book About Living.* New York: Free Press. 2004.

Castaneda, Carlos. *The Eagle's Gift.* New York: Washington Square Press Publication. 1981.

_____. *The Second Ring of Power.* New York: Washington Square Press Publication. 1977.

_____. *The Teachings of Don Juan: A Yaqui Way of Knowledge.* New York: Washington Square Press Publication. 1968.

Chodron, Pema. *Start Where You Are: A Guide to Compassionate Living.* Boston: Shambhala Publications. 1994.

Chopra, Deepak, M.D. *Creating Affluence: The A-to-Z Steps to a Richer Life.* San Rafael, California: Amber-Allen Publishing. 1993.

_____. *The Path to Love: Spiritual Strategies for Healing.* New York: Three Rivers Press. 1997.

_____. *The Seven Spiritual Laws of Success: A Practical Guide to the Fulfillment of Your Dreams.* San Rafael, California: Amber-Allen Publishing. 1994.

_____. *Twenty Spiritual Lessons for Creating the Life You Want: The Way of the Wizard.* New York: Harmony Books. 1995.

Davis, Kenneth C. *Don't Know Much About History: Everything You Need to Know About American History, But Never Learned.* New York: Avon Books. 1990.

Dawidowicz, Lucy S. *The War Against the Jews: 1933-1945.* New York: Bantam Books. 1975.

Dyer, Wayne W., Ph.D. *Change Your Thoughts – Change Your Life.* Carlsbad, California: Hay House, Inc. 2007

Dworkin, Andrea. *Intercourse.* New York: The Free Press. 1987. (A must-read book)

Eisler, Riane. *The Chalice and the Blade: Our History, Our Future.* New York. Harper Collins Publishers. 1988

_____. *The Power of Partnership: Seven Relationships That Will Change Your Life.* New World Library. 2002. (Author suggests practical ways to break free of the dominator model and move into partnership.)

Ellerbe, Helen. *The Dark Side of Christian History.* Orlando, Florida: Morningstar & Lark. 1995. (A must-read book)

Estés, Clarissa Pinkola, Ph.D. *Women Who Run with the Wolves: Myths and Stories of the Wild Woman Archetype.* New York: Ballantine Books. 1992.

Evans, Patricia. *Controlling People: How to Recognize, Understand and Deal with People Who try to Control You.* Avon, Massachusetts. Adams Media Corporation. 2002

_____. *The Verbally Abusive Relationship: How to Recognize it and How to Respond.* Avon, Massachusetts. Adams Media Corporation. 1992.

Farrell, Warren, Ph.D. *The Myth of Male Power: Why Men Are the Disposable Sex.* New York: Berkley Books. 1993.

Ford, Debbie. *The Dark Side of the Light Chasers: Recreating Your Power, Creativity, Brilliance and Dreams.* New York. Riverhead Books. 1998.

Frankl, Viktor, Ph.D. *Man's Search for Meaning.* New York: Washington Square Press. 1959.

_____. *The Unheard Cry for Meaning in Life.* New York: Washington Square Press. 1978.

Gage, Matilda Joslyn. *Woman, Church and State: A Historical Account of the Status of Woman Through the Christian Ages with Reminiscences of the Matriarchate.* Amherst, NY: Prometheus Books. 1893 Classic. Reprinted in 2001. (Introduction by Sally Roesch Wagner, Ph.D must read book.)

_____.

Graham, Dee. *Loving to Survive: Sexual Terror, Men's Violence, and Women's Lives.* New York: University Press. 1994. (An excellent resource on Societal Stockholm Syndrome and alternatives to John Gray's Mars & Venus theories).

Goleman, Daniel. *Emotional Intelligence: Why it Can Matter More Than IQ.* New York: Bantam Books. 1994.

Hannah, Maureen, Ph.D., and Barry Goldstein, J.D. *Domestic Violence, Abuse, and Child Custody: Legal Strategies and Policy Issues.* New Jersey: Civic Research Institute, Inc. 2010

Herman, Judith, M.D. *Trauma and Recovery: The Aftermath of Violence—from Domestic Abuser to Political Terror.* New York: Basic Books. 1997.

His Holiness the XIV Dalai Lama. *The Art of Happiness.* Putnam Publishing Group. 1998.

_____. *The Dalai Lama's Book of Wisdom.* Hammersmith, London: Thorsons. 1999.

_____. *Ethics for the New Millennium.* New York: Riverhead Books. 1999.

Hopcke, Robert H. *There are No Accidents: Synchronicity and the Stories of Our Lives.* New York: Riverhead Books. 1997.

Hudson, Valerie, Ballif-Spanvill, Bonnie, Caprioli, Mary and Emmett, Chad F. *Sex and World Peace: How the Treatment of Women Affects Development and Security.* New York: Columbia University Press. 2012.

Huffer, Karin, M.S., M.F.T. *Overcoming the Devastation of Legal Abuse Syndrome: Beyond Rage.* Fulkhort Press. 1995.

Jacobson, David. *Of Virgins and Martyrs: Women and Sexuality in Global Conflict.* Maryland: The John Hopkins University Press. 2013.

Kern, Alice. *Tapestry of Hope.* Cathedral City, California: Limited Edition Books. 1988.

Kerns, Phil. *People's Temple, People's Tomb.* Plainfield, New Jersey: Logos. 1979.

King, Stephen. *Rose Madder.* Penguin Books. 1996.

Kingsolver, Barbara. *The Poisonwood Bible.* New York. Harper Collins Publishers, Inc. 1999.

Lew, Mike. *Victims No Longer: Men Recovering from Incest and Other Sexual Child Abuse.* New York: Harper & Row Publishers. 1988.

Mahmoody, Betty and Hoffer, William. *Not Without My Daughter.* New York: St. Martin's Press. 1987.

Manis, Andrew M. *A Fire You Can't Put Out: The Civil Rights Life of Birmingham's Reverend Fred Shuttlesworth.* Tuscaloosa: University of Alabama Press. 1999.

Mate, Gabor, M.D. *In the Realm of Hungry Ghosts.* Berkley, California: North Atlantic Books, 2010.

McWhorter, Diane. *Carry Me Home: Birmingham, Alabama:* The Climactic Battle of the Civil Rights Revolution. New York: Simon & Schuster. 2001

Miller, Alice. *The Drama of the Gifted Child: The Search for the True Self.* New York: Basic Books. 1997.

Moore, Thomas. *Care of the Soul*. New York: Harper Collins Publishers. 1992.

_____. *Soulmates: Honoring the Mysteries of Love and Relationship*. New York: Harper Collins Publishers. 1994.

Mousseau, Marlin and Artichoker, Karen. *Domestic Violence is not Lakota/Dakota Tradition*. Pierre, South Dakota: South Dakota Coalition Against Domestic Violence and Sexual Assault. 1997.

Muscio, Inga. *Cunt: A Declaration of Independence*. Seattle, Washington: Seal Press. 1998.

Myss, Caroline, Ph.D. *Anatomy of a Spirit: The Seven Stages of Power and Healing*. New York: Three Rivers Press. 1996. (Her information is good, but her attitude towards trauma victims lacks empathy.)

Nueberger, Thomas S. *When Priests Become Predators: Profiles of Childhood Sexual Abuse Survivors.*

Wilmingham, DE. Self-Published. Distributors: Ninth Street Bookshop. 2012.

Northrup, Christiane, M.D. *Women's Bodies, Women's Wisdom: Creating Physical and Emotional Health and Healing*. New York: Bantam Books. 1994.

Oriah Mountain Dreamer. *The Dance: Moving to the Rhythms of Your True Self.* New York: Harper Collins Publishers. 2001.

Page, Linda, N.D., Ph.D. *Linda Page's Healthy Healing: A Guide to Self-Healing for Everyone*. Healthy Healing Publications. 2000.

Peck, M. Scott. *People of the Lie*. New York: Touchstone Rockefeller Center, Simon and Schuster, Inc. 1983.

Porpora, Douglas V. *How Holocausts Happen: The United States in Central America*. Philadelphia, Pennsylvania: Temple University Press. 1990.

Redfield, James. *Celestine Prophecy*. New York: Warner Books, Inc. 1993.

_____. *The Tenth Insight: Holding the Vision*. New York: Warner Books, Inc. 1996.

Richo, David, Ph.D. *How to Be an Adult in Relationships: The Five Keys to Mindful Loving.* Boston: Shambhala Publications. 2002.

_____. *The Five Things We Cannot Change: And the Happiness We Find by Embracing Them.* Boston: Shambhala Publications. 2005.

Ross, Ruth, Ph.D. *Prospering Woman: A Complete Guide to Achieving the Full, Abundant Life.* Mill Valley, California: Whatever Publishing, Inc. 1982.

Ruiz, Don Miguel. *The Four Agreements: A Practical Guide to Personal Freedom.* San Rafael, California: Amber-Allen Publishing. 1997. (A must-read book).

_____. *The Mastery of Love: A Practical Guide to the Art of Relationship.* San Rafael, California: Amber-Allen Publishing. 1999. (A must-read book).

_____. *The Four Agreements Companion Book.* San Rafael, California: Amber-Allen Publishing. 2000.

Rule, Ann. *Dead by Sunset: Perfect Husband, Perfect Killer?* New York: Simon & Schuster, Inc. 1995. St. Pierre, Mark and Long Soldier, Tilda. *Walking in the Sacred Manner: Healers, Dreamers, and Pipe Carriers-Medicine Women of the Plains Indians.* New York: Touchstone. 1995.

Sams, Jamie. *Dancing the Dream: The Seven Sacred Paths of Human Transformation.* New York: Harper San Francisco. 1998.

Scahill, Jeremy. *Dirty Wars: The World is a Battlefield.* New York: Nation Books. 2013.

Sen, Mala. *India's Bandit Queen: The True Story of Phoolan Devi.* New York: Harper Collins Publishers. 1993.

Sharlet, Jeff. *The Family: The Secret Fundamentalism at the Heart of American Power.* New York: Harpet Collins Publisher. 2008.

Shay, Jonathan, M.D., Ph.D. *Odysseus in America: Combat Trauma and the Trials of Homecoming.* New York: Scribner. 2002

Sledge, E. B. *With the Old Breed: At Peleliu and Okinawa.* New York: The Random House Publishing Group. 1981.

Spezzano, Chuck, Ph.D. *If it Hurts, It Isn't Love: And 365 Other Principles to Heal and Transform Your Relationships.* New York: Marlowe & Company. 1991.

Stanton, Elizabeth Cady. *The Women's Bible: A Classic Feminist Perspective.* New York: Dover Publications. 2002

Statman, Jan Berliner. *The Battered Woman's Survival Guide: Breaking the Cycle.* Dallas, Texas: Taylor Publishing Company. 1990. (A resource manual for victims, relatives, friends, and professionals.)

Stearns, Ann Kaiser. *Coming Back: Rebuilding Lives After Crisis and Loss.* New York: Random House. 1988.

_____. *Living Through Personal Crisis.* New York: Ballantine Books. 1984.

Styron, William. *Sophie's Choice.* New York: Random House, Inc. 1979.

Tarico, Valerie. *Trusting Doubt: A Former Evangelical Looks at Old Beliefs in a New Light.* Independence, Virginia: The Oracle Institute Press, LLC. 2010

Turse, Nick. *Kill Anything that Moves: The Real American War in Vietnam.* New York: Metropolitan Books, an imprint of Henry Holt and Company, LLC. *2013*

Wagner, Sally Roesch, Ph.D. *Sisters in Spirit: The Haudenosaunee (Iroquois) Influence on Woman's Rights.* Summertown, TN: Native Voices Press, 2001.

_____. *Matilda Joslyn Gage: She Who Holds the Sky.* Aberdeen, SD: Sky Carrier Press. 1998.

Walsch, Neale Donald. *Conversations with God: An Uncommon Dialogue: Book 1.* New York: G. P. Putnam's Sons. 1996.

_____. *Conversations with God: An Uncommon Dialogue: Book 2.* Charlottesville, Virginia: Hampton Roads Publishing Company, Inc. 1997.

_____. *Conversations with God: An Uncommon Dialogue: Book 3.* Charlottesville, Virginia: Hampton Roads Publishing Company, Inc. 1998.

_____. *Questions and Answers on Conversations with God.* Charlottesville, Virginia: Hampton Roads Publishing Company, Inc. 1999.

Wiesel, Elie. *Night*. New York: Bantam Books. 1960.

Williams, Juan. *Eyes on the Prize: American's Civil Rights Years, 1954-1965*. New York: Penguin Group. 1988.

Wolf, Naomi. *Promiscuities: The Secret Struggle for Womanhood*. New York: The Ballantine Publishing Group. 1997.

Zimberoff, Diane. *Breaking Free from the Victim Trap: Reclaiming your Personal Power*. Issaquah, Washington: Wellness Press. 1989.

Zukav, Gary. *The Seat of the Soul*. New York: Simon & Schuster. 1990. (A must-read book!)

The above listed resources will provide insights and profound wisdom. You will need to sort the information for yourself and "eat the meat and spit out the bones." *Bonsheá* – Coral Anika Theill

Articles, Films and Videos

American Psychological Association *"Fathers who battered the mother are twice as likely to seek sole custody of their children as are non-violent fathers."*

Biblical Battered Wife Syndrome: Christian Women and Domestic Violence

Charismatic Covenant Community: A Failed Promise by Adrian J. Reimers, May 1986.

Did God Only Endow the White Man with Sovereignty? by Jewell Praying Wolf James, April 14, 2000

Every Two Minutes: Battered Women and Feminist Interpretation
Susan Brooks Thistlethwaite, From Feminist Interpretation of Scripture
Edited by Letty M Russell, Westminster Press, Philadelphia. 1985

50 Obstacles to Leaving, a.k.a., Why Abuse Victims Stay by Sarah M. Buel, Clinical Professor of the University of Texas School of Law, Former Domestic Violence, Child Abuse and Juvenile Prosecutor

Frank Schaeffer is a writer and author of *"Sex, Mom and God,"* and *"Crazy for God: How I Grew Up as One of the Elect, Helped Found the Religious Right, And Lived to Take All (Or Almost All) Of It Back."*

Gloria Steinem's speech on October 11, 2012, 40ᵗʰ Anniversary Ms. Magazine

God hates Divorce, but Loves a Broken Jaw by Violet Socks January 2009.

Marital Rape by Dr. Raquel Kennedy Bergen, St. Joseph's University, Department of Sociology, March 1999.

MEA MAXIMA CULPA: SILENCE IN THE HOUSE OF GOD 2012 HBO Documentary investigates the secret crimes of Father Lawrence Murphy, a charismatic Milwaukee priest who abused more than 200 Deaf children in a school under his control. The film documents the first known public protest against clerical sex abuse in the U.S., which led to a case that spanned three decades and ultimately resulted in a lawsuit against the pontiff himself. The investigation helped uncover documents from the secret Vatican archives that show the Pope, who must operate within the mysterious rules of the Roman

Curia, as both responsible and helpless in the face of evil. https://www.hbo.com/documentaries/mea-maxima-culpa/index.html#/documentaries/mea-maxima-culpa/index.html

Respond to Violence: Teach Peace, Not War by Russel Mokhiber and Robert Weissman

Revictimization 2009 Pandora's Project by Louise

Sex and World Peace by Valerie Hudson

Sex and World Peace: Or, What Little Girls Have to Do with Our Wars by Soraya Chemaly

What the Bible Says About Rape by Valerie Tarico

When Those Who Are Supposed to Help You Get Out - Don't by Maria De Santis of the Women's Justice Center, Santa Rosa, CA. The Patriarchy Still Rules! And Still Needs to be Upended! The glaring blind spot is rooted deep in the self-preservation mechanisms of patriarchal rule.

The Burning Times – The National Film Board of Canada, 1990, Donna Read

In the late 1690's the Christian Church revived witch trials in Salem, Massachusetts, instigating a reign of terror on women. Many believe this widespread church and state-sanctioned torture and killing of "witches" set the stage for modern society's acceptance of violence against women. *Burning Times* Film Documentary.

Recommended Websites for Advocates and Trauma and Abuse Survivors

Advocate Web is a nonprofit organization providing information and resources to promote awareness and understanding of the issues involved in the exploitation of persons by trusted helping professionals. They serve as a resource for victim/survivors, their families and friends, the general public, and for victim advocates and professionals. www.advocateweb.org

Battered Women, Abused Children, and Child Custody: A National Crisis

Battered Women, Abused Children, and Child Custody: A National Crisis was created in 2003 by two mothers, Mo Therese Hannah, Ph.D. of Albany, NY, and Liliane Heller Miller of Charlotte, NC. Our on-going goal is to host a national public forum to address the many complex issues facing battered women as they strive to protect themselves and their children during divorce, custody, and visitation disputes. http://www.batteredmotherscustodyconference.org/

Birmingham Civil Rights Institute

BCRI Mission: To promote civil and human rights worldwide through education. The Birmingham Civil Rights Institute (BCRI) documents the struggle of African-American citizens in Birmingham to becoming full participants in the city's government and business community. Because this struggle was a social movement that caught the attention of the world, Birmingham is an appropriate place for an institution that serves the world as a center for study and reflection. http://www.bcri.org/index.html

Coral Anika Theill Website *BONSHEÁ Making Light of the Dark* shares my search for freedom and light in a society based on patriarchal religion and laws. It openly speaks about the ideas and beliefs in our society which foster sexism, racism, the denigration of human rights and the intolerance of difference. My documentation exposes the dark side of human nature when all people are not valued. A healthy society must have the courage to address these issues, speak about them, examine them and bring them to light. Indifference encourages, "silent violence"-the type of violence I experienced in my home, in the community, religious circles and judicial system. Nobel laureate, Elie Wiesel states, "*The indifference to suffering makes the human inhumane.*" http://www.coralanikatheill.com

Garland Waller Productions

Small Justice: Little Justice in America's Family Courts was Garland's first independent documentary. This groundbreaking documentary was the first to explore a national scandal – that men who beat their wives and sexually abused their children all too often get custody in family courts.

Faith Trust Institute

FaithTrust Institute is a national, multifaith, multicultural training and education organization with global reach working to end sexual and domestic violence. Founded in 1977 by Rev. Dr. Marie M. Fortune, FaithTrust Institute offers a wide range of services and resources, including training, consulting and educational materials. We provide communities and advocates with the tools and knowledge they need to address the religious and cultural issues related to abuse. We work with many communities, including Asian and Pacific Islander, Buddhist, Jewish, Latino/a, Muslim, Black, Anglo, Indigenous, Protestant and Roman Catholic. www.faithtrustinstitute.org

Freedom of Mind Resource Center

The Freedom of Mind Resource Center supports those affected by undue influence by providing coaching and consulting services. We offer training and educational resources to support individuals, families, advocacy groups, educational institutions, professionals, law enforcement, government entities, and non-governmental organizations by providing training and educational resources. We also provide information to the media to help the public understand undue influence (mind control) in all of its forms so that everyone can have the tools and support they need to protect themselves from undue influence.

Freedom from Religion Foundation

The history of Western civilization shows us that most social and moral progress has been brought about by persons free from religion. In modern times the first to speak out for prison reform, for humane treatment of the mentally ill, for abolition of capital punishment, for women's right to vote, for death with dignity for the terminally ill, and for the right to choose contraception, sterilization and abortion have been freethinkers, just as they were the first to call for an end to slavery. The Foundation works as an umbrella for those who are free from religion and are committed to the cherished principle of separation of state and church. http://ffrf.org/

Interfaith Alliance:

Interfaith Alliance celebrates religious freedom by championing individual rights, promoting policies that protect both religion and democracy, and uniting diverse voices to challenge extremism. http://www.interfaithalliance.org/

LEGAL ABUSE SYNDROME (LAS) is a form of post-traumatic stress disorder (PTSD). It is a psychic injury, not a mental illness. It is a personal injury that develops in individuals assaulted by ethical violations, legal abuses, betrayals, and fraud. Abuse of power and authority and a profound lack of accountability in our courts have become rampant. Dr. Karin Huffer, author of the groundbreaking book, *Overcoming the Devastation of Legal Abuse Syndrome*, has devoted over 20 years to researching, diagnosing, and treating PTSD and other trauma disorders.

Liz Argate website

Women's legal research library, including articles and references on family law, politics, the U.S. Constitution, free speech, constitutional rights, marriage and divorce, child custody, children's issues, women's rights, women's history, woman suffrage, civil rights, education, law, psychology and child development; Women of Achievement. http://www.thelizlibrary.org

Men Can Stop Rape

To mobilize men to use their strength for creating cultures free from violence, especially men's violence against women. Men Can Stop Rape's pioneering work embraces men as vital allies with the will and character to make healthy choices and foster safe, equitable relationships. http://www.mencanstoprape.org/

National Institute of Mental Health

NIMH envisions a world in which mental illnesses are prevented and cured. The mission of NIMH is to transform the understanding and treatment of mental illnesses through basic and clinical research, paving the way for prevention, recovery, and cure.

For the Institute to continue fulfilling this vital public health mission, it must foster innovative thinking and ensure that a full array of novel scientific perspectives are used to further discovery in the evolving science of brain, behavior, and experience. In this way, breakthroughs in science can become breakthroughs for all people with mental illnesses.

National NOW Family Law Advisory Ad Hoc Committee Website

The National Organization for Men Against Sexism (NOMAS)

The National Organization for Men Against Sexism is an activist organization of men and women supporting positive changes for men. NOMAS advocates a perspective that is pro-feminist, gay affirmative, anti-racist, dedicated to enhancing men's lives, and committed to justice on a broad range of social issues including class, age, religion, and physical abilities.

Sanctuary Model: An Integrated Theory - Sandra L. Bloom, M.D.

Mission: To teach individuals and organizations the necessary skills for creating and sustaining nonviolent lives and nonviolent systems and to keep believing in the unexplored possibilities of peace.

The Sanctuary Model® represents a theory-based, trauma-informed, evidence-supported, whole culture approach that has a clear and structured methodology for creating or changing an organizational culture. The objective of such a change is to more effectively provide a cohesive context within which healing from psychological and social traumatic experience can be addressed. As an organizational culture intervention, it is designed to facilitate the development of structures, processes, and behaviors on the part of staff, clients and the community-as-a-whole that can counteract the biological, affective, cognitive, social, and existential wounds suffered by the victims of traumatic experience and extended exposure to adversity.

Sanctuary for the Abused

Articles, links and resources for victims and survivors dealing with verbal, psychological & emotional abuse and personality disorders.

San Francisco Training Manual – RAPE

Southern Poverty Law Center

The Southern Poverty Law Center is a nonprofit civil rights organization dedicated to fighting hate and bigotry, and to seeking justice for the most vulnerable members of society.

The Washington Peace Center is a multi-issue, grassroots, anti-racist activist support organization working for peace, justice and nonviolent social change in the metropolitan Washington D.C. area. http://washingtonpeacecenter.net/about

Verbal Abuse Website by Patricia Evans, Author

Our goal is to present information and resources to those who strive for truth and clarity in all areas of interpersonal communications. We focus also on providing information and support to those who deal with verbal abuse issues. We believe that through awareness and understanding many issues can be resolved and authentic human bonds established. It takes two to build a good relationship. It only takes one to destroy it. http://www.verbalabuse.com/

Woman Church and State: A Historical Account of the Status of Woman through the Christian Ages with Reminiscences of Matriarchate by *Matilda Joslyn Gage*

In the late 1800's, Matilda Joslyn Gage was a progressive visionary of women's rights. The scope, breadth, depth, and powerful, no-holds barred writing style makes *Woman, Church, and State* my favorite book of all that I have read. She spoke the truth! Her book assisted me in healing from decades of child, marital, spiritual and legal abuse. It has taken academia and only the most radical, feminist pockets of academia at that, 100 years to catch up with Gage. If this work was published today, it would be considered radical. I urge everyone to read Gage's *Woman, Church, and State* in its entirety. Human liberation. http://www.matildajoslyngage.org/

Military Related Articles by Coral Anika Theill

Leatherneck Magazine

Exclusive Interview: The Commandant of the Marine Corps on Post-Traumatic Stress and Traumatic Brain Injury by Coral Anika Theill – Leatherneck Magazine October 2011

Invisible Battle Scars: Confronting the Stigma of PTS and TBI by Coral Anika Theill – Leatherneck Magazine October 2011

World War II: Montford Point Marines - Honoring and Preserving Their Legacy by Coral Anika Theill - Leatherneck Magazine February 2011

Salem-News

Montford Point Marines of WWII Receive Congressional Gold Medal by Coral Anika Theill Salem-News.com June 19, 2012

From Segregation to a Single Corps of 'Green Marines' by Coral Anika Theill Salem-News.com June 19, 2012

Black Marine History Through White Marine Eyes by Master Gunnery Sergeant Robert E. Talmadge, Edited by Coral Anika Theill Salem-News.com – June 19, 2012

Congressional Gold Medal for Montford Point Marines by Coral Anika Theill Salem-News.com November 9, 2011

Salute to the Montford Point Marines: Loyalty, Honor and Courage in the Face of Racism by Coral Anika Theill Salem-News.com July 12, 2010

Rolling Thunder XXV May 27, 2012: Gone but Not Forgotten by Coral Anika Theill Salem-News.com May 21, 2012

Support USMC K-9 Combat Veteran MWD Sgt Beyco by Coral Anika Theill Salem-News.com April 1, 2012

Remembering Fallen Marine Lance Corporal Osbrany Montes De Oca by Corporal Brandon Rumbaugh, Edited by Coral Anika Theill February 19, 2012

United States Marine Corps Brings Leadership Courses to Wounded Warriors by Coral Anika Theill Salem-News.com February 11, 2012

Support the Warrior Games - Competition for Wounded Military Members by Coral Anika Theill Salem-News.com April 13, 2010

Recommended Films and Documentaries

Burning Times
Sing Your Song"- Harry Belafonte
Mea Maxima Culpa: Silence in the House of God by HBO
Eyes on the Prize
Small Justice: Little Justice in America's Family Courts
Slavery by Another Name
Dirty Wars: The World is a Battlefield
The Invisible War
No Way Out But One
What the BLEEP Do We Know
Antwone Fisher
Once We Were Warriors
Mother Wove the Morning
Casualties of War
Green Mile
The Shawshank Redemption
Mystic River
The Education of Little Tree
Sophie's Choice
It's a Beautiful Mind
Not Without My Daughter
Bandit Queen - Foreign Film
Sleeping with the Enemy
Waking Life
Scarlet Letter
What's Love Got to do with It
Seven
Stepford Wives
Dangerous Intentions
The Color Purple
The Joy Luck Club
Sleepers
Samaritan: The Mitch Snyder Story
Fisher King
Dead Poets Society
Awakenings

Out of the Darkness
Nobody's Child
Perfect Mother
Dead by Sunset
Gaslight
Jim Jones - The Guyana Tragedy
A Cry for Help: The Tracy Thurman Story
American History X
Rules of Engagement
Breaking the Huddle
Black Magic Documentary by ESPN
Time to Kill
Little Big Man
Steal This Movie
The Body Snatchers
Powder
One Against the Wind
Jerusalem - Foreign Film
Gandhi
I am Sam
Spotlight
The Keepers
Handmaid's Tale

Documentation and Supporting Evidence

Timeline - Coral Anika Theill 1955 - 2001.

1956 - Hershel Stonebraker – my great-uncle – Charged with First Degree Murder - Tri City Herald – July 19, 1956

Letter to Martin and Kathryn Warner written by Dr. Charles Kuttner.

February 13, 1999. Affidavit of Kathy Y. Warner (Coral Anika Theill).

February 14, 1999. Affidavit of Mr. Jonathan P. Benson, Attorney at Law, Representing Kathy Y. Warner (Coral Anika Theill).

March 29, 1996. Letter to Dr. Jean Furchner, Custody Evaluator, written by Mrs. Debbie Dresler.

Spring 1996. Letter to Mr. Marty Warner written by Mr. Jack Meier.

June 3, 1996. Letter to Pastor Barnhart written by Mrs. Ellen Callen.

June 14, 1996. Letter to Kathryn Warner (Coral Anika Theill) written by Mr. Joseph P. Crawford, Attorney at Law.

August 5, 1996. Letter to Kathryn Warner (Coral Anika Theill) written by Mr. Joseph Crawford, Attorney at Law.

February 26, 1997. Letter to Kathryn Hall (Coral Anika Theill) written by Mr. Joseph P. Crawford, Attorney at Law.

May 19, 1997. Letter to Kathryn Hall written by Mogens, Anne-Marie, Jacob and Christian Theill–Denmark.

July 24, 1997. Letter to Judicial Fitness and Disability Commission written by Dr. Charles Kuttner regarding Judge Norblad.

August 25, 1998. Letter of Recommendation for Kathryn Hall (Coral Anika Theill) written by Dr. Barbara May.

"Criminal Thinking and Behavior Errors"–Adapted from Yochelson and Samenow and Bays and Freeman-Longo

January 4, 1999. Letter to Dr. Barbara May written by Bob and Shirley Walsh.

July 2001. "Shunning in Charismatic Community," by Robert L. Walsh.

March 4, 1999. Billing Statement to Kathryn Hall from Stahancyk, Gearing & Rackner.

May 30, 1999. Letter to Pastor Ron Sutter written by Tashi Smith.

April 24, 2000. Letter to Coral Anika Theill written by Ms. Renee Kim, Grants Coordinator, Department of State Police, Criminal Justice Services Division.

June 14, 2000. "Did God Only Endow the White Man with Sovereignty?" by Jewell Praying Wolf James.

Statement of Court Action in Warner vs. Warner - 95P-20693, 1995 through 2000.

"Problem Statement" Regarding Domestic Violence.

OCADSV Sexual Offenses

Articles and Handout relating to Domestic Violence.

Documentation Available

Time Line - Coral Anika Theill 1955 – 2012.

Statement of Court Action in Warner vs. Warner - 95P-20693, 1995 through 2012.

May 2, 1981. Teaching presented by Mr. Marty Warner to Vine and the Branches Community, (People of Praise) in Corvallis, Oregon, entitled "God as the Center of Our Life–Our First Love."

August 23, 1993. Letter to Kathy Warner (Coral Anika Theill) written by Mrs. Betsy Close.

April 1993 - April 1996. Documentation written by Mrs. Debbie Custis to Hewlett Packard. Re: Sexual harassment by Mr. Marty Warner.

March 9, 1994. Letter to Martin and Kathryn Warner written by Dr. Charles Kuttner.

May 21, 1995. Letter to Warner children written by Mr. Marty Warner entitled, "Warner Household Duties and Responsibilities."

January 4, 1996. Restraining Order and attempted Marital Rape Hearing. Court Transcripts. Polk County Courthouse. Judge Collins Presiding.

January 1996. Affidavit of Counsel. Mr. J. Mark Lawrence, Attorney at Law, Representing Mr. Martin Warner.

January 25, 1996. Point and Authorities in Support of Motion to Recuse Judge Horner.

Written by Mr. J. Mark Lawrence, Attorney at Law, Representing Mr. Martin Warner.

February 1996 - October 1996. Depositions of Kathryn Y. Warner and V. Martin Warner.

February 13, 1996. Affidavit written by Mrs. Karen A. Heintz

February 13, 1996. Affidavit written by Mrs. Therese Vasquez.

February 13, 1996. Affidavit written by Mrs. Kristi Gilsdorf.

February 13, 1996. Affidavit of Kathy Y. Warner. Petitioner.

February 14, 1996. Affidavit of Counsel. Jonathan P. Benson, Attorney for Petitioner.

February 28, 1996 - March 1, 1996. Temporary Child Custody Hearings. Court Audio Tapes.

March 5, 1996. Letter to Mr. Jonathan Benson, Attorney at Law, and Mr. Mark Lawrence, Attorney at Law, written by The Honorable Judge Albin W. Norblad. Re: Warner vs. Warner (95P20693) ordering Petitioner to "return the children she has to the Respondent by Sunday, March 10, 1996 at 12:00 p.m."

March 29, 1996. Letter to Dr. Jean Furchner, Custody Evaluator, written by Mrs. Debbie Dresler.

Spring 1996. Letter to Mr. Marty Warner written by Mr. Jack Meier.

April 18, 1996. Custody Evaluation of Martin and Kathryn Warner written by Ms. Patricia Cox.

June 3, 1996. Letter to Pastor Barnhart written by Mrs. Ellen Callen.

June 7, 1996. Custody Evaluation and Psychological Appraisal of Martin and Kathryn Warner written by Dr. Jean Furchner.

June 14, 1996. Letter to Kathryn Warner (Coral Anika Theill) written by Mr. Joseph P. Crawford.

August 5, 1996. Letter to Kathryn Warner (Coral Anika Theill) written by Mr. Joseph P.

Crawford.

October 14, 1996 - October 15, 1996. Court Videos of Divorce Hearing, Marion County

Courthouse. Judge Norblad Presiding.

February 26, 1997. Letter to Kathryn Hall written by Mr. Joseph P. Crawford, Attorney at Law.

May 19, 1997. Letter to Kathryn Hall written by Mogens, Anne-Marie, Jacob and Christian Theill.

July 24, 1997. Letter to Judicial Fitness and Disability Commission written by Dr. Charles Kuttner regarding Judge Norblad.

August 25, 1998. Letter of Recommendation for Coral Anika Theill; aka Kathryn Y. Hall written by Dr. Barbara May.

September 30, 1998. Claim of Risk. Polk County District Attorney.

December 2, 1998. Affidavit of Vaughn M. Warner, in Support of Respondent's Motion for Contempt Citation.

January 1999 - August 2001. Letter to Warner Children written by Coral Anika Theill.

January 1999 - August 2001. Letters to Coral Anika Theill written by Hannah, Rebekah, Theresa, and Sarah and Rachel Warner.

January 4, 1999. Letter to Dr. Barbara May written by Bob and Shirley Walsh.

February 1999. Letter to Coral Anika Theill written by Rebekah Warner.

March 4, 1999. Billing Statement to Kathryn Hall from Stahancyk, Gearing & Rackner.

April 5, 1999. "Brief Outline of My Life" written by Coral Anika Theill.

April 22, 1999. Certificate of Change of Name. Marion County Circuit Court.

April 23, 1999. Letter to Governor John A. Kitzhaber written by Coral Anika Theill.

> (In response to a newspaper article "Governor Shocked by Domestic Violence Findings, Associated Press, printed in The Statesman Journal).

May 30, 1999. Letter to Pastor Ron Sutter written by Tashi Smith.

June 1999. Affidavit Supporting Motion Order to Set Aside Judgments by Coral Anika Theill.

July 13, 1999. Affidavit by Dr. Barbara May.

July 13, 1999. Affidavit by Dr. Charles Kuttner.

July 20, 1999. Letter to Coral Anika Theill and Mr. Daniel Van Eaton written by The Honorable Judge Charles E. Luukinen.

January 20, 2000. Oregon State Bar. "Oregon Code of Professional Responsibility" (As approved by the Oregon Supreme Court through January 20, 2000.)

January 31, 2000. Letter to District Attorney Mark Hesslinga and District Attorney Donna Kelly written by Coral Anika Theill.

February 10, 2000. Letter to Governor's Council on Domestic Violence written by Coral Anika Theill.

March 1, 2000. Letter to Ms. Beverlee Venell and Governor's Council on Domestic Violence written by Coral Anika Theill.

April 24, 2000. Letter to Ms. Coral Anika Theill written by Ms. Renee Kim, Department of State Police.

June 6, 2000. Letter to Pastor Ron Sutter, Mrs. Ellen Callen, and Mr. and Mrs. Brian King written by Coral Anika Theill.

August 6, 2000, Mr. George D. Amiotte assaults and attempts to murder Coral Anika Theill.

Mr. George D. Amiotte arrested for assault and D.V., Mr. Amiotte placed into custody, Tumwater, Washington, Police Reports, Neighbors Affidavits, Restraining Order, Order to Surrender Weapons,

December 5, 2000. Letter to Ms. Coral Anika Theill written by Mr. Marty Warner.

OCADSV Sexual Offenses. Chapter 743, Oregon Laws 1971, 163.375.

April 18, 2001. George D. Amiotte terminated from Hoy and Nickle Associates, court ordered batterers treatment counselor for failure to attend classes and court orders.

June 12, 2001. Letter to Oregon State Bar Association written by Coral Anika Theill

June 22, 2001. Complaint filed against Mr. J. Mark Lawrence written by Coral Anika Theill.

July 8, 2001. Letter to Oregon State Bar Association written by Coral Anika Theill.

July 30, 2001. Letter to Coral Anika Theill written by Mary A. Cooper, Assistant Disciplinary Counsel, Oregon State Bar Disciplinary Counsel's Office.

July 2001. "Shunning in the Charismatic Community" written by Robert L. Walsh.

October 2001, Legal Promissory Note signed by George D. Amiotte and witnessed by Joanne Trainor, Hamilton, Montana, in the amount **of** $36,000 with 9% interest.

January 2003 – *BONSHEA Making Light of the Dark* published

December 2003. Affidavit by Debbie Custis (Co-Worker of Mr. Marty Warner, reports abuse)

March 2004 – Coral Anika Theill guest speaker for Thurston County Domestic Violence Task Force meeting in Olympia, Washington, for judges, district attorneys, police, sheriffs, advocates regarding the attempted murder incident on August 6, 2000, by George Amiotte and her book, *BONSHEA Making Light of the Dark*

January 31, 2004 - Letter and manuscript to Veteran's Administration directors and employees, including Dr. Leslie Burger, Portland, Oregon, (10N20) Candice L. Benne, RN, Fort Meade, South Dakota, Mr. Joseph M. Dalpiaz, Director, Sioux Falls, South Dakota, VAMC, Mr. Peter P. Henry, Director, Hot Springs and Fort Meade, SD, VAMC, Dr. Robert Petzel, Minneapolis, Minnesota, VISN 23 Director, Dr. James Tuchschmidt, Director, Portland, Oregon, Mr. Timothy Williams, Director, Seattle, Washington, VAPSHCS, and Mr. Jim Willis, Director, Salem, Oregon, Oregon Department of Veterans' Affairs.

2004 - Filed a complaint, with evidence, against Dr. Charles H. Kuttner with the Oregon Medical Board. Oregon Medical Board dismissed the complaint.

2004 – Mason County Summary Judgment awarded to Coral Anika Theill against George D. Amiotte in the amount of **$31,500 with 12% interest.** (Washington State) Mr. Amiotte did not make payments.

2005 – Copy of dismissal of my ex-husband's appeal of our case to the Oregon State of Appeals for $50,000 in additional child support. Copy of my sixty-five-page legal brief in response to my ex-husband's appeal.

July 12, 2012 – Mr. George Amiotte arrested for eluding police, drunk driving and possession of marijuana, Mason County, Washington State. Mr. Amiotte's pretrial date: March 4, 2013

January 2013 – Letter to Black Hills Veterans Administration Director Stephen Distasio regarding the Black Hills V.A. hiring of George Amiotte. No response or comment from Director Stephen Disasio.

January 2013 – Letter to Mr. Tom Schumacher, Mr. Scott Swaim, and Mr. Michael Maxwell regarding their invitation to George Amiotte to be a guest speaker for their 2011 "Serving Returning Veteran's Conference." Copy was sent to Washington State Veterans Affairs PTSD Program Director Dorothy Hanson. On February 25, 2013 I received a letter from Washington State Department of Veterans Affairs, Heidi Audette, Communications Director, stating that she had discussed my suggestion to modify their screening for presenters of their events with their new PTSD Program Director, Dorothy Hanson. She stated that this is something the Veterans Affairs is committed to doing.

March 2019 Letter to Colonel Christopher Shaw, USMC, Re: National Naval Officers Association

October 8, 2020 Letter to the Senate and Judiciary Committee, Re: Judge Amy Coney Barrett

Articles and Handouts relating to Domestic Violence

Time Line 1955 - 2012

1955 - Kathryn Yvonne Hall born in Tawas City, Michigan. My father was in the Air Force. My mother was a homemaker.

1957 - My brother, Donald Alan Hall was born in Lansing, Michigan. We moved to Tulsa, Oklahoma where my father received his A. & E. License.

1959 - 1961 Moved to Lake City, Washington, near Seattle. My father served in the Air Force Reserves at McChord Air Force Base. He also began working for Boeing as a helicopter pilot.

1961 - 1964 Lived in Kennewick, Washington. Attended first through beginning of fourth Grade at Vista Elementary School in Kennewick, Washington. Summer of 1963 lived in Libby, Montana. Survived helicopter crash with father and brother. (Helicopter instrument mal-function) Summer of 1964 lived in Long Barn, California. Attended school for one month in two-room school house in Long Barn. My great-uncle Herschel Stonebraker lived with our family. I was sexually molested by my great-uncle Herschel (my father's uncle) during these years.

1964 - 1965 Moved to Kent, Washington. Attended fourth Grade at Star Lake Elementary School, in Kent, Washington.

1965 - 1967. Attended Fifth and Sixth Grades at Sunnyside Elementary School in Kent, Washington. Participated in Band - Clarinet. Took piano lessons.

1967 Moved to 1940's farm house in Auburn, Washington, Star Lake Rd. Renovated home and cut cord wood on property. Uncle Herschel lived with our family.

1967 - 1970. Attended seventh through ninth grade at Totem Junior High School. Participated in band, continued to take piano lessons. Spent the summer in Kodiak, Alaska with my grandparents and brother.

1970 Confirmed at Messiah Lutheran Church, Kent, Washington. Spent summer in Lewiston, Idaho, where my father was working.

1971 Attended tenth grade at Thomas Jefferson High School in Federal Way, Washington. My high school friend, Cindy (Fowler) Haugland took me to Bill Gothard's Basic Youth Conflicts in Seattle, Washington, as a guest.

1971 Moved after school was out to Vancouver, Washington. Father worked for Federal Government, Bonneville Power, in Vancouver, Washington, as a jet ranger helicopter pilot.

1971 - 1973 Attended eleventh through twelfth grade at Columbia River High School. President of Honor Society. Graduated with a 4.0 - was co-valedictorian. Attended ground school and took flying lessons at Pearson Airport in Vancouver, Washington. Passed my FAA exam and received my solo license. Attended Bill Gothard's Basic Youth Conflicts Seminars in Portland, Oregon.

1973 - 1974 Attended court reporting school at Pacific Business College in Portland, Oregon.

1974 In January met Mr. Martin Warner during the fuel crisis while on the Portland/Vancouver bus.

1974 - 1976 Worked for the Superior Courts of the State of Washington as a bailiff clerk, as a secretary for two Superior Court judges, and as juvenile court reporter. Dated Mr. Martin Warner during these two years. Traveled to Europe for three weeks the summer of 1975.

1976 On April 10, 1976, I married Mr. Martin Warner at St. Mary's Catholic Church in Corvallis, Oregon. Mr. Warner bought a small two-bedroom house on 15th street in Corvallis, Oregon.

1977 Confirmed at St. Mary's Catholic Church in Corvallis, Oregon.

1978 Pregnancy with twins. Attended Bradley Childbirth classes – instructor, Judy Ringle, Corvallis, Oregon.

1979 Sarah and Rachel Warner, our first-born identical twin girls were born at Albany General Hospital, Albany, Oregon. Dr. Charles South and Dr. Robert Kirschner attending physicians. Twins weighed 15 pounds total. Sarah and Rachel were baptized at St. Mary's Catholic Church. Rich and Therese Vasquez were godparents.

Marty and I started attending formation meetings with the People of Praise Charismatic Community in Corvallis, Oregon, formally known as the Vine and the Branches Community.

1981 Aaron Warner, our son, was born at Albany General Hospital, Albany, Oregon. Dr. Robert Kirschner attended the birth. Aaron was baptized at St. Mary's Catholic Church. Paul and Johnette Hessburg were godparents. Spent the night at the hospital in the emergency room: Paroxysmal Atrial Tachycardia (P.A.T.)

1983 Bought a larger home on Taylor Street in Corvallis, Oregon, and moved. Miscarriage, D & C surgery. Dr. Robert Kirschner performs surgery.

Spent the night at the hospital in the emergency room: Paroxysmal Atrial Tachycardia (P.A.T.)

1984 Miscarriage, D & C surgery. Dr. Charles South performs surgery at Albany General Hospital, Albany, Oregon.

I left the People of Praise Community in Corvallis, Oregon.

I became pregnant with my fourth child, my father died suddenly in November, and my husband was asked to leave the community because I would not submit to the community leaders. Mr. Warner becomes a chairperson for Right to Life. Meets Chris and Betsy Close. Sarah and Rachel attend local Lutheran private school.

1985 Theresa Warner was born at Albany General Hospital. Dr. Charles South attended the birth. Theresa weighed 10 lbs. 2 oz. I suffered anterior membrane dystrophy in my eyes. Theresa was baptized at St. Mary's Catholic Church in Corvallis, Oregon. Fred and Maxine Dare were godparents.

I left the Catholic Church. I shared with Mr. Warner that I wanted to separate from him. He threatened me that I would not get to leave with any of the children. We sought marriage counseling, but nothing helped. Betsy and Chris Close and Peggy Stephens of Corvallis, Oregon, and my brother, Don Hall, are aware that Mr. Warner is becoming increasingly violent towards me. They offer their homes as a refuge of safety for me, if I should need to leave with the children.

1986 Mr. Warner leaves the Catholic Church and starts fellowshipping with local Christians. Aaron, Sarah and Rachel attend local Lutheran private school.

1987 Mr. Warner meets Sacred Name believers and adopts this religion. He begins studying Hebrew, teaching the children Hebrew and demanding that I only use the Hebrew name for God and Jesus and that we keep the Sabbath and Feast Days.

Mr. Warner shares Mary Pride book, *The Way Home* with me and is convicted that we should not use contraceptives and that we should homeschool. Three older children are attending private Lutheran school. I suffer from anterior membrane dystrophy. I go to Casey Eye Institute to see a specialist. He recommends wearing a large bandage lens on my eyes.

1988 Joshua Warner was born at Albany General Hospital. Dr. Charles South attends birth. Prepare to homeschool children in fall of 1988.

1988 - 1991 Homeschooling four oldest children.

1991 Rebekah was born at home in Corvallis, Oregon. Mabel Dzata was our midwife. Summer filled with camping trips. Homeschooled the four oldest children. Homeschooling, selling of home, shopping for home in country, packing for move.

Moved to home in country, Independence, Oregon. Unpacked, homeschooled, renovated and wallpapered home.

1992 Hannah was born at home. Mabel Dzata, my midwife was taking nursing exams, so her assistant birthed the baby. Did not feel well after the birth and bled heavily. I told my midwife that I felt like I was dying. I was weak for months afterward. Homeschooled the five oldest children. Suffering from exhaustion and sleep deprivation. My husband was working 14-to-18-hour days. He was rarely at home.

1993 In March I suffered from a serious eye infection, then developed tinnitus. In April I suffered a mental/nervous breakdown, partial stroke and collapse. Briefly saw Dr. Michael May and Dr. Roger Jacobson in June and August. I began to feel suicidal. Marty had his mother, Helen Warner, stay with us to help with the children and the chores. Dr. May gave me a low-dose tranquilizer for sleep. I briefly stayed with Mike and Lynn Eisler. The children were told I had a "sin" problem and nothing was wrong with me. I was told by my husband and his religious counselors that I just needed to repent.

In September, Marty forced me to attend a Bill Gothard Basic Youth Conflict's seminar with his cousin, Dan O'Halloran and his wife, Penny. I was instructed to learn how to become a submissive wife and obey the authorities in my life that God had placed over me. I needed to repent of my sins, and then I would be "well" again. I became so distraught that I tried to hurt myself my cutting my wrists on a grinding wheel. Mr. Warner took me to Bend, Oregon, to see a Christian counselor, Mr. Tom McMahon. Mr. Warner used me sexually on the trip and I became pregnant.

In November I saw Dr. Charles Kuttner. He sent me to Woodland Park Hospital in Portland, Oregon. I saw a Christian Fundamentalist psychologist, Dr. Larson. I was distraught over the fact that I was pregnant, "not mentally well," and locked up. I suffered a miscarriage and Dr. Jess Hickerson performed my D & C surgery. December 23 - Stayed with Mr. Warner's mother, Helen Warner, in Ridgefield, Washington.

1994 In March, Dr. Charles Kuttner, dismissed me as his patient because my husband was not bringing me in for appointments and was leaving me with unqualified people. Mr. Warner enlisted the help of Mr. Bill Heard, a Christian counselor in Roseburg, Oregon. He was oppressive. He also told me I had a "sin" problem that I needed to repent of my disobedience to my husband, etc. I stayed with my friend and adopted mom, Addie Archer, in Longview, Washington for a week. She was kind and understanding.

My husband left me at the "Wings of Love" half-way house on Killingsworth in Portland, Oregon. My brother, Don Hall, visited me while I was staying there and asked permission from my husband to let me come home with him, Don. My husband finally agreed and I stayed with my brother off and on for the next several months.

In September my husband and I boarded a plane to Chicago, Illinois. I was left at Bill Gothard's Institute in Indianapolis, Indiana. I was exorcised daily for "witchcraft." Again, they told me I was in "sin," and needed to learn how to obey my husband and the authorities God placed over me. I scrubbed toilets, washed floors, peeled potatoes, made beds in the hotel, etc. I ran away after several weeks and flew back to Portland, Oregon. My brother picked me up and I lived with him, in Dallesport, Washington, off and on for the next several months.

In October, Mr. Warner, brought me thyroid medication from an internal medicine doctor, Dr. Gallant, I had not seen for over a year. Mr. Warner takes me to a nearby motel and uses me sexually during the night. He returns me to my brother's house in the morning. No contraceptives were used. I was again pregnant.

1994 I return to our home in Oregon in November, but I am too ill with the pregnancy, so I return to stay with my brother and a friend, Hanna Humberd until mid-January 1995.

1995 Return to Corvallis, Oregon in January. I stay with a former neighbor, Stephanie Hawkinson. A friend, Therese Vasquez drives me to my OB/Gyn, Dr. Charles South in Albany, Oregon. He tells me to get a divorce attorney.

On January 20, I returned to my family home with my husband for my son's birthday party. I stay at the home throughout the pregnancy. I feel better mentally and emotionally, but I am weak physically from the past year and a half. I see Dr. Moynihan for counseling in Corvallis, Oregon until the birth of my eighth child. I continue to see Dr. South. I experience toxemia during the last months of pregnancy. All seven children come down with chicken pox before the baby's due date in July.

Zachary is born at Albany General Hospital, Albany, Oregon, on July 13, 1995. Mr. Warner tried to interfere with the physicians saving my life. I was hemorrhaging. I stayed in the hospital, per doctors' orders, for three days. Zachary and I shared a close bond.

My husband attempts to rape me.

In November 1995, I retained an attorney, Mr. Richard Alway, in Salem, Oregon.

In December I got a restraining order against my husband from Polk County in Dallas, Oregon.

1996 January 4, 1996, Restraining Order and Attempted Marital Rape Hearing at Polk County Courthouse. Judge Collins presiding. Restraining Order was lifted. I was ordered to return to my home with my children. Mr. Alway represented me at the hearing. Mr. J. Mark Lawrence represented Mr. Warner.

1996 January 6, 1996, I leave the home with my three youngest children, including my nursing infant at the advice of CARDVA in Corvallis, Oregon and my attorney and lived in hiding until March 10, 1996.

1996 Dismissed Mr. Alway as my attorney. Retained Mr. Gearing in Portland, Oregon, as my attorney.

In February was subjected to several days of depositions by Mr. J. Mark Lawrence, Attorney at Law, McMinnville, Oregon that were mentally abusive and cruel in nature.

February 28, 1996 - March 1, 1996 attended my three-day custody hearing at Polk County Courthouse. Judge Albin Norblad presiding. Began counseling with Dr. Charles Kuttner.

March 6, 1996. Received news by phone that Judge Norblad signed a Court Order awarding all of my eight children to Mr. Warner. I was to return the younger three children, including my nursing infant to Mr. Warner the morning of March 10, 1996.

On March 10, 1996, Candy McGuire and Debbie Custis picked up my nursing infant, Zachary, and my daughters, Rebekah and Hannah, and drove them to Mr. Warner, at his home in Independence, Oregon.

I got an apartment, a job, and continued counseling and participated in an exercise program and visitation weekends with my children. Worked as a hostess at night and warehouse receiver during the day.

1996 - Attended eight court hearings related to my divorce and underwent approximately thirty-five (35) hours of depositions that were oppressive, mentally abusive and 1999 cruel in nature. I also underwent five psychiatric exams to prove my mental well-being to the court. I attended thirteen juvenile court hearings related to my son's probation.

1997 In March I was legally divorced. Survived a car explosion before my trip abroad. Traveled to Denmark to meet my relatives. Worked as a retail clerk, attended modeling school. Began counseling with Dr. Barbara May. Suffer a physical breakdown from exhaustion.

1997- 2001 Assisted my oldest son with his legal matters.

1998 Worked part-time as a model, attended community college part-time. Took courses in drama and professional voice. Received "Model of the Year Award." Took professional commercial, TV, and video classes. Enrolled in belly-dancing classes. Court awarded me custody of my son, Aaron Warner.

Attended a healing workshop by George Amiotte, sponsored by Dr. Charles Kuttner.

Signed an "at risk" form with the District Attorney's Office in Polk County. Moved out-of-state and went into hiding (Aaron was working in Salem and moved in with friends). District Attorney's Office initiated hearings to get my child support lowered. Met Joanna Trainor and began counseling with her. Began writing BONSHEÁ - *Making Light of the Dark*. Worked full-time selling my beeswax art at retail fairs and supplying stores.

1999 In January I went to a court hearing regarding my child support. Mr. Daniel Van Eaton represented Mr. Warner. I was not represented. Was later sued for double the amount of child support and was sued for Mr. Warner's attorney fees. My visitation rights were taken away. Suffer a physical breakdown from exhaustion in February. Started writing my book and sending documentation regarding my story to the media. Moved out-of-state. For a brief time, I lived on the Pine Ridge Reservation. I also stayed, for a short time, in Denmark with my relatives.

On April 22, 1999, changed my name at the Marion Courthouse, Salem, Oregon to Coral Anika Theill.

My court hearings are stayed temporarily by Judge Luukinen because of my frail health. Suffered a physical breakdown from exhaustion in September. Moved to Washington State.

2000 Continued writing my story, BONSHEÁ - *Making Light of the Dark*. Attended retail and tradeshows selling my art. Attacked and was injured by a vicious dog was I was on a walk. Suffered a physical breakdown in August from exhaustion. Worked on designing a catalog for my art.

2000 August 6, George D. Amiotte attempted to murder me in my apartment, Olympia, Washington

2001 Finished writing my story, BONSHEÁ - *Making Light of the Dark*.

Filed a complaint against Mr. J. Mark Lawrence, Attorney at Law, with the Oregon State Bar Association.

2001 Guest speaker at Linfield College, Portland, Oregon. Invited by Dr. Barbara May, Professor of Nursing.

2002 Please see "Addendum."

2002 Received "Writer's Award" from iUniverse.com

2003 *BONSHEA Making Light of the Dark* published

In October 2002 I sent information regarding my book, *BONSHEÀ - Making Light of the Dark,* to all Oregon State Senators and Representatives in honor of Domestic Violence Awareness Month.

March 2004 – Guest speaker at Thurston County Domestic Violence and Sexual Assault Task Force meeting in Olympia, Washington. Invited by Sheriff Dan Kimball.

2004 *BONSHEA Making Light of the Dark* was used as a college text for nursing students at Linfield College, Portland, Oregon.

2008 Gene Deutscher, a U.S. Marine Combat Veteran, nominated me for the 'Woman of Courage Award.' Coral was selected for the award in 2008 by Andrea Harris, impressionist artist.

2010-2011 – Contributing Writer for Leatherneck Magazine

2011 Recipient of the Lester Granger Award from the National Montford Point Association for my advocacy and articles on the Montford Point Marines.

"Never utter these words: 'I do not know this; therefore, it is false.' One must study to know, know to understand, understand to judge." –Apothegm of Nanada

Letters and Documentation

March 29, 1996

(Written by Debbie Dresler to custody evaluator Dr. Jean Furchner. Communication by letter also made to custody evaluator Patricia Cox)

Dear Dr. Furchner,

I contacted both you and Patricia Cox (after my brief visit with Kathy Warner at her home on her first weekend of visitation) because of concerns I had about the children, particularly the hostility expressed by the older children, the aggressive outburst towards my six-year-old daughter by Theresa, and the overall level of tension in that home.

Both of you sought information about my relationship with Kathy and Marty and how long I had known the family, how well I knew the children and other background information. I wanted to be very careful to tell you what I saw directly on the weekend and not to give information about any of the family that I had not seen or heard myself, other than general history of my relationship with them.

The sadness of this situation continues to haunt me. I feel ready now to share more of what I know of Kathy and Marty's relationship because the unusual nature of their relationship makes this such a tragedy for the children.

Marty Warner is a man of intense religious zeal. He has lived his marriage by certain scriptural principles (actually isolated verses from the Bible) that he would freely share with you as he has with me and all of their friends. He believes that these are the irrefutable principles that govern the marriage of a righteous Christian man and woman.

"Wives, be subject to your own husbands, as to the Lord. For the husband is the head of the wife, as Christ also is the head of the church, He Himself being the Savior of the body. But as the church is subject to Christ, so also the wives ought to be subject to their husbands in all things." Ephesians 5:22-24

"But I want you to understand that Christ is the head of every man, and the man is the head of a woman..." I Corinthians 11:3

"For a man does not originate from woman, but woman from man, for indeed man was not created for woman's sake, but woman for the man's sake." I Corinthians 11:8-9

"Husbands, love your wives, just as Christ also loved the church and gave Himself up for her, that He might sanctify her, having cleansed her by the washing of water with the word, that he might present to Himself the church in all her glory, having no spot or wrinkle or any such thing; but that she should be holy and blameless." Eph. 5:25-27

Marty took these principles and interpreted them to mean that any disagreement with his wishes or beliefs was ungodly rebellion against himself and God. He interpreted them to mean that Kathy needed constant correcting and punishing to make her pure before God and that he was the husband that God had given her in order to make her "spot free".

He established a practice of "headship" in their home. This is something that bears asking Kathy about because it has had such an impact on the relationships in that family and the sickness of those relationships. It began when they got involved in a charismatic Catholic community. The men were honored as the "heads" in their homes and the wives were expected to demonstrate their submission or they had to go through a process of confessing and restoration. When Marty was out of town on business, he would assign another man from the "community" to step in as his "head" and monitor Kathy while he was gone. I can only believe she was totally brainwashed to put up with this. The man would come over to see if she was doing her chores and following her schedules. I can't remember how many years they were involved in this, but it was eerie and I only visited her perhaps 4 or 5 times while they were in this group. She finally dug her heels in and refused to be a part of this anymore. She can tell you about all that.

He eventually left that group when she absolutely refused to be a part of it anymore and after some church shopping, I heard from her that Marty had decided they would become their own little church. I don't know how many years that went on, but he persisted in the "headship" practices at home, often accompanied by family Bible study and "encouraging each other's growth" which was often a thinly veiled reason to find more and more ways that Kathy needed to improve. As the older girls got to be around 10 years old, they were enlisted in the process of helping Kathy to meet her responsibilities as a godly woman should. He would ask them whether she had taken a nap (how, with 5 children?), had she raised her voice, had she been available for all their needs, etc.) They also became involved in the homeschooling movement and very enthusiastic about it, but it resulted in constant demands on her time and constant supervision and reporting to Marty.

Kathy had a very warm and gentle style with the children. I last saw the twins with her when they were about 11 or 12, and they had an affectionate bond. Other friends told me that as the twins hit their teen years, they became demanding and critical of her in much the same way as Marty was. She had her hands full with 6 children by then. Other friends know far more about the relationship with the older children and saw them a lot more in these years. The tone in their household when Marty was home was tense. She was quiet and acquiescent and he tended to have a lot of little "needs", this or that for her to find for him. She always responded quickly, as if these little inconveniences he experienced were a top priority.

I saw her fairly regularly after she left the Catholic Church and things were very tense in their home then. I visited her a number of times when they were involved in the closed charismatic community that had all sorts of "umbrellas of authority". During this time, she looked pretty shell-shocked and I described my visits with her to my husband as visiting one of the *Stepford Wives* (an old TV movie about wives, who were replaced by submissive robots by their husbands). The children were well controlled and angelic, but it was difficult to relate to Kathy. She was very tense and didn't talk freely. She told me years later about the months of trauma she endured when she refused to participate in "Community" anymore.

I saw Kathy after the birth of Joshua and then just heard from her by letter after Rebecca. I had children of my own during that time and the distance and number of obligations I had in Portland with two small children kept me close to home. I visited her when my youngest was two and my older daughter was five. Marty was home and made a point of disparaging women who work as ungodly (I worked 20 hours/week as a physical therapist and Kathy had been asking me about my work and how I handled it). He has very strong beliefs that children need to be in the home with their mother and has shared these opinions freely and frequently with the women he works with and women of Kathy's circle of friends who work. It is dramatically different than the stand he currently takes with the care of the children.

I next heard from Kathy by phone in 1993 or 1994. She sounded very depressed and wanted me to return a book that she said she had sent to her women friends at Marty's request. She said it had grieved her and that she'd like me to send it back. She talked about her feelings of hopelessness and wanting to die to get away from the pain. I was very alarmed and called Marty at work the next day to find out what he was doing to address her depression. He said he had found a counselor after looking for a long time for one who agreed with his frame of reference. He said he didn't believe in secular counseling or psychology and that he had sought someone who agreed with him. I asked him what he thought Kathy's problem was and he said that she was "shirking her responsibilities".

Kathy called again about a month later and asked me to come visit her. I went. She was obviously not well emotionally and it was difficult to reach her conversationally. Marty was at first congenial when I came to the house, but became tenser and angry with her as the day progressed. I had come without the children and she had only Theresa and Joshua at home. Marty had split the family up and sent the other children to relatives temporarily. At that time, Kathy mentioned several times that the older children had become increasingly abusive with her, to the point of some physical abuse. She told me that Marty had said it was up to her to "earn" their respect. This seemed like a real loser of a suggestion from the man who set them up to report on her shortcomings as part of his "headship" in the home.

There was an incident with a dog fight that day that Marty attempted to break up and was bitten in the process. I heard an animal scream and when Joshua came in, we asked what happened and he said "Dad hit the dog with a board because he got bit". I left awhile later, feeling like I had never connected with Kathy and sure that she wouldn't get appropriate help with Marty in control. She said he had taken her to see someone in Roseburg or Springfield and that she didn't like him.

I got a call from Kathy last December and was surprised to learn she had had another baby and equally surprised at how good she sounded. She called to tell me she was seeking a separation, that she knew she needed to be away from Marty and that he needed to be away from her to stop the abuse he perpetrated against her. She said she preferred not to talk about it, but it was a lot of mental torment. She also said the older girls were visiting their aunt for about a month and that since she had to initiate this without his knowledge (he would never permit it), she had taken the opportunity of their absence to seek an attorney.

I talked to her frequently over the next month and then took her and the three youngest children in for a few nights when she came to Portland to meet Mr. Gearing. The restraining order had been lifted, Marty was very angry and back in the home and she was very distraught. Things were chaotic, over the next few weeks with the depositions, the attorney visits, getting Rebecca into counseling, and getting her psychiatric evaluations done in preparation for the hearings. Kathy was certain that Marty's big thrust would be her mental health and was pleased when Dr. Kuttner was able to validate how well she was doing. The little children were unsettled, as was Kathy, but this improved once she got through the depositions and was loaned a home by friends who were out of town. I saw her three or four times during those three weeks and took care of the children on several occasions. During this whole time, Kathy would only allow people she personally knew and trusted to take care of the children. Their well-being was a primary concern to her even though it meant a lot of time on the phone before every appointment to line up trusted help.

I sat through the first day of the custody hearings and then was shocked to learn the next week that she had temporarily lost all of the children, including the baby. At the break in the hearing, the twin girls turned their backs on her whenever she was out in the hall. "Shunning" was practiced by the "Community" that Marty had the family involved in when the girls were younger. (Kathy was officially "shunned" by that group for about 6 months until she refused to go sit in the hall during meetings any longer, but many of those people still engage in the practice of officially "shunning" her.)

I went to Kathy at the attorney's office on the day she was given the decision regarding the children and I can't begin to describe the grief of that day. We were all crying. I wondered how she would make it through the next few weeks–her last week before giving up the children and then giving them up. She knows Marty's belief system and what he feels "called" to do to her, just as he knows her weaknesses and the things that she is passionate about. According to his world view, Kathy is a harlot and home wrecker. She is selfish beyond belief to seek anything other than serving him and the children. She is outside her God-appointed "umbrella of authority" and she needs to be punished and brought back into submission. He called her brother during the course of the depositions and said he and his attorney would "have her broken" before the week was over. (Therese Vasquez knows these people) that he is punishing her and that he is "holding the children as hostages" to get her back in the home. He has told co-workers at Hewlett-Packard that he is "going to destroy her" and that she "deserves to be punished".

Kathy loves her children deeply and wants nothing more than to be their mother. Marty knows this and this is how he will punish her. Power over his wife has been the basis of his marriage with her. Now the courts have affirmed this power and he sees the hand of God in this. The tragedy of this divorce is that he will never allow her to have a healthy relationship with the children. He has custody now and can present the divorce and her absence as he sees fit. This is a family that uses the language of religion and the fear of God as motivation as a matter of course in their conversations. Mommy is evil and disobeying God by leaving the family. Mommy would rather work than be at home with them (the meaning of that in this household is clear).

The other belief that Marty clings to is that Kathy must be mentally ill or she would never leave him and the family. He has been heard to share this with the children. How are the children supposed to relate to Kathy in this context? No one has ever shaken Marty from any of his beliefs. Men that he has had friendly relationships with over the years have tried to talk to him about the extreme beliefs he holds and the effect they have had on Kathy and the children, but he cannot be budged. I think that Marty is aware at some level that he had a lot to do with Kathy's breakdown several years ago because he persists in bragging to people that he can "break" her again. I was with Kathy at the attorney's office for a good part of her depositions because I was taking care of the baby, so I heard a lot about what was being asked of her by Mr. Lawrence and a lot of the questions seemed to be asked directly to humiliate her and hurt her.

When I stopped by the home briefly on Sunday the 24th of March, I was again overwhelmed by the daunting task she has of trying to hang onto some kind of relationship with her children. She knows that he has absolute power in that home. The twin girls were standing in the kitchen, arms folded across their chests, glaring at us all. Parts of the house were locked off. The phones were all locked away. (I had come to the house because I couldn't reach her by phone and she had asked me to contact her). My girls had played with Theresa and Joshua and were getting along beautifully, until Theresa's angry outburst and lashing out at my little one. It was a strange and awful atmosphere that day.

I don't think that Marty has any idea what kind of damage the children experience as he sets out to punish her through them. I know children will feel anger towards the parent who initiates a divorce but she is not in a position to affirm her love for them and show them and tell them that she loves them dearly. It would be all but impossible for the little ones to understand a mother who is there for 2 days then disappears for two weeks again. This has got to be very frightening to them since she has been the primary caregiver in their lives.

Marty has told the court that he loves Kathy and they welcome her back in the home with flowers and open arms. He tells others he will destroy her. As Kathy held her eight-year-old son in her lap as I was leaving on the Saturday of her visitation, the ten-year-old girl stood across the room and glared at him. I had the impression that a campaign is already going on in that home to turn the children against her. If the children remain in Marty's custody, they will eventually have nothing to do with her. He is very intense and determined in his beliefs. I think that Marty would be unable to come up with a plan for how he will share custody of the children with her in a way that allows both of them to love and raise the children. If he is to be the parent in charge of their upbringing, it would be a revelation to see if he could demonstrate the ability to help the children adjust to this difficult situation with a healthy attitude towards their mother.

Kathy's deficiency as a parent errs on the side of perhaps too much gentleness and too many kids to manage simultaneously in a household where disrespect towards her was the norm modeled by her husband. As she has gotten away from Marty, I have seen her grow stronger, more self-assured and more collected in her thoughts. Going back into the home for visitation was an incredible challenge for her, but she made it through, stood her ground with the twins and will have had this emotionally wrenching first visit behind her. She knows, however, that the hostility towards her in that home is bound to grow as a final hearing date approaches. It seems there are better alternatives to visiting all seven of the eight children at the home at the same time, especially since the twins drive and have their own car, and since their issues with Kathy are much more grown up than the younger children. The younger children could have a much more nurturing visit with Kathy without the hostility of the twins to inhibit that bond.

I have gone far too long with this letter to you. I fear I overstep in suggesting that the courts' plan is not in the best interest of the children. I got to know the little children very well while Kathy was in Portland. I saw their confusion and their hurt and it tears me up to see that now they have lost her love and comfort. I am amazed that at this point she is actually going out for job interviews and moving ahead with her life. I don't know too many women who could lose so much and still do that. She tells me that there is a certain place of calm in having nothing else left to lose. She tries to look at her situation from various vantages to see it in a way that preserves her sanity. After the attorneys presented the judgment to her, one took me aside and said, "You and the other friends need to watch over her—women jump off bridges over decisions like these". As friends, some of the other women and I may be hyper vigilant about how she is doing, but at this point we feel we are all she has and that is a pretty scary place to be.

I appreciate you taking the time to wade through my reminiscing and opinions.

Sincerely,

Debbie Dresler
Portland, Oregon

Spring 1996

Mr. Marty Warner
Independence, OR 97351

Dear Marty,

This letter is being written after much prayer and thought. Please hear me out. Although I didn't know you well or very personally when we worked together at CH2M, I regarded you as a nice young man with your feet on the ground. After meeting Kathy, I thought you and she were a fine, young couple to whom my daughter Deborah (Dresler) could relate as Christian friends. Through Deborah I move or less kept abreast your family from time to time. I knew you were a Catholic back in those days, as once I had been. I also knew you were a charismatic Catholic at one time, which I might have been also, had the movement broadened to the Catholic church before I left it. I was concerned when I learned you were in a charismatic Christian commune whose leaders exercised absolute control over its members. I realized then you were in a cult, and from this point on your separation from Jesus Christ and the destruction of your family snowballed downhill.

I wondered how you could fall so far from your faith in Jesus and his assurance of salvation (John 3:16). Could it have been because you couldn't quite believe

360

in your good fortune of being saved by faith alone, a gift of God, and not plus works? I know this troubled me until Eph. 2:8,9 leapt off the page of my bible. What demons are you chasing, Marty? If you believe the holy bible is the inspired word of God, how can you believe the words of men who would deceive you, enslave you, and ultimately destroy you and your family? If it's not in the Word it just isn't true. (Rev. 22:18, 19).

You may ask what business is it of mine to butt into your personal life. Just this. I think you may still regard yourself as a Christian, so as a brother in Christ I am following the exhortation to rebuke you (Luke 17:3). Not only have you destroyed your own life, but that of your family, as well. I am appalled by our non-Christian behavior!

How any man can keep his wife in bondage for some 18-20 years, father eight of her children; expect her to raise them by his rigid, undeviating, pre-planned schedules, home school the oldest five while caring for the youngest three, in addition to her regular household chores; push her to the depth of despair (and almost over the edge)–then cast her aside like a piece of tattered clothing–is beyond my understanding.

I think you may be confused by the word "submit" as used in Eph. 5:22-24, which describes wives' submission to their husbands. These verses are based on Eph. 5:21, which says, "Submit to one another out of reverence in Christ." Verses 22 and 24 do not say "be subservient to," enslaved by," or "obey." The word "obey" does not appear in Scripture with respect to wives, although it does with respect to children and slaves. God created woman to be the helpmate of man. Both are equal in the eyes of God. They are to consult each other when making decisions affecting the family (Eph. 5:21). If they arrive at an impasse the husband's will should prevail. However, he is not Lord and Master, right 100 percent of the time.

To take a nursing baby from his mother's breast, to turn your children against their mother and put them in charge of her, and to withhold common acts of decency from a wife you have controlled for most of her married life are the acts of a hardened heart, and are not Christ like. Cults are of the devil, Marty. Who is driving your life?

I don't know where you found those "Christian" lawyers, or how the judge could have ruled as he did. It is neither right nor just. Kathy deserves better. She should not be deprived of the three youngest children. They need their mother and her love. The oldest ones hate their mother, it seems, and may never love her again. I don't know if Kathy can ever forgive you, but if you <u>really</u> want her back, you should get down on your knees, ask God's forgiveness, find a good <u>Christian</u> counselor, and then try to put your lives back together. But <u>don't even try</u> if you don't mean to <u>turn your life around 180 degrees, and are sincere in your resolve</u> to be the Christian husband God intended you to be.

May God grant you wisdom in deciding how you pursue your remaining years. Prayerfully it will be by resolving to abide in Jesus. This is the only way it can be.

Sincerely,

Jack Meier
Bend, OR

June 3, 1996

Bridgeport Community Chapel
16930 Bridgeport Rd.
Dallas, OR 97338

Dear Pastor Barnhart,

I am sharing these materials with you because I think that we at Bridgeport Chapel have an opportunity to learn from the lives of Kathy and Marty Warner. Indeed, if we are to be able to minister effectively to all people who may happen into our fellowship. I think that it is imperative that we learn from the classroom that God has provided us in the Warrens.

Kathy told me that she came to Bridgeport because she so desperately needed sound Christian fellowship and a place to worship in truth. Marty had refused to come and to let her come, but when she insisted, he decided to come too. By doing so he has successfully separated her from the fellowship of a Body which might have ministered to her.

Kathy has tried to attend Bridgeport on the weekends when she has visitation, but Marty's presence makes it impossible. Also, she senses that Marry has talked to many people and no one really knows how to relate to her. She feels hurt, not just by Bridgeport, but by many well-meaning Christians over the years who have believed Marty's story and have made judgment without taking the time to learn the truth. She has told me on several occasions that she did not want their problems to cause divisiveness in the fellowship, but she still hopes that God may use this learning experience to improve the ministry of our church.

Scripture teaches that we are to be wise as serpents; innocent as doves. It is dangerous to be too innocent. Having no reason not be believe Marty, the church reached out to him, as was right. But what if we learn that he is not what he appears to be? What if we, however innocently, have ignored the victim and nurtured the villain?

What is Bridgeport's responsibility to Marty? To Kathy? To the Warner children who have suffered and continue to suffer so much through all of this? That is for our elders to decide. But I sense a real danger to our fellowship if a decision is not made? Every Sunday that Marty is at church, I see him engaging several people in intense conversation. I am convinced that he is a serpent in our midst. Marty is a liar and serves the Father of Lies, even though he truly believes; I think that he is telling the truth. He also believes that he is a Christian, but more enlightened that most. (I have read some of his letters which bear witness to this attitude.)

Marty Warner defiled his wife before they were married. When she stated this in front of Marty, Pastor Ron, you, and me, you will recall that he did not deny it. He continued to misuse and defile her during their marriage. Marty needs to be rebuked, not embraced by this fellowship. I Corinthians, chapter 5 teaches clearly how the church is to handle immoral people who pretend to be Christians. I am convinced that if we all knew the real Marty Warner, we would see that the entire list presented in verse 11 of that chapter applies to him. Verse 13 commands emphatically, "Remove the wicked man from among yourselves."

Do you doubt that these things are true? In light of what is at stake, isn't it imperative that the truth be learned? Kathy provided Brian King with a list of Christian people who knew the Warners well. I have personally met and talked at length with several of these people. They are truly godly Christians and have fruits in their lives which bear this out. I encourage you and others of the elders to talk to them. I can give you their names and phone numbers. Kathy's brother, Don, is a wonderful Christian man, and he would be greatly encouraged if someone from Bridgeport cared enough to talk with him about these matters.

Debbie Dresler, one of Kathy's friends and a sweet Christian lady, wrote the enclosed letter to the child custody experts working on the Warner case. The other document is Kathy's spiritual history, which she wrote. The collection of poems and writings are things that Kathy handed out to people through her business as a testimony and a way of blessing others. I include them so that you may know a little of the Kathy Warner that I know.

I'm sorry for writing such a long letter. I am sharing it only with you and Kathleen, but I hope that you may share it with Pastor Ron and the other Elders as the Lord leads.

I am so sad that we as a fellowship have not been able to minister to Kathy in love. She continues to suffer so much from the removal and alienation of her children from her. I pray that the time may yet come when we can show her Christian love and reestablish her confidence in the Church.

Thank you both for your ministry among us. Your compassion and discernment are an encouragement to me and to Kathy as well.

In His Love,

Ellen Callen
Monmouth, Oregon 97361

(Please note: The fellowship at Bridgeport Community Chapel have taken care of Marty Warner's, (my former husband) every need during the restraining order period and in the months and years that followed and have wholeheartedly supported him. The elders at Bridgeport Community Chapel expressed to me that it was immoral and sinful for me to divorce my husband.)

May 30, 1999

Dear Pastor Ron Sutter,

My name is Tashi Smith, and I am a teacher in the Springfield School District. I am writing to you on behalf of a close Christian friend, who used to attend your church, Ms. Kathryn Hall. I worked for Ms. Hall when she was known as Mrs. Marty Warner.

Ms. Hall is in need, and, although I understand you probably are not enthusiastic about getting involved in an ugly situation, I am writing to you as a last resort for help. I ask that you read this letter carefully with an open mind, and just pray God will reveal the truth. Thank you for listening; this is information that you need to know.

I became involved in the Warner/Hall case a few years ago when I was still studying to be a teacher at Western, and was hired to help tutor the Warner children. I need to share with you that, while working within the home, I immediately noticed how demeaning and controlling Mr. Warner was toward his wife. However, he assured me he was doing everything "for Kathy's own good," so I tried to ignore the matter. But as time passed, I was witness to Mr. Warner's extreme mood swings, angry outbursts, and unrealistic expectations towards his wife. It is not my intent to criticize Marty Warner, but I will tell you the bare essentials so you can get a glimpse of the reality in which Ms. Hall and her children had to live.

At the time I was hired, Kathy had been working for twenty years as a full-time mother of eight kids, ranging from teenagers to a newborn, as well as a full-time cook, housekeeper, and home-school teacher. Any one of these jobs would have been a heavy load for one person alone to handle, yet Kathy was an amazing mother and teacher who always showed compassion and love to her family. While working with Mrs. Warner over the next few months, I found her to be a positive, Godly woman of utmost integrity. I have never met anyone so wise, loving, gentle, hardworking, and giving. As is obvious, I gained a deep respect and admiration for Kathy Warner, and came to think of her as a dear friend as well as a mentor and "mother" in the Lord. I now have known her for almost four years, and I have absolutely nothing negative to say about her sterling character. She is a beautiful, fragile treasure.

How tragic that such a sweet soul would be oppressed by an enraged husband who only treated her with contempt. If the house, the children, or the meals were not perfect, Marry would become violently angry with Kathy. I became extremely uncomfortable working within the home as I witnessed the level of fear both Kathy and the children lived with every day. Although the family scrambled to please Marty, their efforts were never good enough. He was unable to be satisfied, and continued to bark out his commands to his own family. I had to painfully watch Kathy literally beg him for a few dollars she needed for the kids. I saw the children ignored by Mr. Warner until they accidentally did something "wrong" that he did not like. He would violently spank them for the smallest of offenses. I was shocked that someone who seemed so respectable could be so blatantly wicked in his private life.

As you may be aware, Kathy finally gathered the courage to take her children and flee her husband. She was considered a kidnapper, and was taken to court. When I was asked to testify to Mr. Warner's controlling and demeaning treatment towards Ms. Hall in court, I learned that Marty had been violently abusing Kathy physically, emotionally, and sexually for the last twenty years. She had been continually raped and beaten, often to the point of being hospitalized, by her "Christian" husband. She was kept a prisoner in her own house, being allowed to see others only under Marty's supervision and approval.

Friends of the family only hope he did not take his sexual aggressions out on his daughters in the same way. Not believing in divorce, Kathy stayed as long as she could, always trying to please Marty, in hopes that he would change. You may choose to believe that such a pillar of the community as Mr. Warner could not possibly be capable of such behavior, but I am a first-hand witness that he is a smooth talker with much to hide in his private life. Being Mr. Warner's pastor, it is crucial you are aware of who it is you're really dealing with.

Because Kathy had been living under such extreme emotional pressure in her marriage, she had suffered from a nervous breakdown a few years before leaving Marty.

(It was during this time that, despite Kathy's catatonic state, Marty raped her and she became pregnant with her eighth child). It was this nervous breakdown that Marty used against Kathy in court. Marty had always controlled all finances and, having a high-paying job, simply hired a high-power attorney who claimed anyone having had a breakdown must be unfit to care for children. Having been isolated from interaction with the real world for the last twenty years, I think Kathy was made to appear naive, confused, and weak. Can you imagine watching your cherished, innocent, competent friend losing her children to an abusive rage-aholic? I could go into many more gory details, but my purpose is to warn you about Mr. Warner attending your congregation, and to spur you to help.

For the last two years, Kathy has tried to move on with her life, but is continually harassed by her former husband, as he swings wildly from vicious threats to love poems in an effort to get her back under his control. Marty knows the children are Kathy's life, and she has to hear them cry as they ask why "daddy said she didn't love them anymore."

Nice guy, huh? Yet Kathy is a better Christian than I, never uttering an unkind word about her former husband, even when we are alone. Kathy somehow manages to hold firm to her faith despite any circumstances, but despite her Job-like faithfulness, Marty has been continually slapping lawsuit after lawsuit against her in a sick attempt to break her once again. She is so terrified of his obsessive behavior that she recently did what no mother should ever feel she has to do to survive. To escape his constant harassment and persecution once and for all, she was legally advised to cut off all her court-given visitation rights to her children. She now feels completely devastated, empty, and depressed, yet what else could she do to rid herself of him? Fighting him costs money she doesn't have. Kathy even moved out of state to get away from him, yet had to return for all his ridiculous lawsuits.

Here is Marty's latest: Oregon took him to court to lower Kathy's support payments, so he decided to sue her for extra financial support for three children, all over eighteen, and all living on their own, plus $500.00 extra per month for the other kids. Mr. Warner is a long-time wealthy engineer, and Ms. Hall is considered to be unskilled and uneducated within the modern work force. (What kind of job can you get after being locked away from the world in your own house for the last twenty years? "Housewife" doesn't tend to impress many employers.)

Because of Marty's relentless harassment through the court, she now has over $150,000 in attorney fees, and recently has been too emotionally broken and traumatized by this man to even hold a full-time job. She simply doesn't have the money. As a teacher, I am the first person to want what's best for children, but this is ridiculous. Kathy doesn't even have the funds to fight back, yet if she loses, she could realistically face imprisonment. Anyway, we all know the money is not what Marty is really after.

I don't like getting involved in other people's business, but I feel angry that Mr. Warner has been allowed to continue his sick, oppressive, controlling, and appalling behavior towards Kathy Hall, and I want it to stop. I fail to understand why he is not in prison and shunned by his community. Even the court's psychological exam on Mr. Warner states in black and white that he is clearly deceptive and dangerous. Yet most can't seem to see past his slick, smooth talk and "Christianese."

Because Mr. Warner has been unresponsive to the numerous attempts from friends and family to convince him to leave Ms. Hall alone, I am desperately hoping that, as his spiritual head, he might possibly listen to you. I am assuming you feel a responsibility as his pastor, and I am asking you to prayerfully consider approaching him on this matter. I pray God will lead you to speak to him immediately about his compulsive behavior and recommend serious psychiatric help. I believe God is calling this matter into the light, and you are seemingly the only person to whom Marty might listen.

I realize you have no reason to accept me as a person of integrity, so I ask you to simply ask God to reveal the truth as you read this letter and continue to observe Mr. Warner. I am not trying to play on your emotions, but be careful; Marty fits every description of sociopathic behavior, meaning he is extremely good at his disguise and can disarm your questions and concerns with ease. I am not asking much. Please just try to get him to leave this poor woman alone. He has everything, but won't quit until she "pays" for escaping him. Help her. I love her, and I can't see her slowly, painfully dying like this any more. Please take courage and pray for them both. My cherished friend's life literally depends on it.

I am extremely concerned that Mr. Warner will harass me as he has done to other court witnesses, so I need you to guard this letter and my identity from Marty. I will be available at the number below through June 12, 1999, if you wish to speak to me, but you must never allow anyone else to see it. Thank you for your time, and for your attentiveness to this serious matter.

Sincerely,

Tashi (Smith) Gremar

"Shunning" in the Charismatic Community

My wife and our children were active and devoted members of the "People of Praise" Catholic charismatic community in Corvallis, Oregon, from the time it became a branch of the "People of Praise" ecumenical covenant Christian community in South Bend, Indiana, until we dropped out on May 10, 1983.

From the day that I made that decision, to the present time, I have never been contacted by any member of that community in any way! No one; not the leaders, the Catholic priest who was the head of the group in Corvallis at that time, or any of the people in that group, ever made any attempt to contact me to find out why I had elected to leave! When I dropped out, I told my "head" that I would not come to any more meetings, or be a part of the "People of Praise" and that being a member was bringing more discord into our family life, than harmony.

It seems rather strange that while living in Corvallis all this time (a community of approximately 40,000), that in the last 18 years in general, and the first few months following my leaving the community in particular, that I have never been approached by any of these people in any way - in stores, at work or in our home, to find why I had made that decision!

What is even more mystifying to me is how this so-called Christian community, supposedly following the way of Christ, would purposely not seek out the member who had strayed and find out why he had left them! Even the bible tells the story of Christ leaving the flock to seek out the stray sheep!

For some time before I made the decision to leave the group I had begun to question, in my own mind, some of the requirements of the community such as; headship and submission (husband and wife), tithing 10% (gross income) to the community, and their dictating how we raised our children.

Initially I (as I'm certain many males would be), was comfortable with the idea of having a "defined" submissive wife. We both had made the decision to join the community knowing that there would be "headship" throughout the hierarchy of the community. (i.e.) Every husband was "head" of his wife and family, every husband was under the "headship of some other (community appointed) "head". These men, were in turn under some form of male "headship" all the way up the (somehow appointed) chain of command to the Priest, who then was in submission to the leadership of the People of Praise community in South Bend, Indiana.

Giving the tithe of 10% of our gross income was quite a monetary strain on our budget (we had seven children, four of which were teenagers at that time) but since it was for "God's work" was accepted that. However, after a while, it became questionable to me if God really needed that money more than we did in our single-income family! A good portion of the tithe ultimately went to the leaders in South Bend whose children all were supposedly going to the university!

My wife and I also had to account for the scheduling of our time, day and night seven days a week, which was dominated by the community activities and their scrutiny. Our children became very much aware of how our family life, which previously was acceptably challenging yet harmonious, had become more fractionalized after joining the community.

I finally realized that the "commitment" of time and money that these cults put on their members deceivingly gives them control and power over the misguided members- so, we left. Now in our family, we look back on and sometimes discuss those days in community and are thankful that we are all in agreement on the decision that was made. "Friends" like that are not worth the price, and shunning is not God's way.

Robert L. Walsh
Corvallis, Oregon

February 3, 2002

Dear Coral,

Thank you for your recent mailing regarding *Bonshea*. I received your prior letters and meant to contact you sooner but, to be honest; I think I wasn't sure what to say.

Your case definitely "stayed" with me and I recall vividly a lot of what occurred during my brief time trying to help you. I still remember taking Marty Warner's deposition and I recall thinking what a cruel person he seemed to be. I remember the boxes of evidence you brought to my office and the story of you being dropped off in an unknown part of northeast Portland by Marty for "counseling." I remember the hearing with Judge Norblad.

I plan to order your book. I think it is a story which needs to be told. Ideally, the law is supposed to be rational, principled and just. Unfortunately, cases are decided by judges and jurors who are human beings and bring with them their own, biases, life experiences (both good and bad) and human shortcomings. To me this is the only explanation for what Judge Norblad did. I no longer practice family law, but for many years I did, and your case stood out as one where the judge's decision was most clearly wrong. I can't recall another case of a court removing a nursing child from a mother, except in cases where the mother posed a clear threat to the child's safety, such as drug addiction, etc.

I try to avoid seeing things only from my client's perspective, and to instead be objective about the facts of a case. To me, your case was clear through: Marty was an abusive, controlling, inflexible and dogmatic father and husband...who spent his free time at home indulging his religious fanaticism and addressing issues affecting other home-schooling parents, rather than interacting with his own children. You on the other hand, were a devoted mother who clearly did 95% of the hands-on care for the children. You had some post-partum emotional issues after your last child, which Marty exploited to his advantage instead of trying to help you when you needed help. I hope that by writing this I do not upset you or bring up issues you would rather have left alone.

I hope that you have found peace and happiness in your life and have made light of the dark, as your subtitle suggests. You are a good person.

–Jon Benson
Portland, Oregon
Attorney

(Mr. Jonathan Benson was my attorney in February - March 1996 while working for Mr. David Gearing's office in Portland, Oregon.)

Letters to my Son-in-law, Jesse White

Coral Theill's son-in-law, Jesse White, does not believe Mr. Marty Warner abused his former wife, Coral Theill, or the Warner children.

Jesse White wrote on July 17, 2007, *"As for Mr. Warner, I do not believe I have met a man that has influenced more people in a positive manner."*

Mr. White has never spoken to me, contacted me, or met me. He showed up in the family picture a decade after the abuse in the family occurred. I was not invited to their wedding in 2001. In July 2007 he posted a few comments at Salem-News.com informing the editor that the abuse that I detailed in my book, *BONSHEA*, was made up.

Letter to Tim King/Editor/Salem-News.com

Written by Jesse White, Seeking for Justice July 16

Coral Anika Theill's son-in-law July 21, 2007, posted two comments on Tim King's May 7, 2007 article, *"Abuse Under the Watch of Oregon's Justice System"*

Mr. King, thank you for taking the time to expose some of the terrible injustices to women in the United States. To hear the horror stories of the abuse that many women can attest too makes me sick to my stomach. Regarding Coral's story, and others that you may soon write about, I would please ask you to fulfill your journalistic duties and interview those who were involved in both sides of the story.

When stories like these are told it is easy to jump on the bandwagon and see only the author's perspective. If I didn't know this story first hand, I would be right there with you. But the fact is, I have known the family first hand for over 12 years. Granted, I was not a part of this family's life during most of the period that was written about in Coral's book. But I would like you all to know that I have never met a more beautiful and caring family in my life. Each one of Coral's children is living a life that others only dream of. Each one is gifted with amazing talents, strong will, and a love for life. To grow up in a home full of abuse by their father and to turn out so well perplexes me. Although I am not a psychologist, I do not believe that you could have eight children raised in a home where such abuses occur and have all eight turn out to be so full of life as Coral's children.

As for Mr. Warner, I do not believe I have met a man that has influenced more people in a positive manner – beginning with his eight children that he has raised as a single parent and all those that his life is intertwined with daily. In twelve years of being around him and the children daily I have never seen him raise his hand or his voice in an abusive or even semi-derogatory manner, I do not believe that he could just flip an internal switch in his heart that all of a sudden makes him into such a great man. I would like those of you who have read this book and articles written about this book, **to know that much of this story is completely untrue and please do not believe everything you hear. For this injustice that you all are speaking out against is the same injustice you are causing by not taking the time to know the complete story.** If a book were written about you and your family that spread rumors and lies, would you not be upset? Coral's children live this life every day. Knowing that a book is being read and even used as a textbook in a local college is demeaning to their family and completely untrue.

The enormous pain that has been caused by those of you who think you know the truth by reading a one-sided story is a serious injustice. The hurt and pain that my wife has to live with, brought on by her mother, and now recurring with comments posted by those who do not seek the entire truth saddens me to no end. – *Jesse White,* Oregon (Coral Theill's son-in-law)

Second Letter written by Jesse White, July 2007

Hello again. Thank you all for your responses to my comments. It is very interesting to hear how each one of you feels about this issue. To my mother-in-law, I would like to say I am sorry for making the statement that that your book is completely untrue, I was wrong to make this statement. I would like you to know that your daughter has told me many good things about you and she still does call you mother. She has told me about many of your achievements as a young woman, and is proud that her mother could achieve so much.

I realize where her beauty, strong will, and confidence came from. There is no doubt in my mind that you had a very positive influence in your daughter's life for many years. I am sorry if my comments appeared that I thought otherwise, that was not my intention. In my comments dated July 17, 2007, I am sorry if I didn't make it clear whom I was "seeking justice" for. I would like you all to realize it is not for Mr. Warner (he doesn't know I have submitted these comments); it was not on Bridgeport Community Church's behalf (I do not attend and never was a member), and definitely not the judicial system (I am not a big fan).

The pain I was referring to being caused by the book and articles like these was the children's. It is sad that their names, dates of births, and where they have lived have to be brought into this. Classmates, parents of classmates, and even those who have never met them single them out with rude comments about their family life. I believe this is a direct result of having their true names and personal information written in this book. I do not believe they deserve this. I believe divorce should be between the parents and the children not brought into it. This book may have an adverse effect on the children and how they will be treated by those that read it. I believe this could have been avoided by leaving their true identity out. – *Jesse White,* Oregon

Letter from Debbie Custis in regards to Jesse White's Comments – July 16, 2007

I'm writing this in response to Kathy's (Coral Theill's) son-in-law's statement. I'm sure if there are many people out there who "actually" know of this situation and would still like to dispute Coral's life story, Mr. Tim King would interview them. **Frankly, I don't know where you would find such a person.**

Her son-in-law wasn't in the Warner's life nor was he in court for the proceedings during the time Kathy (Coral) was being abused by Marty and the court system in Oregon. I was. I also worked with and for Mr. Warner. Trust me, he can "just flip on an internal switch" when he feels it's necessary to appear to be a well-adjusted, upstanding member of the community. Feel fortunate that you're not a "woman" and that Mr. Warner feels no need to "control" you!

I'm not the only woman in the workplace that has had the misfortune of working for Mr. Warner. I'm just the one in Coral's book. I was told that "women don't belong in the workplace, they need to be at home taking care of their families and when they don't, unfortunate events are the result, that when men and women work together one thing leads to another, and there are problems." I was a recently and happily married woman when that comment was made. Where did it come from?

I was asked on frequent occasions to get Mr. Warner coffee, I was an Ultra-Pure Water Technician, not an Administrative Assistant, and I never once heard him ask one of the guys under his supervision to bring him coffee. I was also forced to listen to Mr. Warner talk about his wife and her problems when he would schedule one of our "private one-on-one meetings" at work. Once again, none of the guys under his supervision were required to have one-on-one meetings with Mr. Warner while he spoke of the personal aspects of his wife's life and his problems with her.

Everything here is public record and I could go on and on. I prefer not to, I'd like to forget, but as long as doubt is cast on the validity of what Coral went through, I'll continue to speak out!! As I stated before, I was worried about Coral just from listening to Mr. Warner talk about her and their personal problems long before I ever met her. In addition, I went through my own personal hell just working under him and at a later date with him. I was finally insulated from him by my new supervisor and the Department Manager because I'd applied for another position within the company to get away from Mr. Warner. At the time they couldn't find a replacement for my position.

Unfortunately, several months ago, I was contacted by yet another woman who has experienced according to her, abuse and emotional trauma at the hands of Mr. Warner (in the work place). Once again, another life emotionally and negatively impacted by Mr. Warner. Why does this keep happening if there's no validity here, sir.

You didn't see Kathy (Coral) with her three youngest children, her patience, the love and the bond that was so clearly there for all to see while she was in hiding from her husband, living from hotel to hotel, with no money, and no food, entirely dependent on friends and yes, even some strangers that wanted to help her. It's easy to be kind, loving, and nurturing during the good times; Coral was all those things during the hard times as well.

You weren't there during the court proceedings. You didn't listen to the absolute absence of feeling for his wife and her trauma in his answer when the judge asked "why would you continue to have marital relations with your wife in her current physical and mental condition." I was there. I was also outside the courtroom walking the baby when I couldn't stand to hear any more of what he said in court.

You weren't there when I talked to one of the twins. One of which could be the wife you speak of now. She deeply loved her mother and father on that day. What happened to change that? Could it be that brainwashing changed that!

You weren't there when the court decided to take Coral's children away. You didn't see a woman sobbing, rocking back and forth consumed with the kind of grief that only another parent could understand and yet, not wholly fathom.

You weren't there when we picked up the three youngest children and delivered them to Mr. Warner. You didn't hear the screams and sobbing of the two little girls in the back seat of my car on the trip to Mr. Warner's. You never had to watch a grief-stricken mother trying to pump painfully engorged breasts because her six-month-old nursing baby had just been wrenched from her.

Tell me something, what had Coral ever done to deserve this? Coral Theill (Kathy Warner) was a warm and loving mother. She was also a good wife. To this day she loves her eight children deeply, even the ones who no longer call her mother.

Coral was the sole nurturer, caregiver, and teacher in that family for many, many years. At least half of those wonderful, talented, children you speak of received their foundation from their mom.

It saddens and sickens me that all of the wonderful things the children learned from their mother; all of the warm and happy memories that should be Coral's legacy to these children have been tossed away like yesterday's garbage.

That, sir, is the real tragedy. – *Debbie Custis,* Oregon

July 2007

Dear Jesse White,

I want to add my voice to those who have addressed Coral's son-in-law. I helped Coral when she was writing BONSHEA and I know that she struggled with what to tell and what to hold back in telling her story. I pressed her to tell as complete a story as possible. She made every effort to protect her children in her writings, but she was past the point where half-truths would do. What your wife does not understand is that the motivation for the whole ordeal – including escaping from her marriage and standing up to her husband - was an effort to PROTECT her children from harm. And the main reason for writing a book was so that someday her children might know the truth.

I suspect that it is hard to accept that there is a darker reality to people who can appear quite virtuous. I urge you to pay attention to the voice in your head that is beginning to warn you things are not as they seem, and watch for the chinks in the facade of this family. Protect your own children from the people who could wield a strap against their sons and daughters, abuse their spouse, and mis-use the name of God to justify their behavior. – *Judy Bennett,* Editor, Oregon

To Jesse White:

I can't help but notice in your first comment; the general message seemed to be: "there is no problem in this family, and Coral is making this up. She is hurting a good citizen, Marty Warner with false accusations". Then after a bit of criticism, the message changed: "yes there actually is a problem, but it should just be kept between adults, and I'm only concerned now because publicity is hurting the children.

This strikes me as rhetoric on both counts. In the first comment, it appears that the situation's basic existence (that Coral was physically, sexually, and emotionally abused within her marriage, criminally assaulted, and legally forced to relinquish custody of her children) was dismissed in totality; but at the same time, illogically, it was implied that if the situation did exist, all blame for it was placed smoothly on the shoulders of Coral herself.

Then, when called on this, in the second message there is a bit of backpedaling and an admission that yes there were problems within the marriage and a redirection to concern over 'the children'. But in no place anywhere did I notice the actual issues be addressed.

Was this woman raped and assaulted, or was she not? Did she relinquish contact with her own children voluntarily, or did she not?

There is not one person I have ever spoken to who questions her devotion to her children. On what logic do you base your belief that she would choose to leave them and have no contact with them year after year? I see the pain it causes, as their birthdays pass, and Mother's Day passes, and she is without them, and they are again without her. I have seen the letters from her children, where they are desperately trying to reach out to her, but are so afraid. It's clear even now they still want her in their life.

On what possible logic do you support this painful separation of woman and child?

Criminals in jail are allowed more visitation time and parental rights than Coral is. I would like to know your perspective on these questions. And I would also like to know, if you all respect her so much as a woman and mother, why then is she not allowed to even send letters to her own children, which might give her the chance to explain herself to them and repair their relationship?

If what she has to say is not the truth, why are you so very afraid of it? If it is the truth, and you really care about her and abuse victims as you say you do, why are your actions not reflecting that? What you are doing to her does not withstand logical question.

One last thought: Don't you think that if she, like some mothers do, simply did abandon her family to live a life of wanton pleasure, she would be off doing that right now, having forgotten all about her children, rather than trying to fix this problem with every ounce of her strength? I am very interested to hear the answers your family chooses to provide for these questions.

If you truly respect women and mothers, I have faith you will explore the answers to these questions with us, and help us learn. – *Oregon Resident*, (Name withheld), Domestic Violence Advocate, July 2007

Letter from Bruce McLelland in regards to Jesse White's comments July 19, 2007:

I am saddened because Ms. Theill's son-in-law besmirches my character and that of others who have taken the time to read *BONSHEA* and posted comments to this space for not seeking the truth. This is a most interesting universal condemnation of the integrity of people he has never met. If Diogenes had encountered Ms. Theill's son-in-law while wandering through the Agora with his torch, would he have ceased his quest for an honest man?

"To paraphrase a cliché: 'Judge a man by the way he treats the waiter, not by the way he treats the chef.' Do the experiences of his former employee, (Debbie Custis) provide the clearest insights into the soul of Mr. Warner? Debbie has nothing to gain by her comments but does leave herself open to criticism. Can Ms. Theill's son-in-law say he has nothing to gain by singing the praises of his father-in-law? Perhaps his bias precludes an appreciation of truth? Perhaps Ms. Theill's son-in-law would be best served by asking questions in search of truth, and not blaspheming the understandings of others? Only through questioning can we truly embrace our faith." - *Bruce McLelland*, Washington D.C.

Response to my son-in-law's, 2007 comments by Coral Anika Theill

Dear Mr. Jesse White,

My intentions in writing *BONSHEA Making Light of the Dark* and sharing my personal story was an effort to reclaim dignity, equality and honor, not only for myself, but for everyone. Crimes were committed against my children and me not only by my abuser, but in a courtroom of law.

When I first conceived my twin daughter, (your wife), thirty-five years ago, I began praying for you, my daughter's husband. I prayed for your parents, too. I have not had the opportunity to meet you or your parents – your choice.

I prayed you would be a gentle man and compassionate man, a man of courage, integrity, wisdom and understanding. I prayed that you would be good to my daughter, Rachel, protect her, and be generous toward her and that you would have "blessed lives" together.

The comment you posted yesterday reminded me of an introduction in one of my favorite books, "*Night*" by holocaust survivor, Elie Wiesel. "When human beings tell victims, who have suffered excruciating pain and loss that their pain and loss were illusions, they are committing the greatest indignity humans can inflict on another. They are treating the victim as if they are a product of some diseased mind. There is perhaps a greater baseness, those who believe that the victim is a product of a diseased mind and that their pain and suffering are illusions."

This is how you are treating me. You have lost compassion somewhere along your spiritual journey.

I will not allow you to place the crimes that were committed in our home by my ex-husband, Mr. Warner, on MY SHOULDERS. You were not there those twenty years before you met my daughter, but neighbors, physicians, co-workers, counselors, hundreds of friends in churches of all denominations were. Many of them would like a word with you, but until you are ready, it would be a waste of time.

When your wedding announcements were sent out several years ago, I, the woman who gave birth to your wife, and raised her, was not invited and I was not welcome, but my mother and grandmother received invitations, two people who abused me and committed crimes against me for the duration of my childhood. My ex-husband was invited to your wedding; a man who has abused my children and women co-workers, committed crimes against me, and legally stalked and harassed me these past seventeen years through the Polk County judicial system, in Dallas, Oregon. (Please see court records at the Polk County Courthouse Clerk's Office, Dallas, Oregon)

It grieves me that you are professing to support women in abusive situations, except for your mother-in-law - me.

I have a name; I have a face. I invite you to enter my personal holocaust because someday you will need to face the truth. Truth is not something you are seeking at this time, as your posted comment dismisses "me" as a fellow human being. Your writing this comment and accusing me of being a liar without ever having met me, talked to me or written me personally are signs of a COWARD.

Abuse Deserves No Privacy

Some people may be pained by having their names appear in print, but I would like to ask you this question, "If one tries to hide truth behind a veil of anonymity, can it really be truth?" I acknowledge that some people may have been hurt by my sharing my true-life story, but I continue to be supported by many individuals in the book for my efforts to help raise the consciousness in our society about crimes and abuse of this nature.

The divorce documents are public domain. There are literally boxes full of court records that document the testimony, under oath, of doctors, witnesses and other professionals that these incidents occurred.

Many details about my children and their birthdates are in the court files. I have sought help from police, sheriffs and advocates due to the crimes committed in our home. My children's names and information and details of the crimes are also included in their files. My children have face book pages; they detail their own names, where they live, birthdates, and year of birth on their own public pages for the world to see.

I wish that divorce was only between adults, but the reality is divorce transcends the couple who took wedding vows, touching, and too frequently, hurting all those within the couple's family and community circle.

I understand why you have chosen the "perpetrator's side," my ex-husband, Mr. Marty Warner, because he asks you do to NOTHING. The fact that so many individuals, including you, have shunned me and sided with my abuser and perpetrator makes a huge statement to the arrogance, ignorance and spiritual poverty that is prevalent in society today. You could be a part of the solution of healing this horrific situation and tragedy.

Your judgmental comments are a blatant reminder to me of "why domestic violence is socially acceptable in America." You are NO FRIEND to domestic violence, rape and child abuse victims. I hope you will someday become more educated before you speak about a subject matter you appear to know nothing about. I believe the most violent element in society is ignorance.

The reason *BONSHEA* exists at all is because I was driven to document my life—for the sake of my children and adults they will grow to be.

I have always found 'TRUTH' not lies, to be a very healing force in my life.

This story is not finished.

Respectfully,

Your mother-in-law
Coral Anika Theill
Author, Advocate & Free Lance Reporter

The letter below, from my close friend and editor, Judy Bennett, was sent to all eight of my children in March 2018 before my final and 50th court hearing on April 11, 2018. My children choose to support their father, my abuser/rapist Marty Warner, in court.

March 6, 2018

Dear Sarah, Rachel, Aaron, Joshua, Theresa, Rebekah, Hannah and Zachary,

I am writing to you because your mother is my friend, Coral Theill - or as you may think of her, Kathryn Warner. As I am sure you know, she has recently gone to court to have a decades old child support order of $3,815.74 dismissed because she cannot afford to pay it. I am hoping that by giving you some of the facts of your mother's life in the past twenty years you will be able to influence your father to dismiss his claim for child support and free your mother from this burden. The hearing is scheduled for April 11, 2018, 1:15 pm, Dallas, Oregon, Polk County Courthouse.

When your parent's divorce was final in 1997, your mother received an existing IRA account which was in her name. She was ordered to pay your father child support in the amount of $500 a month. At that time, the house on Fruit Farm Road was debt free and appraised at $250,000 (originally purchased in 1992 for $105,000 — today it is appraised at almost $500,000). He also had a stock portfolio and other investments. Your father kept all of these assets.

After the divorce, your mother worked various minimum wage jobs for a while, but her health deteriorated and she could not keep working. She made and sold beeswax candles and ornaments at farmer's markets to make money and she drew money from the IRA account to pay living expenses. She did not live extravagantly. She had been out of the workforce for almost 20 years taking care of all of you and your father. He did not believe women should work outside the home. But she made regular child support payments until 2003.

In 1999, your father sued for increased child support. Because your mother did not receive notice of the hearing date she did not show in court and the judge granted your father another $1,074.00 per month in child support, which was twice her income. The court also forbade her any contact with all of her children — at your father's request. Another hearing, in 2003, ended child support payments, but did not wipe out the unpaid child support judgment from 1999 and interest up to that point.

Even though it was established in the 2003 proceedings that your mother was destitute, your father hired an attorney and tried to sue her in 2004, requesting the Oregon State Appeals Court to grant him another $50,000 in child support. The Oregon State of Appeals court denied his appeal in 2005. A year later, he tried again, unsuccessfully, to sue for more money. Through all these legal proceedings, with the exception of the original divorce trial, your mother could not afford an attorney. She prepared her own legal briefs — a huge time and emotional strain. And even though the appeals case and the last suit were unsuccessful for your father, they required a great deal of study and effort for your mother to respond.

Your mother filed for SSI Disability in 2002 at a time when she was living out of her car. SSI was finally awarded in 2005. The monies from the IRA had long been exhausted for living expenses, paying attorney fees and court fees, taxes, helping Aaron with college, penalties for early withdrawal, etc. For the past 13 years she has lived on $550.00 to $780.00 a month plus a subsidy for housing and a small amount in food assistance.

Your mother has been informed that the State of Oregon and Polk County District Attorney child support enforcement intend to take $150-$200 per month out of the $899.00 your mother lives on now. This would not leave enough for basic food and medical expenses. Your mother does not own any property, has no savings or credit cards and no family support. This is the reason she is attempting to have this debt dismissed.

Your father has stated that he would never dismiss this judgment. This I cannot understand. It is obvious that your mother does not have the financial means to pay several thousand dollars and that taking the money out monthly would create extreme hardship. Forgiveness, generosity and compassion are pillars of the Christianity I know, and your father prides himself on being a good Christian. But he shows no compassion or forgiveness for your mother. It seems he has never stopped wanting to punish her.

I do not believe he truly needs this money. Without a doubt it was expensive to raise eight children, but you are all grown now. I hope life has been good for you. I do not know what you have been taught about your mother, but I know her to be a very loving and compassionate person who was absolutely devastated by losing each of you. She had to leave your father in order to survive. She left you because your father exploited the court system which forced her to give you up. She has never stopped loving you. There is a great deal that you do not know about the situation.

Please, as an act of kindness to the woman who gave birth to you - and, in spite of things you have been told, the mother who has never ceased to love you and ache for you, encourage your father to let this go. If you have questions I can answer, you are free to call me at: (503) _____.

Your mother is a creative and intelligent woman with great strength and grace. Her life has been difficult - and one of the greatest difficulties is not having you in her life.

Sincere regards,

Judy Bennett
Monmouth, Oregon

Affidavit by Debbie Custis, filed in Polk County Court 2003

Affidavit by Debbie J. Custis - 2003

Debbie Custis was abused by Mr. Marty Warner,
my ex-husband at Hewlett Packard, Corvallis, Oregon

IN THE CIRCUIT COURT OF THE STATE OF OREGON FOR THE COUNTY OF POLK Kathryn Y. Warner, Case No. 95P-20639

I, Debbie J. Custis, being first duly sworn, depose and say that:

1. The eighteen months that I worked with and for Mr. Marty Warner were the most distressing years mentally and emotionally I've ever experienced in the workplace or plan to ever experience again.

2. I was not personally acquainted with Kathy Warner (aka, Coral Theill) until the latter part of 1995 or the beginning of 1996, although I thought about her and wondered what kind of life she had, because, I felt in my heart if Marty could say and do the things he did to me in the workplace and get away with it, life for Kathy Warner had to be terrible. As time went on, Mr. Warner would single me out to talk about Mrs. Warner and it was not a comfortable situation. Marty made it well known to at the very least, his staff, that (in his words) his wife was having severe mental and emotional problems. I was told Kathy had suffered a miscarriage, needed to have a D &C she felt responsible for the miscarriage because of her severe emotional distress. A very short time later, our group and others were shocked when Marty told us Kathy was expecting another child.

3. Over the course of a few months, Marty told me he felt Kathy wasn't being obedient to God and needed to pray more. She also needed to listen to the members of the church who were trying to minister to her. He told our group when he felt forced to put his wife in a hospital somewhere and she'd run away. I felt sick inside every time he tried to talk to me because of the instances I've described below. By this time, I was suffering emotionally and mentally from just working with him daily and it made me so sad to think of her anguish.

4. I was employed at Hewlett Packard from September 1991 to June 2003. I spent my first nineteen months with them working as a Flex-Force (temporary) employee as an Ultra-Pure Water/Waste-Treatment technician. Marty Warner became our supervisor during the last couple of months I was Flex-Force employee.

5. In April 1993, two full-time Ultra-Pure Water jobs became available. I was offered one position and the other went to someone outside the Hewlett Packard employee pool. The gentleman who was hired had no prior Ultra-Pure Water experience. A couple of days before our new employee arrived, Mr. Warner came to me and I was told, I would be training the new employee. He also informed that he was starting us at the same rate of pay. At that time, I told Mr. Warner I felt that was unfair as I had an Associate degree in the Water/Wastewater field, was State Certified and that I had already worked in the same capacity as the existing HP Technicians at a much lower rate of pay for the past nineteen months. Mr. Warner replied: "Unfortunately, some people feel they have more value to HP than they actually do". That day was the real beginning of eighteen months working for and with a man who undermined my decisions and harassed me based on his gender bias.

6. I didn't start documenting issues and conversations with Mr. Warner until September1993. Several co-workers and my husband had advised me to document what was happening but at that time I was still hoping Mr. Warner would accept me based on my job performance and not my gender. Unfortunately, that never happened.

7. In September, Mr. Warner and I met to discuss the pay level change for DI water technicians. Mr. Warner wanted to meet outside at one of the picnic tables. Marty asked me if I had any questions or issues and I said, "Yes," I'd like to know why he addressed the majority of questions and comments in Staff and Project meetings to Rich and Tom (we as a group, had noticed this for quite some time). I also asked Mr. Warner if he was having a problem with me as a female employee. Mr. Warner's response was: If you and Leonard (he didn't know my husband personally) were to come to me and tell me you had decided to stay home and take care of your family, I'd be overjoyed. I asked Mr. Warner if he had problems with my work and he replied "No, I was doing a good job, we all were."

8. Marty began talking about some of the problems he was having at home. I mentioned having some problems with my son, and Mr. Warner replied: "If we don't do what the Lord wants us to do, we bear bad fruit and that your children need you in the home." When I stated that I didn't feel I was being punished because I'd had to work as a single parent part of

my children's life and that we were not all fortunate enough to be able to stay home during a child's childhood. Mr. Warner went on to say: "He felt men and women, working closely together weren't always a good thing as it could lead to problems if things weren't going well at home. He said, "You might start taking someone a cup of coffee and then he brings you one" (I'm not sure where he was going with this comment, and as it turned out, Marty Warner was the only man who would ask me to bring him coffee over the next year. I felt this was inappropriate and demeaning) I told Mr. Warner my relationship with my peers and the other guys at HP was a brother/sister friendship, my husband and I had only been married two years and we were very happy.

9. 9/24/03 - I responded to a call for an acid overflow and had to advise some of our fabs to halt the dumping of acid immediately. I also called Mr. Warner to advise him of the situation. Marty wasn't available and I left a voice mail message. Two hours later, Mr. Warner came down and kept asking me, "Do you understand the process Debbie? Do you understand Metering pumps Debbie? Do you understand valves Debbie? I kept telling him yes, I understood, we'd done this several times before. A few minutes later he said, I shouldn't have shut down production, it wasn't necessary. Rich Millimaki, our senior technician, had handled this same problem the week before in exactly the same manner and Mr. Warner hadn't questioned his decision in any way.

10. There are many instances documented of Mr. Warner undermining my decisions and excluding me in conversations that directly related to systems I was in charge of and of Mr. Warner asking my two male peers for opinions and information on systems or assignments that were mine and they knew nothing about. These items may still be documented with the Polk County Court from Mrs. Warner's 1996 hearing. If not, I still have the original documentation.

11. At a staff meeting, Mr. Warner told our Senior Technician to start documenting daily routines and all the work we did and the time that was spent doing it. Rich asked if we were going to hire a fourth person Mr. Warner replied: "You never know, Debbie may quit.

12. At another staff meeting, drug testing for new employees was one of our agenda topics. Tom Sibert asked what they tested for, Marty said; "I don't know, and when I told Tom they test for cocaine, etc. Mr. Warner replied. "Yes, Debbie knows all about it."

13. January 1994. Mr. Warner asked me to meet him in the cafeteria to go over my position plan for the coming year. At that meeting Marty told me he realized he was giving me a year and a half's worth of work to

be completed in a year but to do the best I could (Failure to meet the objectives in a position plan directly affect your ranking and pay on your evaluations). Mr. Warner said, He realized I was overwhelmed with projects and work, but when I commented I would need to work until 8:00 p.m. every night and on the weekends to get caught up as it was and that he wouldn't approve overtime, Mr. Warner told me if I wanted to excel at my job, I'd do whatever it took, I wasn't in Junior High or High School anymore where being a "B" student was acceptable. I was at College Level now and being a "B" student wasn't acceptable or enough to excel. Mr. Warner told me if I wanted to excel, I would do whatever it took to get there. I also asked Marty how he could justify my being away from my family for such extended periods of time when he told me that his being away from his family for so many years had caused numerous problems for himself, he just went back to the if you want to excel, you'll do whatever it takes.

14. I did work the overtime without pay and when someone (I believe, it was my previous supervisor) went to personnel regarding all of the problems I was having with Marty and they realized I'd been working the overtime as an hourly employee without being paid, they asked me to figure out what I was owed. Marty came to me and said, "I need to know how many hours it is you feel we owe you." He was angry and wanted to know what I'd discussed with personnel and why I had betrayed him. Even though I told Marty that personnel said, "I didn't have to meet privately with him again," he didn't stop cornering me when he got a chance. Following are a few additional comments Mr. Warner felt he needed to make.

   o That I should pray and ask the Lord where I would be happiest, back in a municipality (I was working in one when I came to HP) or at home.

   o That he didn't know if something was going on with me or I was just going through something that day (It was very clear he was insinuating I was having a PMS day).

   o That the feelings of self-doubt and inadequacy I'd began to feel at his treatment were all in my head.

   o I was being cold to him and he knew I could be warm because I'd shown him warmth.

15. Marty was eventually replaced as the Ultra-Pure Water Supervisor but he remained the System's Engineer for my south site Water systems and the harassment continued. The constant Turmoil and harassment at Mr. Warner's hand impacted every aspect of my personal and professional

life. I began to cry easily and frequently, couldn't sleep, began doubting my decisions and had feelings of inadequacy. In August of 1995, I made the decision to apply for a position in a different department to get away from Mr. Warner and the constant stress. My new supervisor gave me written permission to apply for the job. I applied, was interviewed and was told I had the position. Unfortunately, without my knowledge our Department Manager and my supervisor had informed the hiring manager for my new position they couldn't let me go for six months as there was no one to take my place. When I met with both the manager and my supervisor to discuss the decision they had made, I told them both I'd applied for that job because I needed to get away from Marty and the stress. From that point on, my supervisor kept me as insulated from Marty as he could.

16. I was contacted by Mrs. Warner in late 1995 or early 1996. Kathy knew of me because of Marty and what he'd told her about me, but she was also informed by a friend that worked for HP that the problems between her husband and I had escalated to Personnel involvement. She asked me if I would be willing to talk to her attorney and I said, "absolutely".

17. I received a subpoena from Mrs. Warner's attorney to testify on her behalf on February 9, 1996. Unfortunately, her attorney asked just one question that I can remember. He asked, If Mr. Warner was a very controlling person and I replied "Yes."

18. I was allowed in court after my brief time in the witness stand and was appalled and sickened by the past treatment of Mrs. Warner by Mr. Warner, by the questions that were allowed in court and by the treatment of a woman in such a fragile state of mine. There were times I couldn't stand hearing anymore and would go outside the courtroom and walk with baby Zachary.

19. The day Kathy was forced to turn her three youngest children over to Mr. Warner because she had lost custody; I was the one who took the two youngest girls (Rebecca and Hannah) to their father. They cried or screamed the entire trip. It was one of the most gut wrenching things I've ever seen. A longtime friend of Kathy's took six month old Zachary in her car. When we arrived at the Warner home, Marty wanted to know what he should feed Zachary as he was a nursing baby.

I've seen Kathy Warner go through pain and suffering at the hands of Marty Warner, and the court system that would drive most people insane. I've seen her lose everything in this world that could possibly matter to her except her hope that justice would eventually come to her aid. I've seen Mrs. Warner pick herself up time and time again in her attempt to right an extreme wrong. I've read the book she's written in an attempt to help other victims of domestic violence and hopefully explain to her children why she is no longer in their lives.

I've sat back and watched and listened as time after time she's been denied justice and human compassion from the very people who say they are advocates for domestic violence.

I don't know how to help Kathy anymore and fear that she can't hang on much longer. I'm submitting this affidavit in the hopes that the legal system will understand what happened to Mrs. Warner is real, is cruel and continues. I know it's real because I lived through eighteen months of emotional and mental turmoil, fear and doubt in my professional abilities at the hands of the same man that brought his wife to a state of emotional and mental breakdown.

Signed and notarized/copy available

Charles H. Kuttner, M.D.
213 Water Ave.,NW, Suite 300
Albany, OR 97321
(503)928-1678 Fax:(503)928-1679
Certified in Psychiatry 1978 by the American Board of Psychiatry and Neurology

COPY

3/9/94

Martin and Kathryn Warner
8700 Fruit Farm Road
Independence, OR 97351

Dear Mr. and Mrs. Warner:

It is with regret that I am writing to inform you that I cannot
continue to be Kathryn's doctor. I realize you have an
appointment set for March 16, and I am willing to see you at that
time and will continue to provide care until April 9, 1994, to
give you time to locate another physician.

My reason for withdrawing from your care is that I believe that
Kathryn's mental condition and life are being endangered by
repeated cancellations of appointments and non-cooperation with
agreements we make regarding treatment plan. I consider the
situation analogous to Martin being asked to take responsibility
for a major project which was not progressing well, but allowed
to only occasionally glance at a blueprint and give advice to
well-meaning but untrained personnel at a distant site.

When we last met in my office, 2/14/94, it was my understanding
that I would see Kathryn in two weeks, at which time we would re-
evaluate the medications. I do not know her current situation,
but I believe I made it clear that I was not comfortable with her
being on only BuSpar and Desyrel, but that I would compromise as
long as we could have close follow-through. This was far from an
isolated incident, and I choose to devote my time to working with
patients who are willing and able to work together with me for
the benefit of the patient. I have talked with Dr. Green, and
understand that he, too, is having a problem with regular
followup.

There are, of course, other psychiatrists avaiable to you, and I
would strongly suggest a return to Woodland Park Hospital unless
Kathyrn is actually doing better. I certainly hope she does
improve soon.

Please contact if you desire further clarification, and please
let me know your intentions on whether you wish to keep or cancel
the 3/16 appointment.

Sincerely,

Charles H. Kuttner, MD

cc:Drs. Gallant, Green

393

Charles H. Kuttner, M.D.
213 Water Ave., N.W., Suite 300
Albany, OR 97321
(541) 928-1678 Fax: (541) 928-1679
Certified in Psychiatry by the American Board of Psychiatry and Neurology

7/24/97

Commission on Judicial Fitness and Disability
P.O. Box 9035
Portland, OR 97207

Re: concern regarding Judge Albin Norblad

Dear People:

I have delayed on preparing this letter, due to the seriousness of the concerns I am raising. However, as I continue to consider the effects of this judge's decision, and his reputation, I realize it is imperative that I raise these issues with you.

I am writing with the permission of my patient. Kathryn (Hall) Warner. On 10/15/96, I testified in Judge Norblad's courtroom regarding child custody issues in the dissolution of this lady's marriage. As Judge Norblad himself phrased it, Mr. Warner is a "control freak" who has no interest in changing his behavior. He agreed that Mrs. Warner, on the other hand, had been seriously depressed, but was recovered from that, was making changes and becoming a stronger person. Judge Norblad discussed the decision he was considering, placing the older three children with their father and the younger five children, including an infant who was still nursing at his mother's breast, in the custody of the mother. I commented on my professional approval of that decision.

From all indications I have, no other significant information came out at trial to alter the impressions that the Court already had. Judge Norblad's decision was to abruptly place all the children in the care of the father. The distress this has caused the mother has been significant. I can only imagine the trauma for the younger children, particularly the infant son, who reportedly cried for days and had considerable difficulty adjusting to bottle feeding.

I could only presume that the Judge had some other information that led him to his decision. I attempted to call him to discuss this, but was essentially blocked in doing so by his assistant. I have spoken with other therapists and attorneys in this area, and understand that Judge Norblad has a reputation for making capricious and bizarre decisions, but that no attorney feels safe to question them.

I do not have enough knowledge of Judge Norblad to recognize a pattern. All I know is that I have seen him make one decision which I consider cruel to the children involved, without reasonable basis, and reversing what the judge had previously suggested was going to be his decision. As I hear from more and more professionals (none of whom are willing to be identified, unfortunately), I understand that this one decision is far from an isolated occurrence.

I would appreciate your evaluating this situation. I realize that this one decision will likely not be reversed, but I am not comfortable having the possibility of an impaired judge sitting in Oregon.

Sincerely,

Charles H. Kuttner, MD

395

IN THE CIRCUIT COURT FOR THE STATE OF OREGON

FOR THE COUNTY OF

Domestic Relations Department

In the Matter of the Marriage of:)
)   Case No. 95 P-20693
KATHY Y. WARNER,   )
)
                Petitioner,   )   AFFIDAVIT OF
)   KATHY Y. WARNER
        and   )
)
V. MARTIN WARNER,   )
)
                Respondent,   )

STATE OF OREGON   )
) ss.
County of Multnomah   )

I, KATHY Y. WARNER, being first duly sworn, do depose and say:

1.   That I am the Petitioner in the above referenced dissolution of marriage case.

2.   On December 14, 1995 I obtained a Restraining Order under the Family Abuse Prevention Act (hereinafter FAPA) awarding me custody of the five youngest children of the marriage. The Restraining Order also prohibited Mr. Warner from intimidating, molesting, and interfering with or menacing myself or the children and restrained him from entering the family residence at 8700 Fruitfarm Road, Independence, Oregon.

3.   A hearing was held before the Honorable Judge Collins in Polk County on January 4, 1996, and at that hearing the Restraining Order was vacated.

4.   That on January 4, 1996, Judge Collins also signed a Temporary Protective

1 - AFFIDAVIT
Page

STAHANCYK, GEARING & RACKNER, P.C
ATTORNEYS AT LAW
200 JACKSON TOWER
806 SOUTHWEST BROADWAY
PORTLAND, OR 97205-3304
TELEPHONE (503) 222-9115
FAX (503) 222-4037

Order of Restraint prohibiting the parties from changing the usual residence of the children.

5. Although the Temporary Protective Order of Restraint of Restraint required that neither party remove the children from the family residence, I had then and continue to have substantial fear for the safety of myself and for my children, but especially for my youngest children.

6. I have been the primary parent of the eight children of this marriage.

7. My husband has worked substantial hours during the marriage while I have not worked outside the home.

8. In addition, my husband and I had decided to homeschool our children and I have been the parent responsible for conducting their homeschooling during the day while my husband was at work.

9. In the past my husband has been physically, verbally and emotionally abusive towards me and in the presence of our children. I am currently nursing my seven month old son, Zachary. This is his primary source of food at this time. Additionally, experts inform me that nursing has positive psychological and emotional benefits for the infant. If the court grants the requested custody order for all of the children to remain in the family home, I remain quite afraid for their well being and my safety. Because of the contentiousness of this proceeding, the restraining order proceeding and the deposition of the parties thus far, I fear that the Respondent and I may not be able to safely live in the same residence. Further, as I have already stated, my infant son, Zachary, requires me for nursing. In deposition my husband, V. MARTIN WARNER (Respondent), admitted that it would be best for Zachary to continue nursing and he further indicated that he had no definite plan on how to feed or care for Zachary if the court awarded custody of him to MR. WARNER.

10. Currently their is a pendente lite hearing scheduled for February 28, 1996, to determine custody of the children as well as other issues in this dissolution. I believe any decision concerning temporary custody of the children should be postponed until then as it will necessarily require inquiry into the facts of this case and testimony by witnesses. I include the affidavits of several witnesses to show the court that to require the children to return to the family home would not be in

2 - AFFIDAVIT
Page

STAHANCYK, GEARING & RACKNER, P.C.
ATTORNEYS AT LAW
200 JACKSON TOWER
806 SOUTHWEST BROADWAY
PORTLAND, OR 97205-3304
TELEPHONE (503) 222-9115
FAX (503) 222-4037

their best interest and would possibly place those children in danger. I could present many more

1   witnesses and affidavits to this effect had I received more adequate notice of this hearing. However, I

2   believe that this matter is necessarily complicated and is not appropriate for a ten-minute ex parte

3   hearing.

4   11.   My children are not currently in any danger. They have been with me since

5   January 7, 1996. I have many people who could testify to their safety and to the good care that I am

6   providing them.

7   I make this Affidavit in support of my response to Respondent's Motion for Temporary

8   Custody as well as any other motions which he may present tomorrow which I have not received

9   notice of yet.

10   *KATHY Y. WARNER*

11   Petitioner

12   SWORN TO BEFORE ME this _13_ day of February, 1996.

13

14   Notary Public for the State of Oregon

15   My Commission Expires: 5/2/96

16

17   OFFICIAL SEAL

18   W.C. ELICH
                         NOTARY PUBLIC-OREGON

19   COMMISSION NO. 015555
                    MY COMMISSION EXPIRES MAY 23, 1996

20

21

22

23

24

25

26

3 - AFFIDAVIT
Page

STAHANCYK, GEARING & RACKNER, P.C.
ATTORNEYS AT LAW
200 JACKSON TOWER
806 SOUTHWEST BROADWAY
PORTLAND, OR 97205-3304
TELEPHONE (503) 222-9115
FAX (503) 222-4037

1

2

3

4

5 IN THE CIRCUIT COURT FOR THE STATE OF OREGON

6 FOR THE COUNTY OF POLK

7 Domestic Relations Department

8 In the Matter of the Marriage of:)
)   Case No. 95 P-20693
9 KATHY Y. WARNER,   )
)   AFFIDAVIT OF
10   Petitioner,   )   COUNSEL
)
11   and   )
)
12 V. MARTIN WARNER,   )
)
13   Respondent,   )

14 STATE OF OREGON   )
)   ss.
15 County of Multnomah   )

16   I, Jonathan P. Benson, of attorneys for Petitioner, do hereby depose and say that:

17   1.   I, Jonathan P. Benson, am an attorney for the firm of Stahancyk, Gearing &

18 Rackner, P.C., who represent Petitioner in this matter.

19   2.   On the morning of February 13, 1996, I was faxed a copy of Respondent's ex

20 parte Motion For Temporary Custody. This IS a motion which Respondent intends to present at ex

21 parte in front of the Honorable Judge Nordblad at 8 a.m.i FEBRUARY 14, 1996, In Salem, Oregon.

22 The Motion is supported by an Affidavit which contains 15 separate paragraphs of assertion of fact by

23 the Respondent.

24   3.   In addition, I received Respondent's proposed ex parte Motion for Temporary

25 Protective Order of Restraint late in the afternoon of February 13, 1996, for hearing the morning of

26 February 14, 1996 at ex parte.

Page

STAHANCYK, GEARING & RACKNER, P.C.
ATTORNEYS AT LAW
200 JACKSON TOWER
806 SOUTHWEST BROADWAY
PORTLAND, OR 97205-3304
TELEPHONE. (503) 222-9115
FAX (503) 222-4037

4.   I believe that this is not sufficient notice to allow Petitioner to adequately and
meaningfully respond to the allegations and to the motions. Respondent's counsel, J. Mark Lawrence,
first indicated that he wanted to present motions ex parte on Wednesday, February 7, 1996. I
requested that he forward to me copies of his proposed motions as soon as possible. I subsequently
sent a letter to Mr. Lawrence requesting at least 48 hours notice of the written motion in order to allow
my client to respond to the motion or motions. I sent a copy of this letter by facsimile transmission to
the Honorable Judge Nordblad. I believe that Mr. Lawrence's failure to provide copies of the motions
in a timely manner has unfairly prejudiced my client. To send copies of the motions both the morning
and the late afternoon prior to an early morning court appearance is far to late when Mr. Lawrence first
indicated his intention to present motions ex parte a week before the hearing.

5.   Additionally, I had made several telephone calls to Mr. Lawrence's office last
Thursday and Friday requesting copies of his proposed motions. I believe that the delay in presenting
these Motions to our office has been unfair and unnecessary, and is contrary to the interests of justice.

6.   The Motions and supporting Affidavit present issues of fact which are
controverted by my client and other witnesses. This type of contested, controverted factual hearing is
inappropriate for an ex parte hearing. My client, the Petitioner would have liked to secure the
attendance of several witnesses to give testimony on some of the factual issue but time would not
allow her to secure the attendance of these witnesses.

7.   I believe that because of the disputed factual nature of these Motions and the
necessity for obtaining testimony of witnesses, this matter is clearly not appropriate for a ten-minute ex
parte hearing.

8.   In a telephone conversation on February 13, 1996, I spoke with a psychiatrist
named Dr. Charles Kuttner who has treated the Petitioner since the time she has moved from the family
residence. He stated that in his professional opinion he does not consider Petitioner to be suicidal or to
have any risk of suicidal tendencies. Further, he stated that he disagreed entirely that she is detached
from reality in any way or that she presents harm to the children. Dr. Kuttner could not be present for
the hearing, nor could an affidavit from him be obtained on such short notice. However, I spoke to

Page

STAHANCYK, GEARING & RACKNER, P.C.
ATTORNEYS AT LAW
200 JACKSON TOWER
806 SOUTHWEST BROADWAY
PORTLAND, OR 97205-3304
TELEPHONE (503) 222-9115
FAX (503) 222-4037

Dr. Kuttner and he will be able to testify at the scheduled pendente lite hearing or at any other time

1 given proper advanced notice.

2   9.   Respondent is alleging that Petitioner is currently suicidal and that she presents

3 an imminent danger of physical injury to the children. This is controverted by Dr. Kuttner and the

4 court should not grant the Order without hearing his testimony as this goes to the very heart of the

5 issue of whether or not the children are in imminent physical danger.

6   I make this Affidavit in support of Petitioner's Response to Respondents Motion for

7 Temporary Custody.

8   Jonathan P. Benson OSB 94248

9   Of Attorneys for Petitioner

10   SWORN TO BEFORE ME this ____ day of February, 1996.

11   Notary Public for Oregon

                              My commission Expires:_____

12

13

14

15

16

17

18

19

20

21

22

23

24

25

26

Page

STAHANCYK, GEARING & RACKNER, P.C.
ATTORNEYS AT LAW
200 JACKSON TOWER
806 SOUTHWEST BROADWAY
PORTLAND, OR 97205-3304
TELEPHONE (503) 222-9115
FAX (503) 222-4037

401

STAHANCYK, GEARING & RACKNER, P.C.
Attorneys at Law

Jody L. Stahancyk
David C. Gearing
Laura E. Rackner

200 Jackson Tower
806 S.W. Broadway
Portland, Oregon 97205-3304
Telephone: (503) 222-9115
Facsimile: (503) 222-4037

Joseph P. Crawford*
James M. Hanson, Jr.
Amy Collins White
Susan B. Bowen, Law Clerk

* Also admitted to practice law in Washington

<u>VIA HAND-DELIVERY</u>

June 14, 1996

Ms. Kathryn Warner
4200 NW Walnut Place, #16
Corvallis, Oregon 97330

Re: Warner and Warner

Dear Kathy:

Enclosed are the following documents:
1) A copy of the Dr. Furchner's custody report. As you can see, it recommends that you have custody of the younger four children.
2) A copy of Mr. Lawrence's response to our first request for production.

As I have said repeatedly to you, we will not guarantee you a result. However, it is my opinion that recent developments in your case have strengthened your chances of receiving custody of the four youngest children -- I believe that, in addition to Dr. Furchner's recommendation, Trish Cox has also recommended that you have custody of the four youngest children. We will be able to verify this shortly when we receive Ms. Cox's report. The letter from Mark Lawrence indicates that Ms. Cox's report is enclosed with the letter he sent by mail on June 13, 1996.

The enclosed response from Mr. Lawrence to our request for production is inadequate. I interpret this as a saying that, if you want to know the extent of the assets in your marital estate, you will have to take your husband to court. I believe that Mr. Lawrence and your husband, in an attempt to give you far less than one-half of the assets, will continue to try to make it difficult for you to ascertain the extent of your estate and may hide assets.

You have described your husband to us as a domineering, religious zealot who will do anything to control you and retain control of the children and the marital estate. Based on your statements and his conduct during these proceedings, I believe that he will not cooperate with you regarding the welfare of the children or with the division of the marital estate.

If you do not receive custody of your children I believe you will have little contact with them and they will become more and more estranged from you. The twins already are openly hostile to you and are extensively involved in this divorce. Theresa, at only 10 years old, has already adopted their point of view. You have agreed with me in the past that, if your husband ends up with permanent custody of children, all of the children are likely to end up with the same attitude towards you that the twins now have.

402

Kathy Warner
June 14, 1996
Page 2

You have stated that you wish to terminate our services because you feel that you can no longer afford to pay us. You have also instructed me to lien your property in order to secure the fees that you owe us. I commend you for not asking us to continue to perform services on your behalf if you feel you can not afford to pay for them.

I understand that this process is expensive. It has been unnecessarily expensive in your case because of the behavior of your husband and his attorney. Nonetheless, when you first came to this office you provided us with countless names of individuals who you believed had relevant information about your case and instructed us to speak with them. This was expensive. Now, because of the fees you have incurred in the past, you have told me that you plan to proceed with this case without an attorney.

The decision of whether to retain an attorney to represent you is your decision to make but you need to weigh it carefully and consider what may be the consequences if you proceed without an attorney. I believe your chances of obtaining custody of the younger children and obtaining your fair share of the marital estate can only be harmed if you do not have an attorney. The stakes are very high in your case and I strongly recommend that, if you can afford it, you have either us or some other attorney represent you.

Very truly yours,

Joseph P. Crawford
Attorney at Law

Enc.

403

STAHANCYK, GEARING & RACKNER, P.C.

Attorneys at Law

200 Jackson Tower

Jody L. Stahancyk
David C. Gearing
Laura E. Rackner

806 S.W. Broadway
Portland, Oregon 97205-3304
Telephone: (503) 222-9115
Facsimile: (503) 222-4037

Joseph P. Crawford*
Amy Collins White
Susan B. Bowen, Law Clerk

* Also admitted to practice law in Washington

August 5, 1996

Ms. Kathryn Warner
4200 NW Walnut Place, #16
Corvallis, Oregon 97330

Re: Warner and Warner

Dear Kathy:

This letter confirms our telephone conversation of August 1, 1996. We discussed that, if you are to be awarded custody of some or all of the children, you will necessarily have further contact with Marty over visitation issues. Furthermore, your husband may initiate further hearings in the future regarding custody and visitation with the children.

You stated that you are no longer requesting custody of any of your eight children because you believe your psychological and mental health can not bear further contact with Marty Warner. For this same reason you have decided not to request specific visitation times with your children but instead will accept general language regarding your visitation rights. You have stated that, once the divorce is final, you will leave the area and will have minimal contact with the children.

I have advised you that, if you choose to fight for custody, you have a good chance of receiving custody of the younger children. This is because you have a favorable custody report from Dr. Furchner and even your husband's expert, Patricia Cox, has recommended that you have custody of your youngest child. Furthermore, even if the court did not award you custody of some or all of the children, it is likely that the court would award you liberal visitation with the children.

I have spoken with Dr. Kuttner regarding your decision to give up custody and visitation. Dr. Kuttner would would like to discuss this decision with you before we convey it to Marty and his attorney. I know you are hesitant to meet Dr. Kuttner because of the cost involved. It is your decision whether or not to meet with him.

In light of Dr. Kuttner's request, I will not communicate your position to Marty's attorney until you tell me to do so. Please contact me once you have discussed this with Dr. Kuttner or once you have made the decision not to consult with Dr. Kuttner about this decision.

Thank you.

Very truly yours,

Joseph P. Crawford
Attorney at Law

JPC:cad

404

STAHANCYK, GEARING & RACKNER, P.C.
Attorneys at Law

Jody L. Stahancyk
David C. Gearing
Laura E. Rackner

200 Jackson Tower
806 S.W. Broadway
Portland, Oregon 97205-3304
Telephone: (503) 222-9115
Facsimile: (503) 222-4037

Joseph P. Crawford*
Amy Collins White
Eric S. Dewey
Joel J. Kent
Susan B. Bowen, Law Clerk

*Also admitted to practice law in Washington

February 26, 1997

Ms. Kathryn Hall
1887 21st Avenue S. E.
#45
Albany, Oregon 97321

Re: Hall and Warner

Dear Kathy:

As you know, Judge Norblad signed your Judgment of Dissolution of Marriage on Thursday, February 13, 1997. As we have briefly discussed before, I believe that you have good grounds for appeal on at least two issues:

1. <u>Child Support.</u> Under the child support guidelines, you should not be required to pay any child support to Marty because you are spending over 35% of the time with the children. If your time with the children were to change, then you would probably owe more support. The law requires that the judge follow the child support guidelines unless he finds a reason to deviate from them. The judge made no findings regarding a deviation from the guidelines.

2. <u>Property Distribution.</u> The court stated that it was going to do a 50/50 division of the property. This was appropriate and in accordance with the law. However, the court did not give you a discount on the taxes that you will have to pay on the retirement accounts when you withdraw the money. There have been at least three appellate cases since 1990 where the Court of Appeals have held that such a discount is appropriate and has modified judgments that did not contain such a discount. In your case, you may have received over $20,000 less than you should have because the judge did not consider the tax consequences.

Although there may be other issues which you may raise on appeal and which the court of appeals might find in your favor, it is my opinion that these are your strongest grounds for appeal.

The judgment was entered on February 19, 1997. You have thirty days in which to file a Notice of Appeal in your case. This is a very strict deadline and once the time has gone by, if you have not filed the appropriate papers with the court, you will not be able to appeal this decision. Please note, Marty has told me that he has no intention of appealing this decision.

Kathryn Hall
Page 2
February 26, 1997

I have made an agreement with Marty that both you and Marty may accept the money and property from this Judgment and still appeal the Judgment. I have done this in order to protect your appeal rights. However, you should be aware there is a possibility that such an agreement would not be enforced. If that were so, if you accept the money and property from the Judgment, you would be precluded from appealing this decision.

We will accept $35,000 as payment in full for representing you through the signing of the Judgment by Judge Norblad provided you pay this amount immediately upon receipt of the funds you receive under the Judgment. If you wish us to represent you in an appeal, we will need an additional $5,000 retainer to represent you. You are of course free to retain other attorneys to pursue the appeal.

Please call me if you have any questions.

Very truly yours,

Joseph P. Crawford
Attorney at Law

JPC:cad

406

Stahancyk Gearing & Rackner
200 Jackson Tower
806 S. W. Broadway
Portland, OR 97205-3304
503-222-9115

March 4, 1999

Kathryn Hall
4742 Liberty Rd S. #297
Salem, OR 97302

#9247352
KATHRYN HALL

Date	Description	Amount
	Interest on overdue balance	$577.55
	Total time and expense charges	$577.55
	Previous balance	$91,161.05
	Balance due	$91,738.60

If you have any questions regarding your billing, we can best help you if you would mark your bill and return a copy of it with your payment for amounts not in question.

Your payment is due upon receipt of this billing. Interest of 9% annually is charged on the unpaid balance, based on the number of days since the last billing. Thank you.

January 04, 1999

Dr. Barbara May MD
1280 Linnwood Dr. NE
Albany, OR. 97321

Ref.: Kathy Hall

Dear Dr. May,

In the approximately twenty years that my wife and I have known Kathy Hall, we have built a valuable friendship which has evolved into mutual concern with, and for, each other. As a result of this, over time, we have occasionally discussed the aspects and challenges of raising both of our growing families. This was done out of sincere concern and respect for both of the families.

Kathy is a lady of distinct integrity who is truthful to herself and others. We have never known her to exhibit an invective nature with anyone, in any way. To be sure, she tends to find positive aspects in every relationship and event, and we have never heard her spread any opprobrious remarks about Marty.

I have known Marty (Warner) for the same length of time, from having worked in relatively close proximity with him at Hewlett-Packard (same building, different departments), and in a much closer relationship in a (so-called) Christian Community environment. My personal experience with Marty is that he not only exhibits a type of "in-your-face" way of verbally communicating with an individual, but his extremely vigorous practice of (Christian) Community teachings, of male headship and control of his family, was evident in our "Men's" Groups and social discussions.

I also personally feel from the casual discussions I have had with Marty, over time, that he has an almost fanatical belief in his need to defend God, personally, in situations where he (Marty) sees his own concepts of Biblical teachings seemingly violated.

We have come to see in Kathy a core of inner strength which gives her the ability to achieve any goal for which she might strive, but like all of us, she functions best in mutually accepting relationships.

Sincerely,

Robert & Shirley Walsh

Robert & Shirley Walsh

Oregon
John A. Kitzhaber, M.D., Governor

Department of State Police
Criminal Justice Services Division
400 Public Service Building
Salem, OR 97310
(503) 378-3720
FAX (503) 378-6993
V/TTY (503) 585-1452

April 24, 2000

Ms. Coral Anika Theill
P.O. Box 253
Hoodsport, Washington 98548

Dear Ms. Theill:

Thank you for taking the time to share your concerns about domestic violence.
Domestic violence is an on-going societal problem without any quick or easy solution.

Your letter was forwarded to the Governor's Council on Domestic Violence and since
that time members of the Governor's Council on Domestic Violence have reviewed
your letter and made independent inquiries concerning the mentioned criminal charges.

Unfortunately they do not have an answer for your very difficult situation. The Council
has learned that the Polk County criminal case was not filed because the district
attorney believed there was insufficient evidence to prove the charges beyond a
reasonable doubt. The criminal justice system must approach the suspect as presumed
innocent and can only proceed with charges when there is substantial independent
evidence, which can prove the case.

The civil divorce case, which had a much lower burden of proof, allowed a lot of
negative attacks against you and most of that evidence would be used against you in
testimony in any criminal case. Reversing the decision of the judge in your divorce is
even more difficult. It appears that the only recourse available to you is to appeal or
proceed with modification. As you know that can only be accomplished through the
assistance of an excellent private attorney, and it seems you have no funds for that
purpose.

The Council does apologize but knows of no clear answers for your situation.

Sincerely,

Renee Kim
Grants Coordinator

409

```
                                            TLW  7/13/01  3:00 PM
Case Register........ Polk County Circuit Court        Status Closed
Case#......  95P20693 State Of Oregon XREL/Warner V Martin
                        Domestic Relations Dissolution
_____

Case Filed Date..... 12/18/95   Starting Instrument.. Petition
Case Started Date....12/18/95   Originating From..... Original filing
At Issue Date.......            Previous Court.......
First Setting Date.. 10/16/96   Previous Court Case#.
Trial Scheduled Date 10/16/96   Master Case Number... 95P20693
Trial Start Date....            Relation to Master... Related Case Same Def
Length of Trial.....            Amount Prayed for.... $.00
Disposition Date....            Termination Stage....
Final Order Date....  2/18/97   Termination Type.....
Reinstated Date.....


                                Judgment Type........ Judgment
                                Judgment Status...... Unsatisfied
                                Judgment Volume/Page. OJIN W

               RELATED CASES
_____
  1 C   95P20693 State Of Oregon/Warner V Martin
  2 C   95P20689 Warner Kathryn Y/Warner V Martin

      ROLE      PLAINTIFF                    ATTORNEY
_____
  1 Petitioner State Of Oregon              Hill Martha
  2 Petitioner Warner Kathy Y               Warner Kathy Y
    Now Knwn   Hall Kathy
    Also Knwn  Theill Coral Anika

      ROLE      DEFENDANT                    ATTORNEY
_____
  1 Respondent Warner V Martin              Van Eaton Daniel H

      ROLE      OTHER PEOPLE                 ATTORNEY
_____
  1 Mediator   Willett

     ENTER DT  FILE DT  EVENT/FILING/PROCEEDING       SCHD DT  TIME   ROOM
_____
  1 12/18/95 12/18/95 Petition
  2 12/19/95  1/28/97 Fast Track Scheduled          3/01/97  5:00 PM
                      CK DECREE
                      Cancelled
  3 12/19/95 12/18/95 Certificate of Residency
                      PET   1 State Of Oregon
  4 12/19/95 12/18/95 Motion
                      temp relief
  5 12/19/95 12/18/95 Affidavit in Support of Motion
  6  1/04/96 12/20/95 Order to Show Cause
             12/20/95 Signed
                      JUD   1 Charles E. Luukinen
  7  1/04/96  1/04/96 Hearing Show Cause Scheduled  2/09/96  9:30 AM C
                      TEMPORARY ISSUES
                      1 DAY
                      PRV   2 Lawrence J Mark
                      Related event #    9
                      Set-Over Def
  8  1/04/96  1/04/96 Notice Hearing



                        PAGE    1
```

```
        ENTER DT   FILE DT   EVENT/FILING/PROCEEDING          SCHD DT   TIME    ROOM
 9      1/04/96    1/04/96   Notice Hearing
10      1/10/96    1/04/96   Affidavit
                             of respondent re: temp motions
11      1/10/96    1/04/96   Order to Transport Prisoner
                             of restraint
                   1/04/96   Signed
                             JUD    2 Collins John L
12      1/10/96    1/09/96   Motion
                             to vacate order (emergency
                             hearing requested)
                             PRV    1 Alway Richard F
13      1/10/96    1/09/96   Motion
                             temp custody and exclusive use
                             of family home
                             PRV    2 Lawrence J Mark
14      1/10/96    1/09/96   Affidavit in Support of Motion
                             RSP    1 Warner V Martin
15      1/10/96    1/09/96   Order
                             granting ex parte motion and
                             order for temp custody &
                             exclusive use of family home
                   1/08/96   Signed
                             JUD    2 Collins John L
16      1/10/96    1/10/96   Service/Acceptance of
                             PRV    2 Lawrence J Mark
17      1/11/96    1/11/96   Hearing Telephonic  Scheduled   1/11/96   1:00 PM 301
                             OBJ TO T/C ORDER
                             JUD    3 William M. Horner
18      1/18/96    1/18/96   Petition Amended
                             PRV    1 Alway Richard F
19      1/18/96    1/18/96   Answer
                             to show cause (Oral Argument
                             Reauested)
                             PRV    2 Lawrence J Mark
20      1/18/96    1/18/96   Affidavit in Support of Motion
21      1/19/96    1/12/96   Motion
                             to disqualify judge
                             PRV    2 Lawrence J Mark
22      1/19/96    1/16/96   Motion
                             for temp use of family home
                             PRV    2 Lawrence J Mark
23      1/19/96    1/16/96   Affidavit in Support of Motion
24      1/19/96    1/17/96   Order
                             vacating order dated 1-8-96
                             for exclusive
                             JUD    3 William M. Horner
25      1/19/96    1/17/96   Order
                             to disqualify judge (CEL)
                   1/17/96   Signed
                             JUD    3 William M. Horner
26      1/22/96    1/22/96   Substitution of Attorney
                             PRV    1 Alway Richard F
                             PRV    3 Gearing David Charles
27      1/30/96    1/29/96   Request Production
                             PRV    2 Lawrence J Mark
28      1/30/96    1/26/96   Motion
                             to recuse Judge Horner
29      1/30/96    1/26/96   Affidavit in Support of Motion

                             PAGE    2
```

411

	ENTER DT	FILE DT	EVENT/FILING/PROCEEDING	SCHD DT	TIME	ROOM
			PRV 2 Lawrence J Mark			
30	1/30/96	1/30/96	**Points and Authorities**			
31	1/31/96	1/31/96	**Response**			
			and objection to motion to			
			recuse Judge Horner			
32	2/05/96	2/02/96	**Response**			
			to objection to motion to			
			recuse			
			PRV 2 Lawrence J Mark			
33	2/05/96	2/05/96	**Affidavit in Support of Motion**			
34	2/06/96	2/06/96	**Order**			
			to recuse Judge Horner			
			JUD 3 William M. Horner			
35	2/06/96	2/06/96	**Hearing Show Cause Scheduled**	2/28/96	9:00 AM	C
			CUSTODY/VISITATION/2 DAYS/			
			JUDGE NORBLAD TO HEAR			
			PRV 2 Lawrence J Mark			
			PRV 3 Gearing David Charles			
			Related event # 36			
36	2/06/96	2/06/96	**Notice Hearing**			
37	2/07/96	2/07/96	**Telephone Call Incoming**			
			Judge Norblad will have hg			
			on Thurs 2/8/96 our TCC will			
			deliver file by 9:45			
			PRV 2 Lawrence J Mark			
38	2/08/96	2/07/96	**Deposition**			
			RSP 1 Warner V Martin			
39	2/13/96	2/13/96	**Deposition**			
			Volume 2 (2 copies)			
40	2/22/96	2/21/96	**Motion**			
			for temp protective order of			
			restraint dated 2-13-96			
			PRV 2 Lawrence J Mark			
41	2/22/96	2/21/96	**Affidavit in Support of Motion**			
			dated 2-14-96			
			RSP 1 Warner V Martin			
42	2/22/96	2/21/96	**Motion**			
			temp custody (dated 2-13-96)			
			PRV 2 Lawrence J Mark			
43	2/22/96	2/21/96	**Affidavit in Support of Motion**			
			dated 2-14-96			
			RSP 1 Warner V Martin			
44	2/22/96	2/21/96	**Response**			
			to rsp motion for temp custody			
			and order of restraint and			
			counter-motion for custody and			
			exclusive use of the home			
			dated 2-14-96			
45	2/22/96	2/21/96	**Affidavit**			
			dated 2-14-96			
46	2/22/96	2/21/96	**Affidavit**			
			dated 2-14-96			
			PET 1 State Of Oregon			
47	2/22/96	2/21/96	**Stipulation**			
			motion for home study custody			
			evaluation and mental eval of			
			the parties and ORDER			
		2/15/96	Signed			

PAGE   3

412

	ENTER DT	FILE DT	EVENT/FILING/PROCEEDING	SCHD DT	TIME	ROOM
			JUD 4 Norblad Albin W III			
48	2/22/96	2/21/96	Motion			
			to amend petition			
49	2/22/96	2/21/96	Order			
			allowing second amended pet.			
		2/20/96	Signed			
			JUD 4 Norblad Albin W III			
50	2/22/96	2/21/96	Petition Amended			
			second amended			
51	2/22/96	2/21/96	Stipulation			
			motion for telephone testimony			
52	2/22/96	2/21/96	Affidavit in Support of Motion			
			dsted 2-19-96			
53	2/22/96	2/21/96	Order			
			for telephone testimony			
		2/20/96	Signed			
			JUD 4 Norblad Albin W III			
54	3/13/96	3/12/96	Order Pendente Lite			
			awarding custody to respondent			
			all children			
		3/08/96	Signed			
			JUD 4 Norblad Albin W III			
55	3/19/96	3/15/96	Opinion Letter			
		3/05/96	Signed			
			JUD 4 Norblad Albin W III			
56	3/26/96	3/25/96	Response			
			and counterclaim to second			
			amended petition			
			PRV 2 Lawrence J Mark			
57	4/23/96	4/23/96	Trial Court Scheduled	10/16/96	9:00 AM	C
			TO BE HEARD BY JUDGE NORBLAND			
			IN MARION CO/3 DAYS			
			PRV 2 Lawrence J Mark			
			PRV 3 Gearing David Charles			
			Related event # 58			
58	4/23/96	4/23/96	Notice of Trial			
59	4/24/96	4/24/96	Other			
			Transcripts from Joe Crawford			
			in LB's Office			
60	5/28/96	5/28/96	Hearing Show Cause Scheduled	6/28/96	8:00 AM	C
			TEMP. CUSTODY HEARING			
			JUDGE NORBLAD IN MC 1HR			
			Related event # 61			
			Cancelled			
61	5/28/96	5/28/96	Notice Hearing			
62	7/09/96	7/09/96	Hearing Telephonic Scheduled	8/08/96	8:00 AM	C
			SHOW CAUSE/JUDGE NORBLAD TO			
			HEAR IN MARION COUNTY/15 MIN			
			PRV 2 Lawrence J Mark			
			PRV 3 Gearing David Charles			
			Related event # 63			
63	7/09/96	7/09/96	Notice Hearing			
64	7/23/96	7/22/96	Motion Compel Production			
65	7/23/96	7/22/96	Affidavit in Support of Motion			
66	7/23/96	7/22/96	Order to Show Cause			
		7/09/96	Signed			
			JUD 5 West C Gregory			
67	7/24/96	7/24/96	Assignment to Mediation			

	ENTER DT	FILE DT	EVENT/FILING/PROCEEDING	SCHD DT	TIME	ROOM
68	7/24/96	7/24/96	Hearing Mediation Scheduled	7/31/96	8:30 AM	C2

* *MANDATORY MUST APPEAR* *
Related event #   69
Related event #   70

69	7/24/96	7/24/96	Notice Hearing			
70	7/24/96	7/24/96	Notice Hearing			
71	8/02/96	8/01/96	Answer			

(in hold file per Carla)
PRV   2 Lawrence J Mark

72	9/11/96	9/11/96	Mediation Partial Agreement			
73	9/11/96	9/11/96	Remove/Mediation Status			
74	9/17/96	9/17/96	Trial Court Scheduled	10/14/96	9:00 AM	C

3 DAYS/JUDGE NORBLAD TO HEAR
IN MARION/RESET FROM 10/16/96
PRV   2 Lawrence J Mark
PRV   3 Gearing David Charles
Related event #   75

| 75 | 9/17/96 | 9/17/96 | Notice of Trial | | | |
| 76 | 9/17/96 | 9/17/96 | Hearing Show Cause Scheduled | 10/09/96 | 8:00 AM | C |

DISCOVERY ISSUES
10 MIN

| 77 | 10/02/96 | 10/02/96 | Miscellaneous Scheduled | 10/14/96 | 8:00 AM | C |

JLC & CEL GONE ALL WEEK
NO CIRCUIT COURT JUDGE TODAY

| 78 | 10/07/96 | 10/03/96 | Motion Compel Production | | | |
| 79 | 6/16/97 | 10/14/97 | Memorandum Trial | | | |

RSP   1 Warner V Martin

| 80 | 6/16/97 | 10/14/97 | Memorandum Trial | | | |

PET   1 State Of Oregon

| 81 | 11/01/96 | 10/31/96 | Opinion Letter | | | |
| | | 10/29/96 | Signed | | | |

JUD   4 Norblad Albin W III

| 82 | 12/18/96 | 12/11/96 | Memorandum Trial | | | |

PET   1 State Of Oregon

| 83 | 1/13/97 | 1/09/97 | Motion Attorney Withdrawal | | | |

PRV   2 Lawrence J Mark

| 84 | 1/13/97 | 1/09/97 | Affidavit in Support of Motion | | | |
| 85 | 1/13/97 | 1/09/97 | Substitution of Attorney | | | |

PRV   2 Lawrence J Mark
PRV   4 Van Eaton Daniel H

| 86 | 1/15/97 | 1/15/97 | Order for Withdrawal of Attorne | | | |

PRV   2 Lawrence J Mark
JUD   1 Charles E. Luukinen

| 87 | 1/28/97 | 1/28/97 | Notice Dism Want of Prosecution | | | |

SENT TODAY

| 88 | 2/13/97 | 2/13/97 | Telephone Call Incoming | | | |

HG 2-14-97 ATTY WILL CALL WITH
STATUS

| 89 | 2/19/97 | 2/18/97 | Judgment Dissolution | | | |

FINAL: 3-15-97 PAGES 22

| | | 2/13/97 | Signed | | | |

JUD   4 Norblad Albin W III
Related event #   91
Judgment #   1

| 90 | 2/19/97 | 2/18/97 | Closed | | | |
| 91 | 2/19/97 | 2/19/97 | Notice Entry of Judgment | | | |

PRV   3 Gearing David Charles
PRV   4 Van Eaton Daniel H

```
     ENTER DT   FILE DT  EVENT/FILING/PROCEEDING_____   SCHD DT  TIME___ ROOM
 92  2/26/97   2/26/97  Order for Withdrawal of Attorne
                        JUD   4 Norblad Albin W III
 93  4/21/97   4/21/97  Hearing Objection Scheduled       5/15/97  8:00 AM C
                        TO QUADRO/JUDGE NORBLAD HEAR
                        IN MARION CO/1 HOUR
                        PRV   3 Gearing David Charles
                        SLF   5 Warner V Martin
                        Related event #    94
 94  4/21/97   4/21/97  Notice Hearing
 95  5/20/97   5/19/97  Order/Qualified Domestic Rel
                        HEWLETT-PACKARD CO TAX SAVING
                        CAPITAL ACCUMULATION PLAN
               5/15/97  Signed
                        JUD   4 Norblad Albin W III
 96  5/20/97   5/19/97  Order/Qualified Domestic Rel
                        HEWLETT-PACKARD CO DEFERRED
                        PROFIT SHARING PLAN
               5/15/97  Signed
                        JUD   4 Norblad Albin W III
 97  8/11/97   7/31/97  Motion Attorney Withdrawal
 98  8/11/97   8/07/97  Order for Withdrawal of Attorne
                        PRV   3 Gearing David Charles
                        JUD   4 Norblad Albin W III
 99  8/29/97   8/29/97  Mediation Partial Agreement
                        5.25 HRS
100  3/06/98   3/06/98  Exhibit Purge Scheduled           4/13/98  5:00 PM 301
                        PET   1 State Of Oregon
                        RSP   1 Warner V Martin
                        Related event #   101
                        Cancelled
101  3/13/98   3/13/98  Notice of Exhibit Purge
102  7/29/98   7/27/98  Stipulated Orders
                        MODIFYING JUDGMENT OF DISSO
                        JUD   1 Charles E. Luukinen
103 10/09/98  10/07/98  Motion Modify Judgment
104 10/09/98  10/07/98  Order to Show Cause
                        JUD   7 Sidney A Brockley
105 10/12/98  10/12/98  Return of Service
                        RSP   1 Warner V Martin
106 10/16/98  10/15/98  Service/Acceptance of
                        PET   1 State Of Oregon
107 10/16/98  10/15/98  Other
                        NO OBJECTION TO MOD
                        PET   1 State Of Oregon
108 10/26/98  10/23/98  Response
                        TO SHOW CAUSE
                        RSP   1 Warner V Martin
109 10/27/98  10/27/98  Hearing Motion Scheduled         12/02/98  3:00 PM C
                        OBJECTION TO CHILD SUPPORT
                        AMOUNT/1 HOUR
                        SLF   5 Warner V Martin
                        DDA   6 Hill Martha
                        SLF   7 Warner Kathy Y
                        Related event #   110
110 10/27/98  10/27/98  Notice Hearing
111 11/05/98  11/03/98  Motion
                        FOR TELEPHONE TESTIMONY
                        DDA   6 Hill Martha
```

PAGE   6

| --- | --- | --- | --- | --- | --- | --- |
112	11/20/98	11/18/98	Certificate of Service			
113	11/20/98	11/17/98	Order			
			ALLOWING TELEPHONE TESTIMONY			
			JUD 7 Sidney A Brockley			
114	12/01/98	11/30/98	Motion Postponement			
			RSP 1 Warner V Martin			
115	12/02/98	12/02/98	Motion Show Cause			
			remedial contempt			
116	12/02/98	12/02/98	Affidavit in Support of Motion			
117	12/02/98	12/02/98	Motion			
			Modify Parenting Time &			
			Support			
118	12/02/98	12/02/98	Affidavit in Support of Motion			
119	12/11/98	11/20/98	Notice Deposition			
			SUBPOENA DUCES TECUM			
120	12/11/98	12/01/98	Affidavit Uniform Support			
			RSP 1 Warner V Martin			
121	12/11/98	12/03/98	Order to Show Cause			
			RE: MODIFICATION			
			JUD 7 Sidney A Brockley			
122	12/11/98	12/03/98	Order to Show Cause Scheduled	12/21/98	11:30 AM	C
			RE: CONTEMPT			
			JUD 7 Sidney A Brockley			
123	12/15/98	12/14/98	Motion Show Cause			
			RE: CONTEMPT			
124	12/15/98	12/14/98	Order to Show Cause			
			JUD 7 Sidney A Brockley			
125	12/15/98	12/14/98	Affidavit in Support of Motion			
126	12/15/98	12/14/98	Order to Show Cause Scheduled	1/25/99	11:30 AM	C
			RE:CONTEMPT			
			CEL/WMH/FRA CANNOT HEAR			
			JUD 7 Sidney A Brockley			
127	12/21/98	12/15/98	Order			
			rescinding telephone testimony			
			rescinded			
			JUD 7 Sidney A Brockley			
128	12/22/98	12/17/98	Affidavit of Mailing			
129	3/16/99	3/12/99	Order for Withdrawal of Attorne			
			JOE PENNA			
			JUD 1 Charles E. Luukinen			
130	4/08/99	4/02/99	Notice Dismissal			
			CONTEMPT CITATION			
131	4/08/99	4/02/99	Notice Intent Take Default			
132	4/15/99	4/14/99	Motion Default Order			
133	4/16/99	4/15/99	Order of Default			
			JUD 1 Charles E. Luukinen			
134	4/16/99	4/15/99	Judgment Modified			
			4 PAGES			
			JUD 1 Charles E. Luukinen			
135	4/16/99	4/15/99	Judgment Modified			
			FINAL: 3-15-97 PAGES 22			
		4/15/99	Signed			
			JUD 1 Charles E. Luukinen			
			Related event # 136			
			Judgment # 2			
136	4/16/99	4/16/99	Notice Entry of Judgment			
			PET 2 Warner Kathy Y			
			DDA 6 Hill Martha			

416

	ENTER DT	FILE DT	EVENT/FILING/PROCEEDING	SCHD DT	TIME	ROOM
			PRV 8 Van Eaton Daniel H			
137	4/30/99	4/29/99	Statement Attorney Fees			
			RSP 1 Warner V Martin			
138	5/17/99	5/14/99	Judgment			
			ATTORNEY FEES			
			JUD 1 Charles E. Luukinen			
139	5/17/99	5/14/99	Judgment			
		5/14/99	Signed			
			JUD 1 Charles E. Luukinen			
			Related event # 140			
			Judgment # 3			
140	5/17/99	5/17/99	Notice Entry of Judgment			
			PET 2 Warner Kathy Y			
			DDA 6 Hill Martha			
			PRV 8 Van Eaton Daniel H			
141	6/10/99	6/09/99	Affidavit in Support of Motion			
			TO SET ASIDE JUDGMENTS			
142	6/15/99	6/15/99	Hearing Motion Scheduled	7/16/99	9:30 AM	C
			SET ASIDE JDT			
			EST 1 HOUR			
			Related event # 143			
			Set-Over Def			
143	6/15/99	6/15/99	Notice Hearing			
144	6/16/99	6/14/99	Affidavit of Mailing			
			6-11-99			
145	6/22/99	6/21/99	Motion			
			ALLOWING ALTERNATIVE SERVICE			
			RSP 1 Warner V Martin			
146	6/22/99	6/21/99	Affidavit in Support of Motion			
147	6/22/99	6/21/99	Response			
			TO SET ASIDE JGMT FOR ATTY FEE			
			& DEFAULT JGMT MOD PARTENTING			
			TIME AND CHILD SUPPORT			
			RSP 1 Warner V Martin			
148	6/28/99	6/28/99	Hearing Motion Scheduled	7/15/99	9:00 AM	C
			SET ASIDE JDT & DEFAULT			
			EST 1 HR RESET FROM 7/16			
			Related event # 149			
			Set-Over Ptf			
149	6/28/99	6/28/99	Notice Hearing			
150	7/14/99	7/14/99	Telephone Call Incoming			
			aff rec'd fr a Dr?			
			PRV 8 Van Eaton Daniel H			
151	7/14/99	7/14/99	Affidavit			
			of Charles H Kuttner, MD			
152	7/14/99	7/14/99	Affidavit			
			Barbara May RN,PhD,PMHNP			
153	7/20/99	7/20/99	Opinion Letter			
			RE: MO SET ASIDE JGMT			
			JUD 1 Charles E. Luukinen			
154	8/10/99	8/06/99	Notice Intent Take Default			
155	8/31/99	8/26/99	Motion Default Order			
156	8/31/99	8/26/99	Order			
			DEFAULT ALLOWING ALTERNATIVE			
			SERVICE UPON PETITIONER			
			JUD 8 Avera Fred E II			
157	8/31/99	8/26/99	Order of Default			
			JUD 8 Avera Fred E II			
			******** END OF DATA ********			

PAGE   8

 # Sexual Offenses

SEXUAL OFFENSES

163.305 Definitions. As used in chapter 743, Oregon Laws 1971, unless the context requires otherwise:
(1) "Deviate sexual intercourse" means sexual conduct between persons consisting of contact between the sex organs of one person and the mouth or anus of another.

(2) "Forcible compulsion" means to compel by:
(a) Physical force; or
(b) A threat, express or implied, that places a person in fear of immediate or future death or physical injury to self or another person, or in fear that the person or another person will immediately or in the future be kidnapped.

(3) "Mentally defective" means that a person suffers from a mental disease or defect that renders the person incapable of appraising the nature of the conduct of the person.

(4) "Mentally incapacitated" means that a person is rendered incapable of appraising or controlling the conduct of the person at the time of the alleged offense because of the influence of a controlled or other intoxicating substance administered to the person without the consent of the person or because of any other act committed upon the person without the consent of the person.

(5) "Physically helpless" means that a person is unconscious or for any other reason is physically unable to communicate unwillingness to an act.

(6) "Sexual contact" means any touching of the sexual or other intimate parts of a person or causing such person to touch the sexual or other intimate parts of the actor for the purpose of arousing or gratifying the sexual desire of either party.

(7) "Sexual intercourse" has its ordinary meaning and occurs upon any penetration, however slight; emission is not required. [1971 c.743 s.104; 1975 c.461 s.1; 1977 c.844 s.1; 1979 c.744 s.7; 1983 c.500 s.1; 1999 c.949 s.1]

Note: Legislative Counsel has substituted "chapter 743, Oregon Laws 1971," for the words "this Act" in section 104,

163.310 [Renumbered 166.180]

163.315 Incapacity to consent; effect of lack of resistance. (1) A person is considered incapable of consenting to a sexual act if the person is:
(a) Under 18 years of age; or
(b) Mentally defective; or
(c) Mentally incapacitated; or
(d) Physically helpless.

(2) A lack of verbal or physical resistance does not, by itself, constitute consent but may be considered by the trier of fact along with all other relevant evidence. [1971 c.743 s.105; 1999 c.949 s.2]

163.355 Rape in the third degree. (1) A person commits the crime of rape in the third degree if the person has sexual intercourse with another person under 16 years of age.
(2) Rape in the third degree is a Class C felony. [1971 c.743 s.109; 1991 c.628 s.1]

163.365 Rape in the second degree. (1) A person who has sexual intercourse with another person commits the crime of rape in the second degree if the other person is under 14 years of age.

(2) Rape in the second degree is a Class B felony. [1971 c.743 s.110; 1989 c.359 s.1; 1991 c.628 s.2]

163.375 Rape in the first degree. (1) A person who has sexual intercourse with another person commits the crime of rape in the first degree if:
(a) The victim is subjected to forcible compulsion by the person;
(b) The victim is under 12 years of age;
(c) The victim is under 16 years of age and is the person's sibling, of the whole or half blood, the person's child or the person's spouse's child; or
(d) The victim is incapable of consent by reason of mental defect, mental incapacitation or physical helplessness.

(2) Rape in the first degree is a Class A felony. [1971 c.743 s.111; 1989 c.359 s.2; 1991 c.628 s.3]

163.385 Sodomy in the third degree. (1) A person commits the crime of sodomy in the third degree if the person engages in deviate sexual intercourse with another person under 16 years of age or causes that person to engage in deviate sexual intercourse.

(2) Sodomy in the third degree is a Class C felony. [1971 c.743 s.112]

163.395 Sodomy in the second degree. (1) A person who engages in deviate sexual intercourse with another person or causes another to engage in deviate sexual intercourse commits the crime of sodomy in the second degree if the victim is under 14 years of age.

(2) Sodomy in the second degree is a Class B felony. [1971 c.743 s.113; 1989 c.359 s.3]

163.405 Sodomy in the first degree. (1) A person who engages in deviate sexual intercourse with another person or causes another to engage in deviate sexual intercourse commits the crime of sodomy in the first degree if:
(a) The victim is subjected to forcible compulsion by the actor;
(b) The victim is under 12 years of age;
(c) The victim is under 16 years of age and is the actor's brother or sister, of the whole or half blood, the son or daughter of the actor or the son or daughter of the
actor's spouse; or
(d) The victim is incapable of consent by reason of mental defect, mental incapacitation or physical helplessness.

(2) Sodomy in the first degree is a Class A felony. [1971 c.743 s.114; 1989 c.359 s.4]

163.408 Unlawful sexual penetration in the second degree. (1) Except as permitted under ORS 163.412, a person commits the crime of unlawful sexual penetration in the second degree if the person penetrates the vagina, anus or penis of another with any object other than the penis or mouth of the actor and the victim is under 14 years of age.

(2) Unlawful sexual penetration in the second degree is a Class B felony.

WHAT IS DOMESTIC VIOLENCE?

Domestic violence is a pattern of behavior used to establish and maintain control over another person. It can include physical, sexual, psychological, social, or spiritual abuse. Over time the abusive behavior becomes more frequent and severe.

PHYSICAL:

- Begins with refusal to meet physical needs of victim (or anyone close to the victim)
- Escalates to murder

PSYCHOLOGICAL:

- Begins with insults
- Often includes crazy-making
- Always accompanies (and frequently precedes) physical violence
- Escalates to suicide by victim

SEXUAL:

- Begins with degrading comments and sexual jokes
- Escalates to rape with murder

SOCIAL:

- Conditions that reinforce the myth that domestic violence is a cultural norm

SPIRITUAL ABUSE:

- Mistreatment of a person who is in need of help, support or greater spiritual empowerment, with the result of weakening, undermining, or decreasing that person's spiritual empowerment.

LEGAL DEFINITION OF DOMESTIC VIOLENCE
RCW 26.50.010 (1)

"Domestic violence" means:
(a) physical harm, bodily injury, assault, or the infliction of fear of imminent physical harm, bodily injury or assault, between family or household members;
(b) sexual assault of one family or household member or another; or
(c) stalking as defined in RCW 9A.46.110 of one family or household member by another family or household member."

The legal definition:

Addresses only part of what occurs;

Is restricted to physical acts;

Does not describe the victim's experience of abuse;

Does not describe how batterers maintain control over their partner.

CRIMINAL THINKING AND BEHAVIOR ERRORS*

Note: This handout was prepared for those committing crimes such as sex crimes, & these are common characteristics

These are ways of thinking or behaving that maintain irresponsibility or hurtful behavior or are used to manipulate others.

1. <u>EXCUSE MAKING</u>: Answers or explanations that are given as a way of avoiding responsibility for one's behavior. Examples: "I didn't know it was illegal." "I couldn't help it."

2. <u>JUSTIFYING</u>: This is like excuse making, but it involves more explaining how things happen(ed) or giving reasons why certain irresponsible behaviors are okay. Examples: "If you can, I can!" "I was hungry. That's why I stole the candy bar." "I just lost control, I wasn't myself right then." "It was an accident."

3. <u>BLAMING</u>: This is a way of deflecting responsibility for one's misconduct onto others. It's a form of excuse making. Examples: "I can't do a thing in this town without getting in trouble. The cops are always watching me." "If you hadn't been so bitchy I wouldn't have hit you."

4. <u>MINIMIZING</u>: Making irresponsible or harmful acts seem less important or insignificant. Examples: "I only did it once" "It was just a little lie." "What's the big deal?"

5. <u>VAGUENESS</u>: This involves talking in a way that is unclear or nonspecific to avoid being pinned down on an issue. It involves using words or phrases that avoid taking responsibility for misconduct. Examples: Questions: "Where have you been, you're three hours late?"
          Answer: "Oh, I got tied up."
          Question: "Did you steal that item?"
          Answer: "Well, I guess you could say I put it in my pocket."

6. <u>PLAYING VICTIM</u>: This involves making others appear to be the aggressors and shifting responsibility and attention onto other's behavior. Making one's self appear to be the injured party is a part of this. Examples: Acting and appearing helpless or too naive to do anything differently. Accusing others with phrases like: "Get off my back, you're always on my case!" "You're trying to make me over into somebody perfect, and I just can't be perfect." Victim behavior may include slouching or looking downcast in order to cause people to feel sorry or come to the rescue.

7. <u>CATASTROPHIZING</u>: Similar to playing victim, this is a type of thinking or behaving where a person maximizes the meaning of negative events in ways that make himself appear to be a victim or draws undue attention to himself. By so doing he justifies not coping with problems. The person using catastrophizing creates a comfortable feeling of helplessness that excuses him from trying, while drawing attention to himself. Chicken Little was a catastrophizer, running around yelling, "The sky is falling. The sky is falling!"

8. <u>LYING</u>: Lies are the most common way of avoiding responsibility. There are three basic kinds of lies:
    <u>Lying by Commission</u>: Saying things that are simply not true.
    <u>Lying by Omission</u>: Saying something that is partly true
    but leaving out major sections to make yourself look better
    or avoid getting into trouble.
    <u>Lying by Assent</u>: Causing others to think you agree when you do not agree or will do something, when you have no intention of doing it. This also involves allowing others to believe something is true, when in fact it is not true. Example: Making an appointment when there is no intention of keeping it. An extra-marital affair where one's spouse has no knowledge of it is usually lying by assent.

Page 1 - CRIMINAL THINKING AND BEHAVIOR ERRORS

9. REDEFINING: This involves making an irresponsible act appear to be a good deed, or at least to make the motivation for the act appear to be acceptable. Examples: "I wasn't really speeding, officer, I was just trying to get to work on time." or "I wasn't sexually abusing my daughter. I was teaching her about sex."

10. ASSUMING: Believing one knows what others feel, think or are doing, without checking out the facts, then guiding one's actions by those assumptions. This is done to support selfishness, disregard for others and misconduct. Examples: "I didn't think you would mind if I missed the group and didn't call." "I assumed you would know I got held up and couldn't make it." "I assumed you wanted to have sex with me. Otherwise, why would you park out here with me?"

11. ANGER: Anger is a normal human emotion and expressing it appropriately is not an irresponsible act. However, if it is used to control, frighten or gain power over others, it then becomes a manipulation. Anger may be used to avoid solving a problem or to intimidate others into backing off and allowing the angry person to unfairly gain advantage.

12. POWER PLAYS: Anger may be part of a power play, but it may also involve such behavior as refusing to listen to what others have to say, abruptly walking away during a disagreement, organizing other people to be angry at each other to avoid coping with a problem, not showing up for an important engagement in order to get one's way or avoid handling a situation responsibly.

13. INGRATIATING: This involves phony courtesy, overdoing being nice to others or going out of one's way to act interested in another person in order to manipulate them. Ingratiating behavior may cover up hidden anger or resentment or may be used as a way of avoiding getting down to work on a problem than needs to be dealt with.

14. CLOSED CHANNEL: Being secretive, close-minded, self-righteous and refusing to discuss certain important topics or receive information from others about one's behavior or attitudes. This is done to conceal the truth or divert attention. It is usually a power or control strategy. Examples: "The subject is closed. We are not going to talk about this anymore." "I have already discussed this with my pastor. He says God has forgiven me, so I don't need to talk about it anymore."

15. "I'M UNIQUE": This is a variation of closed channel. It is a belief or behavior which conveys the notion that normal rules and expectations do not apply to one's self. While it is true that everyone is unique from all other human beings, this strategy is used to avoid responsibility or to reject normal demands that would affect nearly everyone in a given situation.

16. FRAGMENTED PERSONALITY: Similar to "I'm unique," this involves hypocritical behavior where one's actions do not match one's stated values. Most people will occasionally fail to live up to the moral values they hold. The result is usually a guilty conscience. The fragmented personality, however, sees nothing wrong with behavior that is inconsistent with their alleged morals. They believe they are justified in whatever they do.

17. SUPER OPTIMISM: "I think it, therefore it is." The super optimistic person decides that because he wants something to be a certain way or thinks it will be a certain way, therefore it is. This kind of magical thinking permits a person to function according to what he wants, rather than according to the facts of the situation. This often involves placing false expectations on others and not taking into account the need to work out compromises. When super optimistic persons do not get what they want, they often then feel they have a legitimate excuse to explode in anger.

18. BUILDUP: Similar to super optimism, this involves perceiving everything that one does or believes as absolutely correct. Therefore, people who might disagree are, thereby, absolutely

Page 2 - CRIMINAL THINKING AND BEHAVIOR ERRORS

wrong. This black and white type of thinking is used to avoid self-examination, negotiations, or problem solving. It justifies stubbornness and irresponsible behavior.

19. OWNERSHIP: "If I want it, it is mine." This type of thinking or behaving is used to justify taking whatever one wants or treating others as pawns. It may be used to justify child abuse with such thinking as "Whatever I do in my own home is my own business. No one has anything to say about it." or, "She is my kid, I do whatever I want with her

20. DEPERSONALIZING: Similar to ownership, this involves portraying other persons as less than human and, therefore, worthy of hurtful, degrading or illegal treatment. An example may include calling someone degrading names or using another person sexually as if they were simply a body. Depersonalizing frequently comes into play in viewing pornographic material, where women are portrayed as mere sexual objects.

21. DRAMA AND EXCITEMENT: Some criminal or irresponsible acts are done simply for the drama and excitement of them, as a means of reducing boredom, depression or other uncomfortable feelings. This may involve picking a fight, promoting a disagreement between two people or getting over on others with sneaky behavior. Most people enjoy a certain amount of excitement or drama in their lives, but they achieve this through legitimate recreation, or pursing a new business venture or career, rather than achieving excitement at the expense of others.

22. GIVING UP: Allowing one's self to lapse into a state of irresponsibility or hurtful behavior where nothing matters or normal rules do not apply: Examples: Privately telling one's self, "What the Hell, I'm going to do what I want. I don't care what happens." Getting very drunk or stoned is sometimes an attempt to create an excuse to give up. Some romantic songs encourage giving up with such lines as, "Don't worry about tomorrow, it's just you and me tonight."

23. RELIGIOSITY: Similar to closed channel, this involves using religious doctrine to avoid responsibility to gain unfair advantage over another person or avoid solving a problem. Examples: "God is my only judge. No one else has anything to say about this.", or "I prayed about this and God told me I'm right."

24. IMAGE: Placing undue importance on one's status or identity at the expense of others. This usually involves a refusal to admit mistakes or misdeeds, dominating conversations to avoid being challenged and an unwillingness to reach genuine compromises with others. Meeting other's needs in this case is typically a dramatic, self-serving activity.

25. DENIAL: Pretending things are not as bad as they are, and refuting obvious facts to the contrary. This includes avoiding being honest, open, and truthful. Examples: "My problems will go away if I don't think about them." "Hey, I like to drink a little, I don't really have a problem with alcohol." "I've got the flu, not a hangover."

26. COMPARTMENTALIZING: This involves keeping certain thoughts, urges or behaviors away from normal mental review and inspection by the person experiencing them. In certain circumstances this may serve a mentally healthy function such as the victim of extreme trauma mentally keeping memories of the event from normal access. However, if the compartmentalized material involves hurtful, irresponsible or compulsive acts then compartmentalizing serves to maintain that behavior by preventing it from review or change. Compartmentalizing is similar to denial and may be either conscious or unconscious.

* Adapted from Yochelson and Samenow and Bays and Freeman-Longo
LLC:dk 05/23/95

Page 3 - CRIMINAL THINKING AND BEHAVIOR ERRORS

BASIC RIGHTS IN A RELATIONSHIP

from <u>The Verbally Abusive Relationship</u>
by Patricia Evans

The right to good will from the other.

The right to be heard by the other and to be responded to with courtesy.

The right to have you own view, even if your partner has a different view.

The right to have your feelings and experience acknowledged as real.

The right to receive a sincere apology for any jokes you find offensive.

The right to clear and informative answers to questions that concern what is legitimately your business.

The right to live free from accusation and blame.

The right to live free from criticism and judgment.

The right to have your work and your interests spoken of with respect.

The right to encouragement and emotional support.

The right to live free from emotional and physical threat.

The right to live free from angry outbursts and rage.

The right to be called by no name that devalues you.

The right to be respectfully asked rather than ordered.

THE POWER AND CONTROL WHEEL OUTLINING FORMS OF ABUSE

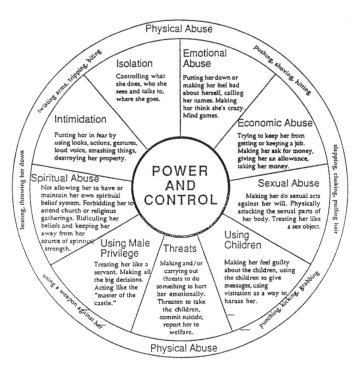

Adapted from Domestic Abuse Intervention Project
Duluth, MN

426

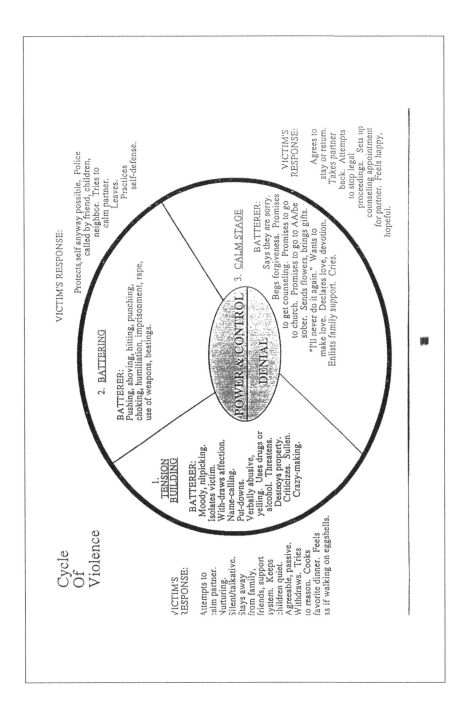

Cycle
Of
Violence

VICTIM'S RESPONSE:

Protects, self anyway possible. Police called by friend, children, neighbor. Tries to calm partner. Leaves. Practices self-defense.

2. BATTERING

BATTERER:
Pushing, shoving, hitting, punching, choking, humiliation, imprisonment, rape, use of weapons, beatings.

VICTIM'S RESPONSE:

Agrees to stay or return. Takes partner back. Attempts to stop legal proceedings. Sets up counseling appointment for partner. Feels happy, hopeful.

3. CALM STAGE

BATTERER:
Says they are sorry. Begs forgiveness. Promises to get counseling. Promises to go to church. Promises to go to AA/be sober. Sends flowers, brings gifts. "I'll never do it again." Wants to make love. Declares love, devotion. Cries. Enlists family support.

POWER & CONTROL
DENIAL

1. TENSION BUILDING

BATTERER:
Moody, nitpicking. Isolates victim. With-draws affection. Name-calling. Put-downs. Verbally abusive, yelling. Uses drugs or alcohol. Threatens. Destroys property. Criticizes. Sullen. Crazy-making.

VICTIM'S RESPONSE:

Attempts to calm partner. Nurturing. Silent/talkative. Stays away from family, friends, support system. Keeps children quiet. Agreeable, passive. Withdraws. Tries to reason. Cooks favorite dinner. Feels as if walking on eggshells.

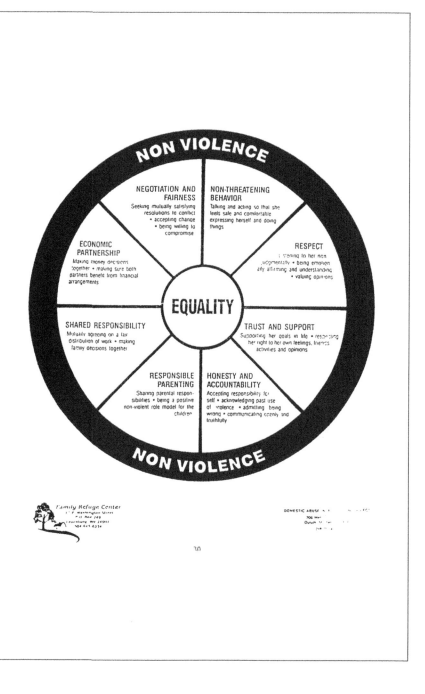

NON VIOLENCE

NEGOTIATION AND FAIRNESS
Seeking mutually satisfying resolutions to conflict • accepting change • being willing to compromise

NON-THREATENING BEHAVIOR
Talking and acting so that she feels safe and comfortable expressing herself and doing things

ECONOMIC PARTNERSHIP
Making money decisions together • making sure both partners benefit from financial arrangements

RESPECT
Listening to her non-judgmentally • being emotionally affirming and understanding • valuing opinions

EQUALITY

SHARED RESPONSIBILITY
Mutually agreeing on a fair distribution of work • making family decisions together

TRUST AND SUPPORT
Supporting her goals in life • respecting her right to her own feelings, friends, activities and opinions

RESPONSIBLE PARENTING
Sharing parental responsibilities • being a positive non-violent role model for the children

HONESTY AND ACCOUNTABILITY
Accepting responsibility for self • acknowledging past use of violence • admitting being wrong • communicating openly and truthfully

NON VIOLENCE

Family Refuge Center
___ washington Street
___ Box 249
___sburg WV 24901
304-___ 6334

DOMESTIC ABUSE ___
706 War___
Duluth ___
___

CHARACTERISTICS OF ABUSERS

from <u>The Verbally Abusive Relationship</u>
by Patricia Evans

The verbal abuser may show a few, many, or all of the following characteristics.
The verbal abuser may be:

irritable
likely to blame his mate for his outbursts or actions
unpredictable
angry or raging
intense
unaccepting of his partner's feelings and views
unexpressive of warmth and empathy
controlling
silent and uncommunicative, or demanding and argumentative
a "nice guy" or charming to others
competitive toward his partner, perhaps engaging in "one-upmanship"
sullen
jealous
quick with come-backs or put-downs
critical
manipulative
explosive
hostile
unexpressive of his feelings

EFFECTS OF VERBAL ABUSE

from <u>The Verbally Abusive Relationship</u>
by Patricia Evans

The partner of a verbal abuser may experience:

A loss of enthusiasm.
A distrust her spontaneity.
A prepared, on-guard state.
A loss of self-confidence.
Internal criticism.
A sense that time is passing and she's missing something.
A tendency to live in the future--"Everything will be great when ..."
An anxiety or fear of being crazy.
A desire to escape or run away.
An uncertainty about how she is coming across.
A concern that something is wrong with her.
An inclination to soul searching and reviewing incidents with hope of determining
        what went wrong.
A growing self doubt.
A concern that she isn't happier and ought to be.
A desire to change herself to make things better.
A hesitancy to accept her perceptions.
A reluctance to come to conclusions.
A belief that what she does best is what she is worst at.
A distrust of future relationships.

EMPOWERMENT OF SELF WHEEL

Transition phase of empowerment

A Self-Healing Perspective for Survivors of Abuse
Transition Phase of Empowerment

ADAPTATION TO NONVIOLENCE

GAINING CONTROL
- Recognizing the negative reality of abuse
- Realizing the need for change
- Exploring options
- Developing safety plans
- Choosing a positive direction
- Seeking support

REBUILDING SELF-ESTEEM
- Believing there is no just cause for abuse
- Letting go of guilt
- Identifying strengths
- Incorporating strengths into daily living

TRUSTING ONESELF
- Taking small risks
- Making decisions
- Accepting outcomes
- Understanding mistakes as opportunities for growth

TRUSTING OTHERS
- Fixing boundaries
- Demanding respect
- Respecting others
- Maintaining a comfortable level of independence

EMPOWERMENT OF SELF

SETTING GOALS
- Focusing on needs of self and children
- Constructing realistic expectations
- Predicting difficulties
- Keeping a positive attitude
- Asking for help along the way

SEEKING NON-ABUSIVE SOLUTIONS TO CONFLICT
- Entitling oneself to expression of opinions without fear
- Reframing negative reactions
- Defining your bottom-line
- Communicating thoughts and feelings directly

BECOMING ECONOMIICALLY SELF-SUFFICIENT
- Assessing financial needs
- Coping with income limitations
- Finding alternative resources
- Establishing steady income
- Attaining peace of mind through financial security

TAKING RESPONSIBILITY
- Setting priorities
- Creating an action plan
- Overcoming obstacles
- Acknowledging successes

ADAPTATION TO NONVIOLENCE

Solitude of Self

No matter how much women prefer to lean, to be protected and supported, nor how much men prefer to have them do so, they must make the voyage of life alone. And for safety in an emergency, they must know something of the laws of navigation. The talk of sheltering women from the fierce storms of life is sheerest mockery, for they beat on her from every point of the compass, just as they do on man. And with more fatal results, for he has been trained to protect himself, to resist, to conquer.

Whatever the theories may be on women's dependence on man, in the supreme moments of her life, he cannot bear her burdens. In the tragedies and triumphs of human experience, each mortal stands alone.

The strongest reason why we ask for women a voice in the government under which she lives, in the religion she is asked to believe, equality in social life where she is the chief factor, a place in the trades and professions where she may earn her bread, is because of her birthright to self-sovereignty, because as an individual, she must rely on herself.

There is a solitude which each and every one of us has always carried, more inaccessible than the ice-cold mountains, more profound than the midnight sea: the solitude of self. Our inner being, which we call ourselves, no eye or touch of man or angel has ever pierced. Such is individual life. Who, I ask you, can take, dare take on himself, the rights, the duties, the responsibilities of another human soul?

--Elizabeth Cady Stanton
January 18, 1892 when she resigned the presidency of the National American Women's Suffrage Association

LINFIELD COLLEGE

Portland Campus

August 1, 2002

To Whom It May Concern:

It is my understanding that Coral Theill is applying for a job at your institution and I am writing to wholeheartedly recommend her. I have known Ms. Theill for several years and think she would be a "good fit" for this job for the following reasons.

Ms. Theill is an expert in the area of abuse and the social injustices that can occur in the wake of abuse. The insights and sensitivity she has gained from her own experiential knowledge will ground her in the reality of others and will help her advocate for them.

Ms. Theill formally researched the topic of abuse and its consequences and integrated her research into a book based on her own experiences. She obtained a Library of Congress number for her book and has sold hundreds of copies. She has been invited to present at many speaking engagements in the Northwest. Many who hear her speak seek her out to draw on her expertise and help them resolve their own situations.

I invited Ms. Theill to be a guest lecturer in a family violence course that I teach. The nursing students said she helped them understand the negative impact that insensitive health care providers can have on someone who is trying to deal with the consequences of abuse. Her examples of the many "do's and don'ts" to observe when working with people in abusive or violence situations were well received by the nursing students. I obtained a copy of her book for our library and several students indicated they had read parts of the book and found it helpful. As an expert in the family violence arena myself, I found Ms. Theill's information in her book to be accurate, touching in the most sensitive of ways, thought-provoking and "apply-able" to practice.

While Ms. Theill does not have formal college credentials, I am of the belief that there are many ways of knowing which inform us about phenomena of interest. I have found her to be a life scholar in this arena and an excellent critical thinker. She takes herself and her work seriously-but not too seriously. She has a delightful sense of humor, is skillful at re-framing events, and has solid interpersonal communication skills.

Additional qualities Ms. Theill demonstrates include her maturity, honesty and integrity. She is organized and manages time very well, and she is conscientious and accountable. She has a good handle on the range of community resources and knows how to access them. Further, I am aware that she was a court recorder for several years which could be a "value-added" aspect of what she would bring to this job.

I am confident that she would be an asset to your organization and I would be pleased to talk with you further about Ms. Theill via phone.

Sincerely,

Barbara A. May, PhD, PMHNP
Professor of Nursing

2255 NW Northrup, Portland, Oregon 97210-2952 • Telephone 503-413-7161 • Fax 503-413-6846

433

Made in the USA
Monee, IL
28 May 2022

97167766R00298